Morris, Gilbert.

A time to weep.

$10.99

DATE			
JUL 30 1996			
NOV 08 1996			
MAR 22 1997			

Also by Gilbert Morris

THE AMERICAN ODYSSEY SERIES

A Time to Be Born
A Time to Die
A Time to Laugh

THE DANIELLE ROSS MYSTERY SERIES

Guilt by Association
The Final Curtain
Deadly Deception
Revenge at the Rodeo
The Quality of Mercy
Race with Death

Number Four in the American Odyssey Series 

A Time to Weep

GILBERT MORRIS

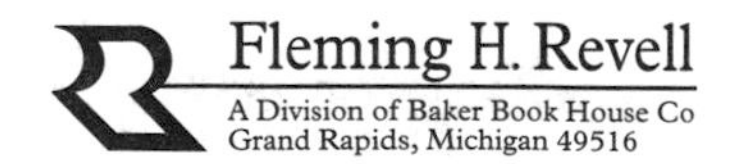

Fleming H. Revell
A Division of Baker Book House Co
Grand Rapids, Michigan 49516

Published by Fleming H. Revell
a division of Baker Book House Company
P.O. Box 6287, Grand Rapids, MI 49516-6287

Printed in the United States of America

Library of Congress Cataloging-in-Publication Data

Morris, Gilbert.
A time to weep / Gilbert Morris.
p. cm. — (The American Odyssey ; no. 4)
ISBN 0-8007-5576-6
1. Depressions—United States—Fiction. 2. Family—United States—Fiction. I. Title.
PS3563.08742T568 1996
813′.54—dc20 95-6950

Scripture taken from the King James Version of the Bible.

To Ron and Linda Fritch

May the Lord give mercy to the house of these two—for they oft refreshed me!

CONTENTS

PART FOUR Summer of Hope

THE STUART FAMILY

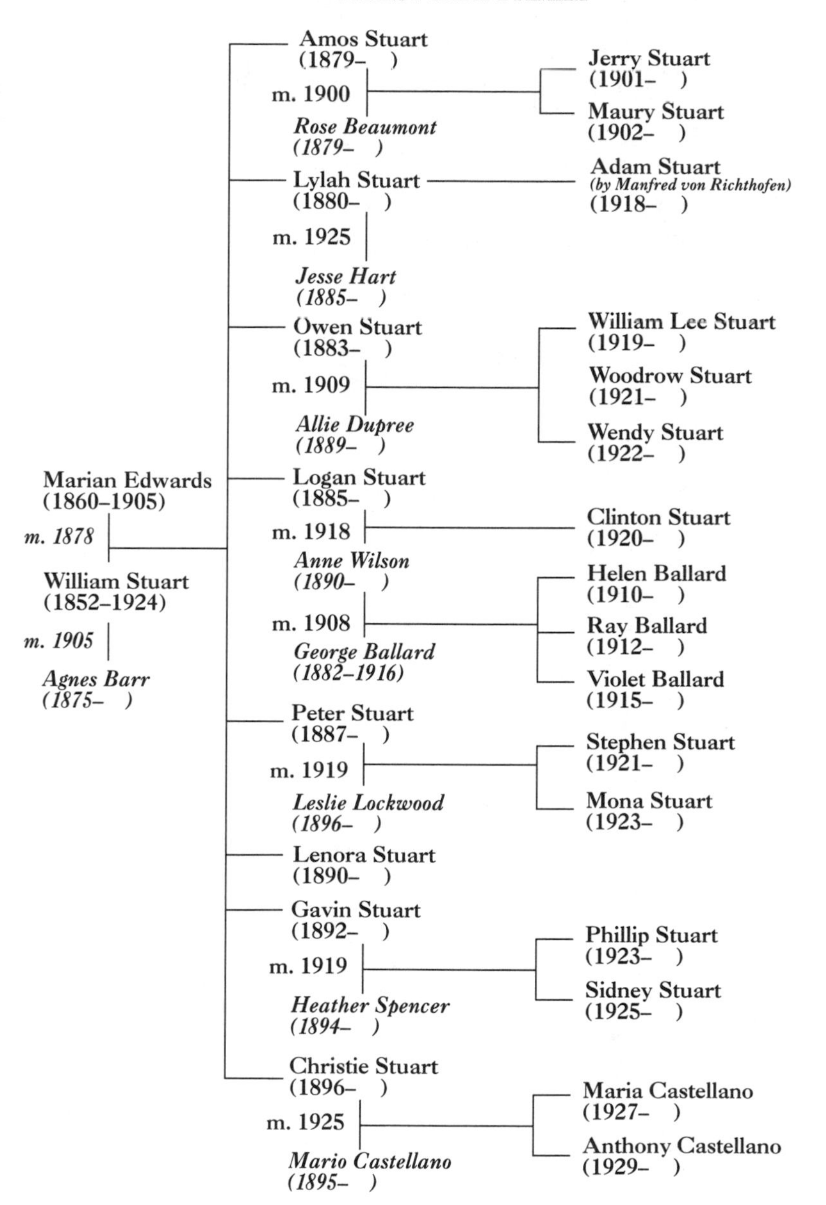

A Time to Be Born	A Time to Die	A Time to Laugh	A Time to Weep	
1900	1910	1920	1930	1940
Spanish-American War	Woodrow Wilson elected president	Lindbergh makes solo flight across Atlantic	The Great Depression	Polio epidemic ravages country
Boxer Rebellion in China	World War I	Stock Market crash	Franklin Roosevelt elected president	Japanese attack Pearl Harbor

Part One
The Ozarks

1960	1970	1980	1990	2000
Billy Graham launches major campaigns	Vietnam War	Jesus People revival among youth	Ronald Reagan elected president	Bill Clinton elected president
Racial segregation of schools declared unconstitutional	Martin Luther King Jr. assassinated	Watergate scandal causes Nixon's downfall	Scandals involving TV evangelists	AIDS crisis worsens

1

HARD TIMES

Violet Ballard took more pains with Cleopatra's sharp hooves than she'd ever spent on the care of her own fingernails.

Stepping back, she stared critically at the sleek, reddish-brown sow and nodded with satisfaction. "I reckon you look pretty enough to win a beauty contest, Cleo," she murmured. She smiled as the huge animal moved forward and shoved against her legs, nearly upsetting her. "Stop that now—you hear me!" she said, slapping Cleo on the back firmly. This was interpreted by Cleo as simply a love pat. She nuzzled Violet roughly with her blunt pink snout, nearly knocking the young woman's legs out from under her.

"I told you to stop that!" Violet snapped. Quickly she stepped outside the barn and closed the door firmly. For a moment she listened. Cleopatra threw her weight against the door, squealing in an outraged series of piggish snorts. Violet spoke to the animal soothingly, for Cleo was capable of tearing the ramshackle structure apart. The barn was already leaning seven or eight degrees in a southwesterly direction, propped up on that side by a series of wooden poles. The whole structure shuddered precariously as the hog moved around trying various avenues of exit.

"Now you just calm down, Cleo," Violet said in a soothing tone. "You'll be all right, but I don't want you to get dirty again. You're too dang much trouble to wash." Turning, she walked away from the barn, her bare feet padding on the hard-packed path that led to the house. She'd risen early in the morning and had come to give Cleo a good cleaning. With nubbins of old corn, she lured the pig into the barn where she had gathered water and soap, and she laboriously washed the red clay from the stiff bristles. She had dried the pig with coarse feed sacks, then had carefully cleaned Cleo's hooves, giving them a coat of lacquer, which had been left over in the bottom of a can.

Stepping up on the porch, Violet entered the house just as light began breaking in the east. She loved to be up in the early, cobwebby hours of the morning savoring the quietness. Her movements were efficient as she poured water into a pan and washed her hands carefully. Strong lye soap bit into a cut on her left hand and she made a face but uttered no words.

Violet was a capable young woman of sixteen, her body strong and healthy, her oval face bearing an early blooming beauty. Her hair was brown, and it gave off auburn tints almost like spun gold. Her dark blue eyes, large and almond-shaped, were her most attractive feature—unless it was her lips, perfectly shaped, full and mobile. She was one of those young women who bloomed early with a startling beauty, and already she had attracted the attention of the young men in the Ozark hills.

Expertly she threw together a breakfast. Singing "I'm Just a Poor Wayfaring Stranger" under her breath in a pure voice, she formed biscuits made of homegrown graham, rolled them to the size of her palm, then popped them into the oven. She'd made the fire before she'd gone out, judging it exactly right. She set the table, and when the biscuits were nearly done, she walked to the hall and called out, "All right, everybody up for breakfast!"

As she walked back to the kitchen, she heard bare feet hitting the floor and her stepfather snorting. *He sounds like a hog snorting,* Violet thought, and a smile turned up the corners of her wide mouth. By the time the family came to sit down at the circular oak table, she'd made thickening gravy created from middling meat. Six large fried eggs decorated a platter, and a jug of ribbon cane syrup sat next to a large mound of fresh yellow butter.

"Well, I don't guess we'll starve with all this around us!" Logan Stuart, aged already at forty-six, was a thin, wiry man with auburn hair and very dark blue eyes. He was not tall, but there was strength in his lanky body and a great deal of inventive quality to his mind. He was what people in the Ozarks call country smart. He could read, of course, but he read people better than he did books. His sister Lylah had once said to their brother Amos: "Logan's smarter than you are, Amos, with all your education. If he'd gone on to school, I think he would have been somebody."

Now, Logan looked around the table, his eyes falling on his wife, Anne. She was five years younger than her husband, a small, plain woman with faded blue eyes and hair an indiscriminate brownish color. Beside her sat Helen, age twenty-one, tall and rather thin. She had flaming red hair and the dark blue eyes of George Ballard, Anne's first husband. There was a patient look about this young woman who was quiet and rarely said much. At twenty-one she was considered an old maid in the Ozark mountains. Most women, by the time they were seventeen or eighteen, were married and at Helen's age had started a family. Helen, however, showed little interest in courtship or marriage. She was not pretty, but there was a wholesomeness about her.

Across the table from Helen sat her brother Ray, age nineteen. He also had red hair and dark blue eyes. He had his father's height, six feet, and there was an impression of strength about him. He was strongly built, his shoulders thick and his chest deep. He had discovered early that he could easily whip any of his peers in bare-knuckle fights, but he had not become a bully, as some young men would have.

He looked across at Violet and grinned. "You been up getting Cleo ready, Violet?"

"Yes, sure have. She looks prettier than Clara Bow." Violet smiled back at him. There was a firm union between Violet and Ray. They had been close since childhood, and as they grew up, Violet had occasionally accompanied Ray on hunting and fishing trips.

"I want to go to town with you, Ray!" Clinton, age eleven, had tow-colored hair and bright hazel eyes. Nobody could quite explain those eyes. Neither Anne nor Logan's people had any eyes like Clinton's.

"You can't go this time, Clint, but I'll bring you something nice back from town."

"You'd better not be spending your money on foolishness," Anne said. Lines of worry swept across her face, for the harsh pinch of the depression had worn her down. Logan had married her after her first husband had died of pneumonia. She had been a pretty woman at the time, with some trace of a light spirit, but when the banks failed in 1929 and times grew hard, Anne seemed to shrivel along with the country. She never grew accustomed to men out of work stopping to beg at the door, and she listened to the radio that Amos had given them—not for the programs that would cheer the heart—but for the bad news that the newscasters often gave: factories closing down, banks still failing, and record unemployment.

There was a lighthearted spirit in Ray Ballard that would not be subdued. "Why, Ma—Cleopatra's gonna bring a fine price! We've been feedin' her good. She's close to four hundred pounds, I'd guess."

"You sure have fed her good." Logan grinned. He studied this tall stepson of his and thought how fortunate he was to have such fine children, even though Helen, Ray, and Violet were not his own by blood. "But the price of hogs is down."

"Not for Cleo," Ray argued. He took a huge bite of egg, followed by a bite of biscuit. He swallowed and then nodded vigorously. "We fed Cleo so good that she's gonna be the best eating hog there ever was."

At the mention of Cleo being eaten, Violet suddenly rose and went to the stove. There was no reason for doing so, and Logan glanced at her. *She's gotten attached to that pig,* he thought to himself. *She always was that way with an animal. I swear she'd be a vegetarian if there was any way!* Aloud, he said, "Your first job's gonna be gettin' her into that wagon. That ain't gonna be easy."

"Why, she'll mind anything I say," Ray boasted. "I've got it all figgered out."

After breakfast, they all went outside. It was August, 1931, and later on in the day, the merciless sun would beat down on the cotton fields making the earth hard. There had been no rain for some time and they were all worried about the crops.

Violet went with Ray to hook up the mules, and when they were hitched to the spring wagon, he backed them up to the barn door.

"How are we going to get her in the wagon, Ray?" Violet asked. "She can't jump that high—and she's too big to pick up."

"I'll show you."

Ray had spent some time thinking of this. He had built up the sides of the wagon with old two-by-fours, forming a cage-like structure. Now he moved over beside the barn, where his father was standing, and said, "Pa, help me get these two-by-eights in place."

Logan glanced down at the old, warped lumber that had been left over from a shed they'd torn down. "Gonna make a runway, are you, Son?"

"Sure—she'll walk right in there." The two men laid the lip of each two-by-eight over the end of the wagon, forming a runway of sorts. When they were done, Ray looked at it and nodded with approval. "There—that ought to do. Okay, Cleopatra." He opened the door and said soothingly, "Come on now, Cleo, we're gonna take a little trip."

The huge swine poked her head out into the morning sunlight. She was a smart animal, and the sight of the gawking family and the waiting wagon seemed to spook her. She disappeared back into the barn, backing up and snorting and grunting deep in her throat.

"I don't think she's gonna do it," Helen said doubtfully.

"She's *got* to do it," Ray said, his lips lengthening into a line of determination. He went inside the barn and walked over to where Cleopatra stood, her feet planted, eyeing him with tiny intelligent eyes.

"Come on now, Cleo," Ray coaxed. "You can do it."

But Cleopatra didn't want to do it. When the others had gathered in the doorway to watch, Ray finally walked around to push; however, pushing a four-hundred-pound hog is never an easy task. Cleopatra stood grunting in her throat while Ray lost his temper, shouting, "Get in there, you ornery pig!"

Cleo, incensed at his tone of voice, turned around and ran against him, knocking his feet out from under him. He sprawled on the floor but came to his feet at once. Cleopatra retreated into the depths of the barn, wedging herself into the angle where two sides met.

"That's gonna be a job," Logan observed. "She's too big for all of us to pick her up—and strong, too. I don't think it's gonna work, Son."

Ray was angry. He stood still, gritting his teeth, trying to think of something. This was a big moment for him. He and Violet had carefully raised the pig for this time. They had fed her well, and now he had big plans for what he was going to do with the money. He was going to take a young woman named Amy McFarland to a dance. He'd boasted to Violet, "I'm gonna buy her flowers and put a spoke in Tyrone Seaton's wheel!"

He and Tyrone had been running themselves ragged chasing Amy, and this was to be the biggest dance of the year. Ray had timed the sale of the pig so he would have cash to put on a big show.

Now, however, it looked like the dance and Amy were going to be Tyrone Seaton's victory. A feeling of helplessness seized Ray, and he kicked at a clump of straw angrily. "Aw, shoot!" he said. "We've gotta get her in that wagon somehow."

"I can get her in. The rest of you go on outside." They all looked with surprise at Violet, who was smiling at Ray. "She just needs to be sweet-talked. A girl likes that, you know."

This amused Logan hugely. "Who's been sweet-talking you, Violet? It must have been that Buckman boy."

Accustomed to his teasing, Violet said, "You just go on out now and have the board ready to throw over the back."

The family retreated obediently. When they were outside and had concealed themselves, Ray shook his head, muttering darkly, "I don't think that'll work."

Logan grinned. "Bet it will. Violet does what she sets out to do. Never saw a more stubborn critter in my life!"

Inside the darkened barn, Violet made no attempt to approach the pig. She stood in the middle of the floor and waited, humming to herself. Cleo watched suspiciously, snorting and grunting, but finally, when nothing happened, she exited the dark angle of the barn. She came forward, stopping in front of Violet with all four hooves planted. Violet reached out and began to tickle her under the chin, which the pig loved. Cleo lifted her head and the young woman began speaking to her softly and gently. "Now there—there's a nice pig! You're going to get into the wagon like a nice, well-behaved pig, aren't you, Cleo?"

Violet began taking steps backward and Cleo, anxious to have her neck scratched, began to follow. They got to the door and Violet, who had planned for this, reached into her pocket and pulled out a handful of corn. "Here's your favorite food," she said, holding it out. Cleo snorted and moved forward, gobbling the corn greedily.

Soon Violet stepped out, backing through the door, and the pig followed. Violet had filled her pockets full of the grain, and when she felt her heels hit the incline, she merely backed up, saying, "Come on—I've got lots of it! Come on, Cleo." She backed into the wagon, saying in the same tone of voice, "Be ready, Pa. I'm gonna dump this out, then I'll step out while she's eating it."

"All right, Daughter—we're ready."

It worked perfectly. Violet dumped all the grain from her pockets on the floor and while Cleo was gobbling it down, Violet stepped outside. "Now, Pa! Quick—be quick!"

Ray and Logan quickly slammed the two-by-sixes used for the back of the cage in place.

Cleo whirled and immediately threw herself against the gate, but it held strong.

Ray walked over and picked up Violet, putting his arms around her and swinging her around. "You're some punkin', Sis!" he said, his eyes sparkling with admiration. "I don't think we would've ever done that. I'm gonna bring you somethin' pretty back from town—see if I don't!" He leaped into the seat and said, "I'll be back before dark." He lashed the mules up, saying, "Giddyap, Blue! Come on, Caesar!" and the wagon rattled off, the silence of the morning air punctuated by Cleopatra's shrill, frantic grunting and the crashing she made against the two-by-fours.

"Sure hope she don't break out of that thing." Logan scratched his neck, then looked at Violet and saw that she was deflated. Knowing that she was grieving over the loss of the pig, he walked over and put one arm around her and squeezed her. "You've got a big heart, Daughter. Never saw a bigger one."

The day passed slowly, as they all did. Violet worked hard on the new dress she was making to wear to the dance. Her mother had somehow come into some attractive blue cotton dress material, and Violet worked on it most of the day. Her mother spent some of the afternoon in bed, and Violet thought again, *Ma's not looking well. She needs to see the doctor.*

But in 1931 there was little money for doctors—not unless someone was dying.

Violet, as she made the final stitches in the dress, thought of the last two years. She remembered the day that the stock market had crashed. She had been fourteen then and had not understood it at all. She remembered her stepfather looking grim and saying, "Well, that tears it. We're gonna see hard times."

The times had always been hard for Violet, or so she had thought. But the depression that swept America in '31 was something frightening. Money was almost nonexistent and there were no jobs to be had. The newspapers carried pictures of the breadlines that had appeared in the poor districts. Bleak settlements, ironically known as "Hoovervilles" after the unfortunate president, began to spring up on the outskirts of cities and on vacant lots. They were composed of makeshift shacks of all sorts of material—even cardboard—but mostly of scrap iron and packing boxes, anything that could be picked up free from the city dump. Sometimes whole families of men, women, and children evicted from their homes slept on automobile seats carried from junkyards. They warmed themselves before fires of rubbish and over grease drums. Sometimes Violet was frightened of the homeless people who came through—thumbers on the highway—and she had seen men clinging to freight cars when she had, on rare occasion, gone into Fort Smith. There were huge armies of drifters always on the move, searching aimlessly for any place that there might be a job.

Violet tried to throw off her gloom as evening drew on. Helen was working on *her* dress for the dance, and Anne was reading aloud to Clinton. Logan sat in a chair reading his Bible after a hard day in the field.

"It's time for *Amos 'n' Andy*, Pa."

"Well, I don't know—the battery's about run down. I hate to use it up. Might want to hear the news."

"Well, I'd rather hear *Amos 'n' Andy* than the news anytime. Let's hear it, Pa—please?" Violet pleaded.

Logan grinned and shrugged his shoulders. "Might as well use it up, I guess. Amos said he would send a new battery down in a week or two."

He walked over to the table and turned on the battery-powered radio, wondering what it would be like to have a house with electricity. *Just plug a radio in—wouldn't that be something!* The battery was always running down at the most inconvenient times, but soon Violet and Logan and the others were listening to the most popular program on radio, the work of two white men, Freeman F. Gosden and Charles J. Correll, portraying their idea of an African-American dialect. The program had taken the country by storm, so that one could hardly walk a block in an American town at that hour without hearing, "I'se regusted" and "That's the proposition" issuing from window after window. Violet and Logan laughed at the antics of Andy Brown and the Kingfish, and finally, as the music issued the sign-off, the battery gave its last gasp of energy and the voices trailed off.

Shutting off the switch, Violet sighed. "Well, I guess that's it till we get a new battery. They're so funny, aren't they?"

"They sure are!" Logan agreed, then lifted his head. He had extraordinary hearing and said, "I hear a team coming."

"It must be Ray!" Violet cried. She put the dress down on the chair and ran to the front door followed by Logan. "It's him!" she cried.

The two stood on the front porch and watched as the team pulled the wagon down the dirt road, a pillar of dust behind it dissipated by the slight breeze that the night was bringing on. Something about the manner of the thing disturbed Logan. He saw that Ray was slumped on the seat, and he murmured under his breath, "Something's wrong, Daughter!"

Violet had noted the dejected slouch of her brother and a jolt of fear ran through her. "Yes. I hope it's not bad news."

They waited on the porch until Ray stepped down from the wagon. He tossed the lines down with a disgusted gesture. There was something in the way he walked that told them he was angry, and when he got close enough they saw that his features were twisted with bitterness.

"What's the matter, Ray?" Violet called out. She ran down the steps and took his arm quickly. "Something wrong?"

"Yes, there's something wrong!" His voice was thick, unlike his usual tone. He stared at Logan and said, "Do you know what I got for Cleo?"

Logan shifted his weight. All prices were down and he had been fearful that Ray would be disappointed. "Well, I don't expect you got as much as she was worth."

"As much as she was worth—" Jamming his hand into his pocket, he rummaged around, then brought it out. "That's what I got! That hog weighed nearly four hundred pounds. After shipping and yard expenses, this is what they gave me—ninety-eight cents!"

"Oh, Ray!" Knowing how much hope Ray had put into this venture, Violet was shocked. She put her arm around him to comfort him, but he was so angry that he pushed her aside and stepped back.

"That's what I got for her!" He gritted his teeth. "Ninety-eight cents! And I had to take it because we don't have any feed for her. Ninety-eight cents and I took it!" Suddenly, with a rash gesture, he threw the coins against the house. They hit the side and rattled, then fell to the porch, some of them falling between the cracks.

Logan bit his lip, not knowing what to say. The depression had hit all the Stuarts hard. Even his brother Amos, who was a successful writer in Chicago, was feeling the pinch. His older brother Owen was an evangelist, and he had felt the pinch more than any. Collections had gone down to practically nothing. Logan thought of Lylah, his sister who was an actress and who had gone into the business of making movies. His last letter from her had lacked the cheer that her letters usually had. *The whole family's going down the drain,* he thought grimly. "Well, don't fret, Ray. We'll make out somehow."

Giving Logan the hardest glance he'd ever given his stepfather, Ray turned and walked away mumbling, "I'll go unhitch the team."

Violet came to stand beside her stepfather. "It's hurting him real bad, isn't it, Pa!"

"He was counting on it big." Logan sighed and said, "Wish I had the money to give him. He sure wanted to take Amy a present for the dance."

But Ray did not attend the dance. He refused to go, and the air was thick with his discontent that night. Violet went along with her sister, but neither of them had a good time. They saw Amy McFarland squired by Tyrone Seaton, and Helen shook her head. "He's not near as handsome as Ray."

"No, but his people have money though." There was anxiety in Violet's tone as she said, "I'm worried about Ray. This might make him real bitter."

The two went home from the dance, and Helen went to bed at once. Violet went out to sit on the porch with Ray. Carefully she said nothing about Amy.

Ray, however, turned to her and asked, "I suppose Tyrone took care of Amy for me?"

"Well, they did dance together some."

"I bet they did."

Stillness fell over the farm. The only audible sound was that of a bullfrog croaking down at the pond. Overhead the sky was black with millions of stars scattered across it. Ray sat silently for so long that Violet wondered if he would ever speak. Finally he did, and she was shocked.

"I'm leaving the farm."

"What! Why, you can't do that, Ray!"

"I'm leaving, Violet. I've had enough of this grubbing for nothing!"

"But the radio and the newspaper say it's no better anywhere else."

"It's got to be better than this!" The bitterness in Ray's voice was clear and sharp and harsh. It disturbed her deeply, so deeply that she couldn't think of anything to say. Finally, he said more gently, "I didn't mean to be so rough. It's just—I get so tired of all this!"

Violet was shaken by his announcement. "You'll change your mind after a while. You can't leave your home."

She was mistaken, however, and three days later, Ray stood in the yard saying good-bye to the family. He had argued it out with Logan, but no words had been able to change his mind. Now, he bade them all good-bye and said, "I'll try to get a job and send some money back, Pa."

"Don't worry about that. You just take care of yourself, Son."

Ray turned and hugged Violet almost fiercely, hurting her. He whispered in her ear, "Don't worry about me—I'll be all right. You just take care of yourself, Sister—and the family."

And then he was gone, walking down the road a sturdy figure, but somehow pathetic as he carried the thin cardboard suitcase with all his possessions in it. They watched until he disappeared down the road to Fort Smith.

"What'll he do, Pa?"

"Reckon he'll hop one of those freights and go up north. But it won't be any better there."

Violet looked at her stepfather, noticing that his lips were pinched and his eyes were pulled down tight. There was a sadness in him, and he reached over and pulled his wife closer. She was crying as he led her back inside the house.

Violet did not go in. Clinton came over and he was crying too. "Why did he have to leave? Why'd Ray have to go, Violet?"

"I guess he just couldn't stand it any longer, Clint." Then she tried to shake herself free from the gloom, knowing that she would be hard put to keep Clinton from grieving, because he idolized his brother. "Come on—we'll go down to the bank and fish some."

In November, winter had come like a wolf-lean specter that lurked up in the hills of the Ozarks. Logan's cotton crop had come to little. It had been burned out by the blistering sun so that they ginned less than half of what he'd hoped for. Nothing had been said, but everything grew tighter around the Stuart farm. There were no trips to town now, and food became scarcer. They'd put up vegetables from the garden and knew well that their store had to last them until the next harvesttime.

Ordinarily, Ray would have helped at hog killing time but he was gone, and Violet had said that morning, "I'll help you slaughter the hogs, Pa."

"No, you don't have to do that. I know how it grieves you."

"I don't mind. It'll be all right," Violet said, her lips drawn tightly together.

After breakfast they moved out to the hog lot. Already Logan had decided that the signs were right. He'd never read Caesar, Virgil, or even Robert Browning, but he had read *Greer's Farmer's Almanac* and, as his father had done, killed hogs by the signs.

Somehow, as Violet drew close to the lot where the hogs were kept, there was a feeling of sacrificial preparation. Logan was bundled up in several layers of clothes, as was she, against the cold November wind. The well windlass rattled constantly as they drew water from the depths and carried it to the lot. Logan sharpened the knife on a grindstone, then advanced into the hog lot. He carried a huge mallet in his hand and said, "You don't have to watch this part, Violet."

Violet turned away as he struck each of the two hogs a sharp blow. As soon as they had been stunned, she knew, he cut their throats. She had watched this once. Logan had struck their throats until the great vessels severed and a gurgling, gushing fountain of blood had sent its stream into the cold air. The animals had died quickly, but she could never again stand to watch it. Soon he said, "Now it's all right." She came to help as he attached the legs to a singletree, a plow line thrown over a thick chinaberry limb. The body was hoisted up and scalding water that they had prepared over an open fire was thrown over the carcass to soften the outer skin. Logan was very good at it, and soon the animal was completely clean. It hung glistening in the early morning sun, its belly bulging obesely.

Helen, making several trips with pans, tubs, and buckets, came down to help. The first hog was opened with careful strokes of the knife and the entrails were put into a waiting tub. Each end of the intestinal tract was tied off with a string, and the full tubs were carried to Violet and Helen, where they could wash the intestines, producing chitlins. They hard-boiled these for hours, sometimes dipping them into batter, frying them, and then eating them. Everything moved rapidly. The livers went into one pan, the heart, spleen, and pancreas into another, and the kidneys were separated from the backbone and discarded—no one liked them. Finally, the skull was opened with an ax and the brains were carefully extracted from their secret nest of bone. Logan liked them boiled and scrambled with eggs, served with grits and fresh sausage, although Violet could not abide them.

They continued until the lean meat was diced, to be ground with salt, red pepper, and sage into sausage. Then the hog was halved down the backbone and butchered into standard cuts. The hams and shoulders were reserved for curing along with the middlings. Fat was stripped off in great wads and sheets and cut into squares.

This was the one part that Violet didn't mind. She put the fat in washpots and boiled it down until pure white lard was rendered. It left a residue of brown cracklings, which was used to season the corn bread she loved.

They had just finished butchering the second hog and were washing up when Clinton said, "There comes Mr. Johnson."

This was an event to the family. Twice a week, Harold Johnson came by, delivering mail to the rural routes. They were always hopeful for a catalog from Montgomery Ward or even a circular. And often there was mail from the family.

"Well, Harold, come on and have a bite of fresh corn bread."

"Don't mind if I do," Harold said. He was a tall, thin individual who had lost all of his teeth so that his face looked to be shoved together like a dried apple. He had cheerful blue eyes, however, and he served as a newspaper for those who could not afford one. Shoving corn bread into his mouth and washing it down with buttermilk, he kept them amused.

"They've got a new thing called min'ature golf up in Fort Smith."

"Min'ature golf? What's that?"

"Oh, feller name of Hiram Seeker took some vacant lots of his and made a kind of little bitty golf course. Charges people a nickel to go around them nine holes."

"I'm surprised people have money to throw away on such foolishness," Anne Stuart sniffed. "They'd spend it better on food."

"Well, I guess rich people always look for ways to throw their cash away," Harold said. When he was finished, he searched through his bag and said, "New catalog here." He shoved the Montgomery Ward catalog out and Anne and Helen began looking at it at once.

There were a few letters and finally Harold said, "Well, got one more here."

Something about the tone of his voice caught Logan's attention. "What is it, Harold?" he inquired quietly.

"A postcard," Harold said. He ducked his head and fished through his bag and pulled it out. "It's about Ray."

They all understood that Harold felt it was his right to read postcards. He would never in the world open a letter, but he often said that if people didn't want things read they oughtn't put them on postcards.

"Ain't very good news. Well, I gotta be going." He got up and left as if he didn't want to be present for the reading of the card.

"What is it, Pa?" Violet asked when Logan stared at it too long.

"It's from a woman in Rockford, Illinois," he said quietly. "Ray's been staying with her. He got hurt and now he's pretty bad sick."

A silence fell across the room—Rockford, Illinois—it might as well have been on the moon!

"We've got to help him, Pa!"

"Help him—how?" Never was Logan Stuart more incensed at those who had brought on the depression as now. He longed to do something! Finally he said heavily, "I should write to Christie, I guess, or maybe Amos. Maybe they can spare a few dollars that we could send to him." After a pensive pause he added, "No, I'm too proud . . ."

Violet saw the pain in her stepfather's face. She slipped over to him and said quietly, "Don't fret about it, Pa. We'll do something."

The next morning when Logan arose, he was surprised that there was no breakfast prepared and said to himself, *It's not like Violet to sleep late. She always gets up when the owls are hooting.* He thought also that she was worried about Ray and maybe didn't sleep much last night.

Just then his eyes fell on a piece of paper lying on the table. It was half-covered by a jar of chowchow and he pulled it out quickly. It said: "Pa, I'm going to help Ray. I'm taking my savings. Don't worry, I'll be all right. I'll write you when I get there."

A streak of fear ran through Logan. He knew the dangers for anyone out on the road and for a girl of sixteen—it frightened him. He stood there holding the note and his hand trembled. She had left sometime during the night. He bowed his head and whispered, "Oh, God—take care of Violet."

 2 

On the Road

The small, worn suitcase contained all that Violet thought wise to carry, but light as it was the handle cut across her palm as she trudged along the frozen road. It was the third day since she'd left home, and already she felt a sense of despair creeping up on her. The sharp, bitter wind whipped across her face and she shivered as it cut through the thin coat she wore. It had belonged to Ray at one time, but he had outgrown it, and she had inherited it.

Carefully she left the road and stepped over to a grove of trees where the wind did not whistle quite so keenly. Sitting down, she removed a package from her pocket, opened it, and leaning against a tree, hungrily devoured the sandwich—and wished that there were two or three more just like it. She had stopped at a store and had bought four slices of bologna and a loaf of bread the day before. Now this was the last of it and she knew she would have to stop again. Settling down on her heels, she rummaged through the other pocket of the red-and-black checkered mackinaw and pulled out a piece of paper. It was a map of the United States, not in great detail, but it was all that she had. She had asked about Rockford, Illinois, in Fort Smith and had found out that it was north of Chicago. Running her eyes along the map, she thought, *It's a long way to go—but I've got to get there.*

Replacing the map, she stood to her feet, blew on her hands, and pulled on the mittens, grateful she'd brought them. As she trudged along, doubts assailed her and she wondered again if she'd done the right thing. She was a thoughtful young woman and—as her stepfather had said—close to being stubborn. It showed in the slightly pugnacious tilt of her chin, the firm line of her mouth, and the clear light in her large, dark blue eyes.

Far over to her left, a train whistle blew. She stopped to watch as it gathered speed and passed by. *If I had train fare, I bet that train would take me right to Rockford.* She saw men perched in the boxcars and others, certainly shivering, on the top, and the thought came to her, *Maybe I could hitch a ride!* But she dismissed that and continued trudging along the road.

The first day of her journey had gotten her to Fort Smith because two farmers had given her rides in their wagons. One of them she knew slightly, but she had not told him her story, although he was curious enough. Arriving in Fort Smith, she had gone at once to the train station and questioned the ticket agent. When he had quoted the price of a ticket, her heart sank because she only had twenty-seven dollars—money she had eked out in pennies and nickels over the past three years. She had sold eggs and worked for neighbors, and had been saving for a grand project such as going to college. But now it rested in her suitcase, except for three worn one-dollar bills that she kept in a small purse in her mackinaw pocket.

"What would a young lady be going to Rockford all by herself for?" the baggage agent had inquired. He had bright black eyes like a crow and hopped around shoving boxes and freight onto a cart as he talked.

"Oh, just a trip," Violet had said. She had hesitated, then said, "If a body went in a car, how would he get to Chicago?"

"Well, first of all, he would cross the river at Van Buren . . . over to Missouri . . ." The agent had given complicated instructions, for the road system in 1931 was patchy, and especially so in Arkansas and Missouri. Finally he shook his head. "It ain't easy to get there from here. You'd better take the good ol' Missouri Pacific."

Now as she walked along, Violet wished again that she had

been able to take the train. She looked behind her from time to time, but during the next hour only two automobiles passed by her. She did not know how to ask for a ride and had merely stepped to one side wistfully as the cars sailed by. It was almost noon when she came to a farmhouse and decided to ask how far it was to the next town.

As she stepped up on the porch, a woman came to the door and eyed her carefully. "What do you want?" she asked sharply.

"I just want to know how far it is to the next town."

"More than thirty miles." Curiosity got the better of the woman. She had a round face, smallish eyes, and a mouth that puckered as she spoke. "You ain't gonna make that before dark," she said. "What's a young'un doing out by herself, anyhow?"

Violet hesitated, tempted to tell her story, but decided it was useless. "Thank you very much," she said. "Could I have a drink of water, please?"

"I guess so. There's the well over there. Help yourself." The woman seemed to relent as Violet turned. "I hate to be sharp, but I can't feed everybody that comes along. The road's filled up with tramps all day with their hands out for something to eat."

Violet was offended. "All I want is a drink of water."

"Well, that just may be. Some of 'em are just no good, you can tell that." She hesitated slightly, then turned away into the house. "Get your drink and I'll fix you something to eat."

Violet marched over to the pump, set her suitcase down, and rubbed her aching palm. The leather had worn off around the handle and now the wires that composed the strap were exposed and cutting into her flesh. She began to pump and when the water came, she simply tilted her head underneath the spout. The water was full of iron so that it set her teeth on edge, but she was thirsty so she drank her fill. Standing up, she pulled her handkerchief out and wiped her mouth, just as the woman came out of the house and poked a small paper sack at her. "There—'tain't much, but maybe it'll help a little. Better get off the road before dark and don't be taking any rides from men, especially those in automobiles. They're up to no good!"

"Thank you, ma'am." Violet took the sack and managed a smile. "I appreciate it." She picked up the suitcase and turned to walk back to the road and when she'd gone fifty yards, she looked back to see that the woman was still standing on the front porch, hugging herself from the cold, and watching her.

I guess she does have to be careful with so many strangers going by, she thought. She remembered suddenly how many men had come by their farm, as far off the beaten path as it was. Almost every day it seemed, one came by looking to work for a bit of food. Usually either she or Logan fed them, allowing them to split a little wood to keep their self-respect. Now as she plodded along, a keener sympathy for them came to her. "When I get back," she said aloud, "I'll be careful to be a little more cheerful to them."

A little after noon, a wagon came along driven by a man with his family. The couple had two small children, a boy and a girl, in the back, and the man drew the mules to a halt beside her.

"Well, get in, young lady," the woman said. "Reckon you'd rather ride as walk, wouldn't you?"

"Yes, ma'am, I sure would!" Violet lifted her suitcase into the bed of the wagon and smiled at the two youngsters. At the woman's bidding, she clambered up into the seat. The woman scooted over and gave her room. When Violet uttered a deep sigh of relief, the woman said, "Our name's Thompson. That's Jimmy and Queenie in the back."

"I'm Violet Ballard and I'm mighty grateful for the ride, Miz Thompson."

"You're welcome, Deary. I don't reckon them sorry mules like it much. They hate work worse than any men I ever saw."

"Oh, they ain't bad mules." The man turned his face, leaning to look around his wife. "You going far, Missy?" He was a thick-bodied man with square, sunburned hands and a catfish mouth.

"Quite a ways—all the way to Rockford, Illinois."

The woman's eyes flew open and she put her hand over her mouth. "Land sakes! That's a fur piece. What in the world you goin' there for?"

Violet explained that she was going to see her brother, not going into detail. Mrs. Thompson was as curious as a coon, and Violet paid for her ride by going through her life story almost from birth. Finally, Mr. Thompson said, "Aw, give her a break, Ma. She'll be too tired to walk after answering all your questions."

"Well, a body can be neighborly, can't they?" Apparently Mrs. Thompson was not impressed by her husband's advice, for she kept up a barrage of questions until the wagon pulled up and she said, "Well, we turn off here, Deary. If you're goin' north, it's that away." A kindness came to her eyes. "We live four miles down this here road. Come and spend the night. You can start early in the morning. My husband can bring you back to this here crossroad."

Violet looked up. The sky was growing darker and she was weary. It had been a long day. With a thankful nod, she said, "That would be kind of you, Miz Thompson. I'd be glad to work for a place to sleep."

Impatiently, the man slapped the mules. "I don't reckon it's come to that—where a guest has to work at my house!"

"I didn't mean to offend you," Violet said quickly. "It's the same way at our house. My pa would about die if anybody offered to pay him for hospitality."

"Well, I should think so! Them Yankees may be like that, but not us." The war was not over in this part of the South in the 1930s. "Yankees" were still viewed with suspicion. A Yankee, according to Mr. Thompson, was anyone who came from north of Missouri—and even St. Louis folks were suspect.

But that night, Violet got a good meal and slept on a good cornshuck mattress in the attic. The next morning, she got up to a breakfast of corn mush, biscuits, and eggs, along with plenty of fresh milk. She ate all she could, knowing that it would have to do her till the next stop. When it was time to leave she thanked them shyly. "I wish there were more folks like you in the world," she said. "I wouldn't worry about getting to Rockford if there were."

"Your menfolks—they let you go off like this?" Mr. Thompson demanded. "You're not running away, are you?"

Violet hesitated for a moment, then said, "My brother's in trouble in Rockford. He's sick and someone's got to go take care of him. I'll be all right though."

Mrs. Thompson said, "Well, we're praying folks here, Holiness people. I don't guess you're Holiness, are you?"

"My folks are Baptist," she said. "But most of our neighbors are Holiness folks."

Without further ado, Mrs. Thompson reached out and laid her hand on Violet's shoulder. She began to pray rather loudly, and her husband laid his massive ham of a hand on Violet's other shoulder. The volume of their prayers frightened the girl, but there was a warmth in their hands that seemed to cheer her. When they were through, she blinked, whispering, "Thank you very much. I guess I'll be on my way now."

"Don't you never forget to trust the Lord Jesus," Mrs. Thompson said, walking out on the porch with Violet. "He ain't never gonna let you down."

The experience warmed Violet. These were her kind of people—mountain folks who had been cut off from the mainstream of American life. They still had some of the habits of their Scotch-Irish ancestors who had settled in the Ozarks years before. Until the coming of the radio, only a few years ago, they had lived almost on another planet from the rest of America. The men had gone off to fight in the war and had returned to their lives in the hidden, remote villages and farms of the region. They were sometimes hot-tempered, often intolerant, and could hold grudges for a millennium—but there was a good streak in them, Violet thought as she walked along the road. *They're good people. I wouldn't mind having them for neighbors back home.*

Two days later, in late afternoon, Violet caught sight of a farmhouse almost hidden behind a grove of trees. The night was falling fast and she was exhausted. It had been a hard two days punctuated by short rides from farmers in wagons, but mostly she had walked. She had eaten very little, hoarding the money in her suitcase as much as possible. A winding road overgrown with weeds cut off from the main highway and she followed it, finding a ramshackle farmhouse. It was about as dreary a place as she had ever seen. The yard around it was nothing but hard-packed dirt and was filled with junk of all kinds—piles of rotting boards, cracked dishes, an old baby buggy with no wheels, and other ruined implements of the very poor. She glanced up at a ragged-looking black rooster that watched her with an evil eye as she approached the house.

"Anybody here?" she called out. When she stepped up on the porch, a board collapsed, rotted by long disuse. It scratched her leg and she cried out involuntarily. Carefully she pulled her leg back and took another route. Stepping inside the door, which swung open, she saw that it was a deserted house. There was nothing in it—except a rusty kitchen range. Instantly, Violet's mind put the two together—a kitchen stove and a rooster. She spoke the words aloud and the sound of her voice seemed to stir a ghostly presence. At once, she went outside and eyed the rooster. He was, she saw, an old bird, but that mattered little. Reaching down, she got some stones and began to toss them down, calling, "Chick, chick, chick."

The rooster made some sort of clucking noise and ruffled his wings. He came down off the remaining section of fence, where he had been perched, and moved up to her feet, pecking at the stones. Instantly, Violet stooped down and captured him. For one moment, she held his head in her right hand, feeling his scrawny body. As always, she hated killing anything, but she knew she had to do it. She released the body, swung it around in an expert fashion, and the head came off in her hand. She quickly threw it away with a gesture of disgust. The headless chicken hit the ground and, as chickens always do, began fluttering wildly, legs pumping and wings pounding. This rooster hadn't shown this much life in a long time, she knew. Suddenly she remembered the pastor of the Baptist church talking about people who made a lot of noise in the church but didn't contribute much. Brother Barnham had said, "The most active chicken in the barnyard is the one that just got its neck wrung off!" Everyone in that congregation understood that that brief spasm of life was exhibited in every chicken in that condition and had made the application perfectly to converts who went at top speed for a while—then seemed to just fade away.

Violet had brought matches with her, along with a knife and fork, thinking that she might have to camp out. She broke up small sticks and soon got a fire going. Someone had left a few chunks of oak that had already begun to rot, but it made a hot fire. She discovered a large pot with a hole near the top, which had been jettisoned. The well had no bucket, but she was able to rig one out of an old tomato can. It took several trips to fill the pot but soon she had water boiling. She scalded the chicken, plucked it, and then, using her pocketknife, she dressed the chicken out. "You're going to be good, rooster," she nodded confidently. She put the rooster in the pot and, while it was cooking, read from an old magazine she found. From time to time, she would go over and poke the rooster.

It got to be discouraging. "This old rooster's got to be the toughest bird ever hatched!" she complained. She boiled it until late that night and finally in despair, pulled it out and cut it up. It was tough and unyielding, but she had good, sharp teeth and tore the flesh from the bones. The liver, at least, was good and tender. All in all she enjoyed it thoroughly. She was very tired, so after she had eaten she rolled up her coat to make a pillow and laid down close to the stove. The fire would hold till morning, she knew, and she went to sleep at once.

At dawn the next day, she was on the road again. She had not worn a cap, but wore a scarf over her head. The wind was rising now and she was apprehensive. Snow could come at any moment and in these unknown hills there was something ominous about the wind that gusted through the trees. From time to time she saw animals along the road. Once a fox trotted out smartly in front of her, gave her a bold look, then went on its way apparently unperturbed. Squirrels barked at her from the trees and she wished she had Ray's gun. *I'd have squirrel soup tonight,* she thought wistfully. But she couldn't bring a gun on the trip to Rockford, Illinois.

The weather worsened as she went along, the temperature dropping. She was grateful for the mittens and shifted the suitcase from one hand to the other. She did get a ride in a truck with a man and two women, but it was only for three miles. They had not asked her destination or anything else, and had let her off with scarcely a word.

She stopped at noon at a store that was set at a crossroads and bought a box of crackers, a nickel's worth of cheese, and a large dill pickle. Thinking she might lay in a little bit more, she bought an end of a huge chunk of bologna and two cans of beans.

She sat beside the stove in the store and ate the cheese and crackers, and the storekeeper, a jovial fellow of about sixty, gave her a Coca-Cola. "On the house," he said when she shook her head. "Coffee'd go better, but ain't none made." He walked over to the window and looked outside. "It's pretty cold out there. Snow's a coming. Feel it in my bones." He turned and gave her a curious look. "Ain't much on that road for the next ten miles," he said, "and not much then—just a little town. Be you going there?"

Skillfully, Violet avoided his questions. She finished her meal, then picked up the sack containing the food and shoved it in her suitcase. Picking up the suitcase, she said, "Thank you," and walked out the door.

Two hours later, she was looking for some kind of shelter, but the country was barren, covered with scrub trees that offered very little break from the sharp wind. The temperature was dropping again, and suddenly she felt a touch on her cheek. "Snow!" she whispered. "I've got to get out of this."

She hurried along the road, almost stumbling, but saw no shelter. Five minutes later, she heard the sound of a car coming. Standing over to one side, she waited as she usually did—not asking for a ride, but her face turned toward the vehicle. To her relief it stopped. It was a large black car driven by a man who leaned out and said, "Snow's coming! You all alone?"

"Yes, sir. I'm headed for the next town."

"Well, you'd better get in. It's five more miles down the road and the snow's going to be coming quick."

Thankful, Violet got in the door, which the man shoved open, and sat down. "Late for a young lady to be out!" The man was bundled up in a heavy coat. He turned to look at her and grinned in a friendly fashion. His face was round and flushed. He had a short, stubby nose and eyes that were set a little too close together.

"Yes, sir, I just need to get to the next town."

"Well, it's getting cold." He reached down on the seat beside him and held out something to her. When she looked closer, she saw that it was a bottle of clear liquid. "This will warm you up a little bit. It's good stuff!"

Violet had already smelled the liquor that was in the car. She had not been around it much, only at parties and dances where the young men sometimes drank homemade brew. Alarm rose in her and she said, "Oh, no, sir, I couldn't do that!"

"Well, it's good for keeping the cold out." Tilting the bottle, the man took two swallows. He held his breath, then expelled it with a sigh of pleasure. Shoving the cork back in, he put the bottle on the seat and said, "Where you from? What's your name?"

"I'm Violet Ballard and I come from Arkansas."

"That's a long way. Where you headed for?"

"Rockford, Illinois." Violet grew apprehensive as the man started pumping questions at her about where was she going, and didn't her folks care. She answered shortly and noticed that the car was slowing down. She fell against the man when he made a sudden right-hand turn. "Where are you going?" she cried in alarm.

"Shortcut," he said. "Road's washed out up ahead and this will get us there quicker."

Alarm ran through Violet. "Just let me out," she said, "and I'll walk."

But the man laughed roughly and sent the car plunging over a rutted road. It was apparently deserted and very narrow, for branches slapped the sides of the car. "Stay where you are, Girlie," he said. "We're gonna have a good time."

Violet had known fear in her life—of snakes, of almost drowning, and when she'd fallen down an abandoned well—but nothing like this. Terror clawed at her like a cornered animal as she fumbled with the car door. Sensing what she was doing, the man reached over, grabbed her left arm, and yanked her over. She was nearly powerless in his strong grasp. His voice was guttural. He said, "You just stay put, Sweetie! I'm going to show you a few things."

Violet tried to pull away from him, but his fingers bit into her arm until she cried aloud. The car bucked and plunged down the rutted road as she tried to hit him with her right hand. Her blow caught him on the neck. He released her arm long enough to strike her in the temple with a hard fist. The blow drove her against the car door, and bright lights seemed to spin in front of her eyes.

Then the car was stopped and the engine shut off. She heard his door open and began to try to find the door handle on her own side, but his hands were on her. She cried aloud as he dragged her into the backseat, "Help me! Somebody help!"

"Scream all you want to, Honey. Ain't nobody gonna hear you out here."

Violet felt his hands pulling at her clothing. Her jacket came open, and she reached up to hit him again. He pinioned her easily with his strong left arm, then reaching out, grabbed the top of her dress. With one motion he tore it away, and terror, like a cold wind, pierced her.

Almost all hope left her then. She was alone with a wild beast of a man in an abandoned place, but Violet had courage. He was still holding her arms pinioned. She wrenched loose and with her left hand she jabbed at his eyes. He uttered a cry of rage, and for a moment dropped his hold and reached up to grab his eyes. He cursed, but Violet forced open the car door and stumbled away into the darkness. Bushes and vines grabbed at her and briars scratched at her legs and tore what remained of her dress, but she plunged ahead. She was strong and hearty, and fear was an added spur. Behind her she could hear him yelling, and for a time could hear him crashing through the bushes. But he was a town man, she could tell, and was not familiar with the woods.

She ran until her breath was raw in her throat, then she stopped and leaned against a tree, trembling at every nerve. The cold bit at her as she listened hard. Nothing. Then she began to weep silently, putting her hands over her face. She felt dirty and defiled at the touch of the man's hands. She pulled her coat together, but he had ripped the buttons off. As she made her way through the woods, she held it together with her hands.

The cold numbed her face and she looked around, straining to see through the darkness. Faintly she heard a car start, and for a time she stood there not knowing what to do. Then she made her way through the woods back toward the road. When she got to the narrow road, she thought she was at the wrong place. The car was gone, and she walked down the road not knowing what she would do if she saw it, whether to run back into the woods or not.

Suddenly she remembered—*My suitcase! It's in his backseat.* Frantically she ran down the road peering through the murky darkness, but could see nothing. Back and forth she went, uncertain of the spot. Another wave of fear rushed through her. Not like when the man had been pulling at her, but fear of being alone in a strange place with no money, no clothes—nothing!

Her legs began to tremble with exhaustion and her stomach was knotted up. She looked up and saw that a few feeble stars gleamed through the clouds overhead, but it was a moonless night. She began to walk along the road, clutching her coat around her, tears running down her face. She had never felt so alone in her whole life, and she tried to pray but could not think of any words. She'd said her ritual prayers since she was a child, taught them by her mother, but now they did not seem to be enough.

Finally she made it back to the main road and looked up and down it. There were no lights from the south. Far ahead she saw lights, but they were the lights of a disappearing car. She plodded slowly along and finally the darkness closed in on her completely. Groping her way to the side of the road, she sat down with her back against a huge tree, and as the wind moaned through the branches overhead, Violet Ballard put her face on her arms and struggled with fear.

 3 

A Friend

The woods that night had been a nightmarish place for Violet. At dawn she had stumbled along the road while weariness dragged at her and the cold numbed her. Finally, she had seen a shape looming to the right and had found a chimney—all that was left of a house that had been burned to the ground. Off to the back of the chimney, however, was what had been a feed bin used to store corn. It had a top that lifted and she had crawled into it seeking relief from the piercing cold. It had been relatively warm inside the bin and she had stayed there, falling asleep. Finally, through the cracks of the warping lumber, the sun touched her eyes and she had crawled out stiffly, hungry and totally confused.

The road led on, but she had no idea what lay before her. Surely there would be *someone* in the next town who would help! Then she thought of the rough tramps who passed through constantly and doubt filled her.

For thirty minutes she walked down the road, clutching the mackinaw to her breast. The dress, she saw, was hopelessly ripped and she had no needle, thread, or even a pin to put it together. Her face burned as she thought of the terrible experience. *Maybe if I go to the police,* she thought, *they'll help me get my money back.* But the idea of going into a strange town and seeking help from the police was so foreign to her thinking that she put it aside quickly.

Twenty minutes later, she came to a creek that meandered across the land. A wooden bridge arched over it and she looked down, suddenly reminded of how thirsty she was.

She left the road, walked down to the creek, knelt down, and pressed her face against the water. She had done this many times at the many creeks in the mountains near her home. The water was so cold that it numbed her face and tongue.

"Water's cold, ain't it?"

Violet was so startled that she jerked back and scrambled to her feet. There, underneath the bridge, sat a man. He was wearing a cap pulled down over his face and ears, and by the look of his ragged clothes he was evidently a tramp. Fear shot through Violet. She was alone and this man was huge! He had to stoop as he came out from under the cross members of the small bridge. "Creek had ice on it this morning—jest a skim."

Violet saw that he had a youthful, round face and innocent-looking blue eyes, but he was so big that he seemed to dwarf her. His bare hands, which he took out of his pockets and blew on, were the size of small hams. She began to back away and, without speaking, headed back to the road. "Won't be no wagons for a couple hours," the man said. "My name's Bailey."

Violet reached the road and looked back and saw that he stood there watching her. The fact that he made no move reassured her, and she took a deep sigh of relief. At least it was daylight now, and she was not in the woods. Surely he wouldn't try to harm her. "What wagons?" she asked.

"Farmers goin' to town. They'll usually give a feller a ride."

Violet looked down the road, but it was barren—no cars, no wagons, not even a farmer riding a mule. She shivered violently as the cold wind whipped about her, despair filling her heart.

"Say, you look cold. I'd better catch up a fire." Without turning to look back at her, the huge man called Bailey walked along the creek, picking up sticks as he went. The creek bent in a curve and she lost sight of him for a moment. Standing there alone, she didn't know what to do. She held her arms across her chest, shivering. She kept watching where the man had disappeared and soon she saw a thin tendril of smoke arise from where the creek bent. It grew larger, and suddenly he appeared, motioning. "I gotta good 'un!" he yelled. "Come get warm!"

Violet hesitated. She looked down the road again, then forward. Nothing was there. *I've got to get warm*, she thought. *Surely he wouldn't bother me in daylight.*

Cautiously she went alongside the bridge and followed the creek to the bend. It was only twenty feet away and the tramp already had a good fire going. He was breaking large chunks of a dead oak, and she noticed he snapped them as if they were nothing. She moved close to the fire and held out her hands. It caused her jacket to fall open, and she flushed and pulled it together. It was awkward, but he paid no attention to her. Finally, the fire was roaring and she huddled close, letting the warmth seep into her.

Looking at her with his large, round eyes, Bailey said, "What's your name?"

"V–Violet, Violet Ballard."

Bailey thought this over. His lips moved as he framed the syllables and he nodded. "That's pretty," he said, then he moved away without a word, leaving her there. Violet was startled at his sudden disappearance, but he was back soon, carrying a blanket roll. He unrolled it and pulled out a pot and two cans of beans. Carefully he arranged two of the burning logs so he could balance a blackened saucepan on them. He reached down and dipped a little of the creek water into the pan, then pulled out his pocketknife. Removing the tops of the cans, he dumped the contents of one into the pan, then the other.

All this time he had not said a word, and now he sat down and watched the beans carefully. There was something odd about his silence, something that troubled Violet. She asked timidly, "Did you stay under the bridge all night?"

"Yep, I did. It got cold. Started to make a fire once, but then I didn't."

He sat there watching the beans until finally they started to bubble. He rummaged through his bedroll and said, "I ain't got but one spoon. We'll take turns." He took one of the cans, emptied half of the beans into it and handed it to her, along with a worn spoon.

"I couldn't take your breakfast," Violet protested. The beans smelled good, and she was very hungry.

"Go on—eat 'em. You look hungry."

Violet took a spoonful of beans, which were very hot. She put them in her mouth gingerly, after blowing on them, and then chewed them. "They're very good," she said, swallowing. "Thank you very much."

He did not answer, and she finished the beans in silence. When she handed the spoon back, he ate the rest of the beans out of the saucepan, seeming not to notice that they were bubbling with heat. Then he washed out the pan in the creek, put it back in his blanket roll, and only then did he turn his attention to her. There was a halting in his speech. It seemed as if he had to think carefully about whatever he said. Soon Violet realized that he had a hulking body, but somehow he was very slow in the mind.

"Thank you very much," she said. "I'd better get up on the road."

"Ain't no need of it," Bailey said. "We can hear a team coming from a long way off." He held his hands out over the fire, squatting on his heels, and asked, "Been on the road long?"

"Not too long. Have you?"

He looked at her in surprise. "Oh, I'm always on the road."

"Don't you have a home?"

"A home?" He looked puzzled over that and shook his head. "No, I ain't got no home. Ain't had one in a long time." He brightened and said, "I got a watch, you want to see it?"

"Yes, I'd like to."

Bailey reached his massive fingers into his shirt pocket and came out with a large gold watch. "Look at that! Ain't that a hummer?"

"It's very nice. Where did you get it?"

"It belonged to my pa—at least I think he was. Look, the back comes out!" Carefully turning the watch over, he showed her the inscription. She read aloud, "To Ronald A. Bailey, for faithful service, Missouri Pacific Railroad."

"Is that you, Ronald Bailey?"

"No."

"Is that your father?"

"I guess—I don't know. My ma said he was. I never seen him though." He turned the watch over fondly, rubbed it with his thumbnail as if it were some sort of talisman, and then put it back in his pocket. "It's all I had when I left home—that and a dollar bill. Ma couldn't keep me anymore, so I left and went out on the road."

He spoke cheerfully enough and changed subjects abruptly. "There's a tater field back down the road. You sit here and I'll go see if they left any."

Violet sat by the fire, adding wood from time to time, and soon he was back, his pockets bulging. "I found lots of taters," he said. "We can bake 'em. I could eat about a dozen of these myself. How about you?"

"I'm still hungry," Violet admitted. "If we put some mud around them and put them in the hot coals they won't burn so bad."

He looked at her with admiration. "You're smart," he announced. "Show me how."

Violet had done this on hunting trips with Ray and Logan. Soon six of the potatoes were lightly coated with mud and she showed him how to build a hot fire over them. They took over an hour, and he was anxious. "I've got some salt," he said. "Let's eat 'em now."

When she agreed, he pulled one of the potatoes out, juggled it with his hands. "Hot!" he grinned. He opened his pocketknife, split the potato open, and handed her the spoon. "You use the spoon and I'll use the knife."

The white hot flesh of the potato was delicious and Violet ate two of them. Bailey ate the other four and grinned and patted his stomach. "Good!" he said. "I'd better go get some more to take with us."

"Take with us?"

He stared at her. "Well, you're going down the road, ain't ya? We might as well go together."

His innocence struck Violet. "You don't even know me."

"Sure I do!" Bailey nodded earnestly. "You're Violet and I'm Bailey." An uncertain look crossed his face. "You don't want to go with me?"

Suddenly the fear of being alone struck Violet. She looked at the babyish face of the big young man and said, "Bailey, haven't you noticed that I'm—not a boy?"

"Course I noticed. You think I'm dumb?"

"No, not at all, but you didn't say anything."

"I guess I know a girl when I see one! What's that got to do with anything?"

Violet started to explain, her face flushing. "Well, sometimes, Bailey, men—they want to bother young women."

Bailey stared at her as she explained, then shook his head. "I've seen some of that." He looked down at his hands, his fingers almost as large as small bananas, then he looked up at her. "Are you ascared of me?"

Violet swallowed and looked right into his eyes. "You wouldn't hurt me, would you, Bailey? You promise?"

Bailey grinned cheerfully. "Why, shoot, Violet—I wouldn't hurt you—and nobody else will, for that matter. Now I'll go get some spuds. We'll take all we can haul with us. There's a town down the way; maybe we can get something else there."

Violet sat beside the fire, a lump in her throat. She had been emotionally scarred by the vicious attack the night before—and now this huge, innocent child of a man had restored some of her faith. When he came back, she said, "I'll try not to be any trouble, Bailey."

He grinned at her and shrugged his massive shoulders. "So will I, Violet. Look at all the taters I got. Must be twenty or thirty here." He had stuffed his pockets full and now said, "We better stuff some of these in my bedroll. Don't you have a bedroll?"

"No, I don't. I don't have anything."

"Aw, that's too bad. I've got two blankets, so let me fix one for you." He unrolled his bedroll and Violet spotted a brown sweater. She thought of the condition of the front of her dress. "Bailey, could I put on that sweater?"

"Sure you can. It's way too little for me. A lady gave it to me, but I can hardly get my head through it."

Violet grabbed the sweater, turned her back and slipped into it. Once it was on and covering the front of the ripped dress, she felt more secure. When she turned, Bailey was carefully arranging some of the potatoes in the second blanket. He tied it with bits of string and said, "Now, you just carry this over your shoulder. There'll be a wagon along pretty soon. If there's not, we can walk into town."

He carefully extinguished the fire and they went back to the road. As they walked along, Bailey whistled in an expert manner. When she commented on it, he said, "That's the funny thing—I can't read, but I can hear a song and then whistle it." He whistled through "Bye, Bye, Blackbird," and, to his delight, she sang along with him. "Why, that's plumb pretty," he said when she'd finished. "I've never heard anyone sing as pretty as you."

As they marched along, he was silent. Finally he said, "I'm glad you're with me, Violet. A feller gets lonesome." After another silence, he said, "Most people don't like me."

Violet did not want to be counted among those. "I can't understand that. I think you're very nice, Bailey." She looked up then and said, "Look! Isn't that a town up ahead?"

He nodded and the two picked up their pace. He had to adjust his steps to hers and once forgot, leaving her behind. He slapped himself in the forehead with his meaty hand and grinned at her. "I've got to remember. I've got me a friend now who's not as big as I am."

"Well, it looks like we've got to find something to eat, doesn't it, Violet?"

"I guess so, Bailey." Violet was tired. For four days, they had walked along the road and she had grown confident that there was no harm in the huge young man. She'd also discovered that people gave them strange looks. *We do look odd*, she thought, glancing over at him. Bailey wore shapeless black trousers ripped along one knee, and his bulky coat barely met over his arching chest. She looked down at her own ragged skirt and at her shoes that were scuffed. Her clothes offered little protection from the cold. People looked at them when they entered towns and she soon found out what they thought.

One police officer said, "We don't need none of your kind here." He was a tall, lath-lean man with a hook nose and a shaggy cavalry mustache. His eyes fell on Violet and he said harshly, "We don't need no bad women in this town. Just move on out!"

When they were on the road outside of town, Bailey said, "Why'd he call you a bad woman?"

"Oh, I don't know, Bailey," Violet said sharply. "People just think bad things."

It had troubled Bailey, and he'd asked her several times. Usually he forgot things quickly, but he remembered that sheriff and could not get the incident out of his head. Now as they trudged along, Bailey said, "Look! There's a camp. Maybe we can get something to eat."

He led Violet off the road, and she stopped abruptly when she saw a group of six or eight tramps. They were gathered around a fire over which bubbled a pot of stew.

"Nothing for you here," a hulking tramp said. He had a black stocking cap over his ears and small, mean-looking eyes.

"Wait a minute! Maybe that lady wants something." The tramp who spoke was much smaller. He had a sharp face like a weasel and hadn't shaved in some time. "We've always got something for ladies, ain't we, Bo?"

The larger tramp looked down at his companion and, catching the look on his face, he said, "I guess."

Bailey moved in quickly and Violet followed apprehensively. "I'm not hungry," she said. "You eat something if you want, Bailey."

"Aw, now," the big tramp said. "We wouldn't let a road sister like you go hungry." He searched around and found an empty can and put some of the stew in it. "You just eat that now." He handed it to her and his hand fell on her shoulder. He squeezed it, adding, "We don't see many pretty ladies down this way."

Violet pulled back quickly and handed the can to Bailey. "Here, Bailey, I don't want any."

Bailey looked at her, his large eyes wide with surprise. "But you got to eat something!"

The big tramp said, "You take your stew, big boy, and get on down the road." He looked at the bulky figure of Bailey and reached down and picked up a walking stick made of hickory. It was a heavy instrument, blunt and lethal. "We'll take care of your girlfriend."

Bailey stared at him, confused. Things were moving too fast for him. And then it happened.

The small tramp rose to his feet and went over and grabbed Violet, who cried out at once, "Bailey!—"

"Let her alone!" Bailey said. He was holding the can of stew in his left hand and took a step forward. One of the other tramps rose and went to Violet's other side, taking her other arm. He had broken teeth and a wolfish look in his eye. "Get out of here before you get your skull broke!"

When Violet cried out again, Bailey tossed the can to the ground, spilling the stew. "You fellas get away from her!" he said.

A ragged laugh ran around the other tramps. Two more of them got up and came to form a menacing ring around Bailey and Violet. The big tramp lifted his cudgel and slapped it into his fist. It made a meaty sound and he snarled, "Get out of here, you big ox, or I'll crush your skull!"

Despair ran through Violet. She struggled to get away and when the weasel-faced man twisted her arm, she cried aloud.

For all his size, Bailey moved quickly. He didn't close his fist, but struck the small man in the chest with a blow that drove a "whoosh!" out of the tramp, who went backward, rolling to the ground.

Instantly, the hulking tramp raised the cudgel and brought it down across Bailey's shoulders. It made a thumping sound, but to the amazement of the tramps, the blow was totally ineffective. Bailey seemed not to have felt it. He turned and, reaching out, closed his hand on the fist that held the club. "You shud'na did that, Bo," he said, almost pleasantly, and then began to squeeze.

Violet wrenched herself away from the tramp holding her arm and stood speechless. The larger tramp looked almost fragile next to Bailey's bulk—and something terrible was happening!

His eyes bulged out and his mouth opened like a fish. A whiny noise issued from him as he tried to pull away, but his hand was buried in solid concrete. "Lemme go! You're breaking every bone in my hand!" he cried out. He reached out to strike Bailey with the other hand. Bailey, confused, squeezed all the harder. The big tramp reached out and touched Bailey's hand, screaming mindlessly, a high, frightened cry.

"Let him go, Bailey! You're breaking his hand," Violet said, running to stand beside him and putting her hand on his arm.

Bailey at once released his grip. The cudgel fell to the ground and he ignored it. The big tramp sank to his knees, cradling his broken fingers with his other hand, making guttural noises in his throat. Bailey looked down at him and said, "Didn't mean to do that." He looked around at the other tramps who were staring at him. "You fellers shouldn't oughter hurt women. It ain't nice." He paused to wait for their replies and when there were none, he turned calmly and said, "Come on, Violet, we best be on our way."

When they were clear of the hobo camp, Violet tramped along beside Bailey wordlessly. Her heart was still fluttering. She well knew if it hadn't been for the massive strength of the big man she would have been savaged. She put her hand in his and he looked down at her in surprise, then smiled.

"Thank you, Bailey," Violet said finally.

"You're welcome."

Violet smiled at his brief reply and the two walked along the road holding hands for some time.

The next week was an education for Violet. She learned how to beg, for one thing. Determined not to be a burden on Bailey, she went from house to house asking for work in exchange for something to eat. Sometimes she received an astonished stare and often a curt refusal. More often, however, she was offered a meal and inevitably she would say, "My brother will do any heavy work you've got. We're both pretty hungry."

The first time Bailey heard her say this, he said, "You called me your brother."

"Well, I guess you are in a way."

"Do you have a real brother?"

"Oh, yes, I've got two." She'd told Bailey about Ray and described eleven-year-old Clinton to him. Afterward, he wanted to know about the rest of her family. He sat quietly as she spoke. When she was finished, she looked at him, saying, "Well, you know all about me now."

"That's a fine family. You ought'a go home."

"I've got to get Ray home. We're very close, Bailey. I've got to help him."

Bailey hunched himself over the fire. They were camped out in an abandoned barn, one of the best places they had found. The fire crackled and sputtered, and he added another stick to it. They had eaten a good meal—a can of corn, some turnips they had found in a field, and a loaf of bread and a jar of jelly for dessert. A kindly woman had given them half a pound of coffee, and Violet had used it sparingly. Both of them sat there soaking up the warmth of the crackling fire and sipping the pungent brew.

"I ain't never had a friend—not really."

Violet grinned at him. At times she was able to close out the difficulties that lay behind her, as well as those that lay before her. Now she took another bite of bread mortared with plum jelly and chewed it with pleasure. "It's good to have friends," she said.

"I bet you have a lot of 'em, don't you, Violet?"

Violet nodded and said, "Yes, I do—back home." When he didn't answer, she saw that there was a sadness in his moon-shaped face. "When we find Ray, you can come home with us, Bailey. There's lots of work to do on our farm and plenty to eat. And you'd like my family."

Bailey gave her an odd look. Her words seemed to trouble him, for he fumbled in his pocket and pulled out the watch and looked down. He did this when he was nervous or wanted reassurance, Violet had noticed. Finally, he looked up and said softly, "I don't reckon I'd like anything better."

From far away, the cry of an owl came to them. It was a lonely sound and made both the young man and the young woman feel glad that they were sheltered by the abandoned barn. The fire was warm and cheerful, and when Violet rolled in her blanket and went to sleep, the hulking form of Bailey remained stationary. He stared at the fire for long periods and from time to time, he'd look over at Violet, and at such times his lips would turn up in a smile. He was a lonely human being—a child trapped in the body of a giant, feared by most—and without skills and without a future. He looked at Violet again and whispered, "I reckon I'd like it better than anything!"

 4 

"I'M A STUART!"

"I just got a call from Pete."

Amos Stuart came into the kitchen where his wife, Rose, was studying a cookbook. He paused for one moment, abruptly aware of how she'd kept her youthful good looks. Her ash blond hair had a little gray, but her dark blue eyes were sharp and clear as ever.

"What did Pete say?" Rose asked. Laying the cookbook down, she turned to face him. She was proud of this husband of hers and seldom failed to show it. She wouldn't have cared if he'd been a ditch digger, but Amos was a celebrity of sorts. His name was at the top of prestigious columns in the Hearst chain of newspapers, and his novel, published the previous year, had attracted favorable attention. Now, however, she saw that he was concerned. "Is Pete sick?"

"No, but Leslie is." Leslie was his brother's wife. She had not been in good health for some time. Amos frowned, leaning over on the counter. He was wearing a pair of shapeless trousers and a worn white shirt that Rose had tried time and time again to throw away. He cared little about fancy dress, and it was a mammoth struggle to get him into formal attire to attend some of his more important appointments.

"She's been sick for over a month, he says, and can hardly get around."

"What's wrong with her?"

"I don't know, but it sounds serious. The doctors aren't too optimistic."

"They're having a hard time, aren't they? Maybe we can help them out with a little more money."

"Maybe so. You've been good to help my family."

"Why wouldn't I? They're my family, too. I'm a Stuart, aren't I?"

Amos leaned over and kissed her soundly. "The best-looking one of the Stuarts, I must say."

She flushed, for his compliments still had the power to move her. "Be serious, Amos. What can we do?"

"Well, it's Stephen and Mona. Pete's having trouble taking care of them. He can't work on that wildcat oil rig of his and care for two small children."

"Maybe we could afford to hire them some help. You'll see Pete at the reunion, won't you?"

"I don't know if he'll be able to come. He doesn't have a cent." A line of worry appeared on Amos's brow and he shook his head dolefully. "That rig he's running takes every dime he can get his hands on. I wish he could leave it and go to work for a big oil company. But in these times there haven't been any good offers."

Rose took off her apron, folded it, then laid it down. "We'll see if we can do something." She reached up and put her hand on his cheek. "As smart as you are, you won't have any trouble."

"The smartest thing I've ever done," he grinned, "was to marry you!"

"You may be right about that!" she quipped, a saucy light in her eyes. A thought came to her, and she said, "Jerry's coming over for supper tonight."

"You'd better cook enough for a regiment then. I've never seen anyone eat as much as he does. What about Maury? She's been so busy with those suffrage protests I don't think she's taken time to eat." Maury was their daughter. At the age of twenty-nine, she still lived at home, though she came and went with total independence.

"She'll be here, too. I thought since we'll be in Arkansas for Christmas that we would give them their gifts tonight."

"Why, it's a week till Christmas!"

"Doesn't matter." She made a face, adding, "Things are so tight that I didn't spend much this year on gifts. Anyway, this will be our celebration."

Jerry Stuart strode breezily into the room, going over to kiss Maury soundly on the cheek. Stepping back, he studied her carefully. He was a tall man of thirty, with the blackest hair possible, and green eyes. He was wearing a pair of gray slacks and a navy blue coat that set off his athletic figure. He shook his head as he said sadly, "You can find more ways to look ugly than any good-looking woman I ever saw, Maury."

Maury had the good looks of the Stuart family. She had red hair, the same green eyes as Jerry, and a shapely figure. She had the temper to go with her red hair, and now it flared. "Don't you start on my clothes, Jerry!"

"You look like an undertaker! Why don't you go see Mae West in that new movie of hers, *She Done Him Wrong*? Now there's a gal who knows how to catch a guy's eye!"

"She's nothing but a cheap floozy!"

"Yeah, but she's a real curvy eyeful." Jerry reached out and took the sleeve of Maury's black dress as if it were a dead worm. "Where'd you get this little number? From the Salvation Army?"

"There's nothing wrong with this dress!" Maury snatched her arm back, aware that he was teasing her as he always did. Actually she was aware that her taste in clothing was not good. The dress was an old one, since school teachers could not afford expensive new clothing. Defensively she snapped, "I suppose you want me to wear one of those short skirts like that—that woman you brought here last month?"

Jerry came over and put his arm around Maury. "Aw, Sis, I'm just kidding." Squeezing her affectionately, he said, "It's just that I think you're the best-looking girl in town and I'd like to see you dress up and primp a little more."

"You don't need a new dress to teach school," she said gruffly. "And the school doesn't permit teachers to wear makeup."

Jerry reached over and grabbed her. "You don't need to teach school. I thought you were going to marry ol' What's-His-Name?" He knew Clyde Baxter's name well enough, but had disliked him so intensely he deliberately chose to ignore him. Jerry Stuart was a careless fellow, but if anything worried him more than his own failure to find his place in life, it was Maury's choice to remain single. At the age of twenty-nine she was still attractive, but had passed up every opportunity to get married.

"Ol' What's-His-Name," Maury said with distaste, "was about as interesting and fascinating as a bowl of cold oatmeal. Come on into the dining room. We've been waiting for you."

Maury led Jerry into the dining room where he was greeted by his parents. As he sat down, he waited until his father asked the blessing, then began loading up his plate. "I'm a growing boy," he said, aware of Maury's incredulous stare. "Got to keep my strength up."

"Up for what?" Maury sniffed. "You're not working, are you?"

Jerry was not disturbed. He grinned back at his sister and said, "I'll have you know that I've got a respectable job now. I'm a substitute pilot for Royal Airlines."

"Will you be flying much?"

"Not unless one of the regular pilots gets sick." He put a fork full of mashed potatoes in his mouth, swallowed it, and said slyly, "I would like for one of them to get pleasantly sick."

"What do you mean by pleasantly sick?" Maury demanded.

"I mean, I'd like one of them with no responsibilities and with money in the bank, a fellow who doesn't need to fly anyhow—I would like for him to get sick enough so he wasn't able to fly. Then I could fly in his place. Why don't you pray for that, Mom?"

"I'll do no such thing. I wish you'd get a regular job."

"Might be a good idea," Amos shrugged. "The way this depression is going, not many people are going to travel by air."

Jerry's face lengthened for a moment. "That's a fact. Pilots are a dime a dozen. But it'll get better. It's bound to; it can't get any worse."

"Yes it could. We could be hungry and out on the street," Rose answered quickly. She was distressed that this fine-looking son of hers had so missed his way. He had no profession and though he was an excellent pilot, he'd been too unstable to keep a job. And even worse, he had no feeling for God—so it seemed. She'd stopped long ago saying much to him, and now she had to bite her lip to stop the sermon that leaped to it.

As they ate, they talked about the family. It was Rose who said, "Your aunt Leslie is ill. We've got to do something about it."

The conversation turned to Pete, who had always been one of Amos's favorites. There had been a goodness and steadiness in this brother of his and he had always admired him. "Money is tight, but maybe we can spare a few dollars to hire some help of some kind to take care of the kids."

Maury had been stirring her coffee idly. At his words she looked up and said abruptly, "No need of that. I'll go down and take care of the children for Aunt Leslie."

If Jerry had not spoken, her parents might have persuaded her against such a venture. They had been concerned about Maury. She had finished college, floated around with about half a dozen jobs, and had finally settled into a teaching position for which she was ill-suited. Her natural good humor had been blunted by the limitations of the work. Amos and Rose had often thought aloud that she would not teach school for long. "But what about your job? You can't just quit in the middle of the year!" Rose exclaimed.

But Jerry ran over his mother's words. "You! Why, you couldn't keep those hooligans for two days!"

Maury's eyes narrowed. "How do you know what I can do? I keep twenty-five hooligans, as you call them, every day."

"You don't do it living in a shack in Oklahoma. I've been down there," Jerry said, shaking his head. He did not stop eating, but spoke around the steak as he mumbled. "It's terrible the way they live. They don't even have an inside bathroom." He looked over at his father and winked. "Can you imagine Maury in an outside privy, Dad?"

Maury had been only half serious, but Jerry's words irritated her. "I can stand anything," she said icily. "Nothing can be worse than putting up with that schoolroom every day!"

"That's what you think," Jerry nodded. He began to outline the hardships of the life that Pete and his family were going through. He'd spent a little time with them on a flight down through Oklahoma and had seen their privations. "I haven't seen a worse place than that part of Oklahoma," he ended his speech.

"Jerry, hush!" Rose said sharply. Turning to Maury, she said, "You're not serious, are you?"

Maury had not been particularly serious, but Jerry's words had fired her. "Yes, I'm serious—and don't worry about school. My substitute is already convinced that she can do better than I can." She was an honest girl and grinned abruptly. "And she probably can, too! She loves the little 'hooligans'!"

The argument that began at supper lasted for two days. It was on Jerry's return that he once again warned her that she wouldn't be able to stand it, and Maury spoke out in anger. "Everyone thinks I'm some kind of a spoiled brat. I'll admit I've had things easy, but I'm a Stuart!"

At once, Amos came to stand beside her and said, "Of course you're a Stuart, and you can do anything you put your mind to!" He put his arm around her and kissed her cheek. "If you really could go for a while, Maury, I think it would be wonderful. Leslie has always liked you, and the kids would like you too. It would be a fine thing."

Maury hugged him, grateful for his warm support. She loved her father fiercely and responded to his approval. "All right then, I'll go. That's all there is to it."

She cast a triumphant glance toward Jerry, who was leaning against the door, his handsome face half smiling. "I think it would be good for you," he said slowly. "There's one-holers and two-holers."

Maury stared at him. "What on earth are you talking about?" she demanded.

"The outdoor privies! Some of them are one-holers and some are two-holers. You see—"

"I don't want to hear anymore of that nonsense," Maury said hastily. "I'd go even if I had to walk on my own two feet to get there."

"Well," Jerry said lazily, "no need for that. I'll fly you down—" he turned to his father, saying, "if you'll pay for the gas, Dad."

"Where would you get a plane?"

"Tom Mackelhaney told me I could have use of the old Stedman." He referred to an ancient two-seater, a crop duster. "It throws oil in the face of the passenger in the front cockpit." He grinned again at his sister. "If you're going to the oil fields it wouldn't hurt you to get acquainted with a little of that stuff. I'll pick you up at six o'clock in the morning."

Maury stared at him. "You knew I was going, didn't you?"

"You never could resist a dare." He grew serious for a moment, then said, "I'm glad you're going. I think a lot of Uncle Pete and I really think he needs the help." He came over to her, hugged her, then kissed her smooth cheek. "You're a good-looking gal," he said. "Some guy's missing a big chance with you. Hate to see a good woman wasted. Be ready at dawn and bring a sack in case you throw up. I don't want you to have to clean that plane out, and I'm certainly not going to."

"Will this thing fly?" Maury stared doubtfully at the plane that Jerry patted fondly.

"Of course it will fly." Jerry gave her an insulted look. "With a pilot like me how could it not? Are you scared?"

Maury shook her head, her lips drawn into a stubborn line. "Just show me how to get into this contraption."

"Well, it's going to be quite a trick in that skirt."

Gritting her teeth and struggling with the skirt, Maury managed to get into the front seat. Jerry clambered up on the wing and handed her a soft leather helmet with huge goggles. As she wrestled it on over her heavy mass of hair, he strapped her in. Then he got into his own seat and she heard his voice. "You sure you want to do this?"

"Yes!"

He started the engine, and Maury nearly leaped out of her seat at the roaring explosion. Jerry ran the engine briefly, then slowly taxied the plane out on the runway. The frail craft trembled as Jerry revved up the engine, and they went bumping along clumsily for what seemed like a long time. Finally Jerry shouted, "Here we go!" and suddenly there was no roughness. Looking out over the sides, Maury saw the ground fall away. She gripped the edge of her seat convulsively, expecting to fall at any second.

The air was freezing and the ground beneath was white with snow. Soon, however, Jerry began to point out parts of the city that she had seen from the ground. It looked so different from the air, and Maury forgot her fear. Finally he wheeled the plane around and began to gain altitude.

The roar of the engine almost lulled Maury to sleep—but it was too cold for that. After the first wave of fear left her she enjoyed looking down at the earth. Snow covered it and it was a beautiful white wonderland. Rivers made black, curling, serpentine forms, breaking the pristine whiteness of the snow. Mountains jutted up at the sky, and ahead white clouds dotted the blue horizon.

They had to stop frequently for fuel, but Jerry was in a hurry. "I know it's cold and uncomfortable, but it's quick," he said. "This is the last stop. Can you make it, Sis?"

"Sure I can, Brother."

He leaned over and kissed her cold cheek. "You're all right," he said and went back to rev up the engine.

They landed on a small field in Oklahoma. Jerry said, "Can you make it by yourself, Sis? I've really got to get back."

"Yes, I'll have someone call me a taxi."

"Well, I can do that! You're a taxi!" he laughed.

"You fool!" Maury threw her arms around him and hugged him tightly, whispering, "Thanks, Jerry." She released him and looked up into his green eyes, so much like her own.

He looked down at her and said, "We green-eyed, good-looking Stuarts have to take care of each other, don't we?"

He clapped her on the shoulder and winked playfully, and then turned and walked back to the airplane.

Maury watched him take off, and when the plane was a mere dot in the sky, she turned and walked inside a small hangar. It was cold inside, but in the manager's office a wood-burning stove glowed with a cheery appearance. "I need to hire someone to take me to my uncle's," she said.

"Might cost quite a bit."

"I can pay," Maury said coolly, "but I'm in a hurry."

The manager called out, "Harry, this lady needs to be hauled somewhere. You take her, will you?"

Harry turned out to be a loquacious Oklahoman who wanted to know everything about Maury. He fancied himself a Romeo and made himself totally available. "While you are here, you and me could go out and see the sights. What do you say?"

"I'll have to think about it."

"Sure you will. Here's the number. Just call the airport. I'll show you a good time, Sweetheart."

He followed her instructions, which she had gotten from Jerry, and soon pulled up in the middle of what seemed to be the most desolate land that she'd ever seen. A ramshackle house of some sort stood at the bottom of a half-finished oil derrick, and everything looked incomplete, worn out, and depressing.

"How much?" she asked.

"Have to have three dollars. It was a long trip."

She gave him four dollars and said, "Thanks!"

"Don't forget—you got my phone number. We'll have us a hot time, Baby!"

Maury picked up her suitcase and started up the path to

the house. When she was ten feet away, Pete came out. She remembered him instantly, though she had not seen him for several years. "Uncle Pete!" she greeted him, putting down her suitcase as he came to her and put his arms around her.

He leaned back and shook his head. "You look good, Maury! A sight for sore eyes!" Doubt came to him and he shook his head again. "I ain't sure about this. It's awful rough here. You ain't used to it."

"Well, I'll get used to it," Maury said firmly. "Come on now, where are the kids? I haven't seen them since they were in diapers."

She stepped into the house—which was a depressing experience. It was the very barest, minimum sort of shelter, and little housekeeping had been done. She ignored the wallpaper, which was old newspaper that was peeling off in spots, and she turned to face the two youngsters who stood regarding her with wide eyes.

"Well, this is Stephen and this is Mona. Kids, this is your cousin Maury."

Stephen, at the age of ten, was a small copy of his father, lank and with a head of shaggy black hair that needed cutting. "That's a funny name," he said loudly.

His sister, Mona, two years his junior, immediately slapped at him. "Don't talk like that, Stephen. It ain't polite."

An argument ensued and Pete at once said, "You kids hush up." He turned to Maury, saying, "Give me your suitcase. We fixed a room for you—it ain't much, but at least you'll have a little privacy."

"That was our room. Now we've got to sleep in here," Stephen grumbled.

"You hush!" Mona said. She came over and touched Maury's coat gently and said, "I hope you like it here. Do you like to play dolls?"

"I love to play dolls." Maury nodded. She looked over at the boy, who had a mulish look on his face. "I'm sorry to take your bedroom, Stephen, but maybe I can make it up to you."

"Sure you can," Pete said hastily. "I'll go see if Leslie's awake. The doctor left some sleeping medicine that just knocks her for a loop." He disappeared through one of the two doors that broke up the back side of the larger room. Soon he reappeared and said, "Come on in—she's awake."

Maury went inside and was appalled by the room. It was piled high with dirty clothes, and the smell was terrible. "Hello, Aunt Leslie," she said. "It's been a long time."

Leslie Stuart had been a pretty girl once, but whatever disease had come had thinned her down so that her cheeks were hollow and her eyes were almost hidden in the crevices of their sockets. "Hello, Maury," she whispered. There was a glaze over her dark brown eyes and the drug had slowed her reactions down. "I'm sorry you had to come. Haven't been able to take care of the house."

"You just don't worry about that, Aunt Leslie. That's what I came for. I was sick of teaching school, so this will be like a vacation for me."

Some vacation, Maury thought grimly. She was sitting at the table late one night after the kids had finally gone to bed. She had been in Oklahoma for only five days, and it seemed like every bone in her body ached. She had never lived under primitive conditions before, and now she was learning how difficult it was for the very poor to just stay alive. Washing clothes, for example, was a nightmare. It consisted of building a fire under a huge, black pot that Pete had rigged up, and stirring them with a stick. Her hands, she noticed, were raw from the harsh soap and the freezing December wind. She saw that her nails, which she had always kept immaculate, were cracked and broken.

She wanted to lean her head down on the table, but she seemed to hear Jerry's mocking voice telling her she was too soft. Defiantly, she straightened up, saying, "It could be worse." But there was an honesty in this woman and she added, "But I don't know how!"

Leslie was very ill; Maury saw that now. She had not tried to talk to Pete about it, for it was not necessary. She saw the look of worry in his fine gray eyes and did not want to add to his burdens. He was engaged in a tremendous struggle to drill an oil well almost single-handedly. She had watched enough to know that it was a gargantuan task that kept him busy sometimes as much as twenty hours in a day. He had to patch up old equipment, and he spent much time out scrounging for things he could not afford to buy. What he did find was worn out and practically useless, but he moved stubbornly forward, improvising with what he had.

"He's quite a man," Maury whispered to herself, thinking of Pete. He was still out working on the rig. She could hear his hammer ringing on metal, and she made light of her own hardship. Finally, she got up and began to heat the stew on the woodstove. When he came in, she said, "Uncle Pete, sit down and try to eat something."

Pete's face was lined with fatigue and pinched white with the cold. He pulled off his gloves awkwardly and held his hands over the stove, then slumped down in the chair. "Sounds good to me." His voice slurred with weariness. He ate the stew slowly and then drank bitter black coffee fixed just the way he liked it.

Maury sat down beside him, nursing a cup of coffee that lacked the cream Maury had considered a necessity until now. "Did the kids behave themselves?" he asked, rousing himself.

"Yes, they did. When they got home from school, I helped them with their homework."

"I bet they hated that."

"Stephen did, but Mona's a darling."

A grin touched Pete's lips. "Steve's like I am—he needs education with a two-by-four."

They talked for a while and finally she asked, "When are you leaving to go to the reunion?"

"I'm not going."

Maury stared at him with shock. "But you have to go—you

all promised." She referred to the promise that all the sons and daughters of Will and Marian Stuart had made when Will had died. She'd heard it over and over again from Amos. "We all promised that every Christmas—no matter what—we would be there." It had become a tradition with them.

"Why, you've got to go, Uncle Pete!" Maury urged.

"No money and no time." He looked helpless for a moment, strong man that he was, and finally said, "I just can't quit, Maury. I've just got to bring this well in. It's the only hope I've got." He looked down at his rough hands and shook his head. "I've got to do something for Leslie and the kids. She needs a doctor, and they need everything."

Maury did not argue, but the next day she took time to go to a store where she made a collect phone call. She finally managed to get her father on the phone.

"Dad," she said, "Pete says that he's not going to go to the reunion."

"Why, he's got to go," Amos's voice crackled over the phone.

Maury had made up her mind. "Wire me some money and I'll get Uncle Pete a ticket on a train to Arkansas. I'll have him there even if I have to knock him out and drag him."

"All right! Tell Pete not to worry about the money. We'll take care of it. We Stuarts have to stick together."

After a little more talk, Maury hung up. She felt a lot better. "At least," she said, "I know this is right. Uncle Pete deserves something." She felt a warm glow of pride, knowing that getting her uncle to the reunion was her doing. But she thought of the pile of dirty clothes at the house, and wearily turned to go face the grim realities of life at a wildcat oil rig.

 5 

CHRISTMAS IN THE OZARKS

Snow had laid ragged white strips on the hills that held the Stuart house. At three in the afternoon tiny granules had begun to fill the air, and now the flakes—as Owen Stuart looked out the window—were getting larger. He was a big man with broad shoulders, a reminder of the days when he had been a prizefighter. He wore a blue sweater, and from the right sleeve a gleaming steel hook extended, a memento of the Great War. He turned and spoke to Logan, who was standing beside him staring out the window. "I have about a million memories of this place," he said. "Do you remember the time we shot the black bear? Right over there where the old barn used to be?"

"Yup," Logan said. "I was only seven and that varmint just about scared me to death."

Gavin Stuart rose from the rocking chair where he had been looking at old photos and came to stare out the window with them. "I've always been sorry I didn't get to see that," he remarked. "It must have been exciting." Gavin was still a fine-looking man at thirty-nine. His wife, Heather, had stayed home with their children, Phillip and Sidney, as Phillip was ill.

The three men stood talking quietly until Lylah Stuart came in from the hall to announce, "It's time to eat! Come and get it before we throw it out."

Her name was Hart now. Her husband, Jesse, was sitting over at the library table that had come from the old Methodist parsonage. He was writing, as he usually was, but looked up, grinning. "Just bring it in here and wait on me like a good wife should."

"That's right," Amos said, and grinned. "Movie stars ought to wait on their worthless husbands."

Lylah Hart was a beautiful woman—at the age of fifty-one she looked no more than thirty-five. She had auburn hair and violet eyes that were deep-set and wide-spaced. She was, in fact, a star of movies, and she had produced a successful picture entitled *The Gangster.* It had been a thinly disguised screen biography of Al Capone. Now she looked over at her brother Pete and thought of the time he had shot Hymie Holtzman, who was trying to kill Amos. She ignored Amos's teasing and went over beside Pete. Putting her arm around him, she said, "I wish you'd hurry up and get that oil well in. I could use some money for my business."

Pete grinned at her thinly. "Just get some big star like Rudolph Valentino to star in your movie like you did for *The Gangster.*"

"Well, in the first place he's dead," Jesse Hart said. Jesse had crisp brown hair that was slightly curly and a neat, short beard. He leaned back in his chair and stroked his square face thoughtfully. "And in the second place, he'd be wrong for the role."

"Who's big in movies these days?" Owen demanded. "I can't keep up with these pictures. Besides, most of them aren't worth seeing."

"You preachers all think like that," Logan said. "And I guess you may be right. There's some pretty raw stuff."

"More reason for making good ones," Lylah said strongly. "Come on in and let's eat."

But Owen was still staring out the window. "I remember the morning you left to go to Bible school, Lylah. Remember that, Amos?"

Amos laughed aloud, humor dancing in his eyes. "I guess I do! You and I caught her smoking out behind the barn."

Lylah's eyes flashed. "Let's not start telling stories. I might have a few to tell on you two."

At once Jesse straightened up. "Let's have them," he urged. "I'm always needing scandals on the famous Stuart family."

Lylah went over and grabbed him by the ear, pulling him protesting out of the chair. "Never mind that—you come along and eat."

They were soon gathered around the table and it was Owen who asked the blessing. "Well, there it is. The best meal we could put together," Anne said. She and Helen and the other women had worked on the meal all day long.

"It's a good meal!" Lenora Stuart spoke up. She was wearing the black uniform of a Salvation Army lassie. An accident while horseback riding had crippled her years ago, but her work in Chicago with the Salvation Army brought her satisfaction. Christie was the youngest of Will and Marian Stuart's children. She had married Mario Castellano. "I wish Mario and the kids were here. All he ever wants to eat is Italian food."

"How's Mario doing?" Amos inquired. He had an interest in Mario's family, the Castellanos. Nick, the eldest brother, had taken Amos in when he was practically starving, but since then, the two had gone in different directions. The Castellanos had grown powerful in the gang world. Only Mario had managed to escape. He had fallen in love with Christie and had firmly turned his back on the family business—bootlegging and the rackets.

"Mario's fine," Christie smiled. "His practice is going well. I just hope Maria and little Anthony are behaving themselves. Mario spoils them too much."

"What about Nick and Eddy?" Owen asked. He was carving the turkey expertly. He grasped the fork in his left hand and had fastened the gleaming, razor-sharp carving knife in his steel hook. Years ago he had learned to do practically anything a person with two hands could do. "I worry about those fellows a lot. I think a lot of them." Owen felt a bond with Eddy due to the time they had served together in France. Owen prayed earnestly for the Castellanos—for their safety and especially for their salvation.

Amos shook his head. "They're still involved in the rackets. I wish we could talk to them—but you know how they are."

The talk ran around the table and they enjoyed the meal tremendously. They were a close family. Amos looked around thinking, *This is the first year we've met without the children. Maybe it's best this way. But we can bring them next year, I guess.*

Amos's gaze went around the faces. He studied Owen, an evangelist now, who spoke to thousands. He knew that out of the offerings that came in, Owen only kept enough for his family. The rest he used to help struggling young ministers. Owen held a congressional medal from the Great War, although he himself never mentioned it.

Amos's eyes shifted to his sister Lylah. He admired her beauty and loved her dearly. He was thankful daily that this sister he was so close to had finally accepted the Lord after going her own way for so many years. He wondered about her son, Adam. Very few knew that the movie star, Lylah Stuart, had been involved in an affair with Baron von Richthofen and that Adam was the result of that brief affair. *I wonder if Lylah's told him yet who his father is.* Amos had told his sister that she was making a mistake by keeping his father's identity a secret from Adam, but, though she was now married, Lylah thought it would be better to keep it quiet.

Amos's eyes moved around the table, stopping on Logan. He was a farmer and had been chosen by the rest of them to stay on the old home place. *Too bad he hasn't had more of a chance,* he thought. *He could have done better than any of us. I guess he's worried about Ray and Violet—that's enough to drive a man crazy—not knowing where his children are, out there in this world somewhere.* He spoke up, asking, "Any word at all about Ray and Violet, Logan?"

Logan glanced at Anne and she replied quickly, "We've gotten one postcard from Ray. Violet ain't got where he is in Rockford yet, but I guess she'll get there eventually."

"I wish you had let me know," Amos said with some irritation. He tapped his water glass with his fork nervously. "We could've helped."

Logan's jaw was stubborn. "You've helped enough," he said. Amos glanced at him and saw that it was the end of that conversation. He shifted his glance to Lenora and Christie, then looked at Pete. "Tell us more about the oil business," he said. "I keep hearing about Indians who never had a dime getting rich out there."

Pete shook his head. "Most of that's just talk. When Indians do have land, some big company like Kingman manages to force them off it."

"Kingman?" Owen asked. "Who's that?"

"Kingman Oil Company," Pete said grimly. "They've been trying to buy me out, and they ain't real partic'lar how they go about it."

"I've heard a little about that," Amos said. "From what I hear, the big outfits, like Kingman, hire a bunch of thugs who make it rough on those who won't sell out. They giving you any trouble?"

"Some." Pete's face turned hard, but he said no more.

After the meal, they sat in the parlor and opened presents—simple gifts, none that were expensive—and there was a great deal of laughter and joking about some of them. "I remember," Owen said, "when I was about six that we made presents for each other. There was no money then."

"I remember that," Lylah said, half closing her eyes. "I wanted a doll and didn't get it." She hardened her jaw and said, "That's why I want Adam to have everything—everything I didn't have."

"I'm not sure that's best," Owen protested. He leaned back in his chair and held up the pocketknife that Amos had given him. It was a good one, and he loved knives. Amos had said jokingly, "You only have five fingernails, but you still need a good knife to clean them with." Now Owen said slowly, "I've seen it happen often—people want their children to have it easier so they spoil them and pamper them."

Pete said grimly, "I'm not likely to spoil and pamper Mona and Stephen. Not with this depression going on."

"It's got to end sometime," Logan said desperately. "Things can't keep on going down."

A knock on the door sounded, and Christie said, "I'll get it." She walked to the front door and opened it. She was greeted by a man who threw his arms around her and picked her up off the floor and kissed her soundly on the cheek. "Merry Christmas! How's the best-looking woman in the country doing?"

"Denton! You put me down!" Christie protested, laughing. "I'm an old married woman now."

"You still look good to me," Dent said. He put her down, but kept hold of her arms. At thirty-one, Denton DeForge was tall and as lean as he had been at eighteen. He had jet black hair and dark eyes to match and was as fine looking as ever.

Christie hugged him suddenly and said, "I remember the time you kissed me in the kitchen. It scared me to death!"

This delighted Dent. "I always remember that! I heard you got that family of yours started." He was delighted again with her blush and said, "You're just as bashful as ever. Come on, I've got presents for everybody."

Christie took his hand and pulled him into the dining room, where he was warmly greeted. He was a favorite of the younger Stuarts who had grown up with him. Lenora came over and kissed him. "You haven't been caught yet by some woman? I'm surprised at you, Dent! I thought you'd be the first to go."

"Too contrary to live with," Dent said and grinned complacently. He leaned over and kissed Lenora right on the lips. "How about you and me going out and partying a little bit and getting rid of these squares, Lenora?" He winked at her.

"You tried hard enough to get me to do that, didn't you, Dent?"

"Never made it though! Too bad." Dent could joke about these things, for though he had been a wild young man, he had been converted in a revival meeting. Most of it was the result of being witnessed to by Lenora. Now he handed out presents and joined in like one of the family.

After the presents had been opened, Logan pulled Denton to one side. "I'm worried about Violet," he said.

Dent's cheerful grin faded. He scratched his head and said, "Me, too. If I had known she was going, I would have kept her home."

"I don't think you could have," Logan said. "You know how stubborn she is."

"Well, she doesn't have any business traipsing around. It's rough enough for a man, but a woman—well, what she needs is a husband."

Logan stared at him. "For a long time I thought that might be you."

"Aw, I'm too old for her. And I'm too ornery for any woman to live with—stubborn, have to have my own way—just a boring old bachelor." Dent was not through with the question, however. He had been fond of Violet ever since Logan had moved his family to the farm and felt that he had had a hand in her raising. "She may think she's a woman, but she's not. She's led a sheltered life here. I have half a mind just to go find her and bring her home."

"You'd never find her."

"I reckon that's so, but you let me know as soon as she gets settled down." Denton DeForge had some stubbornness himself and now his dark eyes glinted. "If I get a chance, I'll go get her and bring her home. And I won't take any sass either."

Logan suddenly slapped Dent on the back. "By george, I believe you would!"

Almost at the moment that the family was talking about Violet, she was seated on the floor of a railcar wishing desperately that she were home. She and Bailey had found slim pickings on the road and finally had taken to riding the rails. It had been hard for her to learn the tricks of climbing onto a moving train. This was a world of which she knew nothing. Some of the bulls, as they were called, were brutal. She had seen them club men off trains. She'd also seen a group of angry riders seize one of the railroaders and throw him from a speeding train. On the other hand, some of the bulls were friendly enough and even helped the homeless men and women from time to time.

She'd found that there was danger in it, too. People got killed if they were careless. The cars were recklessly loaded and sometimes the load would shift with a sudden lurch of the train. A far more common accident occurred when riders misjudged the speed of a train. They made their grab for the ladder and often their legs were crushed.

As the train clattered along, she turned to Bailey, who was sitting beside her. They were on an open car filled with big sacks of lime that farmers would use to fertilize their fields. As the train slowed down, three men jumped onto the car. They stared at the pair, but said nothing. Once again, Violet was happy that Bailey was with her. More than once, men had approached her, but Bailey had scared them off, sometimes by just putting his huge forefinger on their chests and pushing them backward, and sometimes by doubling up his fist and holding it up before them. This was a lethal weapon that most men did not care to taste.

The train picked up speed and she said, "We've passed Chicago. We ought to be getting close to Rockford soon."

"Okay!" Bailey didn't care. They had passed farms and small towns, brown with withered cornstalks. They'd passed rivers, low and sluggish, or sometimes filled with brown water. It was all the same to him. Now he was whistling "Bye, Bye, Blackbird" perfectly on pitch. He turned and grinned. "Sing it, Violet!"

Violet glanced at the men at the other end of the car and shrugged. She began singing the song, keeping up with his melody. It had become fun for them to do. He was amazed at her ability to know the words to so many songs. She was equally amazed at his ability to whistle so many tunes. He couldn't read a note of music or a word, but he had the uncanny ability to remember any melody.

They slept for a while. When they woke, Violet pulled out a piece of bread. Borrowing Bailey's pocketknife, she cut it up into chunks. They kept each bite in their mouths a long time. Finally she handed him the rest of hers and said, "Here, Bailey—you eat this—I never liked the crusty part."

Two hours after dark, the train jolted to a halt. There were sounds of loud voices in the car next to them, and Violet sensed trouble. "Come on, Bailey. I think we're going to have to leave."

She was correct. Two bulls stuck their heads in and said, "Get off the train! And stay off—the whole lousy lot of you!"

One of the men at the other end of the car complained. "Aw, we ain't hurtin' nothin'," but it was useless.

"You're getting off, and don't try to crawl on again. This stuff of free rides is over! We've got our orders and the company isn't fooling."

Leaping to the ground, Bailey turned and helped Violet by catching her and steadying her as she hit the ground. All along the length of the train, figures were piling out of the cars. Some of them were running on the tops of the cars like frightened rats.

The air was filled with shouting and cursing, muted by the noise of the engine screaming in the night. Stumbling away from the cars, Violet was startled by a movement to her right. Turning, she saw a line of men walking toward the car, most of them carrying clubs, sticks, and pitchforks. One of them even had a shotgun.

"You ain't coming in here!" one of them shouted. "Take your empty bellies somewhere else. We've got enough of your kind. If you come this way, we'll club you down!"

One of the free riders demanded hoarsely, "What do you want us to do?"

"That ain't our business. We have enough to do to take care of ourselves. We can't feed a bunch of bums."

Violet touched Bailey's massive arm. "Come on, let's walk down the tracks."

They left at once, followed by others. They knew that in some towns, rail riders had been beaten into insensibility by mobs such as the one that greeted them. When they were out of sight of the town, one of the hobos glanced at the two. "Well, there ain't but one thing to do now."

"What's that?" Violet asked.

The hobo grinned. He was a sharp-faced man, smallish and quick. "We'll catch that same freight."

"The man said not to," Bailey said.

"It's a long way to Rockford. I ain't walking it."

"You're going to Rockford?"

"Sure. This train goes right through there. All we've got to do is get on."

"Let's try it, Bailey." Hope ran through Violet and she said, "All we've got to do is get on one more train." As it happened, it was easier than she thought. The train seemed to be feeling its way down the track, moving less than five miles an hour. And then by some sort of miracle, it ground to a halt. None of the hobos knew why, but immediately they all piled into a car and pulled the door shut. One of them whimpered, "If they find us here, they'll beat us half to death!"

Violet whispered, "They won't find us—God's going to take care of us." She had little faith, but almost at once, the train started moving and picked up speed and was soon rushing on toward Rockford.

Bailey turned to look at her with wonder in his round blue eyes. "Was it God who took care of us, Violet?"

"I think so."

The rooming house had been difficult to find. Violet and Bailey had wandered down the streets of Rockford looking for it, discovering finally that the address Violet had was incorrect. A grocery store owner had stared at them suspiciously when they had gone in to ask for Mrs. Jensen's rooming house.

"It's supposed to be on Jackson Street," Violet said. "But I can't find it. I've walked up and down and nobody knows a Mrs. Jensen."

"Maggie Jensen," the grocery owner shook his head. "Her place ain't on Jackson Street—it's over on Jimerson Street. Take that road right out there, go six blocks, and turn right. Follow the car tracks until you hit Jimerson, then turn left and her place is the sixth house—a big brownstone house on the right."

They had plodded along and now finally stood before the house, and sure enough, a small faded sign said, *Maggie Jensen's House—Boarders Taken.* "I'll wait here for you," Bailey said. "People get scared when they see me."

"No! You come with me," Violet ordered. She marched up the steps and knocked on the door. It was opened almost at once by a stern-faced woman in her fifties. "Yes, what do you want?"

"I'm looking for my brother, Ray Ballard."

The woman's eyes narrowed. "He ain't here no more."

Violet's heart sank. "But we got a postcard—"

"I tell you he ain't here. He was, but he had to leave a week ago. He couldn't pay his rent, and I can't afford to keep people who can't pay."

"Who is it, Ma?"

A heavyset man wearing thick spectacles came to stand beside the woman. "You looking for Ray?"

"Yes, do you know where he is?"

"Well, I ain't for sure, but chances are he's in that hobo jungle under the big bridge out south of town. That's where most of them go who can't pay."

"Thank you," Violet managed, and turned away dully. As they moved down the street, Bailey said, "That won't be hard. I know how to find hobo jungles."

Violet looked up at him and patted his arm. "Well, I guess we'd better go find it then."

It took the best part of three hours, but finally, sure enough, Bailey said, "Look—there's a bridge and there's some hobos!"

The two walked quickly toward it and one hobo, who was frying something in a pan, looked up at them. He spoke cheerfully, "Come in out of the cold. Welcome to the Rockford Hotel." He waved at the bridge and the people crowded together underneath.

"I'm looking for Ray Ballard."

At once, the hobo stood up. "Why, sure!" He pointed and said, "He's right over there. How do you happen to know Ray?"

"He's my brother," Violet said. Bailey followed her as she made straight for the corner of the bridge, ignoring the stares from the men. She had not gone far when she saw a sleeping man with a ragged blanket pulled up underneath his chin. Her heart seemed to stop and she whispered, "Ray!" Going to him, she fell on her knees and put her hand on his chest. "Ray—it's me—Violet!"

The sleeping man shook his head and opened his eyes groggily. He focused them and suddenly said, "Vi! Is it you?" He struggled to a sitting position and she threw her arms around him. He felt her tears on his whiskered cheek and when she drew back, he said, "What in the world are you doing here? How did you get here?"

"I came to get you. I'm going to take you home."

Ray stared at her incredulously, taking in her ragged clothes and sunken eyes. "You mean you bummed it all the way from home?"

"Yes! Now tell me, how are you? Are you still sick?"

"I'm about over it. I'm a bit hungry, I guess."

"We'll fix that!" She turned and said, "Bailey—" reaching into her pocket and handing him a dollar bill, almost the last of the three dollars she had stuck in her coat pocket. "Go get all the beans and bread you can buy with that. This is my brother Ray."

Ray looked up at the hulking man and blinked. "Well, glad to know you." He looked at Violet, his eyebrows raised. "Who is this?"

"This is Bailey." She rose and went to Bailey and pulled

him forward, looking up at him proudly. "He's kept me safe all the way, Ray. If it hadn't been for Bailey, I just wouldn't have made it. Shake hands with him, Ray."

Ray felt his hand swallowed by the massive fist of the young tramp. He looked in the mild blue eyes and swallowed. "I guess I owe you for this, Bailey."

"Aw, it wasn't nothing," Bailey mumbled. He turned and lumbered out, clutching the dollar in his fist. "I'll be right back," he said. "There was a store a ways back."

"He's a rough-looking fellow. He could do considerable damage if he set his mind to it."

Violet went over and sat beside Ray, holding his hand. "It's like I said, he's kept me safe, Ray. I think he's an angel of some kind—a mighty big one." She laughed, filled with relief at finding her brother. "I'm so glad to see you. Everything will be all right now."

"I just don't see how we're going to get out of this," Ray said hopelessly. "I don't want to go home a failure." He was much better now. The slight store of money that Violet had left had bought enough food to give him some strength, but the temperature was dropping. The three of them sat huddled around the campfire under the bridge talking about what they should do. It was settled that Bailey was going with them. Ray had learned to appreciate the young man, but he was still discouraged. He suddenly sat upright and said, "Maybe I could get a job with Uncle Pete at his oil rig. I'm sure he could use the help." He looked at Violet. "Bailey can take you home, but I'm going to Oklahoma."

Violet stared evenly at Ray and replied, "I'm going with you. I almost lost you once. I won't let that happen again."

Bailey had listened to the two talk for hours. Finally, he got up and said, "I'm going out for a while."

"What! It's cold! Stay here by the fire, Bailey," Violet had protested.

But Bailey shook his head and left without another word.

He returned late that afternoon. Coming to a halt in front of them he said, "Come on—we're going."

Violet and Ray had glanced at each other astonished. "Going where? What do you mean, Bailey?"

"I found a feller going to Oklahoma. You said you have an uncle there, didn't you? Somewhere around Oklahoma City?"

"Why yes, my uncle Pete. But how are we going to get there?"

A smile pulled the corners of Bailey's mouth upward. "It's a surprise! Come on—get all your stuff together."

"I don't know what he's talking about, but he does, I guess," Violet said. It was not the first time that Bailey had found some way to get them out of a predicament, but this seemed too far-fetched. "Come on, let's see what he's got," she said to Ray. The three of them gathered their pitiful belongings together and moved out from underneath the bridge. When they got to the roadway at the top, they saw a huge bobtruck parked with the engine throbbing. A man was standing there, his arms crossed and a cap pulled down over his ears. He looked up, snapping with considerable irritation, as Bailey approached. "Hurry up! I ain't got much time," he said.

"What is all this?" Violet said. "You're going to give us a ride to Oklahoma?"

"That's the deal. My name's Purdy. Two of you can ride in front, but one of you will have to ride in back with the load. I've got a little space back there." He gave Ray a rough glance, then added, "The looney here told me that you've been sick—you'd better lie down back there. It'll be warmer than this blasted cab."

Violet protested, but the man was impatient and said, "Either get in or stay—it don't make no difference to me."

"You're going to Oklahoma?" Ray asked.

"If you ever get in I am."

That settled the matter. Violet settled Ray down in the space in the back. The truck was loaded with bathroom fixtures that were crated up, but there was a space, eight feet square or less, long enough for him to lie down on. "This will be fine for me," Ray said, wrapping blankets about him and bundling one for a pillow. "I can sleep real good. It sure is warmer than under that bridge!"

Bailey and Violet scrambled into the cab. Purdy engaged the gears and the truck shuddered as he pulled out. The cab was relatively warm, and Violet said, "We sure thank you for giving us a ride."

"Don't thank me—it's a business deal."

"A business deal?" Violet stared at him, but he shrugged his shoulders and said no more.

They drove straight through to Oklahoma, the weather growing warmer as they moved south. Ray slept long hours, exchanging places with Bailey to ride in the cab from time to time. They had eaten all their provisions, and when Purdy pulled over to the side and set them off in Oklahoma City they had not eaten for twelve hours. Purdy said, "Here we are in Oklahoma City. Best I can do," he said.

Violet tried to thank him as she did before, but he said nothing. He climbed into the cab and the three of them watched the big truck rumble off.

"Well, it's warm here—at least warmer than Illinois," Ray said. "Let's find Uncle Pete."

"That shouldn't be too hard. If I have to I'll make a collect call to Uncle Amos." She looked up at the sky and said, "It's getting pretty late. Maybe we should do that now. What time is it, Bailey?"

Bailey stared at her and shrugged his shoulders.

Violet was puzzled. He always took great pride in pulling his watch out and announcing the time. "I don't know," he said.

"Well, let's see your watch," Violet insisted.

Bailey looked down at his battered shoes, mumbling, "I ain't got it."

All of a sudden, Violet understood and tears came to her eyes. "You gave your watch to that trucker to bring us to Oklahoma, didn't you, Bailey?"

"Aw, it just got in the way."

Violet felt a sudden fresh affection for this huge man who had so little. She turned to Ray and whispered, "It was the only thing he had and he was so proud of it." Turning back to him, she said, "You shouldn't have done it, Bailey."

Bailey summed up his feelings in one sentence. "I guess that's what friends are for."

Ray watched the scene and finally cleared his throat huskily. "Well, let's make that call. We've got to find Uncle Pete." He threw his arm around the massive shoulders of the big man and grinned. "Welcome to the Stuart family, brother!"

 6 

Dent Takes a Vacation

Logan pulled the slip of paper out of his pocket, unfolded it, then handed it to Denton. "Just got this here telegram from Pete and thought you ought to know about it, Dent."

Quickly, Dent scanned the telegram that said: "Ray and Violet are here with me. Both fine. Don't worry." Handing the telegram back, he said, "Well, that's a load off my mind!"

Logan nodded slowly. "Mine, too, of course. But I'm still worried about them—and about Pete, too."

"What's the trouble, Logan?"

"It's hard times for Pete. He's got his family there—his wife's sick. Amos's daughter Maury's there trying to help, but Pete don't need two extra mouths to feed."

"Why don't they come home?"

"Same old story—too stubborn. Ray wants to make it on his own. Violet would probably come, but I don't want her hitchhiking across the country."

A broad smile suddenly split the face of Dent DeForge. He was a restless man, the best mechanic in the county, or anywhere else for that matter, as he often boasted. He frequently took off just to see what the other side of the hill looked like, coming back when he ran short of money. He was in demand in Fort Smith and had offers of good jobs in Little Rock and St. Louis, but he liked the hills and the hunting and could not seem to stay away from the Ozarks for long.

"Why, I guess it's about time for me to have a little vacation."

"A vacation?" Logan stared at Dent in consternation. "What're you talking about?"

"Well, I just got a Model T Ford, and right now I'm in between jobs. Besides that," he said defensively, "I always did want to see one of those oil wells. Reckon I'll just mosey on over to Oklahoma and take a look-see around. I'll pick up Violet and bring her home. I'll try to get Ray to come, too."

"Do you think you could do that, Dent?"

"Do it! Why, there's nothing I can't do!"

"Except be modest, I reckon."

"I'll leave first thing in the morning. Have them back here in no time—after I have a little vacation, of course!"

The family was eating supper when a knock came on the door of the shack. The room was crowded to its extremities. In addition to Pete, Stephen, Mona, and Maury, the latest arrivals were crowded around the table. Ray, Violet, and Bailey seemed to fill the whole room—especially Bailey!

They had been there for almost a week. Ray had suffered a relapse and had spent most of his time sleeping in the bed that he shared with the two kids. Bailey bunked in a storage shed, and Violet slept on a pallet in the main room.

"I wonder who that could be?" Pete said. He got up wearily and moved to the door. Opening it, he found a tall man standing there who looked to be around thirty years old.

"Are you Mr. Stuart?" he asked.

"Yes, I'm Pete Stuart. What is it?"

"Could I come in for a minute? It's cold out here!"

"Come on in." Pete stepped back and let the man enter. He was tall and wiry, and when he pulled off his fedora hat they saw that he had curly brown hair. He had a craggy face, not handsome, but honest looking.

"My name's Ted Kingman," he said, then paused. He seemed to be intimidated by the mob he'd found inside the tiny house.

"Any relation to Horace Kingman?" Pete demanded.

"Well, uh—yes, he's my father, as a matter of fact."

"Have a chair," Pete said. "No, have two chairs. I didn't know we had such important company coming," he said sarcastically.

Not seeing any chairs that weren't being occupied, Kingman said, "Well, I've come at a bad time. I've been trying to get around to several of the small owners."

"You don't look like a knee breaker to me," Pete said.

"A knee breaker?"

"Naw, I guess you'd be the other end. Don't tell me, let me guess—you're a lawyer?"

Kingman had fair skin and blushed at the accusation. "As a matter of fact, I am an attorney."

"Just out of law school, I guess?"

"Well, yes."

"And just gone to work for Daddy!"

Violet and Ray were shocked at the harshness of Pete's barrage of questions. They both knew him to be a kindly, sensitive man, and his anger caught them off guard. They'd heard him speak of Kingman Oil Company being aggressive, but this was the first representative they'd seen.

"As a matter of fact, I just thought we could do some business, but maybe it'd be best if I stop by tomorrow."

"I don't think we've got anything to talk about," Pete said firmly. "Now, if you'd like to sit down, I think we have a gizzard left from the chicken."

Kingman glanced down at the table and his eyes ran around the occupants of the chairs and the boxes that served as chairs. He found something that shocked him—perhaps the poverty that had not existed at Yale, or anywhere else he knew. Still, he stiffened his shoulders and said, "Well, it won't take but a minute. It's about a lease."

"I know. Your ol' man wants me to lease this place to him."

"Yes, that's right," young Kingman said eagerly. "We'd be glad to pay you top price."

"I bet," Pete said. He walked over to the door and said,

"Good-bye, Mr. Kingman. Go tell Daddy that there's nothing shaking."

"But the others have mostly all signed . . ."

"I'll bet they have—after your ol' man's goons busted 'em up."

A flush swept over Kingman's face. "It's all purely business," he said stiffly. "I'm making you an honest offer."

"And I'm making you an honest offer." Pete jerked open the door and said, "Go back and tell your daddy that he'll not get this place!"

Kingman swallowed hard and looked around the table. "Well, I'm sorry to have disturbed your meal," he said lamely and turned and left the house.

"You didn't have to be so mean, Pa," Mona scolded. "You'd have paddled me if I'd been that mean."

"No, I wouldn't—not if you'd been that mean to Kingman Oil Company," Pete grinned, sat down, and took a swallow of coffee, which had grown cold, and set it down. "That's just the first move—the second really. I got a letter from Kingman a few days ago offering to buy me out. That's the way it starts. Then you get a visit from a nice, clean, smooth-talking lawyer."

Maury said, "He's not very smooth. As a matter of fact, he acted downright embarrassed. I've been around a few lawyers and he's about the most unassured one I ever saw."

"I guess young tigers are cute," Pete said, "but when they get older they get to be man-eaters. Just give Mr. Ted Kingman a little time and he'll be as ferocious as the rest of 'em."

Later Maury asked Pete, "Why don't you just sell out, Uncle Pete? There must be something better than burning your life out at this awful place."

Pete leaned against the wall and looked down at Maury, who sat peeling potatoes. The house was quiet for a change. Most everyone was outside on a rare break of good weather. "It'd be hard for you to understand, Maury. I don't mean anything by this," he added, "but you've always had everything."

Maury dropped her eyes. "I know," she said. "That's what Jerry says—that I'm spoiled rotten. He said I'd never make it here."

Pete reached over and patted her shoulder. "Well, when I get ahold of that young man I'll straighten him out about that," he said warmly. "You've been a godsend to us. I don't know how we would've made it without you, Maury. I know how rough it's been for you—the outhouse—I know you hate that."

"Well, I'm not fond of that element, but I've made it."

"Sure you have—but it's been hard on you. The thing is that you'll be going home when Leslie gets better, back to an easy life. How would you like to have a lifetime of this?" He waved his hand around the rough shack and his eyes were filled with pain. "This is all I've got to look forward to, and Leslie and the kids. My only hope is to get that well in."

"That's not certain, is it?"

"No, but nothin' is. It's the only chance I've got. Somehow I just know that there's oil down there! I've been in the oil fields for a long time now and I've never had a feeling quite like this. I know it's there—if I can just hang on!"

Maury was suddenly very fond of her uncle Pete. "You'll make it," she said, looking up with a warm smile. She reached out and took his hand and squeezed it. "We Stuarts are pretty tough. If I can put up with an outdoor toilet, then anything's possible!"

Pete laughed and squeezed her hand in return. "I've got a few things to tell your daddy about you next time I see him," he said warmly.

The next day, a dusty Model T pulled up in front of the shack. Violet was looking out the window as she washed dishes and she cried out, "Ray, it's Dent!"

"Dent?" Ray came out of his chair and, hurrying over to the window, peered outside. "That son-of-a-gun! You might know he'd show up when you least expect him."

Violet rushed to the door and threw it open. "Dent DeForge—what in the world are you doing here?"

Dent had raised his hand to knock, but dropped it and said, "Well, I came to visit and see what an oil well looks like." There was a tremendous bustle then as Dent was introduced to the whole family. The kids took to him immediately. He was that kind of man. He'd told Violet once, "You can always trust a man that kids seem to like—like me."

She'd snapped back, "That's not so! Kids trust anybody, even a gangster!" However, she'd been impressed about how all children hung on him.

"Well, Little Sister," as he was fond of calling her, "here I am! See, now that you've worried your poor ol' parents to death, you can start on me."

"I didn't mean to worry them—and don't call me Little Sister!"

Ray winked and grinned at Dent. "She always did hate for you to call her that."

"Why, I've practically raised this child," Dent said in mock astonishment. "That's gratitude for you. Here I've been like a father to her!—"

"You're not my father and you're not my brother." Violet flushed. "And I don't want to hear anymore about that!"

Pete had come in and heard the last of this and said, "Dent, you're not going to make anything off of her—but I'm glad to see you."

"Well, can't stay long," Dent said airily. "Looks like you have enough free boarders as it is. Thought I'd just see an oil well and take these wanderers back to the mountains where they belong."

Violet and Ray exchanged a glance and Violet said, "We've got another now. You got room for an extra passenger?"

"Why, that car will carry anything I put in it!" At that moment, Bailey came in, and Violet went to stand beside him. "This is Bailey. He's going back to the mountains with us." Immediately, Dent grinned and as he shook Bailey's mighty hand, he said, "Well, we might have to take turns getting out and walking. You're a big one, Bailey."

"He was very kind to me on the road," Violet said sharply. "If it hadn't been for him, Ray and I wouldn't have made it." She patted Bailey's arm affectionately, as she would a child.

Instantly, Dent understood her cue and now said, "Shoot—glad to have you, Bailey. We've got plenty of time, so we can see a little of the country on the way home."

Later when Violet talked with Dent, she told him of her misfortune and how Bailey had saved her life. "We can't just leave him here." She told him about the watch and said, "I've got the driver's name and as soon as I have the money I'm going to buy the watch back."

"Well, that's just like you, Violet. You always were an honest child."

Violet turned to him and said, "I am not a child! I am a woman—can't you see that? Will you please stop treating me like a baby?" Violet had been able to sew up her dress, and it set her figure off admirably.

Dent blinked after a casual glance and then grinned. "Well, we'll have to talk about that. You've grown up to be a fine figure of a woman—but I still think of you as my little sister. Can't forget that I had to fish you out when you fell in the creek!"

Violet later complained to Maury, who laughed at her. "He sure is fine looking. I might go after him myself!"

"You'd have to change your ways," Violet said grimly. "Would you like to go out in the middle of the night to hunt coons? That's what he asks me to do mostly, or trotlining. I hate baiting them with that stinky old crawfish bait!"

Maury seemed to find this amusing. "But he's so good looking that I guess a woman would have to put up with some deficiencies in a man, including baiting a trotline. It wouldn't be too bad." She saw, however, that the girl was offended. Going to her, she put her arm around Violet and said, "He's a fine man. I talked to him some, and Pete thinks the world of him, says everybody does."

"He is fine. When I was growing up, Ray thought it was sissy to have a little sister tagging along, but Dent never did.

He'd take me everywhere he went. Sometimes he'd make Ray stay home when we went hunting and it would make Ray mad." She thought fondly of those times for a moment and then said, "If he just wouldn't treat me like a baby!"

Dent had seen at once that there was no room for him in the crowded shack, so he found a room down the road and invited Ray to stay with him. It had taken some of the pressure off of the small cabin, and Ray was more comfortable there.

Pete had been amazed at how quickly Dent had learned the mechanics of an oil rig. "I've never seen anybody pick up anything so fast," he said in amazement, on the third day of Dent's visit. "You'd think you'd been drilling wells all your life."

"Oh, I guess I'm smart enough with machines and stuff," Dent shrugged. He disliked being praised for this and said, "You say you're going to get some more pipe? Lemme' go with you. That truck of yours needs to have some work done on it, but I'll do that tomorrow."

"All right. I'll tell the others we won't be back before five o'clock. It'll take us that long, I reckon."

The two men ate a good lunch, piled into Pete's old ramshackle Ford truck, and left.

It was late afternoon and supper was almost ready when Maury said, "Seems like it's late for Dent and Uncle Pete to be getting back."

Ray had come to spend the time with the kids. He was feeling much better and both the children loved to play games with him. Bailey always sat and watched, for he could not understand the mechanics of some of the games. He looked up suddenly and said, "I think I hear the truck coming."

"That's them all right," Maury said, looking out the window. "Better get the food on the table, they'll be hungry."

They heard the truck stop, and then a door slammed. When the front door opened, it was Dent. He had a white bandage over his left eyebrow and his right eye was discolored. "Trouble," he said. "Make a place for Pete—he's been hurt."

"What happened?" Maury demanded, but then at once fixed a cot for Pete as Bailey hurried outside. He was back almost at once carrying Pete in his arms as he would carry a child. Pete's leg was encased in a cast and his face was bruised and scarred.

"Who did this? What happened, Pete?" Leslie moved slowly over to touch him as Bailey laid him down.

Pete's mouth was so swollen he could hardly speak, and one eye was almost completely closed. "Kingman's men," he grunted. "They jumped us. If it hadn't been for Dent, they might've killed me."

"I wish I'd had my .38 with me," Dent remarked. "But it was in my suitcase. It won't be there anymore, though," he added grimly. "I'll be carrying it in my pocket from now on!"

"What happened?" Ray asked quickly, although he sensed the answer already. They all listened as Pete, obviously in pain, grunted out the story.

"They lay in wait for us when we went for the pipe. They picked a fight with me and had got me down." A smile came to his tortured lips. "There were four of 'em and all of a sudden Dent came roaring out of the store. He'd picked up an ax handle and he busted two of 'em's heads and they went out. The other two jumped him and it was quite a battle, but he broke one's arm and the other 'un lit out. I was out of it. They had already broke my leg."

Every eye turned to Dent. He said with embarrassment, "It wasn't much of a fight. If they hadn't caught Pete off balance, we'd have mopped up the floor with 'em."

"What about his leg?" Leslie whispered.

"I took him to the doctor. Leg's broke; not the worst kind of break, but he'll be off it for a while."

A silence went over the room. Everyone knew exactly what this meant. "I guess that means we'll have to take Kingman's offer, won't we, Pete?" Leslie touched his bruised lips gently. "I know you hate it."

Pete closed his eyes and clenched his fist. "I truly do hate it! But that's all there is to do."

After a brief silence, Dent said, "Nope—I decided I've had enough vacation. You need a good hand on that rig until you get on your feet. I reckon you can sit in a chair and tell me and Bailey and Ray what to do." He looked over at Bailey and said, "Bailey there's got the back for it and Ray—we can find some use for him, I reckon."

Pete looked at the man in astonishment. "You couldn't do that, Dent!"

"Tell me why I couldn't!"

At that moment, Violet felt more pride in Denton than she'd ever felt for anyone, except Bailey. She reached out and touched Dent's arm gently. "You can do it," she whispered. "We can all help."

Dent grinned and stared around the room defiantly. "I guess I can become an honorary member of this Stuart club." He looked across the room at Maury and winked with his good eye. "I might even make some time with that good-looking Maury Stuart there! What do you say, Sweetheart? We might even party between hitting oil strikes."

Maury laughed aloud. It was a merry sound, and she came over unexpectedly and kissed Dent right on his bruised mouth. "I think we might be able to work that out," she said.

Violet stared at the pair and when Ray whispered, "They make a handsome couple, don't they?" she turned an angry look on him.

"Don't be silly! She could never be a mountain woman."

It was Pete who said slowly, "I don't think you understand what this means. That Kingman bunch will use knives, dynamite, guns—there ain't nothing they won't do."

He went on to explain how impossible it was, but when he was finally finished, Denton DeForge only had one thing to say. "I reckon us Stuarts can handle anything those Kingmans can throw at us!"

Part Two

Hollywood

 7 

AN OLD FLAME

A harsh January wind was sweeping across Chicago as Jerry brought the ancient two-seater in for a bumpy landing. The wind caught the airplane, sharply shoving it to one side so that he had to struggle to bring it back onto the runway. Gritting his teeth, he held the ship in place, striking the earth in a series of hard bumps—hoping the tires didn't blow.

Taxiing the plane up to the hangar, he shut the engine off, stretched, and climbed stiffly out of the cockpit. The mechanic on duty came up grinning. "You didn't win any prizes on that landing, did you, Jerry?"

"Nope. No prizes. Guess I'm losing my touch."

Entering the hangar, he left a note thanking Mackelhaney for the use of the plane, then left, shivering as he stepped out into the icy wind. There had been considerable snow, but it had melted off. Now winter was crouched over Chicago, waiting to fall upon the Windy City. He longed to take a cab, go to his parents' house, bury himself in his room—but his cash was practically gone. He caught a bus that went within four blocks of the house, then walked the rest of it. As soon as he stepped inside, his mother came to put her arms around him and kiss him. "You're frozen!" she exclaimed, reaching up to touch his ears. "Why didn't you take a cab?"

Jerry pulled his hat off and tossed it at the hat rack. To his surprise, it caught on one of the pegs. For all his expertise as a pilot, he had never been able to hit that hat rack. Shrugging out of his overcoat, he handed it to Rose, who hung it up. "I've got plenty of time," he said. "No use wasting money."

Rose paused to give him a careful glance, then nodded. "Come into the kitchen. I'll fix you something to eat." She led him in, where he thawed out while she warmed leftover roast and potatoes. Rose sat down, and Jerry gave the details of his flight to Oklahoma.

She listened carefully, noting the lines of fatigue around his eyes. When he was through eating she said, "Now, you go take a hot bath and go to bed. Leave those clothes out so I can wash them."

"All right, Mom. I think I will. I need to get up early in the morning to go looking for work."

"You'll find something," Rose smiled, assuring him. She pushed his black hair back off his brow where it had a tendency to fall. She noted again the stubborn look about his face and wished that there was some way she could change this element in her son's character. *But he's like Amos,* she thought, *and all the other Stuarts—stubborn as mules!* "Go to bed now. I'll fix you a nice breakfast in the morning."

The next day, Jerry rose early, ate breakfast, and gave his report, again, to his father. "Going out to see if I can't round up some work. May be late getting in."

Amos reached into his pocket and pulled out a billfold. "Here, you must be running low."

"No, I'm okay," Jerry said shortly. He shook his head and both Rose and Amos saw his face set into a determined mode. "You've taken care of me enough. Time I started making my own living."

After Jerry left, Amos shook his head. "He's worried about a job—and I guess he's got a right to. There must be twenty million men out of work."

"But he's a skilled pilot," Rose said. "Surely there must be something."

Amos got to his feet and went to stand beside her. He let his hand trail across her ash blond hair for a moment. "I guess that field's overcrowded," he muttered, "just as all the rest of them. I wish he'd forget about flying. It's not too late for him to go to school, learn a profession. We can help him."

"He'll never do that."

"No, I guess not. But I can hope." He smiled, leaned over, and kissed her. "I'll be going to New York. I've got to meet with Hearst. He wants a special story on prohibition."

Rose's mouth tightened. "I suppose he's decided to end it." She did not like Hearst, who was an arrogant man. "It's not working very well, I'll admit."

"No, the country was never really in favor of prohibition," Amos said. "It'll be voted out sooner or later. Till it is, all it accomplishes is to make racketeers like Capone rich."

"And the Castellanos, too."

"Yes, I guess that's right. Nick and Eddy seem to be prospering. It'll catch up with them someday, though. That kind of wrongdoing has a way of bringing everyone down who's involved with it."

"It hasn't brought Capone down."

"They'll get him, too, sooner or later," Amos said. He kissed her again, got his coat, and left the house. As the cold wind struck him, he wondered about Jerry. *If a man only has one son*, he thought, *I guess he worries about him more than if he had a dozen!*

For three days Jerry searched everywhere he could think of for work. He'd been flying for a long time, first as a stunt pilot working for his uncle Gavin. He had even flown in bootleg liquor for Nick and Eddy Castellano for a time.

He had flown crop dusters, as second pilot on fledgling airlines, and as an airmail pilot. During these years, he had met almost everyone involved in the small world of flying. But, as he ran through his list, despair soon set in. At three o'clock he was standing in the office of Johnny Pesky, who ran a transport service of sorts. "I'll work cheap, Mr. Pesky," he said. "I need a job pretty bad."

Pesky was a small man who had flown in France during the Great War. He had not been an ace but had a vivid scar on his right cheek, a memento of those times. Taking the stub of a cigar out of his mouth, he looked up from his desk and said sadly, "If I had a job, Jerry, I'd take you in a minute. You're a good pilot." He puffed on the cigar, sent the purple smoke rising in the air, then jammed it back between his teeth, shaking his head. "Trouble is, there just ain't nothing. Have you tried over at Southern?"

Jerry refused to let the fatigue and doubt show on his face. Smiling confidently he said, "Oh, sure, I tried there. Marty may be able to use me in another month. Well, thanks, Mr. Pesky."

"I'll call you if anything comes up. How's Gavin?"

"Still flying with Northern Airline. Don't think it's gonna last much longer, though. It's on its last legs, he says."

Pesky stared down at the desk, planted his palms flat, stared at them for a moment, then shook his head as he looked up. "Not many people have the money to fly these days. More of them are riding the rails."

"It'll have to end someday. Times'll get better."

As he stepped out of the office, he felt that the times had him in a vise, but the depression had done that to the whole country. A memory flashed into his mind. He'd been in New York, and on the Lower East Side he had seen a line of men waiting for a bowl of soup and a piece of bread at Jerry McCauley's mission. There must have been two or three hundred men there, each of them representing a failure of some kind.

"I could be one of those guys in that line," he muttered. "I've got to find something!"

To keep his spirits up, he started whistling "When the Moon Comes over the Mountain" slightly off key. Usually he was able to shake off depression. This time, however, he couldn't do it. As he walked along, thoughts came to his mind that he could not shove aside:

I'm sick of being a failure. Here I am, thirty years old, and what have I got? Nothing. A few clothes, not a dime in the bank—noth-

ing to show for my life. His lips grew tight as he moved along, noting that everyone's clothes were worn and unpressed. Very few were sharp dressers anymore. *Uncle Gavin and Uncle Owen at least did something in the war. Owen got a Medal of Honor and Gavin was a hero. They've got that to look back on. They've got families, too. I don't have anything!*

Again the long line of men waiting for soup flashed into his mind. He shook his head angrily and turned toward the north side of town.

He walked all the way to a restaurant where he could not afford to eat, but the owner had part interest in an air circus that was operating in the South. It was a small chance and would pay practically nothing, not to mention being dangerous. But desperation drove him there.

He stepped inside and took off his hat, aware that the waiter was looking at him with a jaundiced eye. *Probably tell me to go around to the back door,* he thought bitterly.

As he started to speak to the waiter a voice called, "Hey, Jerry!"

Turning, he saw Eddy Castellano coming out of the main restaurant. At forty-two, Eddy was heavier than the last time Jerry had seen him. He had the typical Italian dark hair and eyes and olive skin. He was wearing an expensive suit, and a diamond ring glittered on his finger as he reached up and clapped Jerry on the shoulder. "Hey, Kid! Long time no see. Come in for a bite?"

"No, Eddy, I wanted to see Mr. Taylor."

"Taylor, he ain't in town, Kid. He's gone to Pittsburgh." Seeing the slight shadow fall across Jerry's face, he said, "Hey! I already 'et but you come on. I'll buy you a steak and you can bring me up-to-date on all the family. I'll do the same for you with all of us Castellano types."

Jerry protested, but Eddy would not take no. He grasped Jerry's arm and practically dragged him into the restaurant. When they were seated at the table, which was covered with a snowy white tablecloth and had a single deep red rose in a crystal vase, Eddy said, "Hey, Tony! Bring my friend here the best steak you got! Potato be okay, Jerry? Sure, and a bottle of that wine like I just had." He settled back, lit up a huge cigar, and asked at once, "How's the family, Kid?" He sat puffing while Jerry gave him a quick rundown. Finally he leaned forward and said, "I guess we're kinda in-laws now, since my kid brother married into the Stuart family."

Jerry grinned abruptly. "I think so. How's it feel having foreigners mix in with your bunch?"

Eddy laughed loudly, "Ah, you always were a kidder! But let me tell you, Nick and me are proud of Mario, and Ma is too. You'd think there never had been nobody got married! And now, they've got a couple of kids. I think Ma's bored everybody to death talking about those newest grandkids of hers."

"They're doing fine. Christie's real happy." Jerry hesitated, then said, "Mario's in his own office now?"

Instantly Eddy's smile disappeared. He took the cigar out of his mouth and nodded shortly. "That's right," he said curtly. "He ain't got nothing to do with me and Nick." Bitterness tinged his voice and he said, "That what you wanted to hear?"

Jerry looked directly at the gangster. "That's what you wanted, Eddy, you and Nick, to keep Mario out of the rackets."

Eddy stared at the younger man for a moment and then the smile came back. "Yeah," he said. "Course that's what we wanted. The kid's doing great. Now, how about you?"

Jerry hesitated and shrugged his shoulders. "Not much going on in the flying racket. I'm looking around, though."

"Hey! You need a job?"

"Sure, you know of anybody that needs a pilot?"

"Naw, not nothing like that. I'd tell you if I did. But there ain't no sense going around without work. Me and Nick can always use a good man."

Jerry sat back and stared at Eddy Castellano in disbelief. "Eddy, I worked for you at one time and nearly got myself killed. Now you want me to do it again?"

"Hey, Kid, it's a legitimate business."

"It's illegal to sell alcohol."

"Who cares about that?" Eddy said sharply. "All the swells in this town are buying the booze we sell 'em. If it's against the law to sell it, it must be against the law to buy it. Look, I can fix you up where you won't be involved with any of the rough stuff. We need a few smooth, good-looking guys like you. You ain't no lawyer, but I don't trust them anyway—except for Mario."

"No thanks, Eddy."

"Wait a minute!" Eddy held up his thick hand. "Let me talk to Nick. He knows lots of guys, and so do I. Not all of them are in the rackets. It don't have to be flying, does it? Times are pretty rough."

Jerry felt a warmth toward Castellano. Eddy was a hood and a gangster—along with his brother Nick—but their lives and the Stuarts' were intertwined. He had heard his father tell, many times, that if it hadn't been for Anna Castellano he might have starved to death, both he and Rose. They had come separately to the city and Anna had taken them in, fed them, and given them a place to stay until they could make their own way. He knew that both Nick and Eddy took great pride in their friendship, such as it was, with Amos and Owen. Now he said, "Sure Eddy, I'll take anything that's honest. I could get a job, I guess, flying in Mexico or somewhere with a revolution."

"Don't do that, Kid," Eddy said. "Let me look around, okay? Hey! Here's your steak."

As Jerry was eating his steak, Eddy snapped his fingers, saying abruptly, "Hey! You see the paper today?"

"No, I've been all over town looking for work. What was in it?"

Eddy grinned knowingly. "Old friend of yours has hit town."

"What old friend?"

"Cara Gilmore. I guess you remember her, don't you?"

Jerry stared at Eddy's knowing grin and nodded. "Yes," he said, "I remember Cara." She had been his first love, and echoes of their affair still sounded deep down in his chest from time to time. She had been a stunt flyer and wing walker with Gavin's air circus when Jerry himself had first learned to fly. Jerry and Cara had had a torrid affair, but she had left, causing a vacancy in his life that nothing had really replaced.

"What's she doing in Chicago?" he said, careful to keep his voice neutral.

"She's made some kind of flight, long distance from someplace to someplace," Eddy said carelessly. "I'll get a paper. Just a minute."

Eddy went to the desk and soon came back bearing the newspaper. Putting it down before Jerry, he said, "There it is. Still a looker, ain't she?"

Jerry looked at the picture that took up a large part of the page. It detailed a long-distance flight that Cara had made in an airplane belonging to a famous industrialist. Their names had been romantically linked for several months, something that hurt Jerry every time someone mentioned it. He studied the picture. Cara was wearing jodhpurs and her trademark, a long-sleeved shirt, and she carried a soft aviator's helmet in her hand. The wind was blowing her curly hair and her smile was the same. He read the story carefully, then looked up. "Yeah, she still looks good."

"Hey! Maybe her boyfriend can give you a job flying one of them airplanes around. You ought to check it out. Well, I gotta go, Kid. Nick and me'll see what we can turn up."

"Thanks for the meal, Eddy."

"All in the family, Kid," Eddy grinned.

He left the restaurant and Jerry sat drinking coffee, rereading the story. Finally he folded the paper and put it in his pocket, a determination forming in him. "Wouldn't hurt to see her one more time," he said to himself. As he left the restaurant, he wondered what it would be like. He had wondered this many times, but the thought of actually seeing her again stirred him as nothing had for years.

He left the restaurant and recklessly spent a dollar of his remaining cash taking a taxi to the airport. The article had said that Cara would be doing a flight there, an exhibition, and then giving an interview and a speech on her adventures.

When he got to the airport he found that a crowd had already gathered and that the plane was in the air. He watched as the sleek, silver monoplane flashed over the field and pulled up sharply, the engine roaring. Cara did a full loop, pulling out only a few feet from the ground. It was so close that Jerry clenched his teeth and flinched. "Too close," he said. "She always was a fool for taking chances."

For the next half hour, Cara rolled the plane into snaps and dives and outside loops of all sorts. Jerry watched with admiration. Finally she brought it in for a perfect landing, taxied up the runway, and climbed out.

The crowd was held back by police, and a handsome gray-haired man holding a microphone interviewed her.

At the sound of her voice, Jerry felt memories wash over him. She had a husky voice that somehow always stirred him. Now she laughed and told of her adventures on the long-distance flight. He felt some of the excitement come back to him that he'd felt when he'd first seen her.

Finally the interview was over and two police officers moved in front of Cara, making a way for her through the crowd. Jerry did not speak, but when she was even with him, she turned her head and her eyes met his. Shock ran through her, he saw, and he grinned and said, "Hello, Cara."

"Jerry Stuart!" Ignoring the police officers, Cara turned and grabbed him by the lapels of his overcoat. "You good-looking thing!" She reached up, pulled him down, and kissed him, and a light flashed just as she did.

Cara whispered, "Come on, Stuart. We've got things to talk about."

"Is this a friend of yours?" the interviewer asked quickly.

"Oh, yes, this is Jerry Stuart. We're old friends." She winked at the gray-haired man and said, "He's almost as good a flyer as I am. Come on, Jerry. Let's get away from this."

Jerry accompanied her to a car that was waiting, a flaming red Duesenberg.

"This thing's not as big as a battleship," he murmured, sliding into the leather seat beside her, looking around. "But it's not much smaller either."

"It belongs to a man who wants me to fly across the ocean," she said. She started the powerful engine and roared away with squealing tires. She threaded her way through the traffic of Chicago, and forced Jerry to tell about himself. Finally, she pulled up in front of the Palmer House, the fanciest hotel in Chicago, and got out of the car. Then the doorman took it saying, "Good afternoon, Miss Gilmore."

"Hello, Max. Come on, Jerry," she said. She led the way, through the magnificent lobby, up to her room, which was really a suite. As soon as they were inside, she threw her arms around him and pulled his head down. Her lips were as warm and soft as he remembered them. And the firm contours of her figure pressed against him. A riotous emotion ran through Jerry Stuart. He held her tightly and when he lifted his head and looked at her, he said huskily, "I've missed you, Cara."

"Welcome home, Jerry," she smiled and pulled his head down again.

 8 

TROUBLE WITH ADAM

Bonnie Hart finished waxing the linoleum on the kitchen floor, then paused and arched her back. She replaced the cleaning materials, moved into the living room, and stopped in front of the new radio that Lylah had brought in a week earlier. It was an Atwater Kent and was different from the old Edison radio that it replaced. Leaning over, she studied the two dials that composed the controls, then glanced up at the separate round speaker covered with brown fabric. Turning one dial, she sought a station, and the speaker blared at her, "It's *Little Orphan Annie* time!"

Bonnie winced and said out loud, "I refuse to drink another cup of that awful Ovaltine, even for a secret Little Orphan Annie decoder!"

As she continued turning the dial, a smile touched her lips, for she and Adam, her thirteen-year-old charge, had fought over this. By sending in the tops from cans of Ovaltine, it was possible to get secret decoder pins and other paraphernalia straight from the hand of Little Orphan Annie herself. Adam complained constantly that the members of the family weren't drinking enough Ovaltine.

She picked up a radio station from San Francisco. Rudy Vallee's nasal voice was grinding out his theme song, "My Time Is Your Time." Restlessly she searched over the dial and finally stopped in the middle of a broadcast. She frowned as the name Lindbergh caught her ear. Sitting down, she listened with a sense of sadness as the announcer said, "The most intensive manhunt in American history has been mounted in the search for the infant son of Charles A. Lindbergh. The twenty-month-old boy, Charles Jr., was snatched from his crib in his family's home in Hopewell, New Jersey. Police have no clues concerning the kidnapping of the son of the famous transatlantic aviator. A homemade ladder, down which the infant was carried, and a note pinned to the windowsill demanding fifty thousand dollars for the child's safe return are all that they have to work with. Colonel Lindbergh has said that he would be willing to pay the ransom. President Hoover has ordered all federal law enforcement agencies to assist in the search, and more than one hundred thousand officers, aided by civilian volunteers, have joined the search along the entire eastern seaboard. Colonel Lindbergh . . ."

Bonnie listened as the announcer went on, and she whispered, "What kind of monster would steal a sleeping baby?" She bowed her head and prayed quickly for the child and for the family. She had formed this habit long ago of praying as things happened instead of storing them up.

Coming to her feet, she reached out and turned off the radio. Glancing out the window, she saw Adam moving slowly along the sidewalk. Something about the way he kept his head down alarmed her. He usually came running home from his ball games, shouting and demanding something to eat. She stood there waiting until the door opened, and at one glimpse of his face she cried out, "Adam! What happened to you?"

"Nothing." Adam Stuart ducked his head and quickly covered up the left side of his face with his hand. He turned to go, but Bonnie rushed across the room to him. Pulling his hand down, she saw he had a scrape along his cheek and also that his nose had been bleeding.

"Have you been fighting?"

"Oh, it wasn't anything," he said sullenly.

Adam Stuart, the only child of Lylah Stuart Hart, was of average height, about five-feet six. He was trim and showed promise of a sturdy build. Usually he was a cheerful, good-natured boy, but now there was a gloomy look in his face.

"Come along. Let me clean you up," Bonnie said firmly.

"Aw, it doesn't matter. Let me go, Bonnie—"

But Bonnie pulled him into the bathroom and soon had cleared away the traces of the fight. "Now, come along," she said. "I've got cookies and milk for you."

"I don't want any," Adam protested.

Nevertheless, she took him into the kitchen and sat him down and put the plate of chocolate cookies and a glass of milk in front of him. Adam picked up one of the cookies, nibbled on it, but his mouth was tight, and he refused to meet her eyes.

Bonnie knew Adam better, perhaps, than anyone. She had been hired by Lylah to keep the boy while Lylah went to work in Hollywood. After Lylah and Jesse, Bonnie's brother, had married, they left the small cottage and moved into a larger house. Bonnie still kept Adam, and at the same time did research for her brother's books. She sat down now at the kitchen table and said quietly, "I wish you'd tell me about it. Maybe I can help."

"You can't help. Nobody can."

"What was the fight about?" She hoped it was some sort of boyish argument. Adam had been in those kinds of fights before but had ignored them, remaining cheerful. Somehow she felt it was more serious than that.

Suddenly Adam looked up. He had a strong jaw and light blue eyes. His light brown hair was neater than that of most boys. There was some of Lylah in him in the wide-spaced eyes and the squarish face. He had her short nose. But there was a part of him that did not resemble Lylah.

"Who is my father?" Adam said suddenly.

It was not the first time Adam had asked her this question, and Bonnie shook her head saying, "I don't know, Adam."

"He must be pretty bad, whoever he is, if my own mother won't tell me."

"You don't know that. There could be all kinds of reasons. Besides, Jesse is your dad now. Don't you like him?"

Adam dropped his eyes and pushed the cookies around on the plate. They could hear the cries of children playing outside, and a noisy truck went rattling by. "Sure, I like him fine, but he's not my dad—not my real dad, that is."

Bonnie was almost frightened by the intensity of the boy's desire to find out about his father. She was aware that there was something in Lylah's past that had been rather wild. She was relatively certain that Lylah had not been married to Adam's father, but for all the warmth of their relationship, Lylah had never spoken of this part of her life. It was as if she were afraid to talk about it. Bonnie had only seen Lylah frightened one time. That was when Adam asked her this same question. He had been only five years old, she remembered. Lylah had put her arms around him and said, "Someday we'll talk about it," but there had been fear in her eyes, Bonnie remembered.

"Come on now, it's time to do your homework."

"Aw, let me listen to the radio, Bonnie."

"All right. For thirty minutes. But you have to do your homework and that's final!"

Adam nodded reluctantly and moved off into the living room, carrying two cookies in one hand and a glass of milk in the other. Soon the sound of Jack Armstrong, or one of his other favorite programs, filtered through. Bonnie went about her own work but was troubled by the talk.

Later that afternoon she found occasion to mention to Lylah what had happened.

"I think you ought to tell him who his father is. It's none of my business, of course."

"Yes, it's your business." Lylah came over and put her arm around her sister-in-law. She was very fond of Bonnie. Lylah had fallen in love, late in life, with Jesse Hart, and after a tempestuous youth, she was thoroughly satisfied in her marriage. At the age of fifty-one she looked much younger. But as she stood with her arm around Bonnie, she said, "I'm afraid to talk to him." She would say no more, and later on when she and Jesse were preparing to go to bed, she turned to him and said, "Adam was asking Bonnie who his father is."

Jesse Hart was five years younger than Lylah. He was a tall man, trim and strong, with hard hands, very square. He had been a writer for years, but only in the past two years had he proved successful. He had learned to write screenplays that were better than most, and his novel was slowly gaining acceptance.

"Was he disturbed—but I know he was!" He came over and sat down on the bed and watched as Lylah ran a comb through her auburn hair. "What did Bonnie tell him?"

"What could she tell him?" There was a slight bitterness in Lylah's voice. "She doesn't know. Nobody knows but you and me, Amos, Gavin, and Owen."

As she sat combing her hair, she thought about the time that her brothers had come into the hospital room in France right after Adam's birth. They had known that the baby's father was Baron Manfred von Richthofen—the famous Red Baron. Lylah had met von Richthofen on a visit to Germany. The two had an affair, but von Richthofen had been killed, and the baby was born after his death. She remembered very well that her brothers had gathered around, Owen holding the baby. When she had expressed her fear for the child's future Gavin had said, "He'll be a Stuart!"

And so now she put the brush down and turned. Her eyes were troubled. "I can't tell him. Not yet, Jesse."

"Why not?"

"We've gone over it before. Some people in this country are still bitter about the Germans. They'd hate him. Especially as the son of Manfred von Richthofen."

"Some would," Jesse said, "but that's passing away now."

"I don't think so. This man Hitler that's rising to power—he frightens me, Jesse. He could lead Germany into another war."

Running his hand through his curly hair, Jesse shook his

head. "He troubles me, too. I don't think he's sane. He reminds me a lot of the Kaiser. He's going to do bad things with Germany if he ever gets in complete power—but that's no reason for not telling Adam who his father is."

The two talked until late in the night, and finally, when they lay together in bed, he held her tightly as she began to sob. He stroked her back comfortingly. "It'll be all right," he whispered. "God won't let us down."

Some of the turbulence of Adam's thoughts were driven away the next day, for Bonnie took him to see one of his idols, Tom Mix, the famous western actor. She had obtained a pass from Lylah, who knew Mix rather well, and had piled Adam in her Chevrolet coupe for a day's outing.

They found the scene being shot inside a strange-looking set.

"Why don't those buildings have any tops, Bonnie?" Adam asked.

"Well, cameras have to have lots of light," Bonnie explained as they moved into a room the shape of a saloon. "So, the sun has to do the lighting for them."

"Won't people think it's funny, seeing a room without any ceiling?"

Bonnie laughed. "Why, you've seen lots of them, Adam. Think of all the times we've gone to see Bob Steele and Ken Maynard and Buck Jones in rooms just like this."

"You mean they didn't have any ceilings in them?"

"Why no, they were just like this. Look!—" she broke off suddenly. "There's Mr. Mix right there!"

"Gosh! It is, isn't it? Look at him! Isn't he something!" Adam breathed almost reverently. He stood transfixed; the director, carrying a megaphone, shouted directions to the actors, then moved back to sit down in a chair made out of wood frame with canvas for the seat and back.

"I know what they're gonna do," Adam nodded confidently. "They're gonna have a fight."

"How do you know that?" Bonnie asked, amused at his assurance.

"Because in the saloons they always have fights. Look," he said suddenly, "see that man all dressed in black? He's the bad guy."

"How do you know?"

"The bad guys always wear black, and black hats. The good guys always wear white hats." Adam rattled on, giving her the benefit of his experience. "And the bad guys need a shave and the good guys like Mr. Mix don't. Gosh, I thought you knew all that!"

"It makes it easy to know how to watch a movie," Bonnie laughed. "I believe you're right."

They watched as Mix acted his part. She knew many stars used doubles, but in the fight that ensued—which included broken bottles and breaking of chairs over heads—Mix was right in the middle of it.

When the scene was over, the director yelled, "All right, that's a take!"

"Gosh! Could we go up and meet him, do you think?"

"Well, I don't know. He probably doesn't like to be bothered—but we'll try."

They made their way across the floor and Mix looked up at them. He was wearing a white suit with many buttons across the front, cavalry style, and the white hat had not come off his head during the fight scene. He was a ruggedly handsome man with heavy black eyebrows, firm lips, and a hard-muscled body. "Well, hello young fella! Came to see the movie made, did you?"

"This is Adam Stuart. I believe you know his mother, Lylah Stuart."

"Oh, yes," Mix said at once and smiled broadly. He put his hand out and said, "I wish we were doing a take outside. I'd let you ride my horse."

"You mean Tony?"

"You know his name?"

"Gosh! Everybody knows your horse's name, Mr. Mix. You're the best actor there ever was."

Mix found this amusing and said, "I wish you'd tell that to that man right over there," he nodded toward the director. "But I guess really I'm more of a cowboy than I am an actor." He spoke the truth. Tom Mix had been an athletic young man with a flair for showmanship. He often said his horse Tony had more of a genius for acting than he did.

As they left the studio with Adam clutching a piece of paper containing the famous man's autograph, he said, "That's what I want to be when I grow up, a cowboy." His eyes were bright and he said, "You think I could do that?"

"I think you can do anything you want to," Bonnie said and gave him a hug as they passed through the gates of the studio. It had been an exciting day for them both, and it accomplished what she had thought—to take the questions about his father off his mind.

The boardroom of Monarch Studio was small compared with those of other production companies. Monarch had been born through Lylah's efforts. The first film she produced, *The Gangster*, had been a hit. A rival said it was only because she had enticed Rudolph Valentino into playing the starring role. Since then, Valentino had died, but Lylah had clung to the studio, learning the producer's trade as she had learned that of an actor. Now, however, as she sat at the table and looked across at Jesse, she felt weary. The two of them had struggled with the finances until they were both exhausted. She turned to Carl Thomas, who at the age of seventy looked not a day older than when he had helped her make her first picture seven years before. Thomas was five-feet five, trim, and dapper. He touched his small mustache from time to time and his black hair was still full despite his age. It was dyed, of course, but he laughed at that himself.

"Well, where do we go from here?" Thomas asked. "Are you getting ready to do another picture, Lylah?"

"I don't know, Carl. I'm tired, to tell the truth about it. I don't know what kind of picture to do."

"How about another gangster movie?" Carl said. "It would be hard to make a better one than your first one, though."

Lylah shook her head. "No, there've been too many of them lately." She leaned back and named them off. "Paul Muni did *Scarface* and then there's Cagney in *Public Enemy.*"

Jesse added, "There's *Little Caesar.* I think that's the best of all of them. Eddy Robinson's new but he's going places in the movie business, quite an actor. But I think you're right; too many gangster movies already. We need something fresh."

They talked for quite a while and finally Thomas said, "Whatever you do, you better make it a good one, Lylah. The competition's getting tougher. The depression's cut down on attendance."

"I know, Carl, but I've tried everything in my head and nothing seems to be good."

Jesse leaned forward. "I've got an idea," he said slowly. "As a matter of fact," he grinned suddenly and looked much younger, "I've got a script."

Lylah stared at him, "A script! When did you have time to write a script?"

"When you weren't looking." Jesse leaned back in his chair, lacing his fingers behind his head. "I've been thinking about this one for a long time. I think it would be a good time to release it, but I don't know."

"What is it, Jesse?" Carl demanded. "Is it a horror movie?" He nodded eagerly. "You know, that seems to be the big thing. We've got Karloff and Frankenstein, and Bella Lugosi and Dracula. I don't see why we couldn't come up with a monster of our own."

"No, not a monster. It's a film about aviation."

Instantly, Lylah grew alert. She was fascinated with aviation. Her brother Gavin had been a flyer with the Lafayette Escadrille and she still remembered his reports of the fierce battles over France.

"What sort of film?"

"It's a simple story. One that's pretty common. The plot deals with a young pilot who loses his best friend in the war. He comes home and, after the excitement of the war, he can't find himself. So he flies for an air circus and the depression hits. Then the aviation world goes down just like every other business. But—"

"Sounds pretty depressing to me," Carl said. "I can't help humming that song, 'Brother, Can You Spare a Dime?' and it's driving me crazy! I wish it'd never been written. We've heard enough about this blasted depression!"

Lylah knew that Jesse was very much aware of what audiences liked. He had a sharpness about him that enabled him to see things, and had proven it with his scripts. "But you're thinking about something else, aren't you, Jesse?"

"Yes. Flying somehow seems to symbolize this country. It's exciting, it's new, and people still go out to air circuses. Look at the long distance flyers like Amelia Earhart. She's on the pages of every newspaper in the country, and people are interested in flying. The airlines are struggling, but they're romantic. You're not trundling along in a beat-up Model T, you're flying up in the air. I thought we could make it a film," he said slowly, "of hope. You can do that with scenes in the air."

"Hey," Carl said, "I think you've got something. I've been to one of those air shows," he shuddered and turned to Lylah. "Your brother, he had one, didn't he?"

"Yes, he did—and you remember Jerry, my nephew. He's one of the best stunt flyers in the business."

"What's Gavin doing?" Carl demanded. "If we could get those two to do the actual flying, we could save money."

The idea triggered a long meeting that lasted not only that day, but several days. Finally, Carl said, "I think we can get the money on this one. It'll be tight, but if Gavin and Jerry can do the flying, and we get somebody that'll be a draw to star, I think we've got a shot on hitting it big."

"I hope so," Lylah said slowly, "because this is all or nothing, Carl. We'll sink everything we have into it and if it flops, we'll all be selling apples on the street corner."

The door burst open and Bonnie, who was wearing her oldest dress as she did the cleaning, looked up. She had her hair tied up with a bandanna and was shocked to see Jerry Stuart enter, followed by Gavin, and a woman she had never wanted to see again.

Jerry came over at once. "Hey, it's us! Look at me, I'm a movie star!" He stood there, his eyes shining, and said, "Where are Lylah and Jesse?"

"They're—they're not home yet from the studio."

"Oh!" Jerry turned and said, "Look who's here. You remember Cara?"

Cara stepped forward, a smile on her carmine lips. "Well, you've grown up. The last time I saw you, you were just a little girl."

"Oh, yeah, she's like a kid sister to me," Jerry said breezily. He did not see the angry look that flashed in Bonnie's eyes as he turned to Gavin to say, "Maybe we ought to go down to the studio."

Gavin shook his head. "We might miss them on the way. Let's go back to the hotel. We left Heather and the kids there anyway. " He turned to Bonnie. "We'll be at the Avon Hotel. Have Lylah call as soon as she gets in."

"All right, Gavin."

Jerry seized Cara by the waist and squeezed her and said proudly, "Cara's going to be a movie star. Maybe me, too. Isn't that swell?"

Bonnie had never felt so grubby and dirty in her life. Cara was wearing a beautifully tailored green dress that outlined her figure well. Her hair was done in the latest style and she looked ready to model for one of the fashion agencies. Very much aware of her dirty apron, her old dress, her hair done up in a rag, and feeling like one of the witches from *Macbeth*,

Bonnie glared at Jerry and said, "Just swell!" She whirled and stalked out of the room abruptly.

"I wonder what's wrong with her?" Jerry asked in surprise. "She's not usually so grumpy."

There was ancient wisdom in Cara's eyes and a light smile tugged at her lips. "Come along, Sweetheart. We've got things to talk about."

 9 

IN DEFENSE OF WINONA DANCE

This sure ain't much country for looks, is it?"

Dent DeForge wiped the sweat out of his face and looked over Violet's shoulders at the landscape. The oil-field country was about as ugly as anything he'd ever seen. He had been traveling around some, looking at the different rigs, and they were all about the same: platforms of all conditions, each with its own walking beam creaking up and down, and its own little steam engine huffing and puffing. Everywhere he saw crud from the slush pits and lakes of salt water pooled under the platforms and in most open spaces. This, along with piles of rotting garbage thrown out by roughnecks, never known for their hygiene, was what he had seen.

Violet had been watching Dent work on the wooden derrick, which was now lying flat on the ground. Pete had taken it down to lengthen it and restructure it and now it lay like the skeleton of some sort of rectangular dinosaur.

"No, it's not very pretty," Violet said. She looked along the length of the derrick, then shook her head doubtfully. "I don't see how you're going to get it to stand up."

Dent finished tightening a bolt, tossed the wrench to the ground, then stood up and stretched his back. "I don't either," he admitted, "but I guess I'll have to try."

Violet was wearing a pair of overalls that had belonged to Pete at one time. She had been sick of the torn dress she had worn and had appropriated the overalls, tucking them up at the legs, and a blue chambray shirt, which she wore with the sleeves rolled up. Despite the roughness of the garb, the curves of her youthful figure were clearly revealed. She pulled her cap down more firmly on her head to keep the continual breeze from blowing it off. "What do you have to do to get it to stand up?"

Dent said cheerfully, "Well, that's a gin pole sticking up in the air over there. These here are gun tackle blocks. These are pulleys running over to the top of the derrick." He pointed to a tangle of blocks and cables that made absolutely no sense to Violet. Getting up, he walked over to the power source, which was a gas engine bolted to the bed of Pete's truck. He stared at it and shook his head. "This thing probably just has a hundred and fifty horsepower, but it's all we got. I've done a little hoisting and hauling, but I don't know. You ready to try it?"

"Let me go get everybody out. They all want to see it."

Ten minutes later, everybody, including Pete on his crutches, moved out to watch the demonstration. Pete's eyes were doubtful and he said, "I don't know, Dent—," and he began to make some complicated suggestions, but Dent shook them all off.

"Nope, we'll try 'er one way or the other. Here we go!"

Starting up the engine, he shoved the throttle forward. The engine began chugging rapidly, coughing from time to time, then Dent threw the engine in gear. The cables were taken up on the drum and grew taut.

Slowly the derrick structure began to rise—very slowly. Pete was straining his shoulders as if he had part of the load. "You see," he said to Maury, who was standing beside him, "the first ten degrees in a lift like this are the hardest. Gravity's against you and you got the worst possible angle on this thing. Even with that gin pole to take the angle away, this is a critical time right here."

All held their breath as Dent advanced the throttle. The small engine chugged frantically, and as a few seconds passed, they could hear a sudden creak.

"Look out!" Pete yelled. "You're picking up the truck!"

And that was what was happening. Instead of the derrick lifting, the strain on the engine that was bolted to the truck lifted up the truck.

"The truck's winding itself up on its own cable!" Pete shouted. Dent made a leap at the engine, shoved at the clutch, and the Ford settled down with a crunching sound as the derrick fell back with a crash, raising a big pool of dust.

A moan went up from the small crowd of spectators, and Ray walked over to where Dent was looking down with disgust at the rig. "I don't think that's gonna do it, Dent. Maybe we could get a bigger engine."

Dent shook his head, then kicked the tire of the truck with a futile gesture of anger. "We'll have to gear it down lower," he said. "That'll mean getting a few more block and tackle rigs—two more, I figger. I saw some down the road there where a fella's sellin' out. I figure we can get 'em for a few bucks. You wanna go along?"

"Sure," Ray said. "Let's go. Be good to move around a little bit."

Finding the equipment was not hard, and after a minimum of bargaining, Dent bought all they needed for five dollars. "Don't tell Pete I paid for these," he cautioned Ray. "We'll just let this be our secret."

"He's pretty hard up, isn't he, Dent?" Ray asked with a worried look. He was pale from his sickness, but there was some color in his cheeks. The hot summer sun beat down on him, and already he was beginning to get a tan. "I don't know if he can do it. How deep do you have to go to get oil?"

"Shoot! I don't know," Dent grinned. "We just get that derrick up and drill till we hit China, I guess. I was gonna take you and Violet on home but I got a letter from Logan—said stay here and help Pete as long as we need to. Look!" he broke off suddenly, "let's stop and get an RC Cola and maybe a Moon Pie. I'm hungry."

They pulled up at a small general store, parking in front

of a powerful-looking truck loaded with drilling equipment. On the side it said Kingman Oil Company.

"That's some of our competition," Dent grinned. "I figure we can put them out of business one of these days."

The store was adjoined to a cafe and Dent said, "Hey, let's go in there and sit down, maybe get a piece of pie instead of a Moon Pie. They always taste like wax to me, anyhow."

They moved inside the cafe, which consisted of a counter along one side with half a dozen tables scattered around. It was a rough enough looking place. As they seated themselves, a small woman with Indian features came toward them. She was wearing a blue flowered dress, half hidden by a white apron. Her hair was pure black and her eyes were large and brown. She was very pretty and both men looked at her with appreciation.

"What'll you have?" she asked.

"You got any kind of homemade pie back there, Sweetheart?"

"I'm not your sweetheart," the young woman said firmly. "We've got apple and cherry."

"Bring us one slice of each. We'll test it out," Dent said. He took off his straw hat and tossed it on the chair next to him. As she walked away, he kept his eyes on her shapely figure. "Now, there's a good-looking woman," he said. "Don't you think so?"

Ray smiled. He was used to Dent's ways. "Yes, she's pretty," he said.

They waited until she came back with the pie. "What's your name, Miss?"

She gave the pair a scornful glance, then turned and walked away.

"I guess that settles your hash," Ray grinned. "You lost some of your charm since you became a roughneck."

The two ate their pie slowly and finished off an RC apiece, and each ordered a second. As they were halfway through these, four men came in, obviously roughnecks. One of them was frightening in his appearance. He was no more than five-feet ten but must have weighed over 220 pounds. He was bald but had heavy sandy eyebrows over pale blue eyes. His nose was flattened and he had a battered, strange-looking ear.

"That fellow's a pug," Dent said quietly, "a prizefighter."

The four men sat down and when the young woman came they all began to make rough remarks to her. She took their orders on a pad and turned to walk away. The largest man, whom the others had called Ollie, grabbed her around the waist and pulled her down on his lap. "How 'bout a kiss to go with the order?" he grinned.

She turned her face away as he tried to kiss her, and she began to struggle. "Let me go!" she cried.

"Aw, now, a little squaw like you shouldn't mind kissing a white man."

"That's right, Ollie. Give 'er a good 'un," a tall, lean man with a sunburned face encouraged. He had a wolfish grin and laughed loud as the big man began to kiss the woman.

She struggled silently, trying to beat the huge roughneck with her fists, but it was useless.

Ray stood up, shoving his chair back, stepped over to the table, and said, "Let her go."

All four of the men stared up at him in surprise. They saw a thin young man with red hair and blue eyes, no more than twenty years old.

"Hey, Ollie," one of them piped up. "You better look out. That's a desperate-looking character."

The big man kept his hold on the woman for a moment, but she took advantage of the distraction to wrench herself away. He stood up at once and caught her wrist and held her.

"You're pretty rough on women. Now, turn her loose," Ray demanded. But that was the last thing that he remembered. He had turned to look at the woman for a moment and noticed that she was staring at him in a peculiar fashion. He opened his mouth to speak again but something that seemed to be traveling with the speed and power of a freight train caught him high on his head. He was conscious of a jolting pain and of flying through the air, but before his limp body stopped rolling, he was swallowed up in the most profound darkness he had ever known.

"I think he's coming out of it."

Ray heard the voice and identified it as coming from Denton DeForge. However, the pain in his head was so tremendous he could not concentrate. He coughed suddenly and the shock of moving his head made the pain worse. He felt a hand on his forehead and a coolness, then he slowly opened his eyes. For a moment, everything was blurred, then two faces swam into focus—those of Dent and the woman.

Dent grinned and there was some relief in his voice. "You all right, Ray?"

"Yeah, I guess so." He looked around and saw that he was lying on a bed. A movement caught his eye and he saw another man in the room, an Indian wearing blue jeans and a white shirt. Sitting up quickly, Ray blinked and groaned as the pain took him again. He lifted his hand, touched his temple, and found it damp.

"What hit me?" he said.

"Ollie Bean caught you. I told you he was a pug."

"I never even saw him move."

The woman put the cloth that she held in her hand back in the pan, then looked at Ray. "I didn't ask for any help." There was antagonism in her voice and she was staring at him unsmilingly.

"That's no way to talk!" The young man who was standing behind her stepped forward. "My name's Johnny Dance," he said. "This is my sister, Winona." Dance was no more than twenty, and was obviously not a full-blooded Indian. He was six feet tall and lean as a lath. He had dark blue eyes that looked unusual in his copper face.

"I think he's been seeing too many movies," Winona said.

Ray was angered suddenly. "Well, I haven't been seeing

the right ones." Suddenly he grinned up at Dent. "What did you do to keep them from killing me?"

Dent reached into his back pocket and pulled out a .38. "I persuaded him to put it off until you were conscious."

"It's a good thing he did," Johnny Dance nodded. "That Bean's a bad one. He would have kicked your ribs loose if it hadn't been for that." He looked over at Dent and said, "You better watch out. He'll get at you one way or another. He's a mean one."

"Aw, he'll have to get in line, I reckon," Dent said cheerfully. He looked at Winona. "I appreciate your help. You're a pretty good nurse."

Ray stood to his feet, his head pounding. He looked at the young woman and said, "Sorry to interfere."

"You make a living protecting Indians?" Winona asked.

Again there was a hard edge to her voice. Ray could not understand her antagonism. "No, I guess not," he said. He looked over at Dent and said, "I guess we'd better get back. Pete'll be looking for us."

At once something changed in the eyes of Johnny Dance. "Pete Stuart?"

"That's right," Dent said. "We're working for Pete now. This is his nephew, Ray Ballard." He suddenly reached over and shook Dance's hand. "Glad to make your acquaintance."

"I've heard about Stuart," Dance murmured. Something moved behind his dark blue eyes and he said, "I heard he got beat up by the Kingman outfit."

"Yeah, that's right. Might have been Ollie Bean behind it, for all I know. If I'd thought of that," Dent said calmly, "I would've put a bullet in his drumstick."

"They're a big outfit. Nobody has ever bucked 'em and succeeded."

Winona spoke. "They have been unpleasant to us," she said. When Ray and Dent looked at her with the question in their eyes, she said, "We have some land. They've been putting pressure on Johnny and me to sell the leasing to them, but we won't do it."

Johnny said suddenly, "That's probably why Ollie came in. To put a little bit more pressure on us." He thought for a moment and said, "I'd like to meet Pete Stuart."

"Come on along. We'll bring you back," Dent said.

Then he looked at Winona. "But I guess you have to go back to your job."

"I can get off," she said. She turned and walked out of the room and the men followed her.

They climbed into the truck and bounced over the rough road. Ray sat in the back with Winona and the violence of one of the chuckholes threw him against her. "Sorry," he said.

Winona did not answer. She had been thinking about what had happened in the cafe. Now she turned to him and said, "You know, most men would have done that anyhow."

"Done what?"

"Tried to get close to me in the back of this truck."

"Hope you don't think I did it on purpose."

Winona's face was a study. "I don't trust white men," she said. "I know them too well. I've fought them off since I was twelve years old."

The truck rolled along, backfiring on occasion, to the cadence of the rattling of the driveshaft. She turned and looked at him, her eyes suddenly large and somehow different. "Thanks for what you tried to do at the cafe. Most white men wouldn't have bothered."

Ray was embarrassed. "Didn't do anything much," he said, "except get knocked silly."

Winona smiled, the first time he had seen her do so. It made her very pretty and she said, "But you tried."

Horace Kingman was tall, thick-bodied, and strong. At sixty-three he was almost as strong as when he had hit the Oklahoma oil fields without a penny to his name. He had fought his way up and now owned land he had once walked across as a beggar. All over the area, wells were pumping, and the money from the oil went directly into his pockets. He had a strong brown face, and when he spoke he seemed to spit his words out. And now he spoke harshly to the men who were gathered in the tent staring down at a chart.

"All right, we've fooled around long enough. Why haven't you got these leases?"

"Some of them are pretty touchy characters, Horace." Ollie Bean was a sergeant at arms, in effect, for the Kingman empire. A former prizefighter, he was a much shrewder man than his brutal face would seem to indicate. He could whip any of the roughnecks that worked for Kingman, and if this failed, he was not opposed to using a club or whatever came handy. He looked now at Kingman and said, truculently, "You told us to stay out of trouble with the law, and we've gone about as far as we can with some of these people."

Kingman stared at him for a moment. He did not tolerate back talk from most of his employees, but Bean had been with him a long time, and Kingman trusted him as he trusted few other men. Now his eyes skipped over to a tall thin man wearing a white suit and smoking a cheroot. He wore a white hat also and looked like a southern planter, down to the string tie.

"What about this, Todd? Is there some way we can get these things through the court?"

Allison Todd removed the cheroot and shook his head. He had a pale face and the red eyes of a heavy drinker. "It'd cost more to buy up the politicians and the sheriffs and the lawmakers than it'd cost to do it some other way. Just trying to save you money, Mr. Kingman," he said sardonically.

Kingman studied the lawyer, then his head swiveled suddenly. He looked toward a young man who was standing back with his hands in his pockets. Kingman studied the young man carefully, for this was no employee, but his only son, Ted. He took in the lean and wiry build, the curly brown hair, and the brown eyes. *He looks like his mother,* Horace Kingman thought, which was to him a liability. His wife had been a weak woman, at least in his mind. But then, all people were weak who would not use their strength to crush their adversaries. There was impatience in the elder Kingman. He had put this son of his through law school and now expected to see the results of his investment. Harshly he barked, "Well, Ted, what about this?"

Ted Kingman licked his lips nervously. Both Allison Todd and Ollie Bean saw what they already knew, that Horace Kingman had cowed his son. Bean had said once to the lawyer, "The kid won't never be no good. He's been ruined by education. He's got no guts."

Bean's words seemed to be true enough, for the younger Kingman cleared his throat and said hesitantly, "Well, Dad—we've got plenty of leases already. I don't see why you're so insistent on having these."

"I want 'em all," Kingman said. His voice was rough and grated like broken glass over his son's nerves. "If you ever let up, they'll eat you alive. Haven't you learned that, Boy? This ain't a game we're playing. There's wolves out there."

"But Dad—"

"Never mind that." Kingman slammed his blunt finger down on the map. "This one, right here! Get Pete Stuart's place and get it quick! You hear me?"

"They seem like good people," Ted shrugged.

Horace stared at him. "You're soft," he muttered. "Soft like your ma."

Ted Kingman knew a moment's flaring, flashing anger. He lifted his head and opened his mouth, and for one moment Horace Kingman was filled with hope that his son would challenge him, take him on head-to-head, man-to-man. That's what he longed to see. To him, Ted was not a man, but a girl wearing trousers. But Kingman saw the revolt die and grunted harshly, "See that it gets done! You know what to do, Ollie." He turned and left the tent.

Bean turned his massive bulk to face the younger man. There was a taunt in the voice that said, "Well, that means rough stuff. You want to take care of it, Mr. Kingman?" He always called Ted "Mr. Kingman" in a mocking tone—whereas he called his father "Horace"—the only one of the hundreds of employees of Kingman Oil Company to take that liberty.

Once again anger touched Ted Kingman. He had not been brought up on the oil fields but in a private school, then he'd gone to Yale and then to MIT. He knew the oil business from the scientific side but felt completely out of it in a situation like this. For a moment, he stood with his fists clenching nervously. He knew the brutality of Ollie Bean, had heard of it all his life. But only since coming to work and seeing the actual savagery of the oil fields had he come to dread the sight of the man. "What're you going to do, Bean?" he demanded.

Bean's neck, thick as a fire hydrant, was merely a post for his heavy head, which he turned now. His shirt bulged with fat, but underneath was solid muscle. He held up his fist and said, "This is all guys like Stuart understand. I'm gonna bust 'im."

"Be careful," Allison Todd spoke up. "If you kill him you might get in trouble."

Might get in trouble, Ted thought angrily. He stared at the two men, then turned and walked out.

"The kid ain't got no backbone," Bean shrugged his thick shoulders. "He ain't gonna make it in this business. I don't know why Horace keeps him around."

Todd did know. "That's his only son. He wants to pass the Kingman Oil empire on to a Kingman and Ted there is the only son he'll ever have, I suppose. His only chance for a grandson, for an empire, a dynasty."

Bean stared at the lawyer. "He ain't gonna get no empire out of Ted," he said. Then he turned and walked out of the tent, leaving the lawyer alone.

You're probably right about that, Ollie, Todd thought. *Ted won't cut the mustard.*

The attack came so suddenly that it caught Dent off guard. He and Bailey were working on the rig at twilight. They had been called to supper but had kept working doggedly. Bailey's massive strength was a handy thing to have. He lifted blocks and pulled cables as Dent directed him, and Dent had just said, "I think this might do it, Bailey," when it happened.

A cable suddenly parted before Dent's eyes and he couldn't understand it—then the sound of the shot followed immediately. Another shot followed, kicking up dust at his feet. "Get down, Bailey!" he yelled, shoving the huge man, who fell obediently to the dirt. Whipping out the .38 he carried in his hip pocket, Dent ran along the length of the derrick. Another shot kicked up dust at his feet, and when he got to the Ford truck, he ducked behind it. Throwing himself underneath, he clawed himself past the driveshaft. From his position he could see a strange truck parked a hundred yards away, and a man on the back holding a rifle.

"Too far for a pistol shot," he said with disappointment. Nevertheless, he lifted the .38 and aimed high over the head of the man with the rifle, who was laying down a steady fire. He held still and pulled the trigger and saw the rifleman hesitate. Dent continued to fire, emptying the .38. He thought he saw glass fly, and he heard a slight yell. Then the truck engine started, and the man jumped to the ground and leaped into the cab. Leaving a cloud of dust, the truck tore off, careening wildly.

Dent came out from under the Ford, and at once the door of the shack opened. Pete came out, struggling with his crutches, followed by Maury and Violet.

They came to stand by him. "Who was it?"

"Too far to see," Dent said. He looked over and said, "You can get up now, Bailey."

Violet ran over to Bailey saying, "Are you hurt?"

Bailey looked at her in surprise. "No, I'm okay." She patted his arm and he smiled. "They shot at us, I think."

Pete whispered, "Had to be Kingman. Since you had that row with Ollie, I been expecting it."

Ray had come out to stand beside Pete. He touched the bruised side of his head and a fiery light of anger came into his mild eyes. "Looks like Johnny and Winona were right. They're gonna try everything." Dance and his sister had met with Pete and warned him that Kingman would stop at nothing.

Pete's shoulders slumped. He looked around at his wife and children and said, "If I just hadn't busted this leg, I'd fight 'em."

"You can shoot with a broken leg." Dent's words were strangely cheerful. He said, "I think I'd better make a trip in the morning. Saw a pawn shop in the next town. Had some pretty good-lookin' guns in it."

Leslie came to Pete. She put her arm around him and looked up at him, worry in her eyes. "You don't mean to fight 'em with guns?"

"Well, it wouldn't do much good to use cream puffs," Denton DeForge said. He seemed careless, but there was something in his dark eyes that was ominous. Violet had seen him like this before. She spoke aloud her thoughts, "I don't see how a Christian can be a gunfighter."

Dent looked down at her and said, "A man's first job is to protect his family. God's pretty plain about that." He looked around and winked at Maury. "Didn't we decide I could kinda be a Stuart, Miss Maury?"

Maury went over and gave him a hug. "We sure did, Dent." She kissed him on the cheek and said, "Get me a gun while you're there, too."

Dent laughed in delight. "Too bad we can't get one of those machine guns like Al Capone's boys have. But shotguns'll do for out here I guess. I'll sure get you a nice one."

His words were light and broke the tension. The next morning, however, he did exactly as he said. By ten o'clock he was back with an arsenal. When Stephen came to Pete and said, "Pa, you gonna let me shoot one of them old Kingman men?" Pete put his hand out and ruffled the boy's hair. "I guess it's your job right now to take care of your mama, Son."

When he saw the disappointment he said, "I'm glad you're willing to fight, and I hope you'll always fight for what's right."

Maury had come to stand beside Dent. He handed her a double-barreled shotgun and a sack. "It breaks down like this," he said. He broke the shotgun open, fished out two shells from the sack and stuck them into the gun, then snapped it back into position. "Pull these hammers back and aim at anything that bothers you."

"I don't think I'd be a very good shot."

"Aw, I'll give you some lessons," he said. He winked at Violet, who was staring at him unhappily. "And you too, Violet. As for being a good shot," he looked at the shotgun and said, "if you get up close enough that doesn't matter much. Just pull the trigger and whatever's in front will sort of disappear." He walked away happily and Maury smiled at Violet. "Has he always been like that? I never saw anybody like him."

"He was wild when he was young, but he got saved," Violet said.

"I'm surprised he hasn't married," Maury said thoughtfully. "He's so good looking."

Violet stared at the woman and said shortly, "Yes, he is," then turned and walked away, her back stiff and her head held high.

 10 

Bonnie Meets a Star

"I'm not sure it's the right thing to do, Carl. After all, she's not an actress."

Carl Thomas was sitting across the table from Lylah, staring into a glass of buttermilk. He made a face, lifted the glass, then drank it down with a shudder. Slamming the glass down on the table, he wiped his lips vigorously with his silk handkerchief, then finally scowled at her. "I hate buttermilk, but it's the only thing that'll make my stomach quit hurting. Why couldn't it be something like champagne?" Tucking the handkerchief back in his breast pocket, he made a dapper figure as he sat straight up in his chair. "I know Cara's not an actress," he said, "but she's got 'it,' like Clara Bow."

"I hate to ask you, but what is 'it' we keep hearing about?" This of course referred to the meteoric career of Clara Bow, a sultry movie star who was thoroughly detested by Lylah. "She can't act, any more than Bingo can." Bingo was the huge dog that Jesse had brought with him when he and Lylah first met.

"Of course Clara can't act." He leaned forward, placed his hand on his chin, a diminutive figure with wise old eyes. "You don't have to when you've got 'it,' and don't ask me what 'it' is. All I know is people pay for tickets to see her. I think they'd buy tickets to see her read a telephone book or peel potatoes or turn back flips."

Lylah laughed aloud. She was wearing an attractive blue cotton dress that fit her rather loosely around the hips and deemphasized her full figure. "I know that. I just hate to admit we have such low taste here in America."

"It's not just here in America." Thomas shrugged as he spoke mildly. "It's always been that way. Oh, yes, there've always been women around with 'it.' Men, too, I suppose."

"I never heard of a man having 'it,' but some of them do, I suppose," Lylah murmured.

She and Carl and Jesse had been besieged by Jerry with pleas to put Cara into the movie, not just as a stunt flyer but as an actor. Lylah and Jesse had been opposed at first, but Carl had called Lylah to one side earlier today, speaking of money for a long time. Finally he had said, "We can't afford big names for this, except maybe one. Brent Peters will take all of our bankroll. We don't have to have Cara play a large role," he had argued. "Just let her be in it. Have Jesse write her a part, just a few scenes. She'll be doing the flying sequences with Jerry and Gavin. Jerry'll be doubling for Brent, so we're saving money all the way around."

Now Lylah finally gave in. "All right, Carl, I suppose you're right. She can't do too much damage. Jerry'll be happy at least. But I'm not happy for him."

"You're worried about him, aren't you?"

"She's a black widow spider!"

"How's that? She doesn't look like a spider."

"You don't know?" Lylah smiled grimly. "A black widow takes a mate, then kills and eats him after he's of no use to her any longer."

A frosty smile touched the lips of the old man. "I have known a few like that," he admitted. "Some of them big stars." He leaned forward and touched her hand. "I'm glad I've known you, Lylah," he said gently. "You're not a spider."

She laughed at him and squeezed his hand. "All right. The next question is, can we do it? Will the money be there?"

They discussed the finances for a while and they agreed it was a grim enough proposition. "Bankers are stingy with money. Your name's worth something and you're playing the character role. And Brent Peters is sort of a male Clara Bow with those bedroom eyes of his."

"Maybe we could lock him and Cara in a room somewhere. They could devour each other and let the rest of the world go free," Lylah said acidly. Then she rose and said, "I'll tell Cara she gets the job."

Cara was pleased at the offer of a role in the movie. Jerry was happy, too. The two of them went out to celebrate, and Hollywood, like all the other large cities in the country, had its speakeasies. The Roaring Twenties had not brought in fine restaurants. The flappers and their boyfriends could not get drinks in those. When prohibition had come, the flaming youth, as they were called, turned from fine restaurants and headed straight for speakeasies that, in addition to serving liquor, had the intoxicating allure of being a little risqué and therefore glamorous.

They got out of the huge Packard that Cara had bought on credit. Jerry helped her out of the car and they headed for the building on a side street of Los Angeles. Jerry knocked on the door, which brought a grunted response, and a panel slid open. A blunt face appeared asking, "Who sent you?"

Jerry had not obtained a reference and simply said, "Joe sent me."

The panel slid back, and then the door opened. It was a rough, unsavory place, dark, with a loud saxophone squawking its fast jazz rhythm in the middle of a six-piece band.

A burly waiter showed them to a table in the crowded room and there, amidst the smell of cigarette smoke, raw whiskey, and sweating bodies, they proceeded to get roaring drunk.

This sort of thing had gone on since prohibition had come to America in 1919. The flood of outlaw liquor struck the country like a tidal wave. Hip flasks uptilted above faces, male and female, at football games. Speakeasies were serving cocktails made of gin on practically every corner. Well-born young women, with one foot on a brass rail, tossed off martinis. Many a keg of grape juice simmering hopefully in a young couple's bedroom closet was subject to periodic inspection by one or the other. The government had not been able to stop the flow, and the beneficiaries of prohibition were Al Capone and the other rapacious criminals who made fortunes off of illegal liquor.

When Jerry and Cara finally stumbled out of the speakeasy, he was half sick. He had not been drinking since he left Cara, and now he slumped beside her in the car. "You've forgotten how to have a good time, Honey," Cara smiled, patting his cheek. She seemed to be able to consume endless glasses of the raw whiskey without being overly affected. Starting the Packard, she roared down the street, and Jerry muttered, "We can't do this when we start flying."

But Cara was humming a tune that had been the theme song of the Roaring Twenties, "Running Wild, Lost Control," and as the Packard made erratic weavings down the street, she sang at the top of her lungs, and Jerry knew that, whatever Cara did, he was as much in love with her as he had ever been.

Jerry, Gavin, and Cara spent the next week working hard on the airplanes that were to be used for the picture. All day they flew, perfecting some of the stunts that would be necessary. Gavin, as usual, was a perfectionist, and Jerry knew that one hint of a weakness as far as alcohol was concerned and he would be out on his ear.

He went out with Cara most nights but drank very little. Their love affair, however, had burst into flame again. There was a weakness in him for this woman. Deep down he knew that she was not a woman whom he could put his faith in. She was loving, generous, fun-loving—and totally unpredictable. Nevertheless, he was drawn to her, as the proverbial moth to the candle.

Gavin had monitored his nephew's flying closely and when Lylah asked about him, he shrugged. "As far as I can tell about him, he's all right. If he's drinking, it's very little, although he's keeping pretty late hours. I can't do anything about Cara, since she's got a contract. I just hope they don't kill each other."

"Not until the picture's finished at least," Carl said cynically. "Then, it's up to them."

The stars of the picture were Brent Peters and Eileen Turner. Eileen was that rare item in Hollywood, a truly sweet, unspoiled young woman. Somehow the ugly side of show business had not rubbed off on her. She was twenty years old, blond with blue eyes, rather superficial prettiness, and had played the same type of role that had made Lillian Gish famous.

Brent Peters was hot at the moment in Hollywood. He bore a slight resemblance to Valentino. He had the same black hair, which he kept greased back, and most of all he had the soulful bedroom eyes that had made Valentino an idol. Peters was only of average height but was muscular, strong, quick, and agile enough to take over the kind of athletic roles that Douglas Fairbanks had starred in.

Bonnie first met Peters when she brought some papers from the house to the set. She found Lylah in her office talking to Peters and Bonnie recognized him instantly. "Oh, I didn't mean to disturb you, Lylah," she apologized.

"That's all right. I don't think you've met Brent Peters. This is my assistant, Bonnie Hart. She's my sister-in-law, also, and has saved my life by raising my son. She's more of a mother to him than I am, I think."

Bonnie put her hand out tentatively and it was grasped at once by Peters. She had never been impressed particularly by the man on the screen, except by his athletic prowess. But then, she had never idolized Valentino either. Now, however, as she looked into Brent's eyes and as his hand closed around hers, she felt a slight shock and stammered slightly, "N–no, I've never met Mr. Peters."

Lylah smiled involuntarily. She had seen this so many times. *I thought Bonnie might be up to resisting Brent but, whatever it is women like, he's got too much of it.* Aloud she asked, "I suppose you've seen all of his pictures?"

"I think most of them," Bonnie said. "I liked them very much."

"Well, I appreciate that." Peters was free and easy in his manner, and his smile seemed genuine enough. "So you're Lylah's assistant? I may be calling on you for a little help from time to time."

"Oh, she was joking about that. I don't know anything about making movies." She laughed. "All I can do is cook and take care of thirteen-year-old boys."

"Do you know Hollywood?"

"Well, we've lived here a long time, but really I don't get out much."

Something changed in Brent Peters's face and he nodded, "Maybe you'll give me the chance to show you the town."

After Bonnie left, Peters said, "Seems like a fine woman. She's been married?"

"Oh, no. She's really devoted her life to me and my son—and to her brother, of course. I really don't know what we'd do without Bonnie."

Peters pulled a platinum case from his inner pocket. He extracted a cigarette and put it in his lips. He replaced the cigarette case, produced a gold lighter, and lit the cigarette. Letting the smoke trickle out of his lips, he said thoughtfully, "You know, we don't see many of that kind anymore."

"You've known a lot of women, Brent."

He glanced at her quickly. "Too many, I think." He said no more, but later on in the week he met Bonnie again on the set. This time Jerry and Cara were present. They had just come in from a flying scene and were wearing their flying outfits.

Cara came over at once and said, "Hello, Brent." She gazed at him, as she did any attractive man, and smiled broadly. "Did you see the stunt?"

Brent nodded. "I wouldn't want to try that. I don't like high places." He laughed shortly and shook his head. "I don't even like to step up on a curb. What you're doing up there scares me witless." He looked at Jerry and asked, "You've done a lot of flying, I take it?"

"Quite a bit."

Bonnie looked up. She heard the curtness in Jerry's voice, and as the conversation went on, she was able to see the little drama. Cara could no more help making up to a man like Brent Peters than she could help breathing. Peters seemed mildly amused by her. He was accustomed to having women fawn over him, and there was a romantic aura around Cara. She was a public figure. Her courage and daring were blazoned across many newspapers. Men seemed to find this irresistible. That and her full-figured sexuality would attract any man.

That night, Jerry arrived in time for supper with Bonnie and Adam. He played checkers with Adam for a while after supper, and finally Bonnie asked, "You and Cara didn't go out tonight?"

"No, she's out with Peters."

After the game was over, Adam went to listen to the radio, and Bonnie and Jerry went out to sit in the swing on the front porch. The air was warm and the two sat talking quietly. Jerry spoke for a time of the difficulty of flying the stunts. Finally Bonnie asked, "You don't like Brent Peters, do you?"

Jerry snapped his head around and grinned. "You always were a mind reader. How'd you know I was thinking about him?"

"I know you're jealous."

"Well, I am. He's a famous movie star and I'm nobody."

"That's not true."

"Yes, it is. Here I am, practically an old man, with nothing to show for my life."

"You're not exactly tripping over your beard, Jerry. You're only thirty-one."

"Thirty-one and washed up!"

Bonnie saw that he was depressed but was impatient with him. "You know what kind of a woman Cara is. I'm surprised you took up with her again. She nearly tore you apart the last time you were dating her."

Jerry shook his head, "You don't understand. You just don't know what it's like, being in love."

"How do you know?"

Her answer, which came sharply, startled Jerry, and he turned to face her. "I didn't know you'd ever been in love. Who was it?"

Bonnie shook her head. She knew that he was sensitive about his relationship with Cara. *I shouldn't have mentioned it,* she thought. She rose and said, "I've got to make sure Adam gets to bed. That's getting to be more of a struggle."

"How about I take you two to the zoo tomorrow? We're not scheduled for any flying."

"I'd like that."

The next day, Jerry appeared driving Gavin's Ford. Bonnie was ready, and Adam was practically in the car before it came to a complete halt. It was a fine morning and the zoo was fun. As they walked into the lion house, Adam wrinkled up his nose. "It stinks in here! I didn't know lions smelled so bad." Nevertheless, he did not miss a thing that day, bad odor or not. They had a lunch of hot dogs and RC Colas and ice cream. Afterward, they walked around a large pond that contained a flock of flamingos. Adam found the birds to be awkward and was amazed they could even fly.

It was a restful day for Jerry, and when they were on their way back to the house, he was startled to notice that Adam had grown silent and sullen.

"What's the matter, Pardner?" he asked, clapping the boy on the shoulder. "Didn't you have a good time?"

"Sure I did, Jerry."

Jerry glanced over at Bonnie, who shook her head slightly, and he said no more. After they got home and Adam ran to the house, he asked, "What's the matter with Adam?"

"He's worried."

"Worried about what? He's got everything—bicycles, toys, good parents."

"He's worried about who his real father is."

Jerry looked up quickly, understanding dawning in his lean face. "I wondered when that would happen. What does he say?"

He listened carefully as Bonnie described the boy's uncertainties and nodded. "I can see how that would be a problem. I've made a mess out of my life but I sure can't blame it on Dad. He's been swell; so has Mom." He looked over at the house and shook his head. "Why doesn't Lylah tell him, I wonder? Do you know who his father is?"

"No."

"Dad knows but he won't ever say."

"I feel sorry for Adam. It's hard on any child—growing up. I read about 'golden' childhood, but I never had any of it." She was speaking softly now and looking down at her hands. There was a sadness in her voice as she said, "I can't remember feeling safe and secure. I had Jesse but he was gone all the time. I still don't feel safe and secure."

"You should get married. Why haven't you, Bonnie?"

"I was kidding last night. I've never loved anybody. I don't think I ever will. I just don't have that kind of love to bring to a man, I guess."

"Hey! Don't talk like that. We're both just late bloomers." His hand came to rest on her shoulder and he shook her slightly. Reaching over, he pulled her face around and saw, with a shock, the tears running down her face. "Hey now! Can't have that." Quickly he pulled his handkerchief out and wiped the tears away. "I don't like it when my buddy's sad. We've been real close, you and me."

Her answer came slowly, "Yes, Jerry." Then she moved away from him. She got out of the car and entered the house without a backward look. Jerry watched for a while, then thought, *I haven't kept up with Bonnie the way I should. Can't understand why she's never gotten married. She'd make a fine wife.* Her tears troubled him. He left the house, driving to the studio. When Cara asked him later that day what was wrong, he thought of Bonnie, but said, "Oh, nothing. A little bit sober today, I guess." She laughed, making a joke out of it, but he could not get it out of his mind.

"I'm not sure I should have come with you, Brent," Bonnie said. She was riding in Brent's Packard convertible, the wind blowing her hair. The day before, he had invited her out to dinner and she had agreed reluctantly. Now, as they sped along, she looked over at him and saw he was smiling at her, his teeth very white against his dark skin.

"I'm not the big bad wolf with long teeth, Bonnie. You don't have to be afraid of me."

Instantly she reacted. "I'm not afraid of you, Brent! I'm not afraid of any man."

"Well, that can be a mistake." he shrugged. "You need to be afraid of some men." He did not elaborate, and he changed the subject at once. "Have you ever been to Ryan's?"

"No, Lylah's told me about it, though."

"It's *the* place to go in Hollywood. I think you'll like it."

New York had produced some fine restaurants in the thirties. The Waldorf-Astoria Hotel had been built on Park Avenue in 1931. Though considered by many to be foolhardy, it had proved to be so successful that Norris Ryan had decided to try his luck with a fancy restaurant in Hollywood. He made his place a replica of the Pump-of-the-Spa in Bath, England, so that the rich and famous were encouraged to come. It had turned out to be a meeting place of all sorts of people, but Ryan knew that at New York's 21 Club, the best tables were saved for celebrities. He therefore arranged the best tables of all for people such as Brent Peters.

As Brent and Bonnie were seated by a genuine French waiter, Brent pointed out some of the guests. "There's John Barrymore, over there, and that's that new fellow, Clark Gable. Not much yet, but I think he's gonna go places—got lots of sex appeal . . ."

Bonnie was stunned by the food, which matched the swagger of the decor. Waiters pushed wagons of hors d'oeuvres, roasts, soups, and ice sculptures through the large dining room. Everything was excessive and flamboyant with displays of culinary pyrotechnics. She stared as a waiter brought out hot dogs on flaming swords. Another waiter brought out twelve ripe olives, each on a long brochette.

"I guess it doesn't hurt the food much," Brent grinned as some flaming crépes suzette startled Bonnie.

Bonnie did enjoy the dinner. Brent, she found out, was a highly intelligent man. He was witty and charming, and many people that she had seen only on the screen stopped at their table to greet him. She danced with him many times and discovered that he was an expert. "I was a professional dancer before I got an acting role," he shrugged. "Sorry way to make a living. You're not bad, Bonnie."

Finally they left, at her insistence, although it was only eleven—and he took her for a long drive. He drove with the convertible's top down. They came to a stop at her house and he shut the engine off. He turned to her and said, "Now, I've warned you to beware of some men and I've said that I'm not a big bad wolf." He laughed softly and said, "Think about those two things."

Bonnie knew that he was going to kiss her. She did not draw back as he put his arms around her and drew her close. She wondered, *Thirty million women would like to be kissed by Brent Peters. Now, I'm going to see if he's different from other men.*

He was certainly expert. His lips came down on her gently at first, then with an added pressure. His hand caressed her back sending slight shivers up her spine. There was, as she found, something to sex appeal. It was not just something that appeared on the screen. She was stirred by his kiss and was a little shocked at her reaction. She kept her lips on his until finally he drew back and lifted one eyebrow. "Well, I intended to frighten you, but I see that's not going to be possible."

Bonnie laughed suddenly. "I wanted to know if a matinee idol kissed any better than John Doe." Her eyes sparkled and she looked very attractive in the moonlight. There was a smoothness in her face, an even symmetry, and her lips curved attractively as she smiled at him. "I must say, you kiss very well—but I'm not sure it's all that much better than Mr. Doe's."

Brent found her comments delightful. He laughed, slapping his hands together. "You're not giving me a fair chance," he protested. "No man can kiss better than all those images that you see on the screen."

"How much of that is real?" Bonnie asked. "Are you really like those dashing heroes?"

"Not at all," he assured her. "We matinee idols are just like all other men. If you prick us do we not bleed?"

"I know that. It's from *The Merchant of Venice.*"

"Right!" He was surprised, then shrugged. "I don't know why I didn't expect you to know that. Have you read much literature?" When she rattled off her list of accomplishments, he nodded. "That's good. Those are the sorts of things I'd like to read. I'd like to try Shakespeare, but I suppose people would laugh."

"Why should they laugh?"

"Oh, it's like, what's this fellow's name—Weissmuller, who plays Tarzan in this new movie, swinging through the trees—'Me Tarzan, you Jane.'"

"Yes, he was a swimmer."

"Fine athlete, but all he has to say is 'Me Tarzan, you Jane.' If he tried to play Shakespeare, I think he'd have some difficulty getting people to accept him."

They talked for a long time and she discovered that, surprisingly enough, there was a little area of doubt in the man. She mentioned this. "I wouldn't have thought you had any doubts."

"Don't be foolish. Every man has doubts—and every woman—I suppose."

His remark caught at her and she sat running her hand suddenly over her hair. "I don't know about all women, but I have mine."

"You've never been in love?"

The question came so quickly that she answered, "Yes—" She caught herself and closed her lips.

Peters was a perceptive man. "Wounded in love," he said softly. "Well, the old idea of Cupid with an arrow seems rather cute, but you know, getting pierced with an arrow really isn't a pleasant thing. Most love isn't either, I think—if there is such a thing as real love."

"Why do you say that, Brent?"

"Most people when they talk about love are saying, 'What will you give me?'" He shifted in his seat, put his hands on the steering wheel, and gripped it tightly. He rocked back and forth for a minute thinking over his words, then turned to her, putting his hand on her shoulder. "Somehow there's got to be a love that says, 'What can I give you?' don't you think?"

She was pleased with the gentleness that she saw in him. "I think that's nice," she said. Then he leaned forward and kissed her again. This time he was more insistent. She pulled away sharply and smiled. "The big bad wolf is showing his teeth. I'll see you later, Brent. It's been a lovely evening." She got out of the car, leaned over and said, "Next time, I'll fix supper. I can cook better than that bunch down at Ryan's."

Brent laughed as she moved away, and as he left, guiding the Packard with careless ease down the street, he was whistling a tune, rather off key, something he hadn't caught himself doing for a long time. He stopped whistling abruptly and grinned. "You'd have to go native if you chased that one, Brent old boy. She's not your typical Hollywood starlet."

The problem exploded, seemingly, out of nowhere. Bonnie had invited Brent in for a meal, and they had enjoyed a fine evening together. It had been pleasant, from her standpoint. She was greeted by Jerry later in the week, and he attacked her at once. "What are you doing running around with that guy Peters?" he demanded. He had met her in the hall at the studio and had pulled her into a small room used for conferences. His eyes were snapping and she could tell there was a tenseness in him she had not seen.

"Why, Jerry, I've only gone out with him twice."

"That's twice too many," he said. "You've got to stop it, Bonnie. You just don't know what kind of man he is."

“I think I do,” Bonnie said rather coldly. “He’s been a perfect gentleman.”

“That’s just his act,” Jerry grunted. He had heard about Peters dating Bonnie and it had upset him. He had gone to Jesse, insisting that he tell her to show some sense. “She’s a grown woman,” Jesse had said, “and has more sense than most men that I know.”

Now Jerry and Bonnie stood squared off like antagonists. Bonnie was filled with burning anger as he continued to tell her how she didn’t know what she was doing. Finally, she shoved by him, stopping at the door and saying, “You’ve run your own life so wonderfully, Jerry, I suppose now you’ve set out to help the rest of us poor mortals to avoid mistakes. Good to know that there’s one in this life so perfect that he’s able to handle everybody’s problems.”

The door slammed and Jerry stared after her. His face was pale and he was shocked to find out how the quarrel disturbed him. He took a deep breath and set his jaw stubbornly. “All right, Bonnie,” he whispered, “but I’m still right and you’re still wrong.”

11

A Narrow Escape

The making of *The Pilot* proceeded with all the difficulties, obstacles, and frustrations that accompany such productions. Since much of the action took place in the air, fine weather was required—not only for safety, but for good lighting for the cameras. Gavin flew the camera plane, while Jerry and Cara doubled for the stars in the other aircraft. Several days were lost when an unprecedented series of thunderstorms swept over the area. This threw the production behind, and it was on a cloudy Thursday morning with the group gathered in the hangar when Lylah finally lost her temper.

Glaring up at the clouds, she spat out the words, "We moved the motion picture industry to California from New York for good weather. We might as well move back!"

Jesse was wearing an old white shirt and a pair of disreputable slacks that he was inordinately fond of. He excused his mode of dress by claiming to be a writer, and all writers are eccentric.

But now he moved over and looked out the hangar door, then turned with a hopeful expression. "It's clearing off. I think in an hour or two we might be able to do some filming. What do you think, Gavin?"

Gavin glanced up at the sky and shrugged his shoulders. "We can get above it, I think, if we have to."

Jerry was sitting with Cara at a table. They were drinking coffee, and both looked a little upset. Cara had put on her lipstick with a shaky hand and now said stubbornly, "Sure, we can do it. What difference does a little rain make?"

Gavin turned and studied her face. At thirty-four she was still a beautiful woman, but hard living had drawn some lines that had not been there a few years prior. She was still a tremendous flier and always had been. But he thought, *She was out drinking again last night. It's going to get her killed one of these days.*

His eyes shifted to Jerry, who looked sullen in the early morning light. *I'd hate for Jerry to go down with her on one of her fool daredevil stunts, but I can't talk to him.* Aloud, Gavin said, "Let's give it a couple of hours, or even until noon. We ought to be able to get in four or five hours of flying."

"Come on, let's go. We can't do any good here, Jesse," Lylah said. She glanced at Gavin and said, "You know the sequence? It sounds pretty dangerous to me."

"Ought to be all right," Gavin nodded. "We've all done it before." He smiled at Jerry saying, "Remember back in the air circus, Jerry? This was your specialty."

Jerry managed a smile and nodded. "It'll be a piece of cake, Lylah, don't worry."

Lylah and Jesse drove back to the studio and spent the rest of the morning working on details. Finally he said, "Let's take a break."

They went out for lunch but could not leave the business behind. Jesse had been drinking iced tea. He set down the glass suddenly and said, "Have you thought what would happen, to the picture I mean, if anything happened to Cara? If she had a crash and couldn't act in the film?"

Nodding grimly, Lylah answered, "Yes, that's why I've had Dick shoot around, getting all the scenes filmed that she's in except for those in the plane."

"I hope nothing will happen, of course. But it's always possible."

"Jerry's making a fool of himself over her," Lylah said. There was a bitterness in her voice and she said angrily, "And

Cara's egging him on. She runs around with Brent half the time and poor Jerry can't stand the pace of that. Pretty hard competing with a movie star with a pocket full of money."

"You know we can't talk to him about that. When a man's blind about a woman, that's about it." He reached over and took her hand and squeezed it. "I'd like to think what would have happened if somebody had tried to tell me to leave you alone."

His words pleased her. "You do have your moments," she whispered. Then she grew more serious. "I'm worried about Bonnie. You know she was out late last night with Brent. She just doesn't know how explosive a situation that can be." The waiter came and filled the glasses with tea. She waited until he left, then took a sip. "Nobody makes tea like Ma used to back on the farm," she said quietly. "I remember it after all these years. I don't know what she did to it. It was better than anything else."

"Maybe your memory of it is better than anything else," Jesse said.

"What do you mean?"

"I mean the past is always better than the present. Our memories of it get softened. You had a tough time on the farm but that memory gets blunted after a few years. The tea probably wasn't as good as that tea in your glass. But it was a good memory and over the years it sort of incubated."

"I suppose that's right. Is it like that with you?"

"There was a hill close to where I lived at home. I remember it was a frightening thing to go down it in a wagon or on a sled. I didn't go back for years and years, and I kept thinking about how dangerous and what fun it was to go down that hill." Jesse's eyes were half shut as he went back over the past, his lips curling in a pleased smile. "Then I went back," he said, turning to look at her, "and I could spit over the thing. It had grown in my mind until I thought it was Mount Everest when actually it wasn't anything like a big hill."

"I *hate* it when you analyze things like that." Lylah laughed at him then. He could always make her smile. That was one of the reasons she loved him. "We'll have to do something about Bonnie; she's old enough so I can't tell her what to do, and neither can you."

"Why, she's in love with Jerry, always has been, even if she won't admit it to herself."

"I think you're right. He's the reason she's turned down some good men. I wish she hadn't, though, because I don't know if Jerry'll ever settle down."

"If he knew the Lord, it'd be different, but he doesn't."

The two sat there and talked over their problems and finally went back to the studio and picked up the tedious work necessary to making a movie.

"Let's go over it one more time," Gavin said. They were standing slightly away from the planes. The engines had been revved up by the mechanics and the skies overhead were clear. Gavin saw a bored look come into Cara's eyes and he reached out and pulled her by the front of her shirt. "Wake up, Cara, you may have done this before, but every time's different."

Cara stared at him, shocked with the sharpness of his voice. "Aw, Gavin, there's nothing to it, is there, Jerry?"

"Well, I don't know," Jerry said. "It's always tricky."

Gavin went over it again, slowly, methodically, as was his fashion. He was a careful man in all things and especially with anything having to do with airplanes. "Listen," he said, "I've tried to tell you this before. Airplanes are treacherous. Back home on the farm we had a mule that would be good for six months just to have a chance to kick you once. That's the way it is with that plane there," he nodded. "There's lots of wind up there today. All it has to do is toss that plane one foot to the side and all of a sudden you're in trouble, Cara. Let's go over it again now."

"All right! All right!" Cara was bored but went over the stunt carefully. "When we get the sign, I get out of the front cockpit. Jerry keeps the plane steady. I crawl up on top of the wing, fix my feet in the stirrups, and hold my arms up straight.

Then he flies level and after three minutes of that, I take my feet out of the stirrups and move out to the end of the wing. And I hold tight to the straps," she added, before he could interrupt.

The top wing of the plane had been strengthened so that a person could move back and forth. This particular scene reproduced part of a flying circus element in the picture. Cara would wear goggles and a cap as a double for Eileen Turner.

"When I get to the end of the wing, he does a turn, and I brace myself, holding my arms out straight. Now, that's all there is to it!"

Gavin stared at her doubtfully. "All right," he said, "let's do it."

Jerry moved at once to the plane and waited for Cara, who came to step into the front cockpit. He handed her up and she laughed at his sober expression. Running her hand down his face, she said huskily, "How about tonight?"

"You sure you're not busy with Valentino the Second?"

Cara laughed and put herself against him. She kissed him soundly, saying, with a promise in her voice, "I like to keep you jealous." She slapped his cheek playfully and climbed agilely into the front seat.

Jerry climbed into the rear seat and looked over to see that Gavin and the camera operator were ready. When Gavin gave the signal, Jerry gunned the engine and took off. Gavin followed, and five minutes later they were above the cloud cover. As Gavin had said, the rain was gone, but it was windy, and it took all Jerry's skill to keep the plane level. Both he and Cara watched as Gavin pulled the camera plane up ahead slightly and thirty feet over their position. Then he gave the hand signal that meant, Do it!

Cara caught the signal, loosed her safety belt, and moved to a standing position on the seat. She was a strong woman and pulled herself out of the cockpit and onto the wing. She leaned forward, missing the full blast of the wind that snatched at her and pasted her thin red blouse against her body. When she had moved to the exact center of the wing, she slipped her feet into the rigging that Gavin had carefully designed. This rigging would be invisible to the audience. It would look as though she were simply standing on top of the wing. Carefully, she judged the wind and came to a full stand, leaning forward, arms outstretched and head lifted.

Jerry thought, *She's good at that, better than anybody who's ever done it.* He struggled with the controls, keeping the plane as level as he could. He had sensitive hands and managed successfully to counter the blast of wind that tried to shove the biplane to one side. *This is what I'm good at,* he thought grimly, satisfied that without him she could not do this stunt. After ninety seconds, what he judged to be the right amount of time, he glanced over at Gavin quickly and saw his uncle give the sign for Cara to move along the wing.

Cara leaned forward and Jerry saw her disengage her feet from the rigging. Along the wing there ran a cleat that she could brace her feet against as she moved outward. Jerry kept the plane at the lowest possible speed and struggled to keep the wing level as she made her way along. She wore no parachute and this was the essence of the trick. Some trick flyers used a tiny steel cable as a safety belt, but Cara had never used that. As Jerry looked down on the earth far below, a chill went through him as he thought of the impact of a body after falling from this height. Sweat broke out on his forehead, but he could not take his hands from the stick, for every move of the airplane was dangerous.

Cara had gotten within four feet of the tip of the wing when it happened. An unexpected countergust caught the airplane and shoved it sideways. Jerry countered instantly, but still the airplane moved sharply and unexpectedly in a different direction. Cara was caught with one foot off the wing, balancing herself, and the shift of the craft threw her off balance. Jerry knew as the plane shifted that it was trouble, and as he wrenched his head to the right and saw her go down, his heart seemed to stop.

She's gone! his mind screamed, and a sickening feeling caught him in the throat. He wanted to scream, but then he saw that she had managed to catch the strap that had been fastened as a safety device along the cleat. Her body was dragged out over the trailing edge of the wing. She held to the strap with both hands, and her body suddenly twisted so that Jerry could see the agonized expression on her face.

She can't get back on. Nobody's that strong, he thought. His mind raced, for he knew she could not hang on for more than a few seconds. It was a nightmarish thing, and for one moment he could not even seem to think. Then an idea came to him. Reaching into the pocket beside him, he grabbed a piece of leather chain he had fashioned long ago. Quickly he snapped it in place over the control stick. It fastened in four spots, holding the stick steady. He had often wished there was such a thing as an automatic pilot, but there was not. So he had devised this himself and at times had played with the device, letting the plane fly itself. But he had never left the cockpit, for the device was very rudimentary. The plane would still buck and be tossed by the wind, for the chain could not make the minute adjustments that his delicate fingers could make.

Without thought, he leaped up in the seat and clambered up on the wing. On his hands and knees he scrambled along on the wing, feeling the plane tilt to the right with his added weight. Cara's body also was driven at an angle as the plane went into a bank.

Jerry had shut out all thoughts of personal danger. He reached Cara and grabbed her wrist, just as her fingers were losing their strength. "Grab my wrist!" he shouted over the screaming wind. Her eyes were wide and her mouth was open but she nodded and loosed one hand from the strap and then the other, grasping his wrist. Her weight nearly pulled him off balance and he struggled to keep himself on the wing. His toes were caught in the cleat, as was his left hand. That was all that was keeping them from falling down to the green fields laid out in the nicely squared rectangles he saw below. He had time to see a river winding and twisting down below catching the gleam of the sunlight. It was beautiful, but it was deadly. Her weight rested now solely on his right arm. With all his might, he struggled and managed to lift her up until her face was even with his. "See if you can throw your leg over the wing!" he yelled.

Cara was a strong woman, and despite her excesses, she kept in good physical condition. She raised her left leg and managed to get her heel over the cleat.

"Great!" Jerry shouted. "I'm going to move up. Move with me!"

Slowly and painfully the two moved back up on the flat surface of the wing. The plane was now tilted at a thirty degree bank and was headed on a slight downward path. "Come on!" Jerry screamed. "I've got to turn you loose! Can you make it?"

"I can make it, Jerry!" she shouted. "I've got the cleat now and the straps!"

Jerry's arm was aching but he made his way back, holding tightly to the cleat. When he got back to the center of the wing, he glanced back and saw that she was right behind him. He stepped back onto the fuselage, moving into the back cockpit, and settling down with a sigh. He was relieved to see Cara fall into the front cockpit, and he looked at his hand, which was shaking. "I didn't think anything could do that to me," he said aloud, his voice muted by the wind noises. Removing the chain, he grasped the stick and glanced over at Gavin. The camera plane had kept its same position and now he saw Gavin point down, signaling to make a landing.

Fifteen minutes later, Jerry shut the engine off and slumped in the seat. He had lost the panic that had struck him after he had gotten back in the cockpit, and now he took a deep breath and crawled out. When he hit the ground, his knees were shaky and Gavin, who had landed first, came running over as Jerry helped Cara down.

Cara's face was chalk white, and she clung to Jerry and gave one sob.

Gavin reached out and put his hand on her shoulder, saying quietly, "That was a close one."

Cara looked up at Jerry. Her eyes were as large as he had ever seen them. "I thought I was dead," she whispered. "When I looked up and saw you—I couldn't believe it!"

Jerry held her for a moment and for once in their relationship, he felt in control. Always before, she had been in control of what happened between them. But now, she was soft and frail, and he had proven himself to be strong. "It's all right," he said, "we made it."

As they stood there clinging to each other, Jerry thought, *I wish it could be like this always.*

Tom Maxwell, the camera operator in Gavin's plane, had filmed the whole thing, and it would be incorporated into the film. "There's never been anything like it," he said enthusiastically. "A man leaving a plane to fly itself and saving her! You couldn't do that again on purpose in a thousand years."

Lylah held Jerry when she had heard of the near tragedy and whispered, "I wish I could give you a million-dollar bonus. You're some man, Jerry Stuart!"

For two days Jerry basked in the glow of Cara's new attitude. She could not do enough for him and seemed to have lost all thoughts of Brent Peters. It was a wonderful time for him, but he was fearful that it couldn't last.

He took Adam to a movie on Wednesday. He'd gotten very close to the boy, and Jesse had encouraged him to spend as much time with him as he could.

They went to see Tarzan, the newest sensation on the screen, and afterward, Jerry rigged a rope in the tree in the backyard, and Adam became a younger edition of the jungle man. Later, they went inside and listened to some of the programs that the boy liked. They listened to a program called *The Shadow.* It began with eerie organ music, and then a deep mellifluous voice said in hollow tones, "Who knows what evil lurks in the hearts of men?" There was a pause and then the voice said triumphantly, "The Shadow knows," and ended with a deeply sinister and mysterious laugh.

It was a scary program even for a thirteen-year-old, and Jerry was amused that Adam kept getting closer and closer to him on the couch. He put his arm around the boy's shoulders and said, "Boy, this scares me to death! How 'bout you?"

Adam stared up at him in disbelief. "I didn't know you ever got scared, Jerry."

"What're you talking about! I stay scared most of the time. It's okay to be scared." He thought for a minute and said, "It's okay to worry, too, and maybe even cry sometimes. I do it myself."

Such a thought had never occurred to Adam. Jerry was one of his heroes. Now he looked up at him and relief cracked his young voice. "You really cry?"

"Sure I do. What's wrong with that?"

"I–I didn't think men ever cried."

"If they've got any sense they do," Jerry smiled. "Women don't have any monopoly on crying. It's okay if you and I do it. If we've got something to cry about, we cry, okay?"

Somehow his words had struck a chord in the boy. Adam dropped his head and said, "I thought it was wrong. I sometimes cry when nobody's around."

"You want to tell me about it, Sport?"

"I worry about who I am."

"I can tell you that. You're Adam Stuart. You're Tarzan the Ape Man. You're the Shadow, Lamont Cranston. You're my cousin and I think you're the finest boy in the country." When the boy didn't answer, he asked quickly, "What do you mean, you don't know who you are?"

"I think my father must have been a very bad man and I'm afraid I might be, too!"

"Hey! Don't even think like that!" Jerry insisted quickly. He pulled the boy closer and said, "I know who half of you is—Lylah Hart—and now you've got a dad. There's nobody in this world I think more of than Jesse Hart, and he thinks of you as his son. You gotta think of him as your dad."

"Oh, I do. Jesse's great," Adam nodded quickly, "but sometimes I hear about people saying things like, 'it's in the blood' and 'heredity tells.' I didn't know what that meant, so I asked Bonnie and she told me. It means you do things that your mother and father do, sometimes, anyway."

Jerry felt out of his depth, but he turned to the boy and said, "Look here, Adam, I want you to remember you're who you are. You can't blame your folks when things go wrong. Look at me, I've got the finest folks in the world and I haven't done anything but play around all my life. It's not their fault, though. So whoever your father is, that's got nothing to do with you. You go right on and be the man that Jesse is, or Gavin, or Owen. That Stuart blood's in you. It's gonna come out all right."

Finally the boy seemed tremendously assured. He hugged Jerry and went to bed, and for a long time, Jerry sat thinking of it.

He listened to the radio a while and was disturbed by the report that featured the news on the Lindbergh baby. The body had been found, the newscaster said. He asked the country to pray for the Lindberghs in their hour of need.

Jerry turned the radio off and sat in the darkness for a while. Finally he heard a car pull up and he went to the window. He recognized the fancy convertible that Brent Peters tooled around town in. He saw Bonnie get out. She waited, and then Peters came to walk beside her up the sidewalk. Their steps sounded on the porch, then stopped. There was silence for such a long time that Jerry grew nervous. He was sincerely worried about Bonnie. *She doesn't know what she's getting into, fooling with Brent*, he thought. A stubborn streak touched him then and he went to the door and stepped outside—just in time to see the two step apart from an embrace.

"I think you'd better go home, Brent. It's time for Bonnie to come in."

Bonnie stared at him, her body gone rigid with shock. Reaching out, she took Brent by the arm and said, "Wait a minute. This isn't my father." She turned to Jerry and said, "Mind your own business, Jerry."

The sight of her innocent face outlined in the moonlight made up Jerry's mind. Reaching out, he pulled her away and, with his free hand, he shoved Brent backward. "Get out of here and leave her alone!" he said harshly. "I know you're a big star and all that, but I catch you around this place again, I'll put you in the hospital."

Brent caught his balance, his face turned suddenly cold. "As Bonnie says, you're not her father, Stuart. And don't touch me again!"

Angrily, Jerry released Bonnie and once again shoved the actor backward. Jerry started to speak, but he had no chance, for a blow he never saw caught him in the mouth. It was a disaster running through his whole body. He fell backward on the porch, hearing Bonnie scream, "Brent, don't!" Then, with his mind still fuzzy, he got to his feet and lunged at Peters, throwing a blow, anger rushing through him.

It was not effective, however. Brent Peters was an athlete. One of his skills was boxing. He had actually appeared in one boxing movie and had been a fine amateur boxer in his youth. He stood off coolly while Jerry threw wild blows. Peters threw sharp, crisp punches into Jerry's face, and finally a cruel right hand threw him to the floor.

"That's enough, Brent," Bonnie said. "He doesn't know what he's doing."

Brent looked at her and said, "I'm sorry. This wasn't of my making." He looked down at Jerry, who was trying to get to his feet, still ready to fight. "I won't fight you anymore, Stuart. You're a fool if you think Bonnie would do anything she shouldn't. That shows how stupid you are." He turned to Bonnie and said, "Good night," and left.

By the time Jerry had gotten to his feet the car had roared

off. He shakily wiped the blood from his lips and looked at Bonnie, seeing the anger on her face. He felt like a fool.

Bonnie said, "Thanks very much, Jerry, for the show of confidence! I guess you think I'm just like the women you run around with, women who go with anybody who asks them! . . ." She was shocked, humiliated, angry, and broken-hearted over the scene. She began to cry, saying things she should not and knew she should not.

"It's all right for you to be with Cara any time you want to. You've got such a filthy mind, Jerry, you don't know that there can be such a thing as a different kind of relationship between a man and a woman. I never want to see you again!"

Jerry stood mute, watching as she entered the house and slammed the door. Bingo, the dog, came around the corner. He sat down and watched Jerry for a moment and then came over, pawing at him and saying, "Wuff?" with an inquiring tone in his bark.

Jerry sat down on the porch steps, pulled the huge dog closer, hugged him, and buried his face in the fur.

"Bingo," he said, "be glad you're a dog. If you were a man you might make the same kind of stupid mistakes I make!"

 12 

THE GOSPEL FOR EVERYONE

For two weeks after his disastrous attempt at a fight with Brent Peters, Jerry avoided Bonnie whenever possible. Several times he encountered her at the studio, and so great was his embarrassment over the confrontation that he had ducked his head, grunted a greeting, and disappeared as quickly as possible. He did manage to see Adam once during that time. He had promised to take the boy to a movie and was determined to keep his word. By carefully questioning Lylah in an offhand manner he discovered that Bonnie spent her Thursdays in a downtown library researching for Monarch and for Jesse's new novel. One call to Adam and the boy was ecstatic at the opportunity.

Jerry pulled up in front of the house and Adam ran out to meet him at once. When he got in the car, Jerry said, "Okay, Scout, I'll let you pick it. What movie do you want to see?"

"*Dracula!*"

"*Dracula?*" Jerry was stunned. He had heard of the movie, of course, which concerned a vampire. He had not seen it, but Cara had, and she told him it had given her nightmares. *If it gave Cara nightmares,* he thought as he sat staring at the boy, *what would it do to Adam—or to me, for that matter?*

"Why don't we go see a western? There's a new Tim McCoy over on Thirty-second Street at the Gem."

"No, I want to see *Dracula.* All my friends have seen it and they say it's keen."

"I heard it's pretty scary. Might give us bad dreams. We'd better go see McCoy."

But Adam held him to his word, and Jerry drove downtown to the Grand, which showed first-run movies. It also featured live big bands and popular singing groups.

Jerry parked, and they went inside and once again were awestricken by the theater. The ceiling rose like a cathedral and the aisles were carpeted expensively, not covered with linoleum like the Gem. As they found their seats, they discovered that each row had a tiny aisle light near the floor. "Well, I won't dump popcorn on anybody," Jerry whispered. The two waited for the film to begin and stared up at the domed ceiling with its painted fleecy clouds and golden curlicues. "I couldn't throw a softball that high," Jerry whispered to Adam. In the center was a huge chandelier. Adam wondered callously how many people it would kill if it fell. To the rear was a huge balcony and it was filled for the performance.

Before the program, however, there was an onstage presentation, a band that played the "Dipsy Doodle." Then, one of the band members walked up to the microphone and put on a cowboy hat and sang, "I'm an Old Cowhand from the Rio Grande." Looking at the program, they found out the singer's name was Perry Como.

"I don't think he'll ever make it," Adam said firmly. "He can't sing as good as Gene Autry."

Finally the movie came on and the two sat spellbound. It was a horror of a movie, all right, and Jerry found himself unable to stop feeling afraid. *This is ridiculous,* he thought, *it's only a movie!* But Bela Lugosi had a way of filling the screen and almost coming right down off it. By the time the movie was over Adam was curled up in almost a fetal position, and Jerry was relieved when the lights came on. "Let's get out of here, Adam," he said. "I need some sunlight."

All the way home Adam remained silent, and when they got there they found Lylah waiting, and Bonnie was there, too.

"Well, what did you two see?" Lylah asked cheerfully. Then she saw that Adam was not smiling. "What's wrong, are you sick?"

"No. Didn't like the movie," Jerry said.

"What was it?" Lylah demanded.

"He wanted to see *Dracula*—"

"Jerry! You didn't take him to see that awful thing? I saw it, and it scared the wits out of me!" Lylah went over and put her arm around Adam. "It's all right. It was just a movie. Come along now. I've got some dessert for you." She gave Jerry a disgusted look, saying, "I thought you had a little sense, Jerry, but I don't think so anymore."

Bonnie was suddenly amused with the hangdog look on Jerry's face. She had missed him and now said, "Don't worry about it. He'll get over it."

Jerry was encouraged by her words. "I didn't want to take him, but I'd told him he could have his choice. I always like to keep my word to the boy."

"Did it scare you?" Bonnie asked, a mischievous light in her eyes.

"I was scared spitless," he said and laughed at his own words. "I never get afraid in an airplane, but somehow that creep up there on the screen sucking the blood out of people—" he shuddered—"I don't know why people go see stuff like that."

"Well, I'd kinda like to see it. Would you like to take me?"

Looking up quickly, Jerry recognized this was Bonnie's way of saying she was sorry for their alienation. "Sure," he said, "and there's another one over at the Rialto. That one's about Frankenstein, the guy with the bolt through his head. Looks like my old algebra teacher in high school."

"You're crazy!" she laughed. "I'm not going to see either one of those."

"I didn't think you would. Don't tell Adam about *Frankenstein*, though, or he'd drag me back, and I don't think I could stand another one."

"Did you know that Owen's having a meeting over in downtown Los Angeles?"

"No, nobody told me about it."

She hesitated, then said, "Believe it or not, you'll never guess who's going with me tonight."

"Who?"

"Brent. He's cynical about religion, but he's curious, too. You want to go along with us?"

Jerry flushed. "You don't think he'd whip me again, do you?"

"No, it was just a misunderstanding. Brent's sorry about it, just like I am, Jerry." She was wearing a simple linen dress, white, with blue trim around the neck, and she looked very pretty. "Come with us. You two can make up."

"It has been pretty miserable on the set having to look over his shoulder because I couldn't meet his eyes. All right, I'll go."

It went easier than Jerry thought. As soon as Brent had come to pick up Bonnie, Jerry went up and said, "I made a fool of myself the other night, Brent. Forget it, will you?"

Peters smiled at once and put out his hand, "Sure, it's all forgotten. Did Bonnie tell you I'm going to church with her tonight?"

"Yes, I'd like to go along, if you don't mind, and if I won't be in the way."

"Sure, come on. You've heard your uncle preach before, haven't you?"

"Oh, sure, he's the best there is. I'm not a Christian myself—but if I ever become one, Owen's the brand I'd like to be."

The three got in Brent's convertible and drove to the church in downtown Los Angeles. It was a very large church, seating at least two thousand people, and it was filled to overflowing when they got there. Brent was nervous. He was recognized, of course, and people whispered as they moved in to take their seats. "I can just see the fan magazines," he whispered to the pair with him. "Brent Peters Hits the Sawdust Trail."

Bonnie patted his arm. "Don't worry, you've had worse things than that said about you."

Peters laughed suddenly and said, "You're right, I have."

They found seats, and the song service began almost immediately. Jerry knew all the songs and sang along. Bonnie had a beautifully tuned contralto voice and once Brent said, "If you ever want to go into the movies, you've got the voice for it."

They sang, "Are You Washed in the Blood?" "The Old Rugged Cross," and other familiar favorites. Finally, the worship service was over and Owen got up to preach. He carried a Bible in his left hand and turned the pages expertly with the hook.

He did not acknowledge the fact that his relatives and the famous Brent Peters were in the congregation. "He never does that," Bonnie said. "Sometimes he'll introduce an insignificant missionary that no one's ever heard of, but never the famous people who come."

"I like that," Peters said instantly. He looked at the strong figure of the evangelist and said, "I read he got a Medal of Honor in the Great War."

"Yes, but he never mentions that, either. Matter of fact, he gets embarrassed about it," Jerry whispered back.

Owen preached, and it was a simple sermon. "You must be born again," he said. The third chapter of John was his text. Over and over again he stressed the fact that there was no hope for people in their own efforts. "Forget about your church membership," he said, staring out at the congregation. "I was a church member for years and as lost as Judas. Being in a church doesn't make you a Christian any more than being in a garage makes you an automobile." He quoted Scripture constantly, from the Old Testament and the New. Over and over again, he would call out, "The blood of Jesus is the only hope any of us ever has. 'His blood can make the foulest clean,' as the old song says."

Finally, the sermon was over and Owen pleaded, "Now, that's the gospel. We're all lost, but Jesus was sent by God to make us right. Once we've turned to him, our hearts are one with God again. All that God asks you to do is to turn from your sin—and that's a lot!—every sin. He wants to free you from the bondage of it. Whether it be alcohol, sex, or the lust for money, whatever your chains are that you haven't been able to break, the Son of God is able to snap them. Will you look to Jesus now and ask him, the same way you'd ask your father for help? Get up out of your seats and come down. I want to pray with you."

While the heads of the congregation were bowed, Bonnie stole a glance at the two men beside her. On her left, Brent had his head bowed but appeared unmoved. He was cynical in things of religion and the sermon had been interesting—but she could tell he was not moved. However, when she glanced at Jerry, she saw that his features were set and his mouth was a tight line. The muscles in his jaw moved slightly. She saw that the songbook he held, he clutched so firmly that his knuckles were white and he was not seeing the words on the page at all.

Instantly, Bonnie began praying for him, that God would save him from his sins.

But the invitation ended and she saw that Jerry was still tense. "Let's go up and see Owen," she said.

"You two go," Jerry said. "I'll wait for you out in the car."

Bonnie was disappointed, but she led the actor down to the front where he shook Owen's left hand firmly. "Glad to see you, Mr. Peters," Owen said. "I've enjoyed your action movies very much."

Peters was taken off guard. "I didn't know ministers of the gospel went to movies."

"Well, I stay away from some of them, but yours are exciting and fairly free of some of the things I object to."

Peters laughed. "I enjoyed the message. I'm not a man of God myself but I admire your stand, Reverend."

Jerry said very little on the way home, except, "Drop me off at my room, if you will. Cara and I have some early flying to do."

"Glad you could go with us," Peters said as he stopped the car and Jerry got out. "I'll see you tomorrow. You're doing a great job with the flying, Jerry. Making me look real good." He laughed and said, "I couldn't get up in one of those things if my life depended on it."

"Just my job," Jerry said. "Good night. Good night, Bonnie."

As Peters pulled off, he said, "Jerry was pretty quiet. What's wrong with him?"

"I think he's running from God," Bonnie said. "He has been for a long time."

"Running from God? I didn't know God was after us."

"Oh, yes. God's always after us. He wants us to be his own, not our own."

Peters digested that in silence. He said no more until finally, when he let her out, he said, "You're a unique young woman, Bonnie. I wish I'd known somebody like you when I was younger. It might have saved me a lot of trouble and heartache."

He drove off and Bonnie went inside the house. She talked for a few moments with Lylah and Jesse, saying finally, "The sermon touched Jerry tonight, I could tell. We'll all have to pray for him."

If the sermon affected Jerry, he showed it little in the days that followed. The schedule was tight, and every day for the next week he flew with Cara. Cara noticed his silence and teased him about it. "I hear you went to hear the preacher. Are you gonna hit the glory trail, Jerry?"

Instantly, Jerry said, "Don't make fun, Cara." His tone was sharp as he said, "I've seen enough of the real thing in my folks, in Owen, and in Bonnie to know that it's real. You know it is."

Somehow this offended Cara. "I guess you're telling me I'm just a no-good tramp," she said sharply.

Her own life had been bad almost from the beginning, and she took his attitude as a personal rebuke. It drove her to excesses, so that every night she was out drinking. There was no lack of companionship, for men sought her company constantly. Brent said once to Jerry before they went up, "I'm not seeing Cara anymore, but she's stepping pretty high." Hesitating, he said, "She's drinking a lot, too, and I wish she wouldn't. Can't you talk to her?"

"I'm the last one she'd listen to," Jerry said.

It was at the end of a hard day's flying that Gavin said, "Let's do one more shot. There's plenty of light."

"Can't we do it tomorrow?" Cara said. "I'm pretty tired."

Gavin shook his head. "Bad weather may be here tomorrow. If we can do this one sequence, we will be mostly through with the hard stuff. The rest of it you wouldn't even have to do, Cara."

"All right, let's get it over with then."

It was a trick they had done often with the air circus. Jerry would fly over a racing convertible. Cara would stand in the rear seat, reach up, and grab a special harness suspended from the wheels. She would fasten herself in and then the plane would rise. The difficulty was in getting from the undercarriage up into the cockpit. Gavin had arranged special safety devices by which she could crawl from the wheels up the side of the fuselage. It was relatively safe.

As they were getting ready for the stunt, Jerry walked over to Cara, who was wearing a long blue evening dress and a blonde wig as she doubled for Eileen.

Jerry saw that Cara's hands were trembling and that there were circles under her eyes. "Cara, you're in no shape for this. Let's put it off till tomorrow or the next day."

Cara looked up at him defiantly. "No, we'll do it right now." She squeezed her hands together and for a moment looked troubled. "All the fun's gone out of it, Jerry—between you and me. I'll be leaving as soon as we get through with these shots."

Jerry was not terribly surprised. Cara was not steady and he knew sooner or later she would leave. "Where are you going?" he asked quietly.

"Paul Yonkers wants me to do a transoceanic flight. I'm going to New York to talk about it as soon as we're through."

Jerry bowed his head. He felt a great loss and sadness. "I'll miss you, Cara," he said very quietly.

Cara looked up quickly. She took one look at his face, reached out, and put her hand on his cheek. "I'm no good for you, Jerry," she said. "I'm no good for anybody really, but especially not for you. Put me out of your mind. It's all over." She turned quickly and went over to the convertible and got in without another look. Jerry walked over to the plane, received his instructions from Gavin, and nodded.

They had practiced the stunt many times, and Jerry waited for Gavin's signal. The plane was only a few hundred feet in the air at the north end of the field. Jerry saw Gavin wave and, at the same time, the convertible started down the runway, which had been blocked off. Jerry brought the plane in low and positioned it right in front of the racing automobile. The difficult part was that he could not see the actual stunt. By leaning over, he could see the side of the convertible, but he could not see Cara.

It had to be done expertly and quickly, for the runway determined the length of the timing.

He leaned over to his left and brought the plane over the car. The car was bright red, and he lowered the plane until it seemed he could almost reach out and touch it. On the left side of the car was a flag that was furled. When Cara had firmly grasped the harness on the undercarriage, the driver would punch the switch that threw the flag out. This was Jerry's signal that she had made the shift and it was time to lift the plane.

Jerry's nerves tingled as he held the plane steady over the racing convertible. Abruptly the flag pumped out and at once his hand moved back on the joystick very gently. The plane began to rise. Jerry's touch was deft on the stick. The ground fell slowly away. He made no sudden moves, for he remembered clearly the closeness of death when they had done the wing-walking stunt.

Suddenly, when he was forty feet off the ground, something changed. It was a very minor thing, but his hand on the stick was extremely sensitive. The plane seemed to lift a tiny fragment and there was a change in the behavior. Instantly Jerry's hand froze and he almost stopped breathing, waiting for Cara to appear. It took her only fifteen or twenty seconds, as a rule, to climb from the undercarriage, and he watched in agonizing silence and tension, waiting for the blonde wig to appear.

It did not. He twisted his head around and there, on the runway, lay a crumpled figure, the blue dress jumping out at him. He threw the plane into a screaming turn and saw a car racing down the runway. Gavin was at the wheel.

"Oh, no! She fell!" The words seemed to echo in his head and he brought the plane in for a landing, the worst he had ever made. It bounced, almost flipping over. Finally, he got it stopped and leaped out of the plane without even turning the engine off. By the time he got to Cara he could only guess, "How is she?"

Gavin looked up. He was holding her head. Cara's face was devoid of all color. She was totally limp, and blood streaked down the right side of her face from above her ear, where her scalp seemed to be crushed. Gavin shook his head. "It's bad," he whispered.

The two men stared at one another. They knew the dangers of their profession, but this struck them both harder than anything had.

"She's got to live, she's just got to!" Jerry whispered.

Cara Gilmore lay in a coma in an emergency room. Jerry, Gavin, and Jesse sat in the hall in stiff-backed chairs. Lylah had accompanied them to the hospital but had gone home to be with Adam. When Jerry was permitted in to see Cara, he would sit beside her still body. Doctors and nurses came and went and he was not aware of them. His eyes were fixed on the still face, the head swathed in bandages.

The doctors talked to Jerry, Gavin, and Jesse from time to time but offered no hope. All Jerry could do was gasp, "She's got to live! She's got to!"

"These things are out of our hands; they're in God's hands at this point," Gavin said quietly.

Bonnie came often and sat beside Jerry. He held her hand until it hurt her, unaware of what he was doing. She said nothing, but spent all of her time praying silently.

It was almost dawn when a doctor informed them Cara was conscious, but that there was no hope. Jerry and Bonnie went into the room to see her. Jerry moved over to the bed, saying softly, "Cara! Can you hear me?"

Cara's eyes opened. They were dim and dull but her lips formed the words, "Yes . . . Jerry."

Bonnie came quickly to the other side and took her hand. Jerry was trying to speak but could not. "She can't live very long. She's dying now," Bonnie said. Quickly she began to say, "Cara, you're not going to live. I want to tell you about Jesus. You've heard before but soon you'll be meeting him face-to-face. It's not too late." She witnessed to the girl quietly and Cara listened. Her lips moved from time to time when Bonnie would ask her a question and finally, when Bonnie said, "Cara, it's so simple. Just say, 'God, I've sinned against you. Save me for Jesus' sake.' If you'll do that, you'll be right with God."

Cara's lips moved and she whispered something. Bonnie prayed fervently for the woman, and finally Cara said, "Jesus," plainly and clearly.

Jerry was weeping and could not stop the tears that ran down his cheeks. He held Cara's left hand tightly, unable to speak. He listened as Bonnie spoke of the love of God and Cara's need for Jesus Christ. His mind was stunned. It was as if he had been shot and paralyzed. He could do nothing but stand bent over the dying woman, his tears running down his cheeks.

"Cara, are you trusting in Jesus? Just say that much to us. It would mean so much to Jerry and me."

Cara licked her lips and looked up at Bonnie. She turned her eyes toward Jerry and a smile came to her. "Jerry," she whispered.

"Yes, yes, Cara, I'm here."

"Jerry, I always loved you," she said. Then her head turned and she looked at Bonnie and nodded. "Jesus, I believe," she whispered.

They stood over her, and for the next fifteen minutes, she was in and out of consciousness. When she finally left, it was almost unnoticeable. She had whispered once the name of a woman that neither of them recognized, and then she had smiled slightly. But the last thing she said was, "Jesus." Then her chest fell and she lay in that ultimate eloquent silence that death brings.

Bonnie put the still hand on the quiet breast, then reached over and put her hand over Jerry's hand. "Jerry, I think she called on God. You've got to hold on to that."

But Jerry's face was a mask of pain. He seemed not to hear her words, holding the still hand in his own until finally the doctors and nurses came and stood over him. He rose and left the room, walking blindly. Bonnie followed him. Outside in the hall she took his arm and turned him around. "Jerry, I know it's hard, but you've got to remember, she did go out trusting God, believing in Jesus."

Jerry stared at her. He swallowed hard and his words and his voice were a hoarse whisper. "I've lost her," he said. There was a doubt and a harshness in his eyes as he turned and walked down the hall without looking back. Something in the set of his back and the way he held himself stiffly brought a stab of grief to Bonnie. She shook her head and wondered how he would take this blow. He had failed at so many things, and now this had come. She was not at all sure that Jerry Stuart would be able to weather this storm.

Part Three

Wildcat Rig

 13 

A STRANGE AFTERNOON

Maury Stuart longed for the things of beauty in life. *Anyone looking for beauty in life,* she thought grimly, *would never choose a 1925 Model T Ford as an object!* Maury had decided to take the children for a ride and a picnic. As she approached the Model T, she realized that the break was more for her sake than for Stephen and Mona—she was sick to death of the harsh reality of the shack where she had been trapped.

"Are we really gonna have a picnic, Maury?" Mona asked anxiously, looking up with her strangely colored green eyes. Her blond hair and innocent face made the nine-year-old an enchanting child.

"Sure we are, Mona—if I can get this car started."

Stephen, aged eleven, with the same tow-colored hair as his sister, nodded confidently. "You can do it, Maury. I know how, 'cause I've watched Pa lots of times."

"Well, I hope you're right, Stephen. Get in now." Maury got the kids settled, then put herself behind the wheel, her mouth set in a grim line and her jaw clenched in determination.

Those who would be born in later years and would know the simplicity of modern automobiles could never understand the fear that rushed through Maury, for driving a Model T was not simple. First, the hand brake on the left side had to be pulled all the way back. The hand brake was on and the engine in neutral. To start driving, the left foot pedal was pushed halfway down at the same time the hand brake was released. At that same time, the gas pedal was pressed down and the left pedal was all the way down for low gear. Then, after gaining enough speed, that pedal was released for high gear. To stop, the left pedal was pushed halfway down to neutral and the center pedal was depressed as a foot brake. To back up, it was necessary to push the left pedal halfway down, or the hand brake halfway back, and then press the center pedal all the way down.

All this was running through Maury's head, and finally, with a shudder and a clatter of the worn engine, she pulled out into the road.

The children babbled incessantly, excited over their trip, as Maury steered the vehicle down the crooked road. The land was fenced off with barbed wire and on most of the fences were signs reading, No Trespassing—Property of Kingman Oil Company.

Driving through the clumps of low hills and emerging into the open occasionally, Maury paid scant attention to the anticlinal domes she passed from time to time. Most of them were a hundred feet high, almost perfectly round, and smooth all over. They were baked brown and covered with a stubble of dry weeds. Each one was enclosed with a Kingman fence. On the tops of some she noted tarpaper shacks. Sometimes a wooden oil derrick lifted itself toward the sky. These derricks were decorated with a tangle of blocks and cables and had nothing of beauty to recommend them.

Finally, after forty-five minutes, Maury brought the car to an abrupt halt at a place that was a little more attractive. A creek meandered between slight hills and under a clump of mulberry trees, where Maury and the children quickly piled out and dabbled in the creek. After a while Maury pulled off her shoes and waded along with the children. The sun was hot, and she knew that her face would be tinged with pink if she stayed out too long. She finally took a seat next to the creek, under the trees, and watched the children splashing merrily.

A school of minnows came darting in the clear water, short silver torpedo shapes that seemed to have a single mind for they all turned left and right at exactly the same instant. "I wonder how they do that?" Maury said aloud as she watched them with interest. She took a stone, flipped it into the water, and watched as they all wheeled instantly right and disappeared.

She lay back on the dried grass and closed her eyes, letting the quiet soak into her. She seemed to have been immersed in sound and fury ever since she had come to Oklahoma. The small cabin was busy at all times, and both inside and outside there was the constant noise of hammers banging and winches screaming as the men worked on the derrick. Accustomed to her own quiet room, to long hours of solitude, Maury did not realize how tense she had become. She lay back, letting all the strain flow out of her as she listened to the murmur of the brook and the babbling of the children's voices. Vaguely she tried to consider how long she would stay at Pete's and when she would go back to Chicago. Somehow it seemed to be admitting defeat to go home and leave Pete in the lurch—even though Leslie was getting better, at least enough so she could help tend the children.

Finally the children came and they ate the sandwiches she had brought and drank lemonade she had made in a jug. "Get your playing done. We've got to go back." As she expected, there was protest, but there was no help for it.

When they got back to the car and the children were seated, Maury set the levers on the wheel, then moved to the front where the worst operation of all took place—cranking the car. She was a strong young woman; nevertheless, it took all the strength she had to turn the engine over. There was also the danger, if the engine did catch, of the crank whirling around and breaking her forearm. "I don't need that!" she muttered grimly, struggling with the operation. Soon she was utterly frustrated, for the engine would not catch. With the sweat running down her face and her dress clinging to her body, she finally sat down on the running board, defeated.

"Can't you start it, Maury?" Stephen piped up.

"No."

Mona turned a troubled face toward her. "Will we starve?" she asked, her voice quivering a little.

"No, we won't starve. We'll just have to wait until someone comes along to help us crank this fool thing!"

Time passed slowly and no traffic appeared, for they were off the main road. Finally Maury looked up and saw a roostertail of fine dust that marked the approach of a vehicle. Quickly she stood up and moved to the side of the road. As the car approached she waved frantically. The car slowed to a halt and a man got out and walked over to her. "Why, hello," he said and pulled his hat off.

Maury wished it had been *anyone* other than Ted Kingman. She thought fleetingly of the difficulties that Pete had encountered with the company and how harshly he had spoken to Ted when he'd called on them. Nevertheless, she said stiffly, "I'm having trouble with this car, Mr. Kingman. Could you help me?"

Kingman looked at the dilapidated vehicle and smiled briefly. "I'll see what I can do, although I'm not an expert." He moved over and went through the routine of attempting to start the car, but after three failures, he lifted the hood. Maury and the children watched as he remained bent over, and when he finally straightened up, he was frowning.

"You've got a magneto problem," he said. "I think you'll have to have a new one."

"Oh, dear," Maury said, biting her lip. "I don't know anything about such things. My uncle Pete will have to fix it."

"Well, I could take this one off and we could get a new one in town. I think they've got plenty—or," he said suddenly, "there's a wrecking yard just outside of town. If we could find a good used one, I think that would suffice."

Maury tried to think. It was a long way back to the rig and she also had little money. "I don't have much cash with me," she said. "Are they expensive?"

Kingman shook his head, "No, we'll try the junkyard first.

Sometimes you can get one for a dollar at the wrecking yard. Get in my car." He looked up and grinned, saying, "You kids, go get in that car over there. We'll have a ride."

Five minutes later they were moving down the road, the children in the back and Maury sitting stiffly upright by Kingman. She could not help feeling that he must be better than his father, for at least he was polite—which Horace Kingman never was, according to Pete.

Kingman, for the most part, kept up the conversation until they arrived at the small town, which consisted of no more than a dozen businesses lining a single street, with several houses flung out randomly surrounding them. "Why don't you and the kids go in the store there while I see if I can find the part." He pulled up in front of a white building with peeling paint and led them inside. A tall, thin woman wearing a brown dress greeted him, and he said, "See if you can fill these kids up on soda pop. I need to find a part for the car." He turned and left, adding, "I'll be back as soon as I can, Miss Stuart."

Filling the children up took two soda pops apiece and Maury herself drank a root beer. It was cold and refreshing as it slid down her throat. The woman in the brown dress was curious and asked questions, but Maury fended them off successfully.

Finally Kingman was back, shaking his head. "Nothing in the wrecking yard, but I called to the next town. They're sending one on the bus. It'll be about an hour or two before it gets here."

"Probably two," the store owner nodded. "You're welcome to wait here."

But Kingman shook his head. "I see there's a picture show going on down there. Kind of early in the day, isn't it?"

"Oh, that's Nelson Jeter. He shows the same old cowboy movies every day," she snorted. She shifted the cud of snuff in her lower lip, her eyes suddenly filled with humor. "He likes to see 'em himself. Reckon he must have 'em all memorized. I can tell you what it'll be, in case you want to go—Bob Steele in *Raiders of the Prairie*."

Suddenly Ted Kingman laughed. "Sounds like a good one. How would you kids like to see Bob Steele?" Of course the answer was predetermined. He said, "How about you, Miss Stuart? You think your heart can stand all the excitement of *Raiders of the Prairie*?"

"I–I suppose so," Maury said, "but it's really too much trouble for you, I'm afraid."

He waved her off saying, "I haven't seen Bob Steele in a long time. Come along."

He led them to the theater, which was nothing more than an empty building with an assortment of chairs (few of which matched), a screen, and a projector in the back. Kingman paid the ten cents each admission for all to a gap-toothed man who said, "You'll like this one, folks. It's Bob Steele and *Raiders of the Prairie*. Can't be beat!"

After they had taken their seats and waited for a few moments, the owner and projectionist came and turned the lights out. Soon, across the screen, the title came in glaring black and white.

The sound track was scratchy at times, booming at times—almost unintelligible. Bob Steele, it seemed, had drifted into a ranch where a young woman who wore calico was tending her ailing father. The villain, a scruffy-looking man with a fierce mustache and small beady eyes, was stealing their cattle.

"Bob'll stop that in a hurry," Kingman whispered to Maury. "I saw this when I was just a kid, along with about fifty other movies he made."

Maury was amused at the crudity of the movie. She leaned over and said, "Look! In the scene just before this, he had his hat on and now it's off."

"I don't think they're fussy about details in this sort of movie. What they want to see is Bob beating someone half to death."

This Steele did. He was a small, muscular man with frosty, pale eyes and tightly curled black hair. He was constantly either leaping on a horse from behind, whipping somebody with his fists, or engaged in a chase.

Finally the movie was over, but the kids said, "Let's see it again."

Kingman looked at his watch and said, "No, the parts ought to be in now—unless you'd like to see it, Miss Stuart?"

"No, I think once is enough," Maury quipped.

They left the theater and went back to the store, where Kingman purchased more drinks. Then he left them to go to the parts store. Ten minutes later he was back with the part. "I guess we can go see if we can put things together."

As they rode back, Kingman seemed happy. He talked about Bob Steele, Charles Starrett, Buck Jones, and Tim McCoy, the cowboy heroes of the movies. "I lived for those Saturday afternoons," he said. "I guess I really wanted to be one of them."

"I guess we all want to be something other than what we are."

Her remark caught at Ted Kingman and he turned quickly to stare at her. He was impressed by the steadiness of this woman. Her red hair caught the gleams of the sun and there was something beautiful in the sweep and line of her jaw. "And what is it you want to be and are not?" he asked.

Caught off guard, Maury turned to meet his eyes and she flushed slightly, then smiled. "I don't know. Here I am an old maid and still don't know what I want to be. Pitiful, isn't it?"

"I don't know that it is. I think most people don't know what they want to be. They miss the boat sometimes."

"Well, you know what you want to be—president of Kingman Oil Company someday."

He did not answer her at once, but turned his eyes back to the dusty road. The silence ran on as the car moved down the road. He skillfully avoided the potholes and the worst of the bumps, and finally he said quietly, "I suppose so. That's what the plan is. Sometimes, though, I think I'd like to try something else."

"What could be better than being president of a big oil company?" Maury was shocked at his hesitancy.

He turned to look at her and said, "Maybe I'm like you. I just don't know what I want to be—well, there's the car."

A few minutes later, Kingman had installed the part. He started the engine and then stepped back. Pulling off his hat, he smiled at her, saying, "I enjoyed the afternoon. Maybe we can do it again some time."

"I doubt that. Our ways don't go together, it seems."

Kingman flushed at her reference to the difficulties that her uncle was having. "I'd like to do something about it. I don't agree with my father. He wants to own every foot of oil-rich land in the country. But I think there's room for the small fellows, too."

"I wish you were president of Kingman Oil." Suddenly Maury put out her hand and when he took it, she squeezed it firmly and rewarded him with a smile. "You've been very gracious. The children and I thank you."

When they returned to the house, Stephen and Mona were bubbling over with the adventure. Pete sat listening to them and said nothing for a time. Finally, however, when he got Maury alone, he said, "Sounds like young Kingman did a decent thing, but he's got bad blood in him. Horace Kingman is rotten through and through—and I guess his son will do anything his old man tells him to."

Maury was staring out the window as he spoke. She turned to him and said, "I don't know, Uncle Pete. He seems unhappy somehow. I don't think he's like his father."

"He's not. According to what everybody says, he doesn't have any insides. He's just a flunky."

Maury did not argue, but all that day and for several days thereafter, she thought about the encounter. Over and over again she remembered his remarks, *I guess I'm like you—just don't know what I want to do*. Somehow she felt a strange kinship with this man who was so alien to everything she knew.

Bailey had found that work on the rig with Pete was a pleasure. Under the blazing sun, he would stay close by the side of his new friend. He had little aptitude for mechanical things, but for passing tools, pulling on cables and ropes, and moving large bulky items, he was unbeatable. Pete appreciated the help, as he still had some trouble getting around, even though his leg was healing nicely, and rewarded Bailey with small gifts whenever he could. One day, Pete returned from town to find Bailey sitting in the shadow of the oil derrick, and Pete grinned at him.

"Payday!" he said and held up a small paper sack.

Bailey lifted his large blue eyes to Stuart saying, "Payday? Oh, I don't want no money, Mr. Pete."

"Well, it's not money—just a present for all the work you've done on the rig with me, Bailey. Here!"

Bailey took the package gingerly and peered into it. He blinked and reached inside and removed the item, holding it up. "Why, it's a book, ain't it?"

"Yeah, a new kind of book. First one ever to come out," Pete nodded. "They call them Big Little Books."

"Well, it don't look like no book I ever saw," Bailey said. The book that he held was a compact volume measuring approximately three-by-four inches, but was very thick, containing over four hundred pages. Such books were published on the concept they would just fit small hands, and the price would be right for those with a little pocket change to spare. But the book was dwarfed in Bailey's massive hands. He held it carefully with his left and ran his blunt forefinger across the title. "What does that say, Mr. Pete?" he inquired.

Pete was startled. He had never thought that Bailey could not read, although perhaps he should have. Quickly he said, "Why, it says, *Dick Tracy—Detective.*"

"*Dick Tracy—Detective.*" Bailey moved his finger back and forth across the words, then looked up. "What's a detective, Mr. Pete?"

Pete laughed and said, "Well, I guess you'll find out when we read the book. I bet Violet would be glad to read it to you."

At once Bailey rose to his feet. "I sure do thank you, Mr.

Pete," he said. He stroked the book lovingly, nodded, and smiled his sweet smile, then entered the house.

Inside he found Violet cooking, preparing lunch, and said, "Look what Mr. Pete got me—a book. It says, *Dick Tracy—Detective*. Will you read it to me, Violet?"

Violet looked up, startled, then took the book from him. She opened it and saw that there were many illustrations. "Yes, I will, and there are lots of pictures for you to look at."

"Can we start now?"

"I don't see why not," Violet said. She sat down and the big man pulled his chair as close to hers as he could possibly get. She began the adventures of the hooked-nose detective, reading slowly. Bailey loved to be read to and she was pleased that Pete had thought of such a thing.

Soon she had a complete congregation listening to her, for Stephen and Mona came to press closely against her on the other side from Bailey, and Ray wandered in along with Pete, and they sat on the boxes next to the children. They all listened as she read the adventures of Dick Tracy and finally she looked around and said, "Well, I've got to cook. We'll have another reading this afternoon." She handed the book to Bailey and said, "It's your book, Bailey. You hang on to it."

Later Violet said, "That was a nice thing, Uncle Pete. Bailey appreciates little things like that." She shook her head sadly. "I never will get over being sorry that he had to give up his watch to pay for our way down here. I wish I could get it back."

"Well, you got that truck driver's name. If he ain't hocked it, you could probably get it back—if we ever get any money."

Pete put his hand on Violet's shoulder and grinned at her. "What're you cooking? You can bake better stuff out of nothing than anybody I ever saw. I don't know what we'd of done without you, Violet—you and Maury."

Violet smiled back, "Why, I'm making an eggless, milkless, butterless cake."

"Sounds awful!"

"Well, it probably will be." She showed him the recipe she had found in a magazine and said, "It couldn't turn out any worse than that Depression Pudding I made where I just dumped everything together—graham crackers and sugar and baking powder. Now that was awful!"

"Wasn't too good," Pete said. He stood there talking to the young woman for a while, then mentioned, "Dent's taking Maury to church tonight. You want to go?"

"He didn't ask me."

Her answer was so short that Pete gave her a startled look. "Why, shoot! You know he'd like to have you go along."

"No, I don't want to intrude." Violet rose, cutting the conversation off. Pete watched her for a moment, then rose and walked outside where Dent was banging away, trying to straighten out a piece of bent pipe.

"You going to meet'n tonight?"

"Sure am, taking Miss Maury. She needs to hear some good old Pentecostal-type preaching."

"Why don't you ask Violet?"

"Violet? Why sure. I don't see why not." He looked up suddenly and said, "Why did you say that?"

"Oh, she's sensitive. I think she's a little bit jealous of the attention you show Maury."

Dent laughed. "That's crazy. She's just a child."

"No, she ain't."

Dent looked up suddenly, his dark eyes fastening instantly on Pete Stuart. "Why, I can remember when she was just a kid—in pigtails."

"She ain't no kid. She's seventeen. She's a young woman and she's trying to learn how to grow up. That's pretty hard for anybody, but the problems she's having are worse than some. Be nice to her, will you, Dent?"

Dent was embarrassed, "I never thought anything else. You know she's always been a pet of mine, Pete. I've told you that."

Pete stared at Dent, taking in the tall, lean form, black hair, and the fine eyes. Dent was thirty-one now and a confirmed bachelor, Pete supposed. Most men who survive encounters with prospective brides until that age remain in that condition. But Pete was a man of sharp insights as far as human character was concerned. He had seen Violet's eyes following Dent and knew that she had a special feeling for the tall man. He could not put this into words, however, and finally said only, "Well, be good to her. She's had a hard time." Then he turned and left.

Dent stared after him, then idly hefted the hammer from one hand to the other. He stared at it for a moment, then shook his head. "I'll have to be careful, I guess. She's probably got some kind of *crush* on me; I think they call it that in Hollywood. That wouldn't do her any good," he muttered. He tossed the hammer down and walked inside saying, "Hello, how about some of that whatever-it-is you got cooked?"

"You'll have to wait till supper," Violet said briefly.

There was something in her manner—a hurt attitude—and Dent blurted out, "I'd like you to go to church tonight. Me and Maury are going over. Good preacher, so I hear."

"No, I don't believe I'll go tonight."

Dent stared at her. Violet's oval face was turned down, and he could not see her dark blue eyes. He was very fond of this young woman, and suddenly was forced to notice that she was not a child, but full-figured, with all the charm of a young girl just entering into womanhood. *She's seventeen,* he thought. *My sister, Beulah, was married and had a baby almost by the time she was that age.* Still, for some reason, he felt depressed and said, "Well, we'd be glad to have you, if you want to go." He turned, went outside, and began hammering on the pipe with unnecessary force. "Blast it! Why do little girls have to turn out to be full-grown women?"

The revival was well attended. It was held in a tent by a strong, bull-throated evangelist who preached for over an hour and a half. Ray accompanied Maury and Dent, and they had found themselves seated beside the Dances, Johnny and Winona.

Ray was a little surprised to see them at a revival, although he could not say why. After the meeting, Johnny asked him to stop by their house the next day, saying that he had some books that Ray might like.

The next afternoon, Ray borrowed the pickup and went over to visit the Dances. Johnny welcomed him in and Winona set a glass of milk and some cookies in front of him.

"You sure can make good cookies," Ray said admiringly.

"She didn't make 'em; I did," Johnny said. "I'm a better cook than she is."

For some reason this amused Ray. "I thought Indians made their women do the cooking."

"That was back in the good old days," Johnny grinned at him. He winked slowly so that Winona could not see it.

Winona ignored their teasing. There was an innate dignity about the young woman. She moved over and picked up a box. "Here are some books," she said. "You said you like to read."

"Sure do, and I've read everything on Pete's place." Ray sorted through the books eagerly and said abruptly, "Hey! I've heard about this one. I read one of this fella's poems in a magazine." He picked up a book and thumbed through it eagerly.

"That's poetry, ain't it?" Johnny asked idly. He shook his head and said, "I got some chores to do. You and Winona can read poetry. Not me!"

As soon as he was gone, Winona sat down. She was wearing an old green dress, worn and tight fitting, that she had almost outgrown. Her slim figure and smooth cheeks made her very attractive. Ray said, "Well, I don't guess you like poetry either?"

"I don't understand it."

"Neither do I, a lot of it," Ray confessed. "But this fellow—his name's Robert Frost—some of his stuff is really good."

"Read some of it."

"Well, all right." He thumbed through the book and paused, saying, "Here's one I really like. It's called 'Mending Wall.'"

He read the poem carefully, and when he put the book down, he looked at her and grinned. "How'd you like it?"

"It seems too simple to me to be poetry," Winona said. She leaned forward and rested her chin on the heel of her hand, her dark eyes fixed on him. "What does it mean?"

"Why, I guess it means—I guess it's about a wall and about putting it together again."

"I thought poetry was supposed to be about love and God and things like that—important things."

"No," Ray said slowly. He tried to put his thoughts together. He liked poetry, and although he had not had training in it, he sensed the power of it. "I think good poetry is about people and the things that happen to them. Like this poem," he held the book up, "it starts out talking about a wall and says, 'Something there is that doesn't love a wall.'" He began to go down through the poem, which related how a stone wall was repaired by a New Hampshire farmer. He stopped and said, "Look! Here it says he's fixing the wall, putting the stones back up, you see, and this man comes to help him and he says, 'There where it is, we do not need the wall.'" He hesitated, then said, "And the guy says, 'Good fences make good neighbors.' And here're the lines that I like, and what I think this whole poem's about. He says, 'Before I'd build a wall, I'd ask to know what I was walling in or walling out.'" He looked up at her and said, "That's what the poem's about. Not just stone walls, but any kind of wall."

Interest quickened her eyes. She pursed her lips prettily and ran her finger along her cheek. "What kinds of walls can there be?"

"Why, all kinds. There's walls where I come from between Baptists and Pentecostals. Supposed to be serving the same God, but there's just a wall between them—can't see it, but it's there."

His words brought a sober look into Winona's brown eyes. There was a hurt in them, something he could not fathom, and he leaned forward saying, "What's the matter? Something wrong?"

"I guess I know about walls," she said. "You can't be an Indian and not find that out."

She stood up abruptly and walked over to the window and peered out, her back straight. Ray was a little shocked at her statement. He had known that she was highly sensitive about her heritage. Laying the book down, he walked over and stood beside her, trying to look into her face. When he could not, he reached out and turned her around. "You don't have to worry about that," he said, "any more than any of the rest of us. White people have walls, too."

"It's different."

There was something vulnerable and soft and yielding in her for once. Ray reached out and put his hands on her arms. They were soft and round, yet firm, at the same time. "Why, you're one of the prettiest women I've ever seen! Any man would be proud to have a woman like you." He hesitated, and in the quietness of the moment, was taken with a sudden desire. Yielding to it, he leaned forward and pulled her to him. She was watching him steadfastly, and he kissed her gently. Her lips were soft and he held her for a moment. Then suddenly, she pushed him back.

"You're like all the rest of them—think an Indian woman is cheap and easy."

Ray was shocked and at the same time angry. He stepped back and stuck his hands in his back pockets. "I always did like pretty women," he said. "Sorry, but that's the way I am. You're no different to me, except prettier than most. But maybe you need to read that poem over. 'Something there is that doesn't love a wall,' the guy says. You've got a wall around yourself a thousand feet high, Winona. If you don't break it down, nobody's ever going to know who you are, and you'll be lonesome all your life."

Winona stared at him, his words seeming to strike against her. Then she turned and walked away.

Ray left. When Johnny came in, he asked, "What'd you two fight about?"

"How did you know we fought?"

"I guess I know you pretty well, Sis. You like the guy, don't you?"

Winona hesitated. She was a very private young woman, sensitive to a fault, and with pride, like a steel bar, running through her spirit. She turned to her brother and nodded slowly. "Yes, I like him, but I guess I've been burned too often."

Johnny felt a sudden wave of sympathy for this sister of his. He looked at her and tried to find the words that would bring some comfort to her. Finally he said, "Well, Sis, you go hide in a cave and live small."

"You think I ought to let him kiss me then?" she challenged.

"Can't say about that. He seems to be a nice fellow. Not that there aren't plenty out there who would take advantage of you. But that kind will take advantage of any woman, white or Indian."

They said no more, but Winona could not get away from the memory of the touch of his lips on hers. He had not been rough and demanding as others had been. There was a gentleness and goodness in him, she sensed, and she thought, *If he tries to kiss me again, I'll see.*

 14 

Kingman Strikes Back

"Governor Roosevelt will see you shortly, Mr. Stuart."

Amos Stuart looked up from his seat in the governor's waiting room and smiled. "That'll be fine," he said, then turned his eyes back to the notebook. It was a habit of his to jot down ideas for stories as he waited, and he looked down at what he had written for a story:

> One vivid, gruesome moment of these dark days I will never forget. I saw a crowd of some fifty men fighting over a barrel of garbage that had been set outside the back door of a restaurant. American citizens—fighting for scraps of food like animals!

It was a depressing thought, and Amos tried to turn his thoughts to something more pleasant. He had been on a trip across the United States trying to get a feeling for the country's mood and had found little to encourage him.

Turning over a page, his lips turned upward into a smile. He had encountered several utterly ridiculous activities, not the least of which was the fantastic epidemic of tree-sitting.

Probably inspired by Shipwreck Kelly, who had made a career out of sitting on flagpoles for weeks at a time, thousands of publicity-crazed boys had begun roosting in trees by night and day in hope of capturing a record—but they occasionally suffered misadventures.

> A boy in Fort Worth fell asleep, hit the ground, and broke two ribs; the owner of a tree at Niagara Falls sued to have a boy re-

moved from its branches; whereupon the boy's friends cut a branch from another tree, carried him to a new perch and enabled him to continue his vigil; a boy in Manchester, New Hampshire, was knocked out of a tree by a bolt of lightning and, undaunted, climbed another tree immediately.

"The governor will see you now."

"Thank you."

Rising to his feet, Amos moved quickly into the office where he found the governor of New York, Franklin D. Roosevelt, sitting behind his desk. "Come in, come in, Mr. Stuart!" Roosevelt exclaimed cheerfully. He did not rise, for he had been stricken in the full bloom of health by polio. His rise to the top of the political arena was an indication of his sheer iron will and determination. He was a wealthy man and able to stir crowds, and now his teeth gleamed in the familiar smile seen so often by audiences. "Sit down! Sit down! Tell me what you've been doing."

Going over and shaking the outstretched hand of the governor, Amos said, "I've been out trying to find out who's going to be the next president." The grip that held his was firm and the eyes were lit up with anticipation. "From what I can pick up, I understand that'll be you, Governor."

Roosevelt laughed heartily and waved Amos to a chair. "Well, I like to hear good things like that! But Mr. Hoover is the president for now." Leaning back in his chair he studied his visitor and said candidly, "I'm not a candidate yet, you understand."

Amos considered the broad face of Governor Roosevelt. "I remember interviewing Teddy Roosevelt," he remarked. "He said the same thing—and then was elected without any trouble." Amos liked Roosevelt tremendously—as he had liked and admired his relative, Theodore Roosevelt. "I would like to see it," he said. "Something's got to be done. The country's going down the drain."

Roosevelt's face grew more solemn, very serious and intent. He had that ability, this man, to put his energies and mind on one object, excluding everything else, a tunnel vision that allowed him to look at any one item with an almost terrifying scrutiny. "How do you think the country feels? Tell me what you've found, Amos."

Amos began to speak of what he had seen. He had traveled extensively and had a journalist's fine eye for picking conditions—a single one—making it graphic and real. As he spoke, Roosevelt sat silently in his chair listening intently. Amos had the idea his words were being filed, labeled, and put into some kind of a cabinet and that Roosevelt would be able to draw them forth when needed. Finally, Amos spread his hands and said, "It's getting worse, I'm sorry to say, Governor."

Roosevelt shifted some papers on his desk, stared at them bleakly. "It's been the cruelest year of the depression," he said quietly. "Twelve and a half million people out of work. Jobless men going from office to office, from factory to factory, getting more hopeless all the time. People have lost their savings, borrowed on their life insurance, sold everything they had to sell."

Amos nodded. "Mr. Hoover's done some good things—but I don't think he has a grasp of how bleak the situation is."

"I believe you're right," Roosevelt nodded. "It's going to take more than tinkering with the machinery to bring this country out of this depression. Something drastic has to be done. Something we've never done in America before."

Amos listened as Roosevelt spoke on for several minutes, and as he listened, he became more and more aware that this man, if he became president, would not sit idly by on the sidelines hoping, as Hoover did, with a rather futile optimism, that somehow things would come right. No. He studied the direct eyes of the governor that had almost a fanatical gleam as he spoke of how government must come to the aid of the country. Finally, Roosevelt seemed to remember himself. He smiled again and touched the tips of his fingers together. He shook his head and said, "But it will take a miracle to get me into the presidency. So far it's just in the planning stage." Leaning forward abruptly, he said, "If it does begin to open up, I trust I can depend on your support—just as Teddy did."

The charm of the man warmed Amos. He nodded at once saying, "Of course, Governor. We haven't had a man like Teddy Roosevelt for some time. I'd like to see another Roosevelt at the helm." He hesitated, then said, "I'll be praying for you."

His remark caught Roosevelt slightly off guard. Roosevelt studied the face of the journalist silently for a moment, then nodded. "I would appreciate that very, very much," he said quietly.

Amos asked, "Do you think America will survive this depression, sir?"

Roosevelt gave him a direct stare and thought hard. "Someone asked at Andrew Jackson's funeral, 'Do you think General Jackson will go to heaven?' And do you know what the answer was?"

"No, I don't, Governor."

"The answer was, 'He'll go there if he wants to!'" Roosevelt leaned forward, his face tense. "We'll survive—if we want to bad enough." Then he said, "I'll appreciate your support, Amos. I'd like to see your story when it's finished."

"You'll have it, Governor, and I think you'll like it. It's harsh, but the country has to be awakened."

Leaving the governor's office, Amos went out with the agony of the depression on his mind. He had seen much to discourage him, but he had an unbounded faith in this country and felt that with a man like Roosevelt in charge, something could be done. Going back to his hotel, he packed his bag. He went to the airport, where he waited for an hour, then got on a plane, and headed for the oil fields of Oklahoma. He had thought much about Maury during his travels and a sudden urge to see her, to speak with her, to find out how she was coping with life in the raw, had come to him. Leaning back and looking out at the fields that unfolded below him, he remembered Jerry saying that she'd never put up with an outdoor toilet for long. A smile touched his lips briefly and he leaned back in his seat until the cadence of the motors wafted him off to sleep.

"I admire you for what you've done, Maury," Amos said, giving his daughter a fond look over the unsteady kitchen table. "I didn't think you'd be able to tough it out."

Maury glanced up at him quickly. She was wearing a plain, blue-flowered cotton dress that clung to her, pasted down to her figure by perspiration. The summer heat seemed to collect inside the house, and from outside the sounds of banging machinery and the voices of children playing floated in through the open window. "I wasn't sure of it myself," she said. A smile touched her well-formed lips and she glanced involuntarily at the window. "Especially the outside toilet! Now *that's* been an experience!"

Leaning back in a cane-bottomed chair, Amos admired this daughter of his. "Jerry was wrong," he said. "I told him so at the time. I said that you'd stay just out of pure bullheaded stubbornness, if for no other reason—just because we all said you couldn't do it."

"Well, now I know your opinion of me, Dad." Maury was snapping green beans, her fingers moving efficiently. "I've learned a lot, though. Look what I've learned about cooking. See, here's a list I made—the menu for the week at Stuart's Cafe." She handed him a piece of paper with a list of meals penciled in:

Monday—macaroni with tomato sauce, apples
Tuesday—boiled fish and biscuits
Wednesday—vegetable salad and baked potatoes
Thursday—potatoes with milk
Friday—baked beans
Saturday—thick soup and corn bread
Sunday—beef hash

Amos nodded. "You've done a good job. Pete told me he couldn't have made it without you."

"It's been a help since Violet and Ray came."

"A help? Seems like it's more crowded to me."

"But Violet takes care of Stephen and Mona. She's like a mother hen with two chicks, and now that Ray's feeling better, he's a big help to Pete and Dent on the rig."

They talked for some time, Maury turning the conversation toward what was going on in the country. She was a bright, alert, highly intelligent young woman, and somehow as she sat snapping the beans, watching him, he was aware that even with all the difficulties of life at a wildcat oil rig, she had a peace about her that he had not seen in a long time. Cautiously he asked, "Have you thought of coming home again?"

Maury's eyes lifted to him quickly and she stopped snapping the beans. "Coming home? Why, no, somebody's still got to help take care of Leslie. She's getting some better, but she still has a way to go till she is at full strength. Why do you ask?"

"Oh, I just wanted you to know that if it gets too hard, you can always come home."

"Back to the nest? No, I don't think so, Dad. Not right now, anyhow."

That was the end of the conversation, and the next day Dent put Amos in his Model T to take him back to the airport. "Come on along, Maury," he said. "You'll want to tell your dad good-bye."

Eager for a break from the monotony of the work, Maury glanced over at Violet. "Could you take care of things till I get back, Violet?"

"Of course. Take all the time you need."

The drive to the airport was interesting. Amos had heard of Denton and was curious about him. He saw in him a free spirit and said, as Dent skillfully avoided the chuckholes in the road, "I wish I could live like you, Dent, just sort of doing what you want to. You never hang on to one job long, do you?"

"Just a professional bum," Dent grinned cheerfully. He

winked at Maury and said, "This daughter of yours is trying to reform me, but I guess I'm hopeless."

"You never thought of getting married?"

"Well," Dent shrugged, "I had to *think* of it a couple of times." Mischief came to his eyes as he said with a straight face, "Some of the young ladies brought it up, don't you see?"

Maury laughed abruptly. "I bet they did!" she exclaimed. "You must have spent a lot of your time running away from irate fathers and jealous boyfriends."

"All part of the game, Miss Maury, but I'm past all that now. Just a confirmed old bachelor."

"I don't believe that," Amos said. He put his arm around Maury and said, "Watch out for this fellow. Those that proclaim they're no danger to a woman, why they're the worst kind."

"I watch him all the time," Maury grinned back. "He's a menace. A single, good-looking man on the loose somehow alerts every woman within a hundred miles. But I think it's Violet that's got her eye on him."

"Why, she's just a kid, a mere child," Dent protested.

Maury did not answer but winked at her father. When they got to the airport, Amos shook hands with Dent and said, "Watch out for this daughter of mine. Don't let her get into any mischief." Then he turned and hugged Maury, kissing her, whispering, "I'm proud of you, Daughter. You're a real Stuart."

Dent and Maury stood watching the plane as it trundled out on the field, twin engines coughing and roaring. It lumbered into the air, and Dent said, "I don't see how one of those things ever stays up. I think your brother must be crazy to do what he does in airplanes."

"He loves it. Just like my uncle Gavin."

Dent gave her a curious look and said, "How 'bout we take in a movie before we go home? It'd be a break for us."

"All right," Maury said, "but I get to pick it out."

The movie she selected was *Dr. Jekyll and Mr. Hyde.* It starred Fredric March, and they sat through the feature saying almost nothing.

When they got outside, it was still daylight and they blinked at the bright sunshine. Dent helped Maury into the car and then cranked it up. As they pulled out, he said little for a time, but when they were in the open country, he said, "Why'd you want to see a thing like that? Awfullest mess I ever saw!"

"Oh, I don't know. I thought it was interesting."

Dent thought of the movie for some time. He had been baffled by the story of how a man could turn into a monster. "Well, I think we should have gone to see Shirley Temple! That would have made more sense." He looked at her and admired her windblown red hair, which she had loosened. "What do you see in a thing like that?"

"Oh, I guess it just reminds me of how in good people there's some bad somehow or other."

"I'd rather look at it the other way," he said. "In bad people there's some good."

"I suppose that's true, too. I don't know," she said finally, shaking her head with a helpless gesture. "I just like to think about things like that."

"How come you haven't got married, Maury?" Dent said abruptly.

His question seemed to silence her. She pressed her hair down and finally began putting it up with hairpins that she took out of her purse. "I don't know," she said, then abruptly turned to look at him stating, "I was in love and it didn't work out. I guess that's why."

"He let you down?"

"Yes, he did."

The bleakness of her brief reply caught at Dent. He was perceptive and now wondered about how far he could press into her private life. He admired all the Stuarts and was aware of some of their problems from being close to the family. He had heard talk about Maury's brief romance, but had never pried into it. He said quietly, "You can't run all men off because one of them turned out to be no good," he said.

"I suppose that's true. But you also can't turn love on and off like you can a light, can you?"

He thought that over for a while, then blew the horn at a mustard-colored dog that ambled out in front of the Model T. When he got control of the car, after swerving wildly, he said under his breath, "Stupid dog! He won't last long!" He remained quiet for a while, then said, "I don't know much about love. I know what it means to love the Lord, but it looks like to me a lot of people make a mistake—man and woman thing, that is."

"What do you mean, Dent?"

"I mean, I see a lot of people get married and they're miserable."

"I suppose that's so."

"Well, it shouldn't be like that. I've seen your uncle Owen and his wife. They never get tired of one another. You notice that? Even when they're just sittin' together, he just has to hold her hand or touch her arm."

"I know. I think that's the sweetest thing I've ever seen." She hesitated, then bit her full lower lip. "I'd like to have a marriage like that. But most of them aren't that way."

"What happened to you and the man?"

At the abrupt question, Maury suddenly put her hands together and squeezed them tightly. For a moment Dent thought she wouldn't answer. Then she said, "He wanted too much of me."

"Why, I thought that was what a woman wanted. A man that loved her so much he wanted her—all of her."

"No, it wasn't like that. He wanted *all* of me, Dent. *All* of my private life. I loved him, but I think there's a part of all of us that's very private, no matter how much we're in love. There's that part of us that responds to God, part of us that's our past. Somehow he wanted all of that, and I couldn't give it to him."

"Sounds like a selfish cuss."

"I don't know." The Ford bumped over a rock, shaking their teeth, then she said finally, "I miss not having a family.

I know that's what part of a woman is for, to have a man, to love him, and to be loved, but there's a part of me that will always be a little separate."

Dent had never seen this side of Maury and said no more. When they got to the house and walked inside, Violet was brushing Mona's blond hair. She gave them an odd look with a glint in her eyes. "You took a long time to take Uncle Amos to the airport," she said shortly.

"Well," Dent said, "we stopped and took in a movie. Let me tell you about it." He straddled a chair and pulled it over in front of Violet and Bailey, who was sitting across from her. As he told the story of the movie, he saw that Violet was not meeting his eyes.

Finally he got up and left, and Bailey followed him outside. "Something wrong with Violet?" Dent asked. "She doesn't seem like herself."

"I think she would like to have went with you," Bailey said simply. His uncomplicated mind put things in starkly basic terms. "She likes you, Dent, and when she sees you go off with Maury it hurts her feelings."

Dent stared at the big man, then shook his head. "No way to tell about how a woman feels," he said. "No matter what a man does, he's always putting the wrong foot forward. Just no way to handle a woman."

"Is that right?" Bailey asked with interest.

"No, it ain't *right* but that's the way it is!"

The attack came so suddenly that there was no time for Pete to respond. Pete had been driven into town by Ray, who had wandered off while Pete made his way to the doctor to have his cast removed. Ray met Pete outside the doctor's office when Pete was finished. The two spent an hour in town and loaded the car with a few supplies and started back. On the way, a large car had suddenly appeared and pulled up beside Pete's truck. Ray, who was driving, yelled, "Hey! Look out!" but his cry was futile. The big car had swerved, crashing against the pickup, and Ray struggled to maintain control of the vehicle. He drove off the road and managed to slam on the brakes, avoiding a large gully.

"It's the Kingman goons—watch out for yourself, Ray." Pete looked over at the young man saying, "If we give them an excuse, they'll beat us half to death."

Ollie Bean got out of the car and moved over to say, "Get out of there, Stuart. We've gotta have a talk."

"We've got nothin' to talk about," Pete said. He maneuvered himself out of the car, using his crutches. His leg was out of the cast, but he would still need to use crutches for a while. Pete watched Bean's face carefully. There was a cruelty in the big man, as he well knew. Pete said, "We don't have any business with you."

"We're going on a little trip, you and me." He looked over at Ray and said, "You run along, Sonny Boy."

"We'll both go," Ray said. His face was pale and he looked around to see that the three other men had gotten out of the car and had circled the pickup. He swallowed hard saying, "I'm staying here."

Instantly, Pete said, "You go on, Ray. I'll be all right."

"Sure, he'll be all right. Now get on your way!"

Ray hesitated, then gave the pickup gas. He drove quickly and furiously until he got back to the shack. Slamming the brakes on, he came out of the truck hollering, "Dent!"

When DeForge saw Ray's pale face, he came down at once, leaping off the oil rig. "What's wrong, Ray?"

"It's Pete! Bean and three of his toughs stopped us on the road. They took him off. I would have stayed, but I couldn't do any good there."

Dent said, "Where'd they take him?" His eyes were glinting with anger.

"I didn't stay to see but it'd have to be their camp, wouldn't it?"

"All right!" Dent stood there silently, thinking hard. "I've been afraid something like this might happen."

"What're they gonna do to him?"

"Make him sign his lease over to them, what else?"

Ray hesitated, then said, "We've got to do something! We've got to get him back! They might kill him!"

"I wouldn't put it past 'em." Dent looked up at the sky and said, "We'll have to wait until after dark and then sneak up on 'em. Come on." He walked toward the house and stepped inside. He saw that Maury and Violet were fixing supper. Leslie was sitting in a chair watching, her face pale with the sickness that had drained her. "Miz Stuart, we've got a problem," Dent said carefully. As he explained what had happened, he saw Leslie's face grow tense. Quickly he said, "Don't you worry, Ma'am. We'll get him back." He walked over to the wall and picked up Pete's shotgun and got a handful of shells from the drawer. When he turned, his face was hard and there was a purpose in him that none of them had seen before.

"What're you going to do, Dent?" Violet whispered.

"Do? Why, I'm gonna get Pete back." There was a finality in his words that none of them could miss. He reached into his pocket and pulled out the .38 that he always carried now, checked the loads, then carefully lowered the hammer. "I think it's time Mr. Kingman Oil Company had a visit." He looked around and said, "Bailey, you take care of things here. Ray and I have got a little job to do."

Bailey had been listening carefully. "Are they gonna hurt Mr. Pete?" he asked.

"They might."

"Then I'll come, too."

Dent looked at the big man, then a tight smile creased his lips. "All right. I won't give you a gun, but with fists like those, you don't need one."

It was full dark when he walked out the door, and the two men followed him. Violet came out, too, and took his arm. "Dent! Be careful. Those men are killers."

"Why, Violet, they couldn't kill me but once, could they?"

He smiled at her and reached out and touched her cheek. "Nice to have you worrying about me, but I'll be all right. You take care of things here." He hesitated a minute and thought of the movie he had taken Maury to, and what Bailey had said. "Maybe you and me ought to go play some of that min'ature golf they've got up in Oklahoma City. Looks like fun. That be okay? Be like old times, wouldn't it? Like when we used to fish and go coon hunting together."

"I'd like that, Dent." Violet was disturbed at the thought of what lay ahead and bit her lower lip. "Be careful," she pleaded.

"Why sure, I'll do that. You take care of things here, and we'll have Pete back in no time."

Pete gritted his teeth. A trickle of blood ran down his jaw, but there was a stubbornness in him. "You can beat me to a pulp, Bean," he said, "but it won't do you no good. I'm not signing that paper."

Bean stood over Pete, who was sitting with his legs stretched out. His hair was mussed up and there was a bruise on his left cheek. Bean looked around at the three men who were watching. "You better sign it. You're gonna sooner or later. We got plenty of time."

Pete felt a sense of helplessness sweep over him, but there was nothing he could do. He thought of his family and how their only hope was the oil that lay under that derrick. Gritting his teeth, he shook his head and said, "I won't sign."

Instantly, Bean moved. Lifting his meaty hand, he sent a blow into Pete's face that drove his head backward and brought a fresh stream of blood from between his lips. There was a great pleasure in Bean's eyes as he said, "Hold out as long as you want to. I don't mind the work."

Before he could say more, the door burst open and a voice said, "Hold it right there, you fellas!"

Bean whirled to see a tall man wearing overalls and holding a .38 in his hand. Instantly he said, "You're in trouble, fella. This is private property."

Dent smiled frostily. "Why don't you throw me out then, Bean?"

Bean looked down at the revolver and said, "I'm gonna make you eat that gun." He touched the gun at his own waist and said, "You fellas get ready."

"You're a dead man if you try it," Dent said.

"So are you. One of us will get you." Bean had no lack of physical courage, and he saw four-to-one odds as being all he needed. "Get ready and we'll take him."

Dent lifted his voice, "Ray, break out that glass!"

Instantly there was a tinkling of glass and Ollie and his three henchmen were startled. They turned to see the double barrel of a twelve-gauge shotgun thrust through the window. It was trained right on the three men and Ray said, "I think I can get all three of 'em, Dent, with both barrels."

The faces of the three men changed at once, and one of them turned pale. He could see the twin black tunnels of the shotgun and said, "Hey, Ollie, they got the bulge on us."

"They ain't got nothing," Bean said. "We can take him."

Dent kept his eyes fixed on Bean's huge form, then called out, "Bailey, come in!"

He waited until Bailey stepped inside, then he said, "You see that fella? He's been hurtin' Pete. I think we ought'a give him a few lessons."

Bailey's round face was a study. He looked down at Pete, at the blood running down his cheeks and his bruised face. "Gee, they shud'na done that, Mr. Pete," he said. His eyes lifted to Ollie Bean and he said, "You shud'na done that, Mister."

Bean was puzzled by the big man, but he was tough to the bone. "Get him out of here and your other guy, too. We'll lay for you and get you somewhere." He put his hand on the .44 in the holster at his side and started to pull it.

The click of Dent's .38 struck sharply on the silence. He said evenly, "You ready to die, Bean? You just pull that gun and you'll find out."

Bean was tough, but he wasn't suicidal. "If you didn't have that gun, I'd show you a thing or two," he mumbled.

Dent moved over and picked the .44 out of Bean's holster. He stuck it in his belt, then moved over to the other three, who were also armed. Holding their revolvers, he picked up a pillow, removed the pillowcase, and stuffed the weapons in there. "You ready to go, Pete?" he asked amiably.

"Sure, just hand me those crutches."

Bailey quickly moved over and handed the crutches to Pete and helped him to his feet. Pete smiled crookedly. "Thanks, Bailey. Glad you came."

But Bailey, as Pete hobbled across the floor, was still looking at Ollie. "You shud'na hurt him like that, Mister," he said. "Now, I'm gonna hafta hurt you."

Ollie looked at the gun in Dent's hand and said, "You gonna shoot me?"

"Why, no," Dent said. "I'm gonna let you beat up on Bailey here like you did on Pete." He stuck the revolver in his pocket and crossed his arms and leaned back. "Wait a minute, Pete, let's watch Ollie beat up on Bailey."

With a snarl, Ollie Bean threw himself at the big man. He had all of his old skills and his blow caught Bailey's face. With a terrific right he struck Bailey a blow in the body that would have destroyed a lesser man. It made a thumping sound, but otherwise had no effect.

Ollie Bean had put men out using less force than that, and he stood there amazed. He'd never seen a man take blows like that and apparently remain unmoved, but he had no time to think further, for Bailey suddenly moved forward. He reached out quicker than Bean could have imagined and gathered up Bean's shirt with his left hand. He drew back his right fist; Bean tried to escape, but he could not move. He saw the fist coming, and it was like watching a train approach. It struck him between the eyes. He'd never felt such a powerful blow. It chilled him down to his feet. He began trying to strike back, but Bailey's huge fist caught him square in the center of the mouth. He felt blood flowing, and suddenly there was a gap between his upper teeth. He managed to spit the teeth out, and he looked up as one more mighty blow caught him right between the eyes. He knew no more after that.

Dent looked down at the bloody face of Ollie Bean. Then he looked at the three men who were watching in absolute astonishment. "Tell your boss," he said, "if he ever touches any of us again, we'll be coming to pay him a visit. Tell him that, will you?"

The tallest of the men nodded slowly. "We'll tell him all right."

When they heard the truck start and roar off, the tall man went to stand over Ollie Bean. "Well," he said thoughtfully, "I guess Ollie got more than he could turn loose of that time."

There was a victory celebration when Bailey, Dent, Ray, and Pete returned to the house. The story had to be told over and over, and finally it was Pete who said, "Kingman won't take this sitting down. I don't know what he'll try next, but it'll be something."

The next day they found out what the something was. It was Violet who was up first, and she heard the roaring. As she ran to the window, she saw a circle of vehicles drawing around the shack. She cried out, "Dent! Wake up!"

Dent and Ray had not gone back to their rooming house the previous night. They'd slept on a pallet next to Bailey on the floor. Jumping up, Dent rushed to the door, then his face grew bleak. He checked the loads in his .38 and walked outside. Men were piling out of the cars. As he walked down toward them, he saw that one was no less than Horace Kingman. Beside him stood Ted Kingman, whose face was pale.

"What do you want, Kingman?" Dent asked. "Come to beat up a helpless man again?"

"I've come to tell you I'm not putting up with your nonsense anymore." Horace Kingman had exploded when he had discovered that Bean had been beaten and had lost the prisoner. It had been at Kingman's orders that Ollie had moved, and now Kingman's face was florid. "This is the last chance. Stuart signs or that's it!"

Pete had hobbled out of the house and came to stand beside Dent. The others had filed out, too, looking silently at the ring of armed men.

"What're you gonna do," Pete asked, "shoot us down?"

Kingman shook his head. "No, it's all gonna be legal. You see that line out there?" He pointed to the circle of men. "You can't cross that land."

"It's a public road," Pete said.

"No, it's not. It belongs to Kingman Oil Company. That's me!" There was triumph in his face. "You can stay here, but we'll starve you out. You can't cross that line without breaking the law."

Pete had known that the road itself belonged to Kingman, who had put it in to service his other wells, but this caught him off guard.

"You can't put us under siege."

But Horace Kingman grinned mightily. "I've already done it. Now, sign or starve."

Maury was standing to Pete's left. She lifted her eyes and faced Ted Kingman. He met her gaze for one moment, then could not hold it. Dropping his eyes, he turned and walked quickly away.

Pete turned to face Dent and Ray and the others and said, "We'd better hit oil quick because he means it. He'll starve us to death."

Dent said, "We'll see about that!" He was outraged at Kingman's tactics, and his fighting blood was stirred. "We'll bring the well in. Don't worry, Pete."

Kingman had followed his son and said, "What's the matter with you? You look like a poisoned pup."

"We don't have to do this, Dad."

Kingman stared at his son, and for one moment tried to make him understand. "You don't understand. You came up the easy way. I had to fight for everything I had. If I hadn't, you wouldn't have a dime right now."

"I'd rather not have a dime than to treat people like this!"

The resistance, as always, infuriated Kingman. "You're not going to show the white feather. You're going to stay and fight it out. I'll see to that!"

He turned and walked away, leaving his son looking after him with a strange expression in his brown eyes.

 15 

"You've Got to Give Her Up!"

Amos never had been able to reconcile himself to Hollywood. As he got off the plane in Los Angeles, he seemed to feel the aura of the place closing in on him. He remembered a statement he had once written that was filled with more bitterness than he thought himself capable of. "Hollywood is a dreary, industrial town controlled by hoodlums of enormous wealth, the ethical sense of a pack of jackals, and taste so degraded it befouls everything it touches."

His mood lightened when he looked up and saw his brother Gavin waving to him, a smile on his bronzed face. Moving across the concrete, Amos grabbed Gavin and the two men embraced for a moment, then grinned at each other.

"I didn't think anything would bring you back to Hollywood, as much as you hate it. Where's your suitcase?"

"I wanted to find out about Jerry. There it is, over there, the brown leather one." Amos allowed Gavin to get the suitcase and the two moved to the big white Duesenberg that sat parked in front of the airport. As they settled themselves, Amos was amused by the car. "I didn't know you'd gotten rich, Gavin. When did you start driving a rig like this?"

"Not mine. Doesn't belong to Monarch, either. We rented it for a scene. I borrowed it just to come and pick you up." Slamming the door, he turned the key and the powerful engine broke into a roar. "Hang on," he said. "This thing's got more power than most airplanes."

As they drove along, Gavin and Amos probed each other, finding out about their families, but then Gavin finally gave his brother a quick glance. "I know you're worried about Jerry."

"Yes. He won't write to us. Or, if he does, he doesn't say anything. What's going on?"

"Blames himself for Cara's death," Gavin said briefly.

"Why? It wasn't his fault, was it?"

"No, of course not. She was doing a dangerous stunt. You only have to slip for a moment and you're gone. The fall shouldn't have killed her, but she hit wrong. Of course, Jerry doesn't see it like that."

The Duesenberg moved along between rows of palm trees as the two men spoke. A white sun in the pale blue sky poured out beams of heat, and overhead a few sea gulls circled in their bent-wing flight. Amos watched them, thinking suddenly how awkward they were in the air, then he queried, "How's it affecting him?"

Gavin shifted uncomfortably, his strong hands gripping the wheel firmly. He had known this was coming, and he had not been able to prepare an answer that would give any comfort to Amos. "He spends a lot of time at her grave," he said. "Goes there every day. I know," he said quickly, interpreting Amos's glance of disbelief, "it's not what you'd expect of Jerry."

Amos brushed his hand across his face. "Well, he was in love with her for a long time. Never got any happiness out of it, though."

"No, and he never would have," Gavin agreed. "She was an unfortunate woman, never had any peace herself and led a bad life. I felt sorry for her."

"Does Jerry talk to you about it?"

"No, he won't talk to anyone about it. He was always pretty close to Bonnie—and she says he's silent as the grave."

"Well, there's the studio."

Gavin drove the powerful car through arches that said Monarch Studio. Amos looked with interest at the people who moved around, some carrying scenery, some dressed in costumes of a desert tribe. "Is this picture about Arabs, or something?"

"Oh, no, that's another movie. We're doing two at the same time; one's just a quickie. Really, we're renting the studio to another producer."

Gavin stopped in front of a large white building with red tile on the roof. "Lylah's waiting for you. I expect I'll be seeing you tonight for dinner." He hesitated, then said, "Don't worry about Jerry, he'll pull out of it," but there was a doubtful quality in his voice, and Amos looked at him sharply. "See if you can get Jerry to talk about her. If he'd just open up, Amos, I think that would help."

"We haven't talked much, and I guess that's my fault. He's always been so caught up with flying. He hasn't ever been able to find himself."

Gavin dropped his eyes. "I wish now I'd never taught him to fly. I wish I'd never let him work for me. I feel responsible. He's got all kinds of sense, Jerry has, but somehow I think he's got to get Cara out of his system before he'll ever be the man he can be."

"I'll see you later for dinner."

Amos stepped out of the car and walked toward the big building. He entered the door and passed down the hallway, encountering the receptionist—a tall, white-haired woman, who asked him instantly, "Yes, sir. May I help you?"

"I'm Amos Stuart. I'd like to see my sister. I think she's expecting me."

"Oh, yes, Mr. Stuart. My name is Miss Holcomb. Come along. Mrs. Hart said to bring you right in."

She opened the door and said, "Mrs. Hart, your brother's here."

Amos entered and the door closed behind him. He went across the room at once and met Lylah, who was wearing a cool cotton dress of pale yellow drawn tight about her waist. The dress fell below her knees in the newest fashion. He took her embrace and then drew back to grin at her. "Well, Mrs. Hart, has your husband straightened you out yet?"

Lylah laughed, a rich contralto sound. She'd always laughed heartily, and her voice was slightly husky. "I think he's given up on even trying. Come in, Amos, and sit down. Are you hungry? I'll have something sent in."

"No, not really." He took his seat and looked around the room. "Pretty plush," he said. "Makes me feel a little bit like a poor beggar." The room was ornate with pale green Italian tile that showed on the part of the floor not covered by a rich Persian rug in an intricate design. The walls were cream, and the light fixtures appeared to be solid gold.

Intercepting his glance, Lylah laughed again. "Those are not gold," she said. "Actually this was done for a set, but I liked it, so I just made my office out of it after the shooting was done. What've you been doing, Amos?"

Amos sat back and the two talked; they had always been close. After a while, Lylah had iced tea brought in. As they sipped it, she listened to his report, then shook her head. "Sounds like this depression's not going to get any better."

"I think Roosevelt will be elected. If he is, he's got enough strength to try something, anyway." He described his talk with Roosevelt to her and after he finished, he asked, "How's the picture?"

Lylah's eyes clouded. She ran her hand down her auburn hair and was silent for a moment. She had a short nose, full lips, and a very rich complexion. She was no longer the leading lady of films, but the startling beauty that had been hers in her youth was still there. "We're having our own little depression right here in the studio, Jesse and I," she said ruefully.

"Things pretty bad?"

"The picture's costing more to shoot than we thought. They always do."

"Will you be able to bring it in?"

"Not at the original cost. We're going to have to squeeze somehow and see if we can't stir up some more money. Carl tells me he thinks he can do it." She sighed and shook her head. "I don't know what we'd do without him. I hope I'm as active as he is when I'm seventy."

The two sat quietly and finally she said, "Amos, I'm worried about Adam."

"Is he sick?"

"Oh, no, nothing like that. He's very strong and healthy. Thank God for that!" she exclaimed fervently. A nervousness came upon Lylah. She got up and moved to the window and stared out. Blinding sunshine was shut out by the translucent curtains that hung in folds, but she peered out through the opening, studied the setting for a moment, then turned to him. There was fear in her eyes, something that Amos had rarely seen in her before. "He's worried about his father, and who he is."

Lylah's words came as no surprise to Amos. They had talked about it before and he asked, "Does he ask about him?"

"Oh, yes, he asks everybody. Jesse thinks I ought to tell him. Amos, what do you think?"

The first impulse that came to Amos was to agree, but he held back momentarily. He was a methodical thinker and liked to let every facet of a problem come before him before he made up his mind. Finally he sighed and shook his head. "It's not my decision. I don't have to raise the boy. I don't know him as you do." He studied her carefully, then asked, "Why do you hesitate?"

"We've talked about it before," Lylah said restlessly. "If his father had been a nobody, just a common citizen, even German, I wouldn't have hesitated. But what will it be like knowing your father was Baron Manfred von Richthofen? Some people haven't forgotten the war yet. They lost husbands, fathers, and brothers, and they hate the Germans.

"Do you think of him often—Manfred, I mean?" Amos asked carefully.

Lylah bit her lip nervously and held her hands tightly in front of her as if to keep them still. "Yes," she said, "I do, I can't help it. I don't even know now what it was. Loneliness—I loved him—and I think he loved me, but it was a mad time. If it weren't for Adam, of course, I'd wish it hadn't happened."

"We can't turn the clock back," Amos said quickly. "I wish I could help you. Rose and I have been praying for you, and so are others."

"Thank you, Amos. I'll have to decide soon. Adam's very disturbed about this." She tried to shake the thoughts out of her mind and smiled with an effort. "Come along, we'll go home. I want you to see how much Adam's grown."

Amos thoroughly enjoyed his visit with his sister, but his meeting with Jerry had been unhappy. Jerry had obviously been under a strain and had remained silent most of the time. On the second night of Amos's visit, something occurred that made him wonder. Bonnie had bloomed into a beautiful young woman. She was twenty-seven now and was one of those women who get better looking as they get older. She came in for supper, her straight black hair done in an unusual fashion, and her blue eyes set off by her olive complexion.

"Well, you're all dressed up," Amos said, admiring her gown. "I take it you didn't dress up just for me."

"I'm afraid not, Amos." Bonnie smiled. "I've got a date with a movie star."

At her words, Jerry, who was sitting across the table from Amos, looked up, and there was a strange expression in his eyes. He said nothing, but kept his eyes fixed on Bonnie.

"What movie star is this? I would hope for maybe Tom Mix. I've always wanted to meet that cowboy," Amos smiled.

"No, not Tom Mix, although I've met him, and he's a nice man," Bonnie smiled. She winked at Lylah and said, "Tell this brother of yours who I'm going with."

"She's been going out with Brent Peters," Lylah said, her voice almost flat.

There was something in his sister's tone and in her gaze that bothered Amos. He saw that Jesse was not happy about the situation either. There was a tension around the table, and Bonnie suddenly stiffened her back. "Well," she said, "Brent will be here pretty soon. He's going to take me to the opera tonight. I'll be going now."

"What was that all about?" Amos asked, as Bonnie turned and left the room. He looked across at Adam, who was eating with a healthy appetite, and realized that the others would not speak in front of the boy. "Did you meet Tom Mix, too, Adam?" he asked quickly.

"Sure I did. It was swell."

"Did you meet any other movie stars?" Amos asked the question and sat there as the boy began to rattle off a list of stars he had met. *He doesn't look bothered about anything,* Amos thought, *but you can never tell about kids. They don't always show what's going on inside.* When the boy was finished, Amos said, "Tell you what! Why don't you take me to meet some of these famous people? I never get to meet anybody. Oh, except the president. I met him the other day."

"President Hoover?" Adam asked quickly.

"Yes. He's a nice man."

"He's getting a lot of bad press," Jesse observed. "They're calling the villages where people live in shacks 'Hoovervilles.' Not fair to blame the president for this depression, I don't think."

"No, it would have hit no matter who was president." The talk turned to politics, and afterwards Amos asked Jerry, "You don't like Bonnie going out with Peters, do you?"

"None of my business. She's a grown woman." The answer was curt, and Jerry turned away at once. There was almost a deadness in him that Amos hated to see.

Later he spoke to Lylah, who said, "Jerry's always been such a–a vibrant young man. Now he seems just lost. We've got to do something! If he only knew God, that would help, but he seems to have put a wall around himself. He won't listen to anybody."

"What about Peters? What kind of a man is he?"

"Actually, not bad for a Hollywood movie star."

"That's like saying that someone's not bad, except for being a bank robber. You don't like him?"

"I don't like Bonnie going with him. She's at a dangerous age and in a dangerous frame of mind. I think she could make a big mistake." Her eyes grew troubled and she said, "I feel like she's my own daughter, but who am I to talk to a young woman about making a mistake?" Bitterness tinged her tone and at once Amos went to her and put his arm around her.

"I think you've done pretty well, Sister," he said. "I'm proud of you." Tears came in her eyes as he kissed her cheek, and the two felt as close as they always had.

Bonnie was aware that her dates with Brent Peters were displeasing to her family. Lylah had talked to her, hinting at the fact that Peters was a smooth operator and not one to make a firm commitment to any woman. "I know that!" Bonnie had said shortly. "That's nothing to me. I'm just having fun."

Lylah had longed to say more, but she had seen the stubbornness in Bonnie's eyes. Later she had said, "Jesse, Bonnie's twenty-seven. She's turned down two or three decent young men. Now I'm afraid Brent Peters may be too much for her. But I can't talk to her. She's sweet, but she's got a stubborn streak in her."

Driving home after the opera, Bonnie was laughing at Peters's description of it. He was a witty man and she liked his company very much. Finally she said, "It was fun, Brent, but I don't think I want to go to an opera again very soon."

"You don't like music?"

"Oh, I think you have to start learning opera when you're very young." A smile touched her lips and she laughed softly. "I can't imagine a world where everybody sings when they want someone to pass the butter."

Peters found this amusing, and when he stopped the car in front of the house, she turned to get out, but he touched her arm and said, "Bonnie—"

Bonnie turned to him, noting that he was serious. "What's wrong, Brent?"

For a moment he said nothing. He was a handsome man in the prime of his life. His black hair gleamed and there was a serious look in his dark eyes. "I've been thinking that you and I might be able to make a life together."

Bonnie was stunned. She had never once thought that Brent Peters would consider her in the light of marriage. "Oh, you don't mean that, Brent. I'm not from your world—I never could be."

"My world's not too great." Peters made no attempt to touch her. He turned toward her, however, and his chiseled face was handsome in the moonlight. "I've never known an unselfish woman before, but I think you are one."

"You're wrong about that!"

"I don't think I am. Most of the time women go with me because—well—I'm a movie star. If I were a mechanic, they wouldn't give me a second look. But I think you're different. Do you feel anything at all for me?"

"Why, I like you, Brent."

"That's a pretty weak word—*like.*" He studied her for a moment, then said, "I won't rush you, but think about me as a man you might marry. I know," he said quickly, "I'm a two-time loser. Twice I've said I loved women and married them. But both times we were looking out for number one." Then he did touch her, but it was a gentle touch. Reaching out, he let his hand rest on her cheek and said, "You're very beautiful—but that's not why I feel what I do for you. You've got something inside you that draws me. I'm pretty selfish myself, always wanting my own way. I've got some bad habits—" He smiled, then leaned over and kissed her smooth cheek. "But the right woman could reform me. Think about it!"

Bonnie did think about it—indeed she thought of little else. But she spoke to no one about what had happened. The next day, she asked Jesse where Jerry was and was told, "At the cemetery, I suppose. He goes there every afternoon, you know."

Bonnie stared at him then said, "I need to take the car, Jesse. I'm going to talk to him."

"That might be a good thing. Go ahead, Bonnie. He's pretty lost."

Forty-five minutes later, Bonnie pulled up beside the cemetery, on the edge of the Hollywood community. The green grass was neatly trimmed and the stones were all evenly spaced. She saw Jerry sitting on a bench next to Cara's grave and went at once to him. He looked up and a strange look came into his face as he rose. "Hello, Bonnie," he said quietly. "Nothing wrong, is there?"

Bonnie said sharply, "Sit down, Jerry! Yes, there is something wrong." She waited until they were seated and then said, "I don't know how to say this, Jerry, except to tell you right out. I never was good with words, like Jesse is."

Jerry was staring at her. She was wearing a light green blouse and a brown skirt. The wind blew softly through her hair and he studied her intently. "What's the matter?"

"You've got to give her up!"

"What?"

"You've got to give Cara up. You can't go around carrying her death on your conscience. It wasn't your fault."

"I–I guess it was, in a way. I should have done something."

"There was nothing you could have done. She was very strong willed. You knew that. Everyone knew that . . ." She went on talking for a while but hope ebbed and finally she repeated, "You've got to give her up, Jerry."

Jerry stared at her bleakly. He stood to his feet and she rose with him. "I can't just throw a switch. You can't get rid of people who are in your heart, can you, Bonnie? Could you do that?"

The question made Bonnie pause and she said quickly, "No, Jerry, I couldn't do that." She turned and walked away, and Jerry slumped on the bench, staring blindly at the polished marble stone.

16

UNDER SIEGE

By the time the siege had lasted three days, Maury was beginning to wonder how they would ever hold out. Water was not a problem, since they had a pump that gave plenty of fresh water for drinking and for washing, but Maury and Violet had begun to cut the food rations down. She was cooking a pot of dandelion greens, which Violet had taught her how to do, when Pete hobbled in and sat down heavily, his face wet with sweat. "What's that cooking?" he inquired.

"Dandelion greens." Maury forced a smile and said, "I never thought I'd be reduced to eating weeds, but Violet says they're good."

"I always liked them." Pete looked at the tall woman carefully and asked quietly, "How are you doing, Maury? Not your cup of tea exactly."

"Pete, I don't see how they can do this to us," she said. "Are they that strong, Kingman Oil?"

"Yes, they are."

"But you have a lease."

"That doesn't mean much."

"Can't you do anything?"

"I could get an injunction. But what if I do?" Pete shrugged. "Kingman will file a countersuit. They'll find something to go to law about. The case will go to the courts." He leaned back in his chair and tapped the cane, which he was able to use instead of crutches, on the floor.

She looked carefully at Pete and said, "Surely the law will be some help."

"No, it won't. The courts will delay everything, extensions, motions, change of venue. Then about five years from now they might make some kind of decision."

"How can they do that?"

"How can they do that?" Pete echoed. "Where've you been, Maury? These people own the courts. That's why nobody comes out a winner in a fight against these big oil companies. They've got you, they've got the money, and they can wait and hold out."

Maury looked up and asked quietly, "What are you going to do?"

"Pray that we hit oil. If we do that, their little siege line won't mean nothin'."

"What would happen then?"

"There'd be people in here in thirty minutes waving contracts in my face to buy all the oil that we could pump outta here. It would blow Kingman away, and he can't stand the thought of that."

A week later Pete was talking to Dent late one afternoon and said, "Dent, we're gonna pull a little stunt tonight."

"What's up, Pete?"

"I've been watching their lines. After dark I think we could sneak out. But first, we're gonna rig a little surprise. Sooner or later, they're gonna try to bust in here. I want to put up an alarm system."

"Wish we had my dogs here from back home. That'd be all the alarm system we need. What's on your mind, Pete?"

After darkness fell, Pete led Dent out, carrying a bunch of sticks that he had broken off into three-foot lengths and sharpened. They made their way halfway down the slope and he drove one into the ground. "Now," he whispered, "drive one in about ten feet away down there."

Dent obeyed, and then they tied a string between the sticks about a foot off the ground. "Now," Pete whispered, "take those cans out and tie two of 'em together about four or five feet apart." He had filled a sack with cans from their own private garbage heap out back of the house, and finally Dent saw what Pete had on his mind.

"If somebody clumsy comes up this slope, dragging his hands or feet across that string, he's gonna set them to jangling."

"Give us a little bit of warning," Pete nodded. "Now, come on. I've spotted a thin spot in their defenses."

The guards had grown careless. Some of them had gathered around a fire, so that Pete and Dent crept through without any trouble. When they were outside the line, Pete said, "Now, the trouble is getting a ride to town."

"What're we gonna do when we get to town?"

"I'll show you. We've gotta have something more to fight back with."

It took only thirty minutes to get a ride. A farmer came by and stopped his truck long enough to pick them up. Thirty minutes later they were in town, in the back room of the hardware store. The owner's name was Rooney, and he grinned at Pete, saying, "I thought you'd be coming to make a buy."

"I don't have much money," Pete warned.

"Well, you gotta have something to fight Kingman off with and I'm the only place you've got to get it from. What do you think about these little dandies?"

Rooney picked up a pry bar and ripped the top off a crate, one of many piled around the perimeter of the room. Lifting off the top, he waved proudly, "How about that?"

Pete and Dent moved in and there, inside the box, were hand grenades, all packed carefully in straw, like eggs in a nest.

Dent took a deep breath but said nothing.

"Finest hand grenades you can buy," Rooney said. "Better'n dynamite! If the blast don't get 'em, the steel will."

Pete reached out, picked one up, hefted it in his hand. "Pretty heavy," he commented.

"Yeah, that's the good thing about them. You don't have to throw them, not on that hill where you are."

"What do you mean?" Pete inquired.

"All you have to do is just roll 'em down. Any time Kingman gives you any trouble, roll a few of these down. You'll see how bashful fellows get when they're facing live hand grenades."

"All right," Pete said, "but you'll have to deliver 'em."

"Can't do that. Kingman won't let anybody through. You know that, Pete."

"We can get 'em in," Dent said suddenly. "Might have to make a few trips but they're not watching very careful. I'll bring Bailey, if I have to. He can carry both of these in one trip."

"How much?" Pete demanded.

"Well, let's see—fifty—we'll let 'em go for maybe twenty-five a case. What do you say?"

Pete paid the man off out of a thin roll of bills. He said, "You'll have to drive us back close to the camp."

It actually went very smoothly. Rooney drove them back, and they deposited the two cases of hand grenades under a shrub and made their way back through the lines. Dent came back with Bailey, who carried both cases as lightly as if they were filled with air.

"Don't tell anybody about this, Dent," Pete said, as they stashed the grenades in an equipment shack under a pile of rusted pipe. "Might make the others nervous."

"What are they, Mr. Pete?" Bailey inquired.

"Something to discourage folks from coming to visit us." Dent winked at Pete and nudged Bailey in the ribs. "Come on, we'll have to go to work early in the morning if we're going to hit that oil."

Somehow Pete Stuart's stubbornness had become a cause to Horace Kingman. He had become accustomed to easy victories, but now the little colony perched on the hill and the sound of the drill slowly cutting its way down through the hard rock infuriated him. He had established a headquarters at the site and had restrained himself for three weeks. Now, as the month was coming to an end, he decided it was time to do something. Calling Ollie Bean and Ted into his tent, he stared at them grimly. "All right, we're gonna make it a little bit harder on our friend Stuart."

Bean shifted his feet nervously. When he spoke, the gap in his front teeth made his words a little fuzzy and hard to understand. He kept his lips closed as much as possible. Nothing had ever embarrassed him so much as being mutilated in this fashion by a single blow from a man. "What's on your mind, Horace?" he said.

"We're gonna make life a little more interesting." Horace Kingman pulled his shoulders back and glanced up in the fading light to where the shack sat on the hill. The derrick was outlined against the gray sky. A few stars, dimly seen, surrounded it as twilight fell. "As soon as it gets good and dark, take a bunch of the fellows, and go shoot the place up."

"You mean, really shoot at 'em?" Bean asked. This time he did smile and nod, the gap between his teeth obvious. "Good! I'll let 'em have it."

"Don't kill anybody, Bean," Horace Kingman warned. "Stuart's got to have a little sense. When he sees bullets flying around those women and kids up there, I think he'll cave in. I don't know what they're eating up there anyhow. They must be getting through the lines."

"No, sir! *Nobody* gets through my lines!" Bean said, stung by the words. "Are you sure you don't want to at least draw a bead on some of the men?"

"Not in the dark, you fool. All we'd need is to have a child shot up there. We'd have every do-gooder newspaper writer in the country down on our necks. Naw, keep your shots high. Wouldn't hurt to knock the chimney down, maybe, something like that. Okay! Go after it."

"Dad, I don't think we ought to do this. There's no point in it. They can't hold out much longer."

Ted Kingman had said nothing more to his father about his opposition to starving out the Stuarts, but now, looking at Bean's piggish eyes, he knew this was something that could explode in their faces. He said as much. "Like you say, Dad, if a woman or child gets hit, you know what the papers will say."

"Ain't nobody gonna get hit," Bean said. "My guys know how to shoot. I'll tell 'em to aim high."

Kingman turned to his son, saying, "I want you to go along. Take a gun and be a leader for once in your life."

The younger man tried to meet his father's eyes, but he was unaccustomed to standing in his way. He said nothing, but later that night when Bean and his men moved out, he went along with them. He had a pistol that had been forced on him by his father, but he had taken the shells out of it and thrown them away. Now, with an empty gun, he moved ahead into the darkness.

Up at the shack, the alarm sounded abruptly. Dent and Pete had been sitting on the front porch late that night talking. Almost everybody else was in bed, except for Bailey, who sat with his back against the wall of the house. They had been quiet for some time when suddenly a tinny sound came to them.

"That's the alarm!" Dent said quickly. "Somebody's coming up the hill!"

"I think they're gonna try it! Quick! Get the grenades!"

The two men raced to the shed and Pete said, "I didn't think they'd be fool enough to try it."

A shot rang through the air and a piece flew off the chimney. "Keep down!" Pete shouted. "Bailey, pick up one of those cases of grenades and follow me!"

The full moon had come out, so as the three men made their way around to the side of the house they could see that men were coming. Now the shots began to echo, most of them hitting the roof of the house. "Gimme one of those grenades!" Pete demanded. "Dent, you put yours down in that gully over there. See where they're coming up?"

"Yeah, I see 'em." Dent grabbed a grenade and ran over twenty feet. The grade fell away shortly into a steep incline. He took a deep breath, pulled the pin, and thought to himself, *I hope this thing doesn't go off when I turn it loose.* He then sent it rolling down the hill. He could not see the grenade, of course, although the moonlight outlined the men brightly. He waited for a few seconds and thought, *The thing didn't work!* Then there was an explosion and a red flash illuminated the landscape. Shouts of pain and alarm followed, and Dent laughed as he called out, "Come on! We got plenty more!" Immediately, a grenade went off to his left where Pete had loosed it at another group.

The three men moved around the house, tossing the hand grenades down. Some of the grenades failed to explode, but others went off stunningly. "Keep down! Keep in the house!" Dent yelled when Violet stepped outside the door. "Shut the door and stay inside!"

Down below the house, Ollie Bean stared down at one of the men who was lying on the ground writhing in pain, holding his thigh. "Get me to a doctor," the man was pleading. "I'll bleed to death!"

Bean looked up and rage stirred in him. "Come on! They can't get away with this!" He led a charge up the hill, but it did not last long. He looked around to make sure that Ted Kingman was nearby, reached out, and grabbed his arm. "Come on, you're going with me!" He jerked the younger man roughly up the slope. When they were within thirty yards of the house, he heard a hissing, and in the moonlight, saw a grenade come rolling down the hill. With a gasp, he turned Kingman loose and threw himself to the ground. Kingman turned to watch Bean and was taken off guard when the grenade went off. He felt a searing pain in his right side and was driven backward to the ground. From somewhere up above, rifle fire began raking the ground, and Bean rolled backward as a shot split the air beside him. Dropping his rifle, he ran down the hill, aware of the vulnerability of their position. "Come on, let's get out of here!" he gasped, and the men, willing enough, gave ground. When they had regrouped at the bottom, he said, "Did we lose any?"

"Bateson got hit in the leg," one of them said, "and I about got a finger shot off."

"Where's the boss's kid?" another man asked.

For the first time, Bean thought of young Kingman. "He's back up there—hit—maybe dead for all I know. Come on, we gotta go tell his old man. Now, maybe he'll let us bust 'em good."

On top of the hill, Dent and Pete waited, each holding a grenade. "I think they pulled out," Dent said.

"I believe you're right. Wait a minute! I heard something!" Pete turned quickly and the two men listened. "Somebody's moving down there. Here, take this rifle and go see about it. Be careful, though, Dent."

Dent moved down the hill and found a man lying on the ground. He was moving and seemed to be armed. "Hold it right there!" he said. "Throw your gun down!"

Ted Kingman gasped, "It's not loaded!" Nevertheless, he tossed the revolver down.

Dent picked it up. "Where are you hit?"

"In the side—here."

Dent leaned forward and saw that Kingman's shirt was soaked with blood. Lifting his head, he hollered, "Bailey! Get down here!" He waited until the huge form of Bailey appeared and he said, "He's hit. We gotta carry him inside."

Bailey picked Kingman up and marched back up the hill. When Pete appeared, Dent said, "One of their guys got hit. We better take a look at him. He's losing a lot of blood."

"I can walk," Kingman protested, but Bailey paid him no attention and carried him straight inside.

"Light the lanterns," Pete said. "We've got a wounded man here."

Maury was closest to the lantern. She struck a match with a trembling hand, lit the wick, then resettled the globe. When she turned around she held the lantern high and moved around to where Bailey had put the man on the couch. His right side was covered with blood and his face was pale. Maury gave a gasp and said, "Ted Kingman!"

Her voice came to Kingman. He opened his eyes and looked around the room. "Hello," he said weakly. He looked down and said, "I–I'm afraid I'm bleeding all over your furniture."

Maury could not believe her eyes. Nevertheless, she said, "Take his shirt off. We'll see how badly he's hurt."

Kingman felt his shirt being removed, and the pain ran through him. It was bad enough that he passed out.

Pete looked carefully at the wound and said, "Well, he's not going to die, but he sure got this side chewed up. We gotta clean it out."

"What about a doctor?"

"I don't think we better try going through that line tonight," Dent said. "They're gonna shoot anything that moves." Looking at the wound, he shook his head. "I think he'll be all right."

Maury looked down at the pale face of Ted Kingman. "I'll get some water heated," she said.

 17 

Mr. Kingman Gets a Surprise

Horace Kingman's face was livid. He had shouted at Ollie Bean until he was hoarse—and for once in his life, Bean made no sharp reply. He saw that the owner of the company was ready to do anything, including firing him! The thought of looking for an easy job that paid as well as the one he had disturbed him, and he finally interrupted feebly.

"But Horace, you were the one that told Ted to come with us. It wasn't my idea."

Kingman did not like being reminded that he had made a bad judgment. He stared at his lieutenant and said, "You botched it, you fool! Now they've got a hostage."

"We can take 'em," Bean said quickly. "There's just a handful of 'em. We're ready for 'em now. Let us have another crack at it."

"You idiot, my son's in that shack!" Suddenly wrinkles appeared on his brow and he fell silent, his mouth making a tight line. Bean stared at him with some confusion, not understanding that particular look. He had seen Horace Kingman in most of his moods, but this was a new one for him.

"Something wrong, Horace?" he asked tentatively.

"I–I don't want anything to happen to Ted." The voice was almost a whisper, and Kingman fumbled in his pocket, pulled out a watch, and stared at it. "We'll have to do something. I'll go get the law! They've kidnapped him, actually."

Instantly, Ollie Bean shook his head. "You don't want to get the law in this thing. I mean, after all, we did a little shooting, too. Better let my boys handle it."

"Your boys have done enough damage. Now I'm going to take care of it. Can't trust fools like you to do anything." He turned away with a worried look still on his face.

Bean moved out of the room, anger on his blunt features. "What's the old man gonna do?" one of the men asked him.

"Gonna use the law to try to get the kid back. Funny thing, though, he looks worried. I never thought Horace Kingman worried about anybody, not even that kid of his."

"Well, if he's got a soft spot in his heart, he's kept it pretty well covered up. I think he'll let the kid go."

Ted twisted away from Maury's firm grip. "Ow," he said, "that hurts!" He was bare to the waist, and she was dipping a wad of cotton in alcohol and applying it liberally to the raw flesh where the shards of metal had plowed ridges along his ribs.

Maury was intent on what she was doing. "Be still," she said with some irritation. "I've got to be sure you don't get any infection." She put her hand on his chest, pushed him down flat on the bed, and firmly bathed the injured side with the alcohol. While she was doing that, Kingman was staring up at her at a loss for what to say. She had done this twice, and both times he had been embarrassed. She had stripped off his shirt as if he were a child and thoroughly cleaned his wound. Now as she bent over him he was fascinated by the determination in her eyes. He noticed that there were small gold flecks, or so it seemed, around her pupils and thought, *I've never seen anybody with eyes like that.* She was very attractive. "Can I sit up now?" he pleaded.

Maury looked at him, then smiled. "All right. I've got to put some bandages back on. Sit up." Reaching behind his back, she helped him to a sitting position. He put his feet over on the floor and held his arms up while she taped fresh bandages on the wound. "We're using a sheet for bandages," she said, "but I scalded it, so it ought to be sterile."

Cautiously, Ted lowered his arms and winced as he touched the side. "Never had a hand grenade go off under me before," he said. "Seems like a pretty dumb thing to be in the way of something like that." He looked at her curiously and said, "Did you know Pete was going to roll hand grenades down on us?"

"No, I didn't know anything about it—but I heard the rifle shots and the bullets hitting the house. I don't think you have a complaint about what comes back down the hill when you do a thing like that."

Actually Ted Kingman was more worried about the attack than she knew. He had been opposed to it from the beginning, and now wished bitterly that he had stood up to his father, but he could not say this to her. When he did not answer, she looked at him. He looked embarrassed and she said, "What's the matter?"

"Could I have a shirt to put on?" he said.

Laughter glinted in Maury's eyes and she said, "Well, you're modest, even if you are a bully." She handed him one of Pete's old shirts. He put his arm through the sleeve, protesting, "I'm not a bully."

"What would you call it? Opening fire on a house with women and children in it."

"I—" He couldn't think of any defense and shook his head.

At that moment, Mona and Stephen came in to stare at him. Stephen's eyes were unwavering and his mouth was turned down in a severe frown. "Is he gonna die, Maury?" he demanded.

"Why no, of course he's not going to die."

Stephen looked at the injured man for a moment and said, "You're a bad man! I thought you were like the good guy in that movie, but you're not. You're like the bad one!"

With this judgment, he turned around and walked away. Mona, however, saw the hurt look on Kingman's face. She reached forward tentatively and touched his hand, which was resting on his knee. "I don't think you're a bad man," she said. "You're not, are you?"

Kingman did not know much about children and had had little contact with them, but the girl's trust pleased him. He reached out and put his hand on her blond hair lightly and mumbled, "Well, I'm not very good, I'm afraid, Mona." He added, "Sorry to disappoint you."

"That's all right," Mona said. "I'm not very good either sometimes." She was very matter-of-fact about it and nodded wisely. "You can be better. All you have to do is want to."

Maury was amused at the child's self-assurance. "There, Ted! There's your philosophy for the day. All you have to do is want to and you'll be better."

Kingman, however, showed no amusement. The words had struck home and touched some deep part of his spirit. It was as if the girl had been given some sort of superior wisdom, and he said stiffly, "I guess she's right. Trouble is, I never wanted to. Not enough, that is."

Mona patted his hand. "You'll do better; I hope so, anyway. Do you like to play checkers?"

Her abrupt change of subject did bring a smile to Kingman. "I love to play checkers, but I'm not very good."

"I am," Mona said. "I beat everybody I play, don't I, Maury?"

"You sure do, Honey. Well, you play checkers with Mr. Kingman while I go help fix supper."

Kingman was amused at the attitude of the child. She brought a battered checkerboard and announced, "We have to use some bottle caps. I lost some of the checkers. Do you want red or black?"

"Which do you like?"

"Oh, I like the black."

"Well, that's good, because I always liked the red." He sat there playing, amused at the seriousness of the child's concentration. She was an intelligent and interesting girl and he enjoyed losing to her, which he managed to do four times in a row. "You're just too good for me, Mona," he said, shaking his head in mock amazement. "I just don't understand it. How'd you learn to play so well?"

"My pa taught me. He's the best checker player in the whole world—except for me."

Maury came in then, saying, "Supper's ready. You want me to bring you something?"

"I can get to the table, I think."

Kingman got to his feet, moving very carefully. His side was hurting him badly, and once when he brushed against something, it brought a sharp gasp from him.

"Maybe you'd better lie down. I don't mind bringing you something to eat," Maury said quickly.

"No, that's all right. I don't want to be a bother."

They entered the crowded main room of the cabin. "Our guest is able to sit up and eat," Maury smiled. "I hope you've got something good, Violet, for the heir of the Kingman Oil Company."

Ted's face flushed at her words, and he sat down cautiously in the chair that Bailey pushed under him. "You sit right down there," Bailey said encouragingly. "You're sure gonna get something good to eat. Violet's a good cook."

The meal was very simple, consisting of beans, fresh baked bread, and salt meat. There was only water to drink, except for the children, who had what remained of some tea. Kingman was startled when Pete Stuart bowed his head and began to pray. "Father, we thank you for this food, for every blessing you've given us. We ask you to bless our lives—" and there was a slight hesitation, "—and bless this guest and give him recovery from his wound. We ask it in Jesus' name."

An "Amen" ran around the table, and Kingman picked up a spoon and began to eat the beans. He discovered he was hungry, but he also discovered that no one had seconds. He didn't need to ask why, for he knew they had been holding out for nearly three weeks on whatever food they had on hand when Kingman Oil had thrown a cordon around the house.

Pete looked up at him and said, "I'm glad you're not hurt worse, Kingman," he said. He frowned and shook his head. "I don't like bullets and hand grenades."

"I don't either," Ted said simply.

"Then why'd you throw all that lead up here?" Dent demanded. "All we're asking here is to be let alone."

Maury listened as Dent probed steadily at Ted Kingman. She began to feel sorry for him and finally said, "Be quiet, Dent. Ted's a guest."

"Ted? Oh! I didn't know we were on a first name basis." Dent was amused at Maury and gave her a second look. A thought occurred to him and he smiled and shook his head, but muttered only, "All right, I'll leave off."

They were just finishing the meal when Ray came in. He had been outside standing watch. "Better come out here! Looks like trouble!"

At once Pete got up and walked out the door. He saw a strange car parked down the hill, and Horace Kingman was approaching with a tall man wearing a white suit. "That's a deputy," he said. "I've seen him in town. Look at that. Kingman's got a white flag. He's not taking any chances."

"I guess we better go hear what he's got to say," Dent said. "At least he didn't bring his gunslingers along."

Pete and Dent walked twenty yards away from the house and waited until Kingman and the deputy, whose name was Smith, got close. "I've come to get my boy," Kingman said.

"Get off my land," Pete said. His voice was hard. "The last time you came up here you were shooting everything up." He turned to look at the deputy. "Smith, ain't there a law of some kind about shooting at unarmed people?"

"Unarmed?" Kingman almost yelled. "Why, you threw hand grenades down at my men and nearly killed two of them!"

Smith looked embarrassed. "Mr. Stuart, looks like there's been a misunderstanding here."

Pete swung his arm around the line of men and cars and tents that surrounded them. "Why don't you talk to Kingman about that? He's the one that's got us under a state of siege. He's the one that sent his gunmen to shoot us up."

He began to excoriate Kingman in no uncertain terms, and

finally Kingman saw that it was useless. "I'm going to get a warrant for your arrest. You've got my boy in there and that's kidnapping."

Inside the house, Maury was standing at the door. At these words, she turned around and looked at Ted, whose face was pale. "Well, you've been kidnapped," she said quietly. She fully expected him to get up and walk to the door, but he did no such thing. "Aren't you leaving? Pete wouldn't stop you, or Dent."

Ted Kingman had a peculiar feeling. The sound of his father's angry voice seemed to have some sort of adverse effect upon him. His side was giving him considerable pain, but he could have walked down the hill. He knew all he had to do was go and he would be taken to a hospital, his wounds dressed, and everything would be back as usual.

Back as usual! Somehow the words seemed distasteful to him. Visions flashed before him of how his father had forced him to come on the raid, of how he had argued with him against bringing pressure on the Stuarts, in any case, and had been shouted down. Somehow Ted didn't want to go back to things as usual. He settled down in his chair and shook his head. A trace of humor ran under the surface of his serious manner and he said, "I'm kind of enjoying being kidnapped. Guess I'll stay a while longer."

Maury was surprised. She glanced across the room at Violet, who was watching Kingman closely. The two women were puzzled.

"I don't understand you, Ted."

"I don't understand myself, Miss Maury," he said. Kingman got up painfully, walked to the door and looked out. He saw his father, big, bulky, overbearing as usual, shouting threats at Pete. "I wish he didn't shout at everybody," he said. "He always shouted at my mother. I hated that!"

Maury was startled at this unexpected revelation. "Does he shout at you, too?"

"He's shouted at me since I was two years old. Nothing I do ever pleases him."

There was a bitterness that marred the face of young Ted Kingman. He walked back to the chair, sat down, put his hands on the table and stared at them. The two women looked at him, then exchanged glances. "Well," Maury said, "he's shouting enough now."

But Kingman's shouting did no good. He cursed and threatened and raved, but Pete just stood there, saying finally, "Go get your sheriff—bring your warrant. We'll be waiting for you."

The deputy said, "I guess we might as well go, Mr. Kingman. Nothing to be done here. We better go get that warrant." He looked at Pete. "Better be sure nothing happens to Mr. Kingman's son, Stuart, that would put you in a bad fix."

Pete did not answer, but when the two men walked away, he turned and strolled back into the house. Looking over to Ted Kingman, he said, "Well, I expected you to cross over and go with your old man."

Ted Kingman settled back in his chair. "I like the cooking here," he said. "I intend to be kidnapped a little while longer."

Dent had just stepped inside and heard Kingman's words. He laughed abruptly. "Never heard of a kidnappee you couldn't get rid of. But," he added, "when the grub gets a little thinner, you may change your mind."

Ted Kingman had a stubborn streak. He had always been able to do anything—except stand up against his father. Now he was wondering what the future held. He looked up and his eyes met Maury's, and for a moment the two of them shared a secret thought. "I like the company here," he said quietly. His remark brought a smile to her lips and she dropped her head, a gesture that Pete caught and filed away.

All afternoon they expected Kingman to come back with the sheriff. Dent pulled Violet and Ray off to one side, saying quietly, "We'll have to give Kingman up."

"He really ought to go," Violet said. "I can't understand why he's staying here."

Ray said, "I can. He's tired of his daddy shoving him around."

Dent gave the young man a quick look. "I think you've

got something there." He hesitated, then added, "We can leave. I'll take you two out of here. They'll let us go."

"Go back home?" Violet asked. The temptation came to her, but she shook her head. "No, we can't leave Uncle Pete. It wouldn't be right."

"That's right," Ray added quickly. "I ain't goin'."

"I declare," Dent said mildly, a smile pulling at his lips, "you Ballards are stubborn as Stuarts! Well, I guess we'll all stay, then. One good thing about it, we aren't gonna get fat and ugly on what we've been eating around here. We're about out of grub."

At half past three, they heard the sound of cars coming and looked out to see Kingman's big black Packard pull up and stop. He got out, and Pete said, "I guess that's the sheriff with him. Come on, Kingman, you've got to go, or you'll have me arrested for kidnapping."

Ted Kingman got slowly to his feet. He walked outside and stood silently as his father and the sheriff plodded up the hill. As soon as they were close enough, his father said, "All right, Ted, we'll get you out of this. Sheriff, serve that warrant."

"No need of a warrant," Pete said. "We never kidnapped Mr. Kingman here. He was hurt and we took care of him. He's free to go whenever he wants to."

The sheriff, however, had been primed by Kingman. He was an elected official and his backing came from the oil man. His name was Jennings, and he barked harshly, "Never mind that! I'm arresting you, Stuart!"

Ted stepped forward at once and took a deep breath. It hurt his side and his lips felt dry. He spoke to the sheriff, but his eyes locked with those of his father. "You ever get slapped with a suit for false arrest, Sheriff Jennings? You won't be wearing that star very long when the county has to pay a hundred thousand dollars."

"False arrest? What're you talking about?" Jennings snapped. He cast a startled look at the elder Kingman, then back to the younger man. "You were kidnapped!"

"No, I wasn't kidnapped. I got hurt and these folks were kindly taking care of me."

Horace Kingman turned red. "Stop that foolishness, Ted. You were kidnapped and that's all there is to it! Now come on, let the sheriff serve the warrant."

A quietness fell on everyone. The Stuarts had gathered in front of the house. All were watching carefully, and none more carefully than Maury Stuart. She had learned through talking to Ted the hold his father had on him, and she knew how rare a thing it was for people to be able to stand up when they'd been cowed all their lives. "Come on, Ted. Do it!" she whispered under her breath.

Ted Kingman straightened up. He was wearing a tattered old shirt, handed down from Pete, and he was pale. He did not look like a millionaire's son. Nevertheless, there was something in him at that moment that Pete Stuart suddenly took note of. He said nothing but watched carefully as the drama unfolded. "I'm not coming—Jennings isn't arresting anybody—and that's final," he said emphatically, staring straight into the eyes of his father.

As always, when Horace Kingman was opposed, he flushed and inflated like an angry bullfrog. "You come right now, or you're out of the business! You're out of my family! I don't need a son who's got no guts!"

Again the harsh words fell on the stillness of the air, but this time there was a quick answer. Ted Kingman lifted his head, straightened his shoulders. "I've been out of your family for a long time. I don't need a father who makes war on women and kids. The next time you come with your goons, I'll be shooting back at you."

Sheriff Jennings said, "Come on, Mr. Kingman, there's no need for a law officer here. Nobody's holding your son prisoner." He turned and walked away.

Horace Kingman glared at his son in stark disbelief. "You'll come around," he whispered. "You've never had it rough. When you get hungry, come in and tell me you're sorry and maybe I'll let you come back in. But don't bother coming unless you're ready to tell me you're wrong! . . ."

They all watched as Kingman went down the hill.

"Hallelujah!" Maury Stuart ran to where Ted stood. She stepped in front of him, and before he could move, reached up, pulled his head down, and kissed him firmly on the lips. Her lips were soft against his and she said, "Good! I'm so proud of you I could scream."

Dent grabbed his battered straw hat from his head and threw it up in the air. He jumped over to where Kingman stood and slapped him on the back, which sent pain down the wounded man's side. Dent was grinning broadly. Then the others of the Stuart clan came around him. Mona came and took his hand. He looked down at her and her eyes were big as saucers. She had not understood what was happening, but now she whispered, "See, you can be good if you want to."

Ted Kingman felt a sudden rush of emotion. "I should have done this years ago," he said. He turned to look at Maury. He could feel his lips tingle from her kiss, and he echoed Mona's words, "I guess Mona's right, you can be good if you want to."

Ted felt Maury close to him. He heard again her words, *I'm so proud of you I could scream!* He thought he had never heard anything in his life that pleased him more!

 18 

DENT FINDS A CHANGE

The siege stayed in place and day by day the intrepid little band bound inside the ring ate less and grew leaner. However, the decision of Ted Kingman to stay with the Stuarts had leaked to the newspapers. As a result, the numbers circling the house grew, but not with employees of the Kingman Oil Company.

"Who are all those people?" Maury asked Ted. The two of them were standing outside the house looking at the tents and trailers and wagons that had been added to the circle.

"I expect some of them own land around here," Ted said.

"Why'd they come here?"

"Don't you know?" Kingman was mildly shocked. "You're smarter than that."

Maury turned to him and studied his face. "Tell me," she said.

"Why, these are people that Kingman Oil has fenced off from their land or stopped from fulfilling their leases so the company could take them over."

"But why'd they come here?"

"Because if Pete Stuart can win, it would mean others could win. That's why it's become sort of a test for my father. Look!" he said suddenly. "Who's that?"

Maury looked in the direction of his gesture and narrowed her eyes. "It's Johnny and Winona Dance," she said. "You don't know them?"

"Oh, yes, I remember. They've got some land around here." Again a bitterness came to his lips. "I suppose they hate us, too."

Maury had grown to understand the sensitivity of Ted Kingman. He was nothing at all like his father, and she wondered how the two of them could even be related. "They don't hate you. It's what your company stands for that they don't like."

"It's all the same in their minds," Ted muttered.

He studied the pair who walked up to the porch. As Pete came out and Ray came forward, it was Winona who said, "You know, I just thought of something Johnny and I did last night."

Ray admired the smoothness of Winona's cheeks, the steadiness of her eyes. She felt his gaze and turned deliberately to face him. Still she had not figured out how a white man could be honest in his admiration of an Indian woman. She feared to trust him, and yet there was something honest in the young man's gaze.

"What is it?" Pete asked. "You think of something, Johnny?"

"I believe I did." He looked over at Ted and said, "But I better not say it, not with him here."

Instantly, Ted ducked his head. "I'll leave."

As soon as he was out of sight, Maury said, "You don't have to worry about him."

"He's a Kingman, isn't he?" Winona said defiantly. "He's the one that's stepping on all of us."

Maury shook her head but made no answer. "What is it that you've done?"

Johnny Dance was grinning. He had a naturally solemn countenance, but something had brought a deep amusement to him. "Winona and I were talking last night. Kingman trucks have been crossing our land to get at their Number Seven rig, the one he stole from our uncle."

Dent had come up to join them and hear this. "You mean that rig's right in the middle of your land?"

"That's right. You see what that means, don't you?" Johnny Dance grinned. "I've already started. We've got a bunch of people throwing a siege line around that rig. We got that bunch trapped in there. They can't come out and nobody can go in. Kingman's not the only one that can put a siege around an oil derrick."

Instantly, Pete said, "I've got to get word off to Amos. The newspapers need to hear about this. It's a way to hit at Kingman I never thought of."

"We can get back through the lines," Winona said. "What do you want? To send a telegram?"

"Yes, to Amos, my brother. He's a newspaperman, and he'll know what to do about this."

There was excitement in the house that day. Kingman felt out of it, but then Maury came over to whisper, "Don't feel bad, Ted. They don't really hate you. They just can't understand how you could leave money and everything you've had to come to this place." She hesitated, then said, "I don't understand it myself."

At ten o'clock that night, Violet and Dent were out at the derrick. Dent was holding a rifle in his hands and she had come to watch with him.

"Do you really expect them to come up that hill again, shooting at us?" she asked quietly.

Dent had been walking back and forth. Now he came over to stand beside her. She was leaning against the derrick, and the heavens were ablaze with stars and the moon poured a silver light down on her. "No," he said quietly. "I don't doubt they'd like to do that, but there's too many witnesses now. I think it's gonna be all right."

There was a quietness on the land. Somewhere far off a dog howled in a mournful way and Dent lifted his head listening. "Wonder what's wrong with him? Reminds me of the way Trigger howls when he's on a coon hunt. You remember Trigger?"

"Of course I remember Trigger. He's the best dog you've got, except for Roy."

"He's better than Roy."

"No, he's not."

"Trigger's the best. Don't you remember that time Roy walked right by that trail and Trigger came along and we found that big old coon up in the persimmon tree?" Dent slapped his side and put the rifle down. "I'd forgotten that. How old were you then, ten?"

"Eleven."

"Those were good times, weren't they, Violet? I hope they come back again." He looked out over the flat countryside and shook his head. "I don't like this country. I need to see some hills—something to rest my eyes on."

"So do I, but I've got to stay and help Uncle Pete. You don't have to, though. He's not your kin."

Dent shook his head. "I've thrown in. I'll have to do what I came to do. That's to take you and Ray home when this is all over."

She said nothing, and for a long time they just sat there. Finally, Dent put his hand on her shoulder and turned her around. "What's wrong, Violet? We're not as easy as we used to be."

"Aren't we?"

"No, you know we're not. We used to have fun all the time. Now seems like I'm always hurting your feelings somehow or other. What's wrong?"

For a moment she said nothing. Then she turned her face up to him. The silvery moonlight gleamed in her eyes and her lips looked soft and vulnerable as she whispered, "I–I can't tell you."

"Sure you can." Dent put his hand on her other arm and held her as she looked up. "We could always talk. Don't you remember when you got in trouble at school? You were afraid to tell your pa or your ma, but you always told me. What is it now?"

"I can't tell you." Inside Violet was struggling to keep from showing her true feelings. His hands on her shoulders were strong and warm, and as she looked up at him, she was thinking, *He thinks I'm just a baby, but I love him so much and I don't know how to say it.*

Dent was concerned. He leaned forward, looking into her face more intently. "You're not in trouble of some kind, are you, Violet?"

"Not what you'd call trouble, but oh, Dent, I'm so miserable and unhappy!" She had been under tremendous pressure since she had left her home. All the long weeks on the road, then the difficulties at the oil rig made her suddenly feel alone and helpless in a way she had not felt for a long time. When she had been fourteen, she had realized she was practically a woman, that she could never go to Logan, or really to Anne, as she had when she was a little girl. There had been one day when she had felt the need to go, but somehow she could not force herself. Since that time, except for Ray and Dent, she had had no one really to share life with.

Looking up at him, she whispered, "I wish I could tell you—" she broke off and knew she could not. To her horror, she felt tears start welling in her eyes and she blinked her eyes to bat them away.

Dent saw she was disturbed. "You're not crying?" he whispered. "What is it?" He felt very protective of her and he did then what he had done many times when she was a child. He pulled her forward and put his arms around her and began to stroke her hair. This was always what she liked when she was a girl, when she had cut herself or been disappointed and she had come to him. Now, he held her—but suddenly he was aware that this was no child. The fullness of her womanly figure pressed against him, and when she put her arms around him and held him tightly, he became agitated and whispered huskily, with some embarrassment for the feelings that rushed through him, "Now, it's all right, Violet."

"It's not all right." Her face was against his chest now and he could feel her trembling. Reaching up with one hand, he pulled her head back and saw that the tears were running down her face. During that one still moment he forgot the years that he had known her as a child. This was no child but a woman, desirable, lovely, young. Obeying the oldest instinct in a man, he kissed her. To his shock and amazement, her lips were warm and receptive, and he knew that never again could he refer to her by any term such as "Little Sister." He felt himself drawn toward her as he had never felt drawn toward a woman and he savored the softness of her form and the pressure of her lips on his.

She pulled back suddenly, whispering, "That's what's wrong with me, Dent. You always treat me like a baby and I'm not. I'm a woman!"

Dent cleared his throat and released her abruptly. "I–I reckon you are, Violet. I didn't realize how you'd grown up. Just seemed to happen all at once, like." He was confused. The revelation of what she was had come to him and he said, "I guess I'll have to rethink what we are, but we can't go back to what we used to be."

Violet suddenly smiled. The moon laid its silver waves on her face, and her dark brown hair and dark blue eyes reflected their gleam. She reached out, touched his cheek, and whispered, "I bet no woman ever kissed you like that." She was shocked at her own boldness and her face flushed.

But Dent was amused. "You're a woman, all right. No question about it. Already starting to learn how to torment a man." He caught her when she would have moved away and ran his hand over her hair. "You're a mighty sweet girl, Violet Ballard. You don't know what it means to me to see someone sweet and gentle, innocent like you." He reached out then, kissed her cheek gently and said, "You better go inside."

"Let me stay for a while. I want to be close to you."

"All right, but you sit down right there. You've got to start behaving proper if you're going to be a full-grown woman."

The moonlight continued to bathe the prairie with its silver beams. It gave a strange ethereal beauty even to the ugliness of the land. The darkness hid the scars, and overhead the stars winked brightly as the two sat. Soon Dent reached down and took Violet's hand and held it, without saying a word.

Although Dent and Violet did not know it, Maury and Ted had been seated on the porch. They had been too far away to hear, but Maury said, "One of these days Dent's gonna wake up and find out Violet's not the little girl she used to be."

"Girl? Why, no, she's a lovely young woman." Ted was startled. "What makes him think she's a little girl?"

"Oh, she grew up with him. She's still a little girl to him. He's older than she is. Practically raised her, according to the way he tells it."

Ted strained his eyes and thought about the pair. "Well, she's very beautiful. Do you think anything'll come of it?"

"I don't know." She looked over at Ted and said abruptly, "You think anything'll ever come of me?"

Startled by her words, Ted turned to her. "I've thought about you a lot," he said, "wondered why you haven't married."

She hesitated, then said, "I almost did once, but he was too possessive."

Instantly, Ted nodded. "I know what that's like," he said. "My father always wanted a son. But it wasn't that he wanted me to be what I am, he wanted me for himself."

"That's exactly what the man I thought I loved wanted. But I'm me, Ted. I can't be anyone else. Just like you're you, you can't be what your father wants you to be, not altogether."

Ted was shocked at the feelings that ran through him. He had never found anyone who could put into words what he felt but could not express. "Something's wrong with love," he said slowly, "that eats away at people. It's a cannibalism, and not love at all." He was rather a deep thinker, and now he tried to piece together what had been going on in his mind, especially over the last few days. "If you love people, you don't love them for what they can give you, you love them for what you can give them."

Maury turned to him, her eyes wide. "That's very wise, Ted. How did you learn that?"

"I guess from not seeing anything like real love. My mother died young and my father—well, he's a very proud man, very ambitious. I remember growing up I'd have given anything if he had only taken me on a fishing trip or done something with me. But he never did. He told me over and over how one day I'd be president of Kingman Oil, and about all the power I'd have." He fell silent then and shook his head. "But he never once told me he loved me, not once. I don't think he does."

Maury reached over and put her hand on his. He at once clasped it and turned to face her. "Maybe he does, but he doesn't know how to show it. He's like a lot of people. They think they have to possess everything."

"I don't believe that's really love—it's something else."

Maury was very much aware he was holding her hand and said uncomfortably, "You're holding my hand, Ted."

"You've had your hand held before. Are you afraid I'll be too possessive? Is that why you've never married, never wanted another man?"

His question seemed to trouble her. She turned to him. "You know, I don't think you would be too possessive. I think both of us have learned the hard way that if we ever do fall in love, we'll have to ask what we can give and not what we can get."

Ted released her hand but remained facing her. "I like that," he said. "The other thing about love, I think, is if you love someone it's not an *if* kind of love."

She was puzzled. "What do you mean, an *if* kind of love?"

"I mean, Dad's always said to me, in effect, I'll love you *if* you'll be the kind of son that would be a good president of an oil company. I'll love you *if* you'll make good grades. I'll love you *if* you get your degree. But love's not like that. Love says, I love you no matter what you do. You think that's right, Maury?"

There was a plaintive quality in Ted's voice. Somehow she felt a pity for him. He was a man, she felt, prevented by his father from becoming what he might have been. Now as he said these things, things she had believed for a long time but had not seen, she slowly nodded. "I think so. I think love says

I love you no matter what you do. I love you for yourself and I expect your love to give me freedom to be what I am."

Ted was staring at Maury as if he had never seen her before. His life had changed so drastically that he was bewildered by it. For a long time he had known that he could not be what his father wanted, but he had tried to be and had failed. Now, sitting beside this lovely young woman who was saying the things that lay dormant in him, he suddenly felt a freedom and a joy that he had never felt before. Reaching out, he took her hand again and squeezed it.

"I think you're right," he said simply. Then he smiled and there was a youthful look of joy on his face such as she had not seen before. "Maybe," he said quietly, "we can help each other find our way."

Part Four

Summer of Hope

19

Last Chance

I think it would be fun to be a cowboy, Bonnie."

Looking fondly at Adam, Bonnie shook her head. "I don't think so, Adam," she said. "It looks exciting, I suppose, on the screen or in books—but I think it would be pretty hard work."

Adam glanced across at the mounted men that were preparing to ride down a replica of an old western street. Bonnie had brought him to one of the studios so that he could watch the filming of a western. He had been fascinated, as most boys were, by the old West and had accumulated a sizable collection of revolvers, holsters, Stetson hats, and neckerchiefs. He drove everyone crazy enlisting them to play cowboy. And now at the age of fourteen, the phase seemed to be growing even stronger. He had pestered Bonnie and his mother until they had finally arranged for him to come and watch the making of an inexpensive western. Now, the boy's eyes were alive with excitement. "Look! They're going to have a shoot-out. See, Bonnie, that man with the white hat coming out of the saloon—he's going to win, because he's the good guy."

"I wish things were that simple in real life," Bonnie remarked. She watched as the director, sitting in a canvas chair off to one side, lifted his voice and said, "All right, roll 'em!"

Actors moved at once in obedience to the call. The lean, muscular man in the white hat stepped forward, then turned to face three men who had separated themselves from the other riders. The tall actor kept his eyes fixed on the trio, and, despite the fact that she was well aware that it was playacting, some of the tension communicated itself to Bonnie. She watched and listened as sharp words were spoken, then the leader of the three yanked a gun from his holster. The actor in the white hat also pulled his gun, and the air was filled with the sharp echoes of revolver fire.

"Look, he got them, all three!" Adam said, carried away by the action. Unconsciously he had reached over and taken Bonnie's arm, and his grip was very strong. Adam had a wide forehead, a squarish face, and his mouth was now pulled tight with suspense. It was a large mouth, and his ears were also slightly larger than usual. All in all, for a fourteen-year-old boy he had a look that bespoke strength—and an unusual determination. Not over average height, he was beginning to fill out with a promise of muscular strength.

As Bonnie glanced down at him, she thought, *He doesn't look like a Stuart. They're all tall and rather lean. I wonder if he's noticed that?* Thoughts ran through her mind, and her brow furrowed as she had a sudden fear that Adam's dissatisfaction with himself was a problem that was not going to go away. To rid herself of the thought, she smiled, saying, "I don't know why you like to watch these western movies. They're all just alike."

"Well, so are the ones you watch," Adam argued. He had a logical streak in him, this young man, and in turn a humorous side as well. Turning his light blue eyes toward her, he brushed his brown hair back with one hand, then shrugged. "I don't know—they're just exciting." He watched as the three villains in black got up from the dust and asked, "Can we go over and meet the actor in the white hat?"

"I don't know him, Adam—he must be new," Bonnie said. "There are so many of them, I can't keep them straight."

"Please, Bonnie! I want to see his gun."

Bonnie nervously agreed. They were visitors on this set, and she herself did not know the director. Nevertheless, the tall actor had leaned up against the outside of the saloon and was rolling a cigarette. He looked pleasant, and she said, "Well, just for a minute. We can't get in the way."

"Come on—let's go!" Adam led the way, and Bonnie followed close behind. As they approached, the actor glanced up at them and shoved his hat onto the back of his head. A smile twisted his lips. "Hello, Pardner! What are you up to today?"

"My name's Adam Stuart. I–I sure liked the way you did the shooting and all."

Bonnie said quickly, "We don't mean to interrupt—I know you're busy."

"Why, that's all right, Ma'am." There was a twangy element in the actor's voice, and he spoke rather slowly and deliberately. He pulled his hat off, nodded at her, then looked down at the young man. "You'd like to be a cowboy, would you? Well, that's what I wanted to be when I was about your age."

"What's your name? I've seen lots of western movies, but I don't think I've ever seen you," Bonnie observed.

"Nope, I ain't famous." Again, the crooked smile. "My name's John Wayne."

Bonnie had never heard the name, but she said quickly, "Adam here is crazy about cowboys and the West. I tried to tell him that being a real cowboy involved a little more than what we see in the movies."

"I reckon that's right, Miss," Wayne said. "It's a pretty hard life." He drew on the cigarette and studied Adam, saying thoughtfully, "Pardner, I don't think you'd like being a cowboy much. That life's all gone anyway. No more big trail herds to take from Texas to Abilene." There was a thoughtfulness in his pale eyes as he shrugged his lean shoulders. "I'd like to have lived back in those days. It'd be more exciting than what goes on now."

"Can I see your gun?" Adam asked eagerly.

"I don't see why not." The tall actor pulled the gun from his holster and handed it over butt first. "Be sure you don't shoot it."

"It's not loaded, is it?"

"Just with blanks, but you see, those blanks can shoot powder for about ten feet. It'd be bad business if it hit somebody in the eye."

Adam held the gun almost reverently. He leveled it to arm's length, aiming it at a blacksmith's shop down at the curve of the street. Wayne watched him carefully and grinned. Then winking at Bonnie, he drawled, "This young fella's got a real steady hand. I reckon he's going to make a pretty good man."

Adam handed the gun back and said, "Thank you, Mr. Wayne."

"Anytime, Adam." A call came from the director and Wayne pulled himself out of the leaning position and settled his hat. Nodding to the two, he strolled to his horse and mounted with a smooth, fluid motion. As he galloped to the end of the street, Adam said wistfully, "He's a nice man, isn't he?"

"Yes, he is." Bonnie turned and led the boy away. On the way she saw an assistant script writer that she knew slightly. They stopped and talked for a moment, and Bonnie remarked, "We just met that actor, John Wayne. Is he pretty good?"

The script writer, a short, pudgy man with a pale face and large, thick glasses, stared at her. "Wayne? Nah, can't act a lick. He'll never amount to a thing in the movie business."

"He seems so nice."

"Oh, yeah, he's a fine guy and can ride a horse better than anybody in the business—but he can't act."

As they moved away from the set, Adam was silent. Finally, when they were in the car driving home, Bonnie said, "Did you have fun, Adam?"

"Yes—but I wish it wasn't now."

"What does that mean?"

"I mean, I wish it was back in the days when there were cowboys, Indians, and cattle drives—exciting and adventurous stuff like that." He sighed deeply and turned to look at her. "There's nothing like that anymore, is there, Bonnie?"

"Oh, I expect there is. But most of life isn't an adventure like that. It's hard work." She nudged him with her elbow. "Like learning that algebra you enjoy so much." She laughed when he made a face and turned her attention to steering the Oldsmobile down the street.

Not often did Gavin Stuart and his sister Lylah argue. They had been close all of their adult lives, and usually their relationship was calm and peaceful, even affectionate. But in Lylah's office the air was thick with tension, and Gavin's lips were drawn tight with something very close to anger as he faced her across the desk. His tone was clipped and sharp as he said, "I've had it with Jerry, Lylah! He's disappeared and I guess we both know where he is."

Lylah was wearing a pale green dress and her hair was done in the latest fashion. She leaned forward and locked her hands together, her eyes troubled. "I know he's got problems, but we have to stick with him, Gavin."

"He's not an actor," Gavin argued. "If an actor does something wrong and messes up a scene, you can shoot it over again." Shoving his hands in his pockets, he strolled purposefully to the window and stared out at the bright sunshine. His back was stiff and he was obviously trying to gain control of himself. Turning back to face Lylah, he said, "If Jerry does something wrong in the air and kills himself—or somebody else—you can't shoot *that* over again and bring them back to life."

Lylah rose and went over to stand beside him. Putting her hand on his arm, she said, "I know it's been hard on you, Gavin—but I'm afraid this is Jerry's last chance. You know him as well as anyone, and you've done more for him than anybody else."

"I've stopped him from getting killed a few times. I wish to heaven I'd never taught him how to fly!"

"He would have learned from somebody else."

"Well, I guess that's right. He's one of those people just

born to fly and nothing would have stopped him. Still, it wouldn't have been my fault if he had gotten himself killed."

Lylah flinched and shook her head. Squeezing Gavin's arm, she shook him lightly. "Don't say that, Gavin."

"It's true enough. But that's not the problem now." He looked down at Lylah and forced a smile. "Didn't need all this along with all your other problems. I'm sorry to bring it up, but we've got to do something."

Lylah bit her lip and turned to stare out the window. She usually enjoyed the sight of the palm trees, the bright sunshine, and the blue skies, so clear they seemed to be painted. Now, however, they brought no pleasure to her. "When did you see him last?" she asked quietly.

"We shot the last stunt three days ago. He was supposed to be here the next day, but I haven't seen him since. We've got to do something, Lylah. We're getting behind and I know the money's running short."

Gavin's words were more accurate than he knew. Only Lylah knew how desperate the situation was. They had run over budget, and she was spending a great deal of her time trying to raise extra funds. Knowing it would do no good to worry Gavin or the rest of the crew, she had said nothing of this. But the figures seemed to fly before her eyes, and she realized that something had to be done. "We're so close, Gavin!" she whispered. "I'd like to see Jerry finish this. He's got a bad record of walking away from things when it gets rough, and that's what he's done this time."

Standing tensely across from her, Gavin nodded. "It's all about Cara, I suppose—he hasn't gotten over her death. He still blames himself, and I can't convince him of anything different. She knew what she was risking."

"I think it goes deeper than that. He was in love with her—or thought he was—for a long time. She hurt him pretty badly."

"Not as badly as if she'd married him."

"Yes, you see that, do you?" Lylah suddenly looked impressed with her brother's insight. "I don't think I've ever seen such a case of blind, foolish infatuation, and it went on for so long. He's known so many fine young women, but he couldn't get Cara out of his head. It was like a bad movie."

Gavin pulled his hands out of his pockets and ran them through his crisp, brown hair. "We've got to do something! For the rest of the stunts I can hire somebody to do Jerry's flying."

Lylah stared at him unhappily. "I hate to do it, Gavin. It's like we're pulling the rug out from under him—and as I said, it might be his last chance. Amos is worried about him. I talked to him on the phone last night."

"I know, but if Jerry gets killed where will Amos be then? I think we'd better drop him." He saw the unhappiness in Lylah's eyes and went over and put his arm around her and squeezed her. "I know how you feel, Sis—and I feel the same way. We both love Jerry—everybody does. He's his own worst enemy." He stepped back and shook his head. "All right, I'll give him one more chance—if I can find him that is. If I can't we'll just have to shoot without him."

Lylah tried to smile. "Do your best for him, Gavin. We owe it to Amos and to each other. After all, he is a Stuart—one of us. I've done far worse than he ever thought about doing." Once again her eyes were filled with dismal unhappiness, and she shook her head, saying, "It's a turning point for him, I think. We'll have to bear with him."

"All right, I'll see if I can find him. You do the same, but we'll have to shoot that scene in the morning, with or without him."

"I'd like to speak with Miss Bonnie Hart, please."

"This is Bonnie Hart."

"This is Sergeant Evans at the Sixth Precinct. We have a young man down here who claims you're a friend of his."

At once, Bonnie knew exactly whom the sergeant meant. "Is it Jerry Stuart?"

A soft chuckle came over the phone. "I guess this ain't the first time you've got a call like this, is it? Well, your boy's down here under arrest for misconduct and drunkenness in a public place. There's no real damage, but someone has to bail him out."

"How much is the bail?"

"Around fifty dollars, I guess. The judge is lenient on things like this."

"I'll be right down," Bonnie said. She hung up the phone and stood there for one moment thinking rapidly. *Jerry must have been afraid to call Gavin. He knows he would boot him out of the picture and ground him if he found out he had been drunk and was in jail. I guess he's afraid of Lylah, too.*

A quick strain of sorrow touched her as she thought of the waste of Jerry's life, but she threw her shoulders back and picked up her car keys. Adam was at school and Jesse was at the studio with Lylah. *It's a good thing I was here to take the call,* she thought, as she got into her car and started it up. The traffic was heavy, and by the time she got to the police station she was more upset than ever with Jerry. Going inside, she marched up to the sergeant and said, "I'm Bonnie Hart."

"Oh, yes, are you sure you want to take him home with you? He's in pretty bad condition. Might not hurt to leave him in for a day or two."

"I'll take him. Fifty dollars, you say?"

"That's right, Miss Hart."

The sergeant took the money and called out, "Bring Stuart out—if he can walk, that is."

Bonnie held on to her purse tightly and nodded to the sergeant, forcing a smile. "Thank you so much, Sergeant. I appreciate your kindness."

"He's a nice young fellow. Just off on the wrong foot, I guess." He studied her carefully and curiosity got the best of him. "Your man, is he?"

"No," Bonnie said quickly. "He's my man-in-law, more or less."

"Ah, well, there he is, Miss." The sergeant grinned broadly and said, "Well, Stuart, I hope you feel properly ashamed of yourself, forcing this lady to come down and take you home in that condition!"

Jerry looked awful. He evidently had not changed his clothes in some time, and at some point he had spilled food all over the front of his shirt. It was stiff and dried now, and he ducked his head as he stared down at it. When he lifted his eyes, Bonnie saw that they were sunk back in his head and that he was a pasty color. At once, she felt a strange mixture of anger and pity. "Come along," she said quietly. "I'll take you home."

Jerry, without a word, followed her to the car. His hand fumbled at the door, then he collapsed into the seat and pulled the door shut. His hands were trembling and his mouth was as dry as ashes. Worse than the nausea that he could not seem to rid himself of was the feeling of disgust with himself—that Bonnie would have to see him like this. He'd given her name reluctantly. She was the only one he could think of who would make bail for him. "Thanks . . . for getting me out," he mumbled.

Bonnie gave him a quick look, then put her eyes back on the traffic. As she threaded her way down the street, she said, "You look terrible. How do you feel?"

"Worse than I look."

"There's nobody at home. You can go in and get cleaned up without being seen," she said curtly.

There was no other talk as she drove home. She wanted to pour recriminations on his head, but her better judgment told her that this was not the right time for that. He sat silently in the car, his head down, his hands clasped loosely in his lap. *There's something so–so pathetic about him*, Bonnie thought. Jerry was usually so neatly dressed and cheerful, his eyes bright, and he was always excited about something. Now everything had been drained out of him. He looked like a bum who had just stumbled into one of the mission houses that the Salvation Army maintained in Chicago. Bonnie had lived in Chicago and had seen many men like this. It frightened her that the emptiness of his eyes might never change.

They pulled up to the front of the house and when they entered, she said, "There're plenty of towels and soap. Why don't you bathe and shave, and I'll fix you something to eat."

"I don't want anything."

"You need something. When's the last time you ate?"

"I've been drinking my lunch for the past couple of days," he said bluntly. She looked at his eyes and there was a desert of pain in them. He stood there almost helplessly and suddenly Bonnie felt a strong maternal instinct, as foolish as that was.

She said quietly, "Go get cleaned up. I'll fix you something—then we'll talk."

Thirty-five minutes later, they were seated at the kitchen table. Jerry's hands were still unsteady as he handled the fork and tentatively took a bite of the scrambled eggs. He looked better—at least he was wearing decent clothes, a pair of dark blue slacks and a white shirt. But there was still such unhappiness in his face that he did not need to speak of it.

But after a while, Bonnie said, "Jerry, you can't go on like this. You're killing yourself."

He chewed thoughtfully and swallowed and shook his head. "Don't ever try to reason with a drunk, Bonnie."

"You are not a drunk!"

A small trace of humor lifted the corners of Jerry's mouth. "I give a pretty good imitation of one."

"No, that's not right. You're not a drunk," she insisted firmly. "You just try to hide from your problems by drinking."

"Sure, that's what drunks do. People that have backbones face them."

"Jerry, you've got to face up to Cara's death. It wasn't your fault. We've talked about this before."

Jerry put his fork down. He leaned forward suddenly and put his face in his hands. Gritting his teeth, he tried to stop the waves of grief that rolled suddenly to overwhelm him. He had not learned to control this. Time and again, he had purposed to put Cara behind him, but at times, her face would come back and the sound of her voice and the touch of her skin. And then loss like a vast, empty desert would envelope him. "I–I can't help it," he whispered. He hated himself for the tears that came to his eyes as he struggled for control.

Bonnie suddenly rose and went to stand behind him. She put her arms around him, hugging him. He had washed his hair, which smelled sweet and clean, and she held him, whispering, "It's all right, Jerry. It's all right to cry."

The words seemed to open a floodgate. His shoulders shook, and he suddenly could not keep the tears back. Without thought, he stood and turned to her and she put her arms around him and held him like she would a child. He was a full-grown, strong man, but there was something helpless and vulnerable about him at this time. Great sobs racked his body and she held him, murmuring sweet terms, meaningless and comforting. For a long time it seemed, he stood there. Again, he took a deep breath and pulled back.

"I guess by now I should be over this."

She looked up into his eyes and saw that they were clearer. Pulling a handkerchief from her pocket, she wiped his tears away and said, "It's no crime for a man to cry. You need to cry sometimes to wash things away. You've never had a loss before like this," she said. "Jerry, God's going to take care of you."

The words seemed to strike Jerry. He looked at her strangely and then down at the floor. When he lifted his eyes, solemnly he said, "It looks like he's going to have to. I've done a sorry job of it myself."

A hope came to Bonnie and she said, "You'll see. Now, you have a picture to finish."

 20 

No Exit

The summer of 1932 would be remembered by many as one of the most sizzling in memory. In Washington, D.C., as Amos Stuart moved along the jumble of tents he saw women and children almost exhausted from the heat poured down by the merciless, pale sun. A sense of despair gripped him when he saw shrunken cheeks of men who had sought work without success. These were men who had fought for the liberties of their country in the Great War but now had become beggars. The camp that he picked his way through was a shantytown located on the Anacostia Flats, just outside of Washington. The hobo settlements under bridges had been called Hoovervilles, and this was a big-scale Hooverville. It occupied some vacant land, with out-of-use buildings scattered around, on Pennsylvania Avenue just below the Capitol. Amos had been back and forth to Washington since June, watching thousands straggle into the nation's capital. Looking around, he made an estimate in his mind. *There must be fifteen or twenty thousand men here and no telling how many women and children.*

The ragtag group made up what they themselves called the Bonus Expeditionary Force. They had come to Washington to petition Congress for prepayment of a bonus for their wartime service. It was not legally due to be paid until 1945, but men with hungry families become desperate, and the veterans had accumulated, causing great alarm among officials.

Amos had interviewed many of the lean men who inhabited the camp. Hearst had sent him to Washington to get the inside story, and Amos had been sickened by it all. His sympathy was with the marchers. They were Americans, all having offered their lives for their country, but now they had become the enemy. Many of the government officials, stirred with alarm, had sent out frantic calls to the White House to do something about the "army."

Amos saw that there was an unusual restlessness in the men. He stopped to ask one tall, lean individual with a hard-bitten face, "What's happening?"

The veteran looked at him bitterly. "What's happening is that we're about to get hit by the American army."

Staring at the man incredulously, Amos shook his head. "Nothing like that's going to happen."

The veteran gave him a hard look. "What world are you living in, Mister? You think those cavalry troops are coming to give us a steak dinner?" He raised his hand toward the lines of United States cavalry that were forming to the east of the camp.

Amos swallowed hard. "They're just to keep order. They won't harm you. What's your name?"

"Gerald Hansard."

"Where are you from, Mr. Hansard?"

"Missouri." The light blue eyes of the veteran were as hard as agates. He looked at the flag that was waving over the troops of infantry that were forming on the western side of the camp. "That flag means nothing to me, Mister. I fought for it, took lead in this leg in France—and this is what it's got me!"

Amos shook his head. "It's not that bad, Mr. Hansard. But it might be just as well if you dispersed and went home. I don't think you're going to hurry the government up."

Hansard closed his lips and a rigid quality seized his figure. "I might as well starve here as back in Missouri," he spat out bitterly.

Amos stared after the man, who turned and walked away to stand by a woman wearing a faded gingham dress holding a child no more than a year old. Amos was shocked and appalled by the poverty and helplessness of the so-called army that now was staring with apprehension at the infantry and the cavalry that were flanking them.

He made his way toward the edge of the camp, where he was stopped by a muscular sergeant. The soldier had his campaign hat pulled down over his eyes, and there was a truculent expression in his face. "Move off to one side, Mister—unless you're one of that army over there."

"What's going on, Sergeant?" Amos asked. At the same time, he looked up and saw two officers arrive in a staff car. His eyes narrowed, for he recognized one of them. A straight-backed man wearing jodhpurs, knee-high riding boots, and four stars got out of the car, followed by a major. "Isn't that General MacArthur?" he asked the sergeant.

The sergeant glanced over his shoulder abruptly and grunted. "Yes." He threw his glance down the line of infantry and whispered hoarsely, "Straighten up, men! The general's here."

Amos had never met MacArthur personally but knew that he was the premier officer in the United States Army. His very presence here indicated that the tension in the White House had become intense. Amos Stuart had an instinct for events—an innate sense that other people did not have. It alerted him like an alarm bell when something unusual was brewing on the political scene. Now he moved back, on the order of the sergeant, but kept as close as he could to the action. *This could be bad—it would just take one incident to set the whole thing off.*

Later that afternoon, somebody threw a brick and there was a scuffle between the veterans and the police. Two hours later, there was more serious trouble as a police officer pulled his gun and began shooting. Two veterans were killed before the police stopped shooting.

Amos moved over to where one of the men was lying and saw that it was Gerald Hansard. The tall man lay with his eyes open but sightless while his wife lay across his chest weeping. The baby was held by another plainly dressed woman whose eyes were filled with grief.

Amos moved away, unable to bear the sight. He had a great love for America, but little for bureaucracy—especially a demonstration such as he had seen. An hour later when an impressive parade came down Pennsylvania Avenue, alarm bells again began to ring inside his head. Four troops of cavalry, four companies of infantry, a machine gun squadron, and several tanks advanced steadily. As they approached the disputed area, the crowd began crying aloud at them. Then suddenly, there was chaos!

Amos could not believe what he saw. The cavalry charged into the crowd, scattering them, and Amos saw one young girl of ten or eleven knocked to the ground by one of the horses. The infantry fired tear gas bombs, and women and children were soon choking from the gas. The troops moved on, scattering everything before them. When they reached the end of the Anacostia Bridge, they met a crowd of spectators who booed them, and they threw more gas bombs at these.

Amos moved quickly to a woman's side. "Come along," he urged. "This is going to get worse." Even as he spoke, the troops moved in and began burning the shacks in the camp. It was growing dark now, and soon the sky over Washington glowed with the fire. Amos stayed close, filing it all in his mind. Even after midnight, the troops were covering the territory with bayonets and tear gas bombs, driving the people like helpless cattle.

Amos never forgot that night—nor did he forget the interview with two officers the next morning. He was only one of a group of reporters who met with General Douglas MacArthur, who gave the official justification for the military action. MacArthur faced them, his lips thin and his eyes cold. He read a prepared statement in a clipped, even tone: "The veterans were a mob, animated by the essence of revolution. They were about to seize control of the government."

Amos glanced at Major Dwight Eisenhower who was standing off to one side listening carefully. An involuntary negative shake of the officer's head caught Amos's attention. He saw that Eisenhower's lips were thin and that he was angry. *Eisenhower's against all of this,* he thought. *But who's going to challenge MacArthur?*

Suddenly, Amos spoke up and said, "I hardly think a few thousand civilians including women and children stood much chance of taking over the government, General."

MacArthur turned his gaze on Amos. "Which newspaper are you with?" he rapped out abruptly.

"The Hearst newspapers, General. I'm Amos Stuart."

The name obviously meant something to MacArthur, but he refused to bend. His back was straight as a ramrod as he said, "The army will restore order under any and all conditions, Mr. Stuart. That is our duty."

MacArthur wheeled around and walked away. Eisenhower cast one look over the reporters, gave a shrug of his shoulders, and followed him. Amos turned away sick at heart. In his mind the first sentence of his article on the Bonus Army formed: *It is a sad day for America when the veterans of the country are butchered by the armed forces—whose duty it is to repel enemy attacks from without, not slaughter civilian citizens.*

Amos left Washington after sending his story off to Hearst. He noticed with a wry bitterness two days later, when another reporter's story appeared in the newspaper, William Randolph Hearst had decided to take the side of the military. MacArthur was presented as a noble soldier doing his duty.

Amos spoke to his boss on the phone and Hearst said, "You've been working too hard, Amos. Take a break! Go to New York or get back to Chicago. I've got things for you to do."

Amos wearily returned to Chicago, where he did not work at all but went to baseball games. He went to one game that pitted the Chicago Cubs against the New York Yankees. Amos was not a baseball fan, but it was a welcome relief from the problems of the nation to go out and sit in the bleachers, eat hot dogs and peanuts, and drink a cold soda, while the gladiators on the emerald green field went through their paces. He kept his eyes, mostly as everyone else did, on George Herman "Babe" Ruth. Ruth was a slum kid from Baltimore with a giant torso, spindly legs, and the ability to knock a ball farther than any man ever had. He had set many records during his career. In 1927, he had slammed sixty home runs that had set a record that seemed forever unbreakable.

After the game, Amos interviewed the ballplayer and found him to be a simple man, profane and full of gusty life. Instead of talking about baseball, Amos asked him, "You made eighty thousand dollars last year, Mr. Ruth? That salary's higher than President Hoover's."

Ruth was eating a hot dog, which he consumed in two bites. A crafty light came into his eye and he grinned broadly. "Well," he said, after a moment's meditation, "I had a better year."

Amos went home to find Rose with a worried look on her face.

"I just got a call from Gavin," she said. "It's Jerry."

"Is he hurt?"

"No, but he almost crashed. You better call Gavin—he'll give you details."

At once, Amos picked up the phone and in a few minutes was speaking to his brother. "What's this about Jerry?" he demanded.

"He's all right," Gavin said quickly. "But he nearly had a bad accident. A lot of people think he was drinking."

"What do you think?"

There was a hesitation on the phone and Gavin's voice was cautious as he said, "He says he wasn't, but he's been different since it happened. I don't know what the problem is—or what to think of him."

"Do you think I'd better fly to Hollywood and talk to him?"

"No—he won't be flying again until I get it straight in my mind. We're almost through with the picture, and I'd like for him to finish it. He's had a bad record of dropping things when they got hard. I'll watch him, Amos, and I won't let him fly unless I'm sure."

"Thanks, Gavin. I'll get back to you later."

"Is he all right? Do you think we need to go to him?" Rose asked when he repeated Gavin's words. Her dark blue eyes were troubled as she came to stand beside him. "What should we do?"

Amos was uncertain. "We've been through so much with him," he said quietly. "For some reason, this time I think he's got to fight it out himself. I don't know what happened out there, but we've got to pray that God will do a mighty work."

"Let's pray now, right now," Rose said quickly. The two of them immediately knelt in front of the couch. They held hands and prayed aloud, then silently. Finally, they got to their feet and Rose said firmly, "God is doing something with our son, Amos; I feel it in my heart!"

Amos nodded. "I think so, too. I don't know what it is, but it's got to be now or never for him!"

Bonnie heard of Jerry's close brush with disaster from Jesse, who came in from the studio early. He said abruptly, "Jerry almost killed himself today. I don't know what kept him alive."

A chill went through Bonnie and she stood silent, unable to move or speak. "What happened?" she whispered finally.

"Well, he was doing this stunt with a new man . . ." He outlined quickly the stunt that should have been rather simple, but Jerry's plane had somehow gotten out of control. It had gone into a dive, and he had managed to pull out less than a hundred feet above the ground. "He would have been dead. There's no walking away from a head-on crash like that," Jesse said curtly.

"Where is he?"

"I don't know. He got out of the plane, and it was like he was in shock. Everybody said he was like a dead man. He couldn't even talk, Gavin said."

"But where is he now, Jesse?"

"He just walked off, and nobody knows where he went."

"We've got to find him. There's something wrong!"

"Well, we can start calling around to his friends. I'm afraid he might go out on a drunk again—and that would be the end for him."

Bonnie had the same fear. She immediately went to the phone and began calling the different places where Jerry might be found. No one had seen him, however, all day long.

Night fell and there was still no sign of him. Lylah came home worried, as well. They had a quiet supper and afterward Jesse and Lylah took Adam out to a movie. When she was alone, Bonnie could not sit still. A great anxiety seemed to drive her, and finally in desperation, she went out and got in the car. She had one idea where she might find Jerry—a small lake on the east side of Hollywood. It was a hidden place surrounded by trees, and very few people knew of it. Jerry had taken her there once to fish for perch that abounded in the small body of water. He had told her while they were there, "This is the quietest place I know. Here's a little bit of sanity in the midst of this crazy Hollywood dump."

As she pulled up on the outside of the grove, a sudden sense of relief washed over Bonnie. "There's his car," she whispered. "He's all right." Stopping the Oldsmobile, she got out quickly and followed a worn path that led through the grove to the pond. The moon shone brightly, so she had little trouble seeing. Finally reaching the bank, she called out tremulously, "Jerry, are you here?"

A moment of silence, then—"Over here." A form suddenly materialized and Jerry asked wearily, "What are you doing here, Bonnie?"

"We–we were all worried about you. I've called everybody. Are you all right?"

"Just dandy." There was a bitterness in Jerry's tone. He turned and walked over to a fallen tree and sat down heavily on it and looked out silently over the lake. There was a defeated look to his slumped shoulders, and he kept his face turned away from her.

Bonnie went over and sat down beside him. She took his hand and held it in both of hers. "What happened, Jerry?" she asked quietly.

The silence ran on for such a long time she thought he didn't plan to answer her. Finally, he turned and said hoarsely, "I went into a dive—the plane was out of control—I don't know what happened. I was headed straight to the ground at top speed. It was rushing at me, Bonnie, and I felt so helpless. I knew I was going to die—" He broke off and looked back out over the water. He was squeezing her hands so hard that they hurt, but she said nothing. He turned back and said, "I was dead, that's all there is to it—and all I could think is what a rotten thing my life's been!"

Bonnie held his hand and they sat quietly for a long time. Finally, he looked at her again and said, "I can't forget the last time I felt like this. It was at the end of Owen's meeting, and he had given the invitation. I felt scared and lonely. That's how I felt when the plane was going down."

"Jerry, I'm so sorry," she whispered. "Your life is empty, but it doesn't have to be." That was all she said, but for a moment she was afraid that it might have been too much. She knew how Jerry hated being preached to. He had heard the gospel for years from his parents, from Owen, from her, and from Lylah. A great fear came to her that he might be one of those with such a hardened heart that he could not hear, but then he turned to her and her heart leaped, for she could see that he was not angry.

"You're talking about being saved," he said simply. "I've heard about that all my life—and I've seen it, too. I saw it happen with Lylah. When she became a Christian, why it was like she was a different woman—I'd never seen anything like it before, Bonnie. Then, I've seen it in you," he said. "You've always had something in you that I've envied—a peace, I guess."

"Oh, Jerry, it's so easy to be saved! God loves you so much that he sent Jesus to die for you. You've heard that a thousand times."

"I know, but it sounds too—well, too easy, I guess. I've always thought you had to do something. I've tried to be better—to quit drinking, go to church—" He shook his head sadly. "That just makes it worse. I just can't do it, Bonnie—I just can't!"

"Good!" she rapped out abruptly.

Jerry's head snapped around. "What do you mean—*good?*" he asked almost angrily. "Is it good that I can't be saved?"

"No, it's good that you recognize that you can't help God save you. Jerry, none of us can help God. If we could have been saved by living good lives or quitting our drinking or whatever was wrong, then there wouldn't have been a need for Jesus to die." She spoke earnestly and he sat listening. She quoted many Scripture passages that he had heard over and over again, but now they struck him in a way that they never had. They seemed to go straight into his heart, and despite himself, he found a hope beginning to grow in him. He listened as she said, "The Bible says, 'Not by works of righteousness which we have done, but according to his mercy he saved us.'" Then she shook her head, saying, "Don't you see? It's not what we do, it's what Jesus did at the cross."

"But how does that help me? Jesus died hundreds of years ago. What does that have to do with me?"

"Jerry, all times are the same with God. He is the Alpha and the Omega, the first and the last. When Moses wanted to know his name, God just said, 'I AM.' That means that he doesn't have a yesterday, tomorrow, or today—all times are the same to him. And when you call on him, that's the time that he hears."

"That's what Owen kept telling me—and Mom and Dad, of course."

"It's true! It's all you can do. If Adam hurt you, then turned to you and said 'Jerry, can you forgive me?' what would you do?"

"Why, I'd forgive him, of course."

"And do you think you're better than God?"

Jerry blinked in surprise. "Why, no, of course not!"

The air was warm and there was a silvery glow of moonlight that fell on Jerry's face. Bonnie wanted desperately to see the pain and the doubt and the fear, which were etched there, erased. She prayed silently, her heart crying out to God and finally she said, "Jerry, this is your time—I just know it!"

"My time?"

"Yes, the time for you to come into the family of God. It's time to have your sins forgiven and to become a follower of Jesus."

"I don't know if I can do it. I've been so rotten, and everything I've tried has failed."

"We're all failures. Some fail harder than others—in the sight of the world, at least," she said quietly. "But God loves you. Jesus is the proof of that. His death on the cross is God's sign that he loves us. Do you believe that?"

"Of course."

"Do you believe the Scriptures, Jerry?"

"Yes, I believe the Bible. I just can't make it work."

"Do you believe it when it says 'Whosoever shall call on the name of the Lord shall be saved'?"

Jerry struggled with that. "It seems too simple," he muttered. "But if it says it, then I believe it. But how do I do that?"

"Just tell God that you're sorry for your life and your sins. Confess them to him and then ask him to forgive you in the name of Jesus. Will you do that, Jerry?"

There was a moment's pause and for one awful moment, Bonnie feared that he would rise and walk away, turn his back on her and on God. She yearned to see him come to himself and find God, but this was as far as she could go. *You can only go so far with anybody,* she thought, *and now it's up to Jerry. Oh, God, draw him as you've never drawn him before.*

Jerry seemed to be frozen. He did not move, but then suddenly, he removed his hands from her and looked at her almost frantically. "Yes!" he whispered hoarsely. "I can't go on like this—I've got to have something in my life besides what I have had."

"It's all right," Bonnie said. "We'll pray." She began to pray quietly, putting her hand on his back, and soon she felt his body begin to tremble, even as it had once before. Then she heard him saying, "Oh, God, I'm so alone—I need you so desperately!" He prayed hoarsely, as if he had to force the words. Finally, she heard him sob, "I ask you to save me in Jesus' name."

They sat there for a long time, Bonnie praying from her heart and Jerry with his face in his hands. Finally, he straightened up and turned toward her. "Bonnie," he whispered, "something has happened to me. I feel as if all the stuff that was in me is gone. Is this it? What you've been feeling since you've been a Christian?"

"Yes, that's the peace of God, Jerry," she said.

He shook his head and wondered, "Will it always be like this?"

"Jesus said, 'I am with you always.' It's just the beginning." She began to talk to him about what it means to be a Christian, how he needed to make his faith in Christ public. "Jesus didn't call people to be secret disciples," she admonished him. "You must openly declare your faith in him to other people. Will you do that?"

Jerry said instantly, "Yes, I'll do that. I don't know how it's going to go." His voice trembled, then he smiled beautifully. "Something's in me that was never there before." Suddenly, he took her hand and pulled her to her feet. "Let's go. I want to tell Gavin about it and then I want to call my folks." He suddenly reached out and hugged her. Holding her close, he said, "Thank you, Bonnie. I don't know how you've put up with me all these years."

She was very conscious of his arms around her, and tears ran down her cheeks. When he stepped back, she said, "Come along, Jerry, we've got some things to do!"

 21 

THE STUART LINE

The premier of *The Pilot* was not as impressive as some opening nights, but it was large enough for Lylah and for those who gathered with her in front of the theater in downtown Hollywood. The spotlights swept the skies overhead with their cone-shaped beams of light. The crowds had gathered outside the theater and were accustomed to greeting Hollywood personalities. They gasped and applauded as the actresses and actors got out of their cars, giving special fervency to their cries for Brent Peters. He was walking with Bonnie, who had agreed to accompany him rather reluctantly. Leaning over, he whispered, "Listen to them crying out my name," then grinned. "If the picture's a bust, they'll throw rotten cabbage at me."

Bonnie looked up at him and smiled cheerfully. "It won't be a bust, Brent. You did a marvelous job."

He looked at her carefully and shrugged his shoulders. "I still think you and I could have made a good life together. I need someone steady like you to keep my feet on the ground."

"No, you don't need me. I'm not cut out for this Hollywood life. Come on; let's go inside and watch the picture."

They made their way inside the theater, and soon the row reserved for them was filled. Jesse and Lylah sat together, with Adam sitting between Lylah and Jerry. The cast was there—and Carl Thomas and others who had worked to complete the picture. Adam whispered incessantly. "You show me the times you were flying the plane, will you, Jerry?"

"Sure I will. I did all the good stuff." He looked down the row to where Bonnie was sitting with Brent and his face stiffened, expressionless. Adam followed his glance and said, "Gee, Bonnie's sure pretty, isn't she? I didn't know she had a dress like that."

"I guess she bought it just for this occasion," Jerry said quietly. "Look, the movie is coming on." He watched as the credits rolled by and smiled faintly to see his name as an assistant—then Cara's name came on and his smile faded. He sat watching the movie, and he was amazed. He had seen bits and pieces of it done. It had been a surprise to him that a movie is not made from front to back—from beginning to end. One of the first stunts in the picture was the last one he had done. It had not been a particularly difficult one, but he remembered how Gavin had urged him to be careful.

He watched the audience as much as he did the picture, attempting to gauge how they were taking it. It was not a picture that evoked a great deal of loud laughter, for the humor in it was rather sophisticated—keen and cutting sometimes. He had to admit that Brent Peters had done a fine job in the lead role. There was pathos in the movie, sadness, grief, and the struggles of aviators against the skies, and the dangers that the world of aviation brought with it. As the screen flickered, Jerry thought of Cara. He remembered her smile, her laughter, her verve.

Finally, the picture ended and Jerry came out of his reverie. The audience was standing, applauding loudly. They continued to do so, and Jerry saw Brent go over and take Lylah's hand. He escorted her to the stage with Jesse following closely behind and spoke into a microphone that was placed in front of him. "Thank you so much, fine friends, for your enthusiasm. I will say nothing of my own performance, but I will say that this picture was a delight to make! It was made by the courage and vision of this dear woman whom you have loved on the screen for years, Miss Lylah Stuart. Lylah Stuart Hart, I should say. She and her husband have brought this picture to birth. Lylah, I congratulate you and Jesse."

Lylah took the microphone, and after all her years on the stage and before a camera, she felt inhibited. She was close to tears, for the film had stirred her. It was a better film than she had thought and she said, "Thank you, Brent. I must say what he has not said himself. His performance in this film is the finest that he has ever given. I must also say that the story belongs to my husband." She turned to Jesse and smiled sweetly. "Without him, there would have been no film."

She spoke for a while, very briefly, thanked them, and then curtsied. "Thank you for your response to our film."

Jerry put his hand on Adam's shoulder and said, "That's some set of parents you got there, buddy. I hope you appreciate them."

"I do." He was strangely quiet, but on the way home, he said, "Mom?"

Lylah put her arm around him. Adam was seated in the middle, and Jesse was driving. "What is it?"

"You did good—both of you. It was a swell story, Dad. I wish I could write like that. I'd write westerns."

Jesse laughed and reached over and ruffled the boy's thick, brown hair. "Maybe you will. There's no time like the present to start."

They parked the car and went in. When they got inside, Adam suddenly turned and said without preamble, "Mom, why won't you tell me who my father is?"

Jesse halted abruptly, turning his head slightly to watch Lylah's face. He saw the shock run over it, and then he stepped to her side. Putting his arm around her, he said evenly, "Lylah, I think it's time."

Lylah took a deep breath, her eyes fixed on this son of hers. He looked so tall and straight—and so much like his father!

Slowly, Lylah nodded and walked over to Adam. "Come and sit down," she said quietly. "I'll tell you about your father."

Jesse took a chair over on one side of the room and watched as Adam turned his face toward his mother. As she began to speak of her early days, her struggles in the theater, and finally about how she had gone to Germany, he wondered if she would be able to keep herself steady, and realized what a terrible moment this would be for her.

Lylah said slowly, never taking her eyes from Adam, "When I was in Germany, a dear friend of mine introduced me to her cousin. He was a baron and his name was Manfred von Richthofen. Have you ever heard of him?"

Adam's face assumed a frown. He'd said nothing during the earlier part of his mother's recitation, but now he said, "I think so—but I can't remember. Was he famous?"

"Yes, he was very famous, Adam." Lylah hesitated. She had no idea how Adam would take what she had to tell him, but she had long known this moment would come. She said quietly, "It was wartime. America was at war with Germany. Your uncle Gavin was a fighter pilot."

Suddenly, Adam opened his eyes wide. "That's where I've heard of him! Manfred von Richthofen! Uncle Gavin's told me that he was the best fighter pilot the Germans had in the war."

"That's right."

The room seemed very quiet. Jesse and Lylah both watched as emotion suddenly seemed to break the boy's face. He looked young and vulnerable, and as he stared into his mother's eyes, he asked in a whisper, "Is he my father?"

"Yes, he is."

Adam looked at his mother, his eyes fixed on her. Neither adult knew what was going on in his young mind, but when he finally spoke, both of them were taken off guard. "Did you love him, Mother? Did he love you?"

Tears filled Lylah's eyes and she nodded, pressing her lips together for a moment. Dashing the tears away, she said, "Yes, I did love him—and he loved me. But I was an American and he was in the army at war with our country. We didn't marry, Adam."

"What happened to him?"

"He was killed—shot down in action. Not long after he died, you were born. Uncle Gavin was at the hospital, and

Uncle Owen and Uncle Amos. I'll never forget that moment," she said in a voice that was almost too quiet to hear. "I was holding you and they stood on each side of the bed. Then they–they put their hands on you and said 'He'll be a Stuart.'" Tears overflowed and she bit her lip to gain control. "Adam, your father was an honorable man and I loved him very much. I was very young—we both were—and it was wartime. We sinned, Adam, but never doubt that he would have loved you if he had lived."

Adam sat quietly beside his mother. He took his eyes from hers and looked down at the floor. The silence ran on and Lylah looked across the room at Jesse. They were both mystified and afraid for Adam, but finally he looked up and said, "If he had lived, Mom, would you have gotten married?"

"I think we would," Lylah said simply.

Adam nodded. His face was pale and his lips twitched slightly. "Thank you for telling me. Why wouldn't you tell me before?"

"I was afraid for you, Adam. It may be difficult for you," Lylah said quietly. "Even now many Americans have hard feelings toward Germans because of the war."

Adam then looked across at Jesse and said something Jesse would never forget. "You've been a good dad to me. I can never forget that."

Jesse swallowed. "Thank you, Adam. I've tried to be. Since I don't have any sons of my own, I feel that God has given you to me—and I want you to know I will always be here for you." He hesitated, then went on. "I studied the life of your father very carefully. Your mother is telling the truth. He was a man of honor and dignity, and you should be very proud of him. We don't always agree with those we love, but love is bigger than a disagreement."

Adam stood up and said, "I think I'd like to go to bed. Good night, Mom." His face was pale, but there was a steadiness in his eyes as he looked at her.

Lylah stood up and embraced him. He pulled her head

down slightly, although he was almost as tall as she, kissed her, then said, "Good night, Jesse."

He turned and left the room, and the two looked at each other. Jesse came over and put his arm around Lylah. They sat down, and he discovered that she was trembling. She began to weep, and he held her tightly.

"I don't know what he thinks—what's in his mind! I should have told him years ago."

"Don't talk like that. It will be all right," Jesse said. He looked toward Adam's room and shook his head. "I was proud of him. He's got strength." He looked at her and squeezed her. "Like his father, Lylah."

Lylah straightened up and brushed the tears away. She put her hand on his cheek and whispered, "What would I do without you, Jesse?"

"You don't have to do without me—and I don't have to do without you. What we have to do now is stay very close to Adam. He's going to need time to let this sink in—and it won't be easy, as you said, but God will see us through it."

Jerry arrived at the house early the morning after the premier of *The Pilot*. When he entered, he found Bonnie in a robe, with her hair wrapped in a towel. She let out a screech and started to run away, but he moved forward and caught her by the arm.

"What are you doing here? Go away—I'm not dressed yet!"

"Well, get dressed," he said, a smile tugging at his lips. He reached up and touched the towel on top of her head. "You look as good as usual, don't you?"

"Get away from me, you beast! What do you mean coming here at this time of the morning?" He held her fast and she looked up. "Do you mean we're going somewhere?"

"Just go get dressed. Put on the best outfit you've got, like I have on." He stepped back and held his hands out. He was wearing a pair of white slacks, a navy blue double-breasted coat, and a spotless white shirt. A new wine-colored tie was neatly tied and he'd had a haircut and a shave.

Bonnie stared at him. "Why are you so dressed up this early?"

"I'll reveal that to you at the proper time. Go get dressed. And remember—wear your prettiest outfit." He went and plumped down on a chair, crossed his legs and then his arms, and then stared at her.

Bonnie blinked and fled to her room. She was mystified by his behavior. "What's he up to?" she muttered. She looked at her wardrobe and said, "Where could he be taking me that we have to be dressed up this early in the morning?"

Nevertheless, she made up her mind to do as he said. She put on a dress that she'd only worn once. Dresses looked softer and longer in the thirties than they had in the twenties, and women's hairstyles were less severe, curled at the back of the head more gaily. As she brushed her own hair, Bonnie wondered what Jerry was thinking. The dress she chose suited her admirably. She slipped on a pair of new pumps, looked carefully at herself, picked up her purse, and left the bedroom.

"Well, you look presentable," Jerry said. "Come along."

Bonnie was amused at him. He had always had the ability to cheer her up and to amuse her. When he opened the door, she got into the car and sat back. He closed the door, walked around—whistling a song everybody else had stopped singing months ago—started the engine, and pulled away from the curb. She was determined to show no curiosity, but when he pulled up in front of the courthouse, she said, "What are we doing here?"

"No questions—just come with me."

He jumped out of the car, went around, and opened the door. When she stepped out, he took her arm firmly and walked up the stairs. It was a busy place and he did not give her the chance to look around. Finally, they entered a set of double doors with frosted glass, but she did not have time to see what was written on them.

A man was sitting behind a tall desk watching them carefully. "Yes, sir," he said when Jerry came up, "what can I do for you folks?"

"We'd like to apply for a marriage license."

Bonnie's face turned pale. She felt her knees begin to tremble and she turned slowly to look at Jerry. "What–what did you say?" she whispered in a voice that was not steady.

"Well, I've decided to marry you," he said. He looked extremely handsome, and the elfin sense of humor in his eyes could not be hidden. "After we leave here, I'm going to take you to some romantic place and propose properly. But I thought we'd get this little bit of business over with. It was on the way, you know."

Bonnie turned furiously. "Jerry Stuart, you are insane!" She stalked out of the office and Jerry called out to the man, "We'll be back! What time do you close?"

"Five o'clock, and don't think I'll stay open late for you, brother. You've got just as much tact as an elephant!"

Bonnie heard the remark and marched back to the car, her head high and her face flaming. She felt embarrassed, and when Jerry sat down beside her, she said through clenched teeth, "Take me home!"

Jerry started the car, still whistling the same old tune. A few minutes later Bonnie said, "This isn't the way home."

"Just one stop before we get there, Bonnie."

She soon recognized where he was going. He pulled up in front of the grove of trees that concealed the pond where she had found him one fateful night. Bonnie said, "I'm not getting out of this car."

Jerry looked at her but said nothing. He got out of the car, walked around, and opened the door. She clenched her teeth together and gritted out the words, "You have no sense of decency, Jerry Stuart! Take me home!" Then she gasped, for he had simply reached in and plucked her out. He was very strong, and though she resisted, he began walking her down the path that led to the woods.

"Have you noticed how thick the pine cones are this year?" he remarked, ignoring the blows she struck at him. "I'm told that means a hard winter, but I don't believe those old superstitions . . ."

He chattered on until finally he stepped out to the side of the lake. The water was blue and clear, and white clouds were ruffling the skies as he said, "Why, here's an old log. Suppose we sit down." He took her over to it, and when she tried to pull away from him, he put his arms around her. Bonnie felt the strength of his body as he held her tight. She looked up to blaze out at him again, then she saw something in his face that made her stop. He was not smiling but was looking at her in a way that she'd never seen him look before.

"Jerry, please take me home," she whispered.

"Bonnie, I love you and I want you to marry me," he said quietly. There was a serene look on his face. After all the years of seeing his frantic attempts to find peace, Bonnie recognized at once that this was the new Jerry talking. He leaned down and said, "I'm going to kiss you, but you can run away if you want to."

She did not run away, but lifted her face. And when he kissed her, it was like coming home. His lips were demanding, but no more so than her own. There was a hardness and strength in him that had not been there, and there was a desire for her that she sensed. She returned his embrace freely. When he lifted his head, he said, "Will you marry me, Bonnie?"

"Yes," she whispered quietly.

Then he kissed her again, but she stepped back. "What do you mean taking me to that courthouse? That was an awful thing to do."

"I wanted you to understand that my intentions were serious," he said. Then he laughed, grabbed her hands, and swung her around. "You should have seen your face! I'll never forget it! For our fiftieth anniversary we'll do the same—go in and ask for a wedding license. I'll bet he'll be just as shocked as he was this morning."

"You idiot!" she giggled. "I was never so embarrassed in my life!"

"You probably will be again," he said. He pulled her close

to him. "I've been the worst fool on earth, but God's done something in me now. I can learn to be a good husband."

"What about Cara?"

He shook his head firmly. "That's in the past. I'm sorry for her. She could've had a better life—but I've put that behind me, all right?"

"All right, Jerry." They walked around the lake, supremely happy, and laughing about everything.

When they went home and broke the news, Lylah said to Jerry, "You don't deserve her—but maybe she can make something out of you."

Jerry grinned at her, then winked at Jesse. "Now that we're practically brothers-in-law," he said, "I wonder if I could get a small loan, enough to get married on and go on a honeymoon?"

"Didn't take you long to become a sponger." Jesse smiled. "All right, where will you go?"

"I'll let the bride decide." But although the two talked about Hawaii, Sun Valley, and other exotic honeymoon spots, they did not come to a decision. That night at supper, they were interrupted by a phone call. They had been laughing and teasing Jerry until even he blushed. When the phone rang, Lylah said, "I'll get it." She'd gone out of the room and had stayed away for a long time. When she came back, Jesse took one look and said, "What is it, Lylah?" They all turned to her and immediately saw that something was wrong.

"That was Amos on the phone," she said. "There's something wrong in Oklahoma. Pete's going down the drain if we don't get to him and help."

"Did Dad say what the trouble is?" Jerry asked quickly.

"A big oil company's freezing him out. They're really under a state of siege." Her brow wrinkled and she shook her head. "I don't really understand it in this day and age, but they are actually having to fight them off with guns!"

Adam had been listening carefully and at this his eyes flew open. He jumped up and ran to his mother. "We've got to go help Uncle Pete, Mom!"

When she tried to pacify him, he said, "No, we've got to go! All of us Stuarts have to stick together. That's what you always say."

A murmur went around the table and Jerry squelched it firmly. "That's what I say, Adam!" He turned to Bonnie. "What about it? You want to get married before or after we have this gunfight with the bad gunslingers—the guys in the black hats?"

"Let's wait till after," Bonnie said. "In the meanwhile you can give me shooting lessons."

They grew serious and the next day, after calls to Owen and Gavin, they were on a plane with Gavin headed to Oklahoma. Lylah put her arm around Adam. "I'm very proud of you, Adam—sticking up for your family like you did."

Adam patted her arm. "Don't worry, Mom. We'll help Uncle Pete, just see if we don't." He hesitated for a moment, then said, "Do you think my father would help if he were here?"

Lylah hugged him very hard and whispered fiercely, "I'm sure he would, Adam. I'm very sure he would!"

 22 

Kingman Meets His Match

After Maury had fixed breakfast for the children, she sat down and began to sort out the feed sacks. It had become part of her work to take the large assortment of these bags and try to make some sort of clothing out of them. Sheltered as she had been from the actual hardships of the depression, she discovered from this activity how important feed sacks were to poor people in 1932. As she sorted the sacks into different piles, she could hear the whining of the engine that sputtered in through the window. It was an irritating noise, but she had become accustomed to it, filtering it out of her mind completely.

Some of the sacks were rather pretty, for the feed makers had discovered that one way to sell feed was to put the product into sacks with colorful designs. Holding up one of them, Maury admired the paisley pattern with a yellow background and red flowery design. The tiny pattern looked like red caterpillars bending over to begin spinning their cocoons. A fanciful thought came to her that it would be nice if those caterpillars could become butterflies and float off into the sky.

"I'm getting to be quite a dreamer," she muttered, a smile creasing her lips. Moving to the stove where a tub of water was boiling, she poured Fels-Naphtha soap into it, then put in several sacks that had the names of the companies stamped on them. She let them boil in the big tub, then rinsed them. The name still came through, so she repeated the action. She had done this before and knew that when the color was gone they could either be used plainly, or for the more fanciful, could be stamped with designs or embroidered for tablecloths or tea towels. *Not much use for tea towels out on this place,* she thought, straightening her back and looking across the room. The men were all gone, Leslie was lying down, and for once there was a sense of quietness in the air. After setting another batch of sacks to boil, she sat down for a moment in the chair, a cane-bottomed rocker, by the window. Picking up the Bible that lay beside it, she opened it, and it fell open to the Psalms. Her eyes fell on the Seventieth Psalm, which began, "Make haste, O God, to deliver me; make haste to help me, O LORD." She studied that for a moment and thought wryly, *That's what we need, Lord—all of us here. If you don't come through, I guess we're all finished.* She dropped her eyes to the second verse that said, "Let them be ashamed and confounded that seek after my soul: let them be turned backward, and put to confusion, that desire my hurt."

Somewhere outside the house, she could hear the children's voices as they called to one another. Farther off she heard a dog barking mindlessly in a steady, rhythmic beat. He seemed to have no need to breathe, for the barking went on relentlessly. She thought about the verse she'd read. *Lord, I don't know how to pray against people, but I guess I'll have to pray against the Kingman Oil Company.* She read the next line: "Let them be turned back for a reward of their shame," then the fourth verse, "Let all those that seek thee rejoice and be glad in thee: and let such as love thy salvation say continually, Let God be magnified." For some time she remained still, thinking about the Scripture. It had become a habit of hers in the long days since the siege started to let the Scriptures filter through her mind.

She'd always been a quick reader and had gone through college by devouring an enormous number of pages per day. When she had come to the Bible, at first she had tried to read it the same way. It had been frustrating, however, and she had found no satisfaction in it. Slowly she had discovered the art of meditation. Her pastor had said once, "It's like a cow that has several stomachs. That cow goes out to pasture and begins to eat. She doesn't chew anything much—just swallows it. It goes into one of her stomachs, then later on she lies down and somehow that unchewed grass comes up into a cud, so she chews it and chews it. That's the way it should be with the Scripture. Put it in your heart, memorize it, and then on your bed or while you're working—think on it."

Maury had found this to be good advice. For the next hour, she did her work while thinking about the verse, "Let all those that seek thee rejoice and be glad in thee." Naturally she wondered, *How could we rejoice out here? We're out of food, burning up in the heat, surrounded by enemies, and poor Pete can't see how we're going to last another day—and I can't either!* She carefully removed the bleached feed sacks, took them outside, and hung them on the line, thinking, *How can any of us rejoice when everything is going wrong?* Still the Scripture came to her, "Let all those that seek thee rejoice and be glad in thee." Then she remembered the last verse of the psalm. "But I am poor and needy: make haste unto me, O God: thou art my help and deliverer; O LORD, make no tarrying." As that last verse floated through her mind, so clear that it seemed to appear before her eyes, a sense of well-being came to her. She looked around the shack and the pitiful conditions and then lifted her eyes out to where the tents of Kingman's men ringed the homestead. She should have been depressed—but somehow the words of the psalm were soothing and encouraging. She whispered aloud, "O Lord, make no tarrying." Then smiling and refreshed, she finished hanging out the sacks. When they were all on the line she walked over to where Ted was working on the rig.

When he saw her coming, he smiled, saying, "Come to help drill for oil?"

Maury returned his smile. She saw that he was tired, for he, like the other men, put in long hours just keeping the rig going. She looked at the shaft turning and screeching and said, "I never have understood how this thing works."

"Well," Ted said, running his hand through his brown hair, "rotary rigs are pretty new. The old way was what they called a cable rig. It operated on a percussion principle. You know if you pick something up and hit with it often enough, eventually it will make a hole. That's what a cable rig does—it just picks up a heavy pipe with a bit on the end and drops it in the same spot. Sooner or later, it'll make a hole in the ground—even through a rock."

"That'd be very slow, wouldn't it?"

"Sure," Kingman nodded, "but the advantage of cable is that you can pull the tool string in the hole and scoop out your digging. This one, the rotary, stays in the hole all the time. You've seen us just adding pipe onto the part that sticks out above the shelf, right here, you see? And we put water in it to flush it clean."

"What happens if you run out of water, or if you don't have any?"

"Then you don't use a rotary rig," he grinned.

He looked very young, and Maury spoke, impulsively. "I can't understand you, Ted."

"I'm not very complicated."

"Yes, you are. You're very complicated." The wind blew Maury's red hair into her face and she pushed it back, frowning. "I always hated red hair," she said. "People always call you 'Red,' and grown people come up when you're a child and ask where you got the red hair."

"You didn't like that, I suppose."

"No, I didn't. Mother says when I was a little girl a woman came up and started stroking my hair and saying things like that—and I just spit on her!"

Ted stared at her in amazement and then laughed out loud. "I don't believe it."

"Well, I did—" Maury smiled and poked his chest with her forefinger. "It's part of the family history. Mama told her I was sick and didn't feel well—but I wasn't," she grinned. "I remember it very well. I was just tired of being pawed and having people ask me those stupid questions."

"I think your hair is beautiful," Ted said quietly. "But I won't ask you where you got it."

Maury flushed at his compliment. She did look attractive as she stood before him. There was a smoothness of her cheeks and a fullness of her lips that lent a beauty to her oval-shaped face. She was a strong woman physically, too, and the breeze outlined her figure against the thin cotton dress that she wore. Ted suddenly thought, *Why, she's beautiful!* and something of his thoughts showed in his face, for Maury flushed again and at once half turned from him. "What do you mean—that I'm complicated?" he asked.

She thought for a moment, then answered slowly, "Why, you could be anywhere you want to, Ted. You've always had all you wanted—money, clothes, cars—and here you are working on this derrick, eating hard beans and canned food." She turned and said, "I don't understand you. You know you can't stay on this drilling rig forever. What about your father?"

The question seemed to trouble young Kingman. He made some unnecessary adjustment to the engine that increased its speed slightly and made the pipe groan within its collar. He poured water over it out of a rusty tin can, then turned to face her.

"I don't know," he said slowly. "I guess I've been spoiled—but sometimes I think I would have traded everything just for the simple life, maybe like you had. But I'm too much of a coward to pay the price for it. I've thought about running away, many times, and going out and being just a cowboy, or a roughneck—or whatever I could do and stand on my own two feet." His face was serious, and she saw that there was a longing in him that he did not let many people see—at least so she suspected.

"Will you go back to work for your father?"

"I suppose so," he said glumly, "but it doesn't thrill me very much."

They stood talking for a long time. Maury had discovered that she liked his company. They thought alike, for the most part, laughing at the same things, and both were fascinated by certain books. Finally, she said, “Well, I’d better go and start thinking about dinner. There are only so many ways you can cook beans.”

The rest of the morning she thought about Ted Kingman, but it was Pete who came to her after lunch and brought her down to earth. “Well,” he said calmly, “I don’t think we’re going to have to put up with this much longer, Maury.”

“What’s the matter, Pete?”

He slumped down in the chair, his face worn, and fingered the straps of his bib overalls. They were paper thin, faded almost white from so many washings. “I thought we would hit oil before now, but we can’t go on. The kids are starving—and you are, too.”

“We can make it, Pete,” Maury said quickly.

“No, I gambled and I lost. It’s the same old story,” he said. “The big fish eat the little fish. Kingman’s won.”

A stab of sadness touched Maury. The past few weeks had been the hardest living that she’d ever known, but she’d grown close to this part of her family, learning to love them. Somehow she felt beaten and her spirit defeated. She raised her head as she went over and put her hand on Pete’s shoulder. “We can hold out, Pete. Don’t give up.”

Pete shook his head. “There’s a time to hold out and fight and take the rough side of life—but I can’t ask my sick wife and my kids to do that. Besides, it’s just a matter of time.” He rose suddenly, saying, “If I don’t hit anything by tomorrow, I’m going to sign the leases over to Kingman and we’ll move on somewhere.”

“If you do that, Pete, you’ll always feel defeated. This is your big chance. You said so yourself.”

But Pete shook his head and left the shack.

Later on, Maury was sitting outside watching Ted at the drill when she was joined by Violet and Ray. “Pete’s going to give up,” she said.

“Oh, he can’t do that!” Violet cried. “He’s worked too hard. We can’t let him.”

"No, we can hang in there," Ray said. "I'll sneak out tonight and get some grub. We can hang on."

That night they had a semi-official meeting. After supper, they were all gathered in the room and Pete said, "I've got to tell you something. If we don't hit anything tomorrow, we're pulling out."

Immediately, Dent sat up straighter. He had been playing checkers with Stephen and his eyes instantly had a combative light. "We can't do that, Pete. We can whip Kingman!"

"Dent, we're starving to death. How much food do you have left, Maury?"

Maury wanted to say that they had plenty, but she was aware of the scant store and cupboard. "Not a lot," she said. "But we can pull our belts a little tighter."

Bailey rarely said anything in groups, but now from where he sat on the floor watching quietly, he piped up. "I ain't gonna quit, Mr. Pete. We can do 'er."

One by one they all expressed their encouragement, but Pete knew the harsh reality that faced them and merely said, "I appreciate all of that. You've all been great, but, this time at least, Kingman's got the best of us."

Maury said, "I was reading the Scriptures this morning, Pete, and the psalmist was praying for help, and the last thing he prayed for was to send help quick. Let's all pray tonight that something will come tomorrow that will help us hold out."

Pete's lips turned upward in a smile. "Your mama and daddy would be proud of you if they heard you say that. You're quite a woman, Maury Stuart!" His eyes fell on Ted Kingman, who was sitting in the angle of the corner on a stool, saying nothing. He had taken Mona up on his lap, for he had taken a special fancy to her, and his hand was stroking her blond hair. His eyes were fixed on Pete, his lips were drawn in a tight line—but he said nothing.

Maury had seen the exchange of glances and wondered, *How does Ted feel? We're the enemy to him, I suppose.* She said nothing about this; instead she said, "Let's pray and ask God to do a miracle."

"Why, sure," Dent said. He was sitting beside Violet and reached around her and gave her a sudden squeeze. "I guess we've seen a few of those, haven't we? Like getting a no-account fella like me saved and under the blood. Why, it won't be anything for God to pull this thing out of the fire!"

Finally, Pete shrugged. "All right," he said. "I've always been a bit cautious about asking God for instant miracles, but I reckon that's the only kind that's going to do it." He bowed his head and one by one they began to pray. It was not a time for wild excitement, but they were fervent prayers. Mona and Stephen joined in. Mona prayed, "Dear Lord, help us get something to eat because we're hungry—and Lord, we need it tomorrow, if you please."

As Ted Kingman heard this prayer, a strange feeling rose in him. Something about the scene was affecting him tremendously. He had never seen Christianity in action—and he certainly had never heard of praying for a miracle. Something was stirring in him—a longing that he could not define.

When the prayers were over and they all went to bed, Ted fell onto his pad in the shed, alongside Bailey and Ray. Pete was taking the watch on the rig and Ted listened to the squealing of steel against steel and the chugging of the engine that monotonously punctuated the night air. He lay looking out through the support that held the shed, studying the stars that sparkled and danced against the velvety darkness of the sky. He had not given thought to God, but he felt that his whole life was threatened by what he had experienced that evening. He slept poorly, waking up several times, for dreams had come to trouble him. Finally, he whispered very softly, "Oh, God, I've got no right to ask you for favors, and I don't for myself, but these folks need your help. I would appreciate it if you would do something for them—and we need it quick, like Mona says." He felt a little foolish, for he'd never prayed before, but then he fell off to sleep and he wasn't troubled by dreams any longer.

Everyone rose early the next day and there was a strange sense of anticipation in the air. Ted went at once to stand his watch at the drill, but there was little to do as the engine droned on endlessly. He kept his eyes on the others, especially Maury, looking for some sign of defeat in her. He could tell little difference in her other than her lips seemed to be drawn together somewhat tighter than usual, and she appeared to be caught up in some sort of thought that was reflected only in her eyes. Bailey came to stand beside him once and the big man was silent, as usual. Finally, he blurted out, "Mr. Ted—"

"What is it, Bailey?"

"I don't like to leave this place. Do you think we'll have to?"

Something in the simple eyes pulled at Ted. He wondered what it would be like to be trapped in a huge body with a mind as simple as that of a child. And yet he was aware that there was more honor and dignity in Bailey than in most people that he had known. "I don't know, Bailey. I hope not."

The sun climbed into the sky until it stood directly over them at noon and then began its slow descent. The shadows grew longer, and finally, at three o'clock Pete, who had been standing beside Leslie in the doorway of the house, straightened his shoulders. "Well," he said, in a voice that he kept even and low, "I guess that's it."

Leslie reached out and put her arm around him. She said nothing, for the struggle had drained her. She was actually feeling better physically than she had before the siege. Her face was pale and she had lost that prettiness of youth, but still there was a glow of love in her eyes as she looked up at him. "You've done all that any man could do," she whispered softly. "I'm proud of you, Pete."

Startled, Pete looked down, and when he saw the look in her eyes, he squeezed her and said, "You're some woman, Leslie!" Then he straightened up. "Well, I'd rather take a beating, but I have to go down and talk to Kingman's men."

Maury and Violet stood together watching as Pete left the house. "I guess he's gonna do it," Violet said sadly. "It just tears me apart inside!"

Maury said nothing, but she felt the same way. When Pete reached her side and passed by, she said, "We'll all go down with you, Pete. We've been together in all this, so we'll stand with you."

Pete stopped and looked at her. "You sure you want to do that? It's not much fun being gloated over—and that's what's gonna happen."

Maury nodded and forced a smile. "Come on, let's go spit in their eyes!"

Ted Kingman heard this. He dropped the wrench that was in his hand and came to stand by Maury. "I guess I'll go with you." His jaw was tense and he dreaded the scene that was to come.

"You don't have to go, Ted," Maury said quietly.

"I guess I do," Ted Kingman said slowly. "I think this is one time I have to let folks know which side I'm on!"

Pete, joined by his tiny army, moved down the slope. Almost at once he saw that Horace Kingman was there. *Like a buzzard!* he thought grimly. He wished that he didn't have to face the big man, but he did.

Kingman came out, flanked by his henchmen, with Ollie Bean standing right beside him. He grinned broadly. "Well, I see you've come to talk business. That's a smart move." His eyes shifted over toward his son. His lips grew tight and he said, "All right, Ted. You've made your point. Now you can come back where you belong."

Ted Kingman stared at his father. He stood thinking of the years of humiliation that he had endured from this man. He was at a crossroads. Turn one way and he'd go back to being the man that he once was. Turn the other way—and it would be hard. He knew that. His father's mercilessness was better known to him than to anybody. He realized that if he did not knuckle under, he would not receive one penny from Kingman Oil Company, and this caused him to pause. A silence had fallen over the group.

Maury looked almost desperately at Ted. *Don't do it, Ted,* she hoped fervently. *Anything's better than going back to him!*

As if he had felt her thoughts, Ted lifted his eyes to her. There was a strange communication that passed between them—one of those moments when people somehow read each other, an epiphany, it's called in the church, when one gets a message directly from God. For a few moments their eyes were locked, then he smiled at her. Turning to his father, he said, "I am on the right side. You're on the wrong side. You've been on the wrong side for a long time, Mr. Kingman."

The use of the term "Mr. Kingman" struck the older man like a blow. For all of his hardness, he yearned for a son—someone to share his life with. Suddenly he knew that this was the end of his dreams. Kingman Oil would grow larger—but what would happen to it after he died? Strangers would take it over he realized, and he wavered, unable to meet his son's gaze. A sense of futility and sadness came over him. He swallowed hard and said, "Now, Ted, we've got to talk about this—"

Ollie Bean suddenly straightened up. "What's that?" he asked, his tiny eyes narrowing even smaller. "Who's that coming?"

Maury, too, had been aware of the sound of approaching vehicles. As the sound grew louder, they all turned and saw the dust rising from the road in huge billows. "Whoever it is," she said quietly to Ray, who stood beside her, "they sure are stirring up the dust."

"Probably more of Kingman's toughs," Ray said, shaking his head almost in despair. "Looks like there's enough of 'em already."

"Who are those guys?" Ollie Bean demanded. "Did you send for someone, Horace?"

"No, I don't know who they are—but they're pulling trailers."

A large Packard had pulled up at the head of the parade. Behind it were three trucks pulling trailers. The Packard stopped and the doors opened. At once, Pete yelled, "Look at that! It's Lylah—and Amos and Rose!"

The two who had gotten out of the car began to smile, and a third person climbed out. The sun touched the gleaming steel hook and Maury said, "It's Uncle Owen and Uncle Gavin, and there's Jerry and Bonnie!"

The new arrivals came quickly to stand beside Pete and his small group. "Hello, Pete," Lylah smiled.

"Lylah, what are you doing here?" Pete demanded. "And you, Owen, Gavin . . . and Amos?"

It was Amos who spoke. "I don't know about Owen, Gavin, and Lylah, but I came to get a story. Hello, Mr. Kingman."

"I don't know you," Mr. Kingman said. "What are you people doing here? This is private land."

"We decided to break the law. The people deserve the news—and you're big news. Everybody wants to hear about how the big, bad Kingman Oil Company's squeezing out small owners. I've brought a photographer along, too. Fellows, you want to set up?"

Other people were coming out of the vehicles, including a photographer with a large camera. He shoved his hat back and asked, "That one there—the big guy?"

"Yes, that's Mr. Kingman." Amos smiled at Kingman, saying in a friendly fashion, "I've seen your picture while doing some background research. As far as I can figure out, you've squeezed out about two hundred small lessees. Is that figure correct?"

Horace Kingman was not someone to be crossed. His face turned crimson. "Get off my land! I'll call the law on you!"

"Good! That'll make a better story." Amos grinned. "My name is Amos Stuart. I'm Pete Stuart's brother and I work for Mr. Hearst. He's been looking for a scandal, and I guess you big oil owners will make a pretty good story. You're going to see your name in print a lot, Mr. Kingman!"

Owen had moved over to stand beside Pete. He nudged him in the ribs and said, "I'm starting a revival meeting in that little town down the road. You suppose you could come?"

"Oh, no, Mr. Kingman won't let us cross his lines," Pete said with a straight face.

"Good!" Amos exclaimed. "That'll make an even better story—Horace Kingman refuses to let people worship."

Kingman seemed to strangle. A movement to his left caught his attention, and he turned to see that motion picture cameras were being set up—all trained at him. He felt trapped and shut in—and for perhaps the first time in his life—helpless.

Lylah said, "There's a new technology called Movie News. We're getting in on it, Mr. Kingman. We'll film this, then go up and take pictures of the hungry children that you won't let food get through to. Oh, you're going to be very well known in America!" she smiled. There was something incongruous about her beauty as she stood on barren Oklahoma land with the shack behind her. And yet there was a power in her as she said, "We'll be setting up our trailers here. Our lawyers will be here, too. There's such a thing as right-of-way, but that's one more thing for my brother Amos to put in the story." Then she went over to Pete and kissed him. "We've got truckloads of food like you never saw. Are we invited to supper?"

A cheer rent the air and Dent DeForge could stand it no more. "Yippee!" he yelled. "The cavalry has come to save us from the vicious outlaws!" He suddenly reached out, picked up Violet, and spun her around wildly. "How do you like that, Sweetheart?" he asked. "I reckon the Lord has heard!"

Maury felt faint. She found that the suddenness of it all had taken her off guard. She was aware that Ted had come to stand beside her, and he leaned over and whispered, "Maury, I never believed in God much and surely not in miracles—but I'd certainly like to know more about it."

"All right, Ted, we'll talk about it." Her eyes were like stars as she reached out and took his hand.

Horace Kingman was a rough and violent man—but not stupid. When he saw the attractive young woman dressed in the cheap dress take the hand of his son, his eyes narrowed. He studied them carefully, then his eyes swept over the movie cameras that were rolling and the still photographs that were being made. He turned, saying not a word, and left.

Lylah called out after him, "We'll be seeing you, Mr. Kingman. Be sure you get your lawyers here as quick as you can. We're looking forward to a big, noisy, wild, and vulgar court battle . . ." Laughter went up from the Stuart group, and even a few hidden smiles from the Kingman faction.

Kingman walked away, accompanied by Ollie. "Well, what do you want to do now?" Bean asked.

Kingman turned to face him. "You see what this means?"

"Well, there's just a few of them."

"A few of them! We'll be on the front page of every one of Hearst's newspapers, not to mention on the screens of half the theaters in America! People are always looking for someone to hate—now the Stuarts found someone—and that's me."

Bean swallowed.

"Do nothing! Don't you do a thing," replied Kingman. He stared back at the crowd that was milling around, at people shouting and hugging, and he felt a strange sense of loneliness when he saw his son standing tall beside the young woman. "That's a dry hole they're on. Let them go bust. It'll all be for nothing."

Ollie Bean had never seen his boss like this. Always before, Kingman had been in control—and had all the answers. Now he watched the man's face and thought to himself, *Horace is getting old—I hadn't noticed that.*

 23 

It's Never Too Late

None of the Stuarts ever forgot the two weeks following the arrival of the clan. For one thing, the newcomers brought supplies of all kinds, including enough groceries to feed a regiment for a year! The very first night that they arrived, the air was thick with the delicious odor of steaks sizzling in skillets, potatoes frying in deep grease, fried pies, and fresh coffee. The trailers served as a base, but Pete's homestead was constantly filled with the sound of laughter and music. Lylah had brought a radio, and the sounds of popular songs of the day lay always either under or above the chatter and talk. These included songs such as, "I Found a Million Dollar Baby in a Five and Ten Cent Store," "Have You Ever Been Lonely?" "Love Letters in the Sand," and a new song from a Broadway success, *Of Thee I Sing.* It was called "A Hot Time in the Old Town Tonight."

Ray and Winona found themselves spending more and more time together. He said once to her, "Winona, you laugh a lot. I thought when I first met you that you were pretty stuffy."

Her brown eyes sparkled as she said, "I didn't think you were the greatest thing either, but I'll always remember you getting knocked down trying to protect me in that restaurant."

Ray grinned and rubbed his chin ruefully. "Maybe I'd better take boxing lessons from Jack Sharkey."

One of the best things that happened—at least in Lylah's mind—was Adam's introduction to what rough living was really like. It was true that there was plenty to eat now, but the outdoor bathroom and the other signs of hard living had come as a shock to the fourteen-year-old. He had been accustomed to comfort and ease all of his life, and now he saw how other people lived. Two days after they arrived in Oklahoma, Adam pulled Gavin aside and asked him to go for a walk. Gavin had known instantly that this was no walk for exercise. As soon as they were out of hearing from those in the house, Adam looked up at him and said, "Uncle Gavin, Mom said you knew my father."

"That's right, I did. Not very well, but I did meet him."

"Did you like him?"

Gavin thought back to those days when he had flown in France in the Layfayette Escadrille—the stark encounters with death high over a checkerboard earth, the sound of bullets piercing the thin fabric of his wooden Sopwith Camel, the smell of burning oil thrown in his face. "Well," he said slowly, "it was a hard time for everybody. Let me tell you about the war."

The two walked for a long time. Gavin spoke quietly about what it was like to wake up every day not knowing if it would be your last day alive. Finally he said, "It was the same for the German fliers. We were on different sides, but I felt real close to them."

"Didn't you hate them?"

"I tried not to," Gavin said. "I don't think they wanted to be there anymore than we did. Sometimes countries do things and people have to go to war whether it's right or wrong."

"My father—he was the best flyer the Germans had?"

"The very best! He had a brother named Lothar who was very good also, but Manfred was the best. Not just alone in a plane, but he became a great leader. The men trusted him. They painted their planes all kinds of crazy colors and they were named the Flying Circus—Manfred von Richthofen's Flying Circus," he mused. "We hated to hear that they were coming because they were fine pilots—all of them."

"Did you meet him, though?"

"I met him once. I was shot down over enemy territory and captured. It would have gone very badly for me, but your father looked me up. I'm afraid I treated him pretty shabbily. I was angry at the war and I wasn't sympathetic for the love he and your mother had for each other. But it didn't matter, he did his best for me." Gavin looked down and smiled, putting his hand on Adam's shoulder. "He was a fine man, Adam. I wish he could've lived. I know he would have been proud of a son like you." Adam said nothing for a long time, and the two resumed their walk.

Later that day, Gavin pulled Lylah aside. "Well, I think it's going to be all right with Adam. We had a long talk—about Manfred." He told her the nature of the talk and saw that her face showed great relief. "I think you can relax now," he said. "He's going to be a fine man—just like his father."

Owen had not been joking about the revival. He was well known enough that all he had to do was announce a meeting, and people would flock from everywhere. The little town closest to Pete's place had no building for a large meeting, but somehow Owen managed to get a tent—a huge one. Every night, from all over that section of Oklahoma the crowds came in. The roughnecks came in their dirty drilling clothes, and the families from the town came to fill the tent.

Violet was surprised when Dent came to her on the first night of the meeting, saying, "Get your Sunday best on, Vi. We want to get down on the amen row. I want to hear some good preaching."

"All right, Dent," she said. "I don't have much to wear, though." She asked to borrow one of Lylah's dresses, a white one trimmed in blue, and when she came to meet Dent, his eyes were wide open.

"I'll be dipped, Violet! Why, you're prettier than a pair of red shoes with green strings!" he exclaimed. "Come on, let's go down and let folks see what a good-looking couple looks like!"

Ted Kingman went along also, accompanied by Maury. He'd spent considerable time with her, but as they entered the tent, he said nervously, "I–I don't know about this, Maury. I've only been to church a couple of times in my life—and it was never like this."

Maury laughed and squeezed his arm. "Don't worry, it's going to get worse."

He looked at her with a wild surmise but saw that she was teasing him. He took his seat and she handed him one of the worn, paperback songbooks, entitled *Heavenly Highways*, and said, "There, let's hear you sing out."

They sang for what seemed like a long time. Ted didn't know any of the songs, but he enjoyed Maury's clear soprano and stole glances at her from time to time. She was wearing a dark green dress that set off her red hair in a spectacular fashion. He had caught the admiring glances from many of the men as he escorted her in and wondered, again, if she would ever trust him enough to marry him.

The sermon was on the subject of repentance. "Except ye repent, ye shall all likewise perish," was the text.

Somehow, Ted expected that Owen Stuart would rake the congregation with allegations of immorality, and would cut them down for smoking, drinking, and going to the movies; however, it was not so.

"Repentance," Owen said, "is not making a list of things you think God hates and then doing your best to stay away from them. That's what the Ten Commandments are—a list of things that reveal a perfect individual. And nobody has ever kept the Ten Commandments—except Jesus Christ of Nazareth."

He paused and looked out over the rough congregation. "Why do we have them, you ask? Why did God give the Ten Commandments if we couldn't keep them? Very simple—to show us that we need him. Have any you fellas ever laid bricks, or blocks, or stone?" He paused and quite a few hands went up. "You know what a line level is then. You put that line up and lay the bricks to it. But ask yourself this—if a wall was crooked, would putting a line up there make it straight? No! The commandments are like that. They show us where we're crooked, and Jesus came to show us a better way. Instead of having a list of things we're not supposed to do and gritting our teeth and plowing at it, Jesus said, 'I have come to be in you and when I am in you, you will know God. For I am in the Father, and the Father is in me. I will be in you and you will be in me.'"

The sermon was not long, and at the end Owen said warmly, "The question is simply this—what do you want the most? What you have—or God? To all of you who do not have God, I know what it's like and I know you're not happy. No one can be happy away from Jesus Christ, for he's the most important of all things. Tonight, if you will come and ask God for his mercy, he will delight to make you his own, and to become yours." He spoke earnestly, explaining that it is necessary to call on God and to turn from sin and to believe in faith that Jesus rose from the dead. Then he said, "As we sing, will you come?"

Ted found his hands trembling slightly as the congregation began to sing:

Just as I am,
Without one plea
But that Thy blood
Was shed for me . . .

He had little idea of what all this meant, but something in him recognized the truth of what he'd heard. He felt Maury's hand touch his, and when he looked at her, he saw tears in her eyes. "Do you feel the need for the Lord, Ted?" she said quietly.

Suddenly, his throat grew thick and he nodded silently. He could not speak for a time, then he managed to say, "I've never felt like this! What is it?"

"It's called 'conviction.' It just means that Jesus wants you to be his own."

"But I don't know how!"

"It's not what you know, it's *who* you know. Do you want to know the peace of God? It will be a different kind of life." Her lips trembled. "But it's wonderful to know Jesus."

There was a moment of intense struggle for Ted Kingman. He understood so little of what he'd heard, but he'd never been shaken as he was at this moment. He did not for one instant doubt the sincerity of Owen Stuart, but it was the words of the Scripture that kept hammering at him, over and over again. Owen had said, "Ye must be born again," and had quoted many places in the Bible to illustrate that. Ted stood wanting to turn and run out of the tent, but knowing somehow that to do so would be fatal. As the people continued to sing, he suddenly took a deep breath. He turned to face Maury and said, "I don't understand much about this—but I know that I need something in my life. Will you show me how?"

"Come on," she said, "let's ask Owen to pray with you."

As they made their way down the aisle, Ted felt like every eye in the world was on him. He also felt like an utter fool. More than once he felt that he would have to turn and leave that place, but Maury's hand was steady on his arm, and when they got to the front, there was Owen, a smile on his lips and light in his eyes.

"Uncle Owen, Ted wants to be born again."

Owen put out his strong left hand and took Kingman's hand. "Let's talk a few minutes. Sit down here, Ted." Maury stood to one side listening. The congregation continued to sing as others came, and the people whom Owen had enlisted to do this work spoke to them. From time to time, there would be a shout of joy as someone found the Lord—and more than once family members came and embraced those who had found Christ. Finally, Owen stood up and turned to Maury. "He's come through! Stick with him, Maury. He's a good man and he's going to need your help."

Maury sat down beside Ted. She saw that there was a far-off look in his eyes and tears stained his cheeks. He looked helpless, almost like a baby, and, without thinking, she put her arms around him. "It's going to be all right!" she whispered. "Now that you know the Lord, everything will be all right!"

From across the room, Amos and Rose watched. Amos said in an unsteady voice, "It looks like we're going to have a larger family, doesn't it, Sweetheart? I never saw Maury act that way before."

Standing next to him Jerry was holding Bonnie's hand. Bonnie's eyes were filled with tears. She and Jerry had been inseparable, and now she looked over at Amos and managed a smile. Rose saw this and came to stand beside her. "Maybe we can have a double wedding and get both of our children married off in one grand swoop."

Jerry grinned and said, "We've got to bring this oil well in first." Then he hugged Bonnie and looked down at her, love shining through his eyes.

Two days later, at ten o'clock in the morning, Pete was sitting beside the ancient engine listening to it chug and groan. Across from him, Bailey was looking at his Dick Tracy book, his huge hands almost concealing the small item. Pete was thinking, *If we never get oil, at least I've found out what it's like to have folks that love you!*

He stiffened. The ground had started trembling, like a miniature earthquake. Suddenly, he knew what was happening. He let out a wild cry: "It's coming in! It's coming in!"

His cry startled Bailey, who jumped to his feet, amazed to see Pete running away from the rig. He followed, not understanding completely, but echoing Pete's words. "It's coming in!"

The house emptied itself instantly. No sooner had everyone gotten out than there was a ripping explosion and a strange *whooshing* sound from the rig.

"Look at that pipe!" Dent yelled. "It's coming out of the ground like a snake."

From down the hill, the oil workers from Kingman, and

others who had come to watch, started running up the hill. It was a frightening sight. Maury reached out and grabbed Ted, saying, "What is it? What's happening?"

Kingman was watching carefully, his eyes narrowed. "We've hit natural gas. It's pushing that column of pipe right out of the ground."

There was a terrible screeching sound of metal tearing and rising. It rose slowly, reaching the height of the derrick, and there it began to buckle. The whole thing was falling to pieces, the pipe joints banging as they cracked free and the lengths of pipe falling away, only to be replaced by more pipe. The casing began to fold and to gather in on itself so the derrick could no longer confine it. The derrick began to break apart with popping crossties and legs working apart as the casing sought to expand.

"It's going! It's going!" Pete yelled, doing an Indian war dance. He grabbed Leslie when she came out of the house and said, "It's come in, Sweetheart—it's come in! Look at that!" The old derrick tottered and slowly collapsed to the ground with a massive crash. It seemed to shake the earth, and still the casing continued to climb out of the steaming wreckage.

"I never saw anything like that!" Ray breathed, holding on to Winona unconsciously. They stood together and watched as the pipe rose high into the air.

"Me either," Winona murmured. "What happens next?"

"I don't know—but something's sure gonna happen."

Finally the casing was completely expelled, covering the wreckage of the rigging platform. There was a moment's quiet and they all stood completely still, for there was a rumbling with something sinister about it; from deep down in the bowels of the earth it came. Pete held his breath and then suddenly, he yelled, "Look! There it is!" and then from the pile of casing came a little mud that seemed to bubble up. It seemed to cough and sputter, and some rocks shot into the air. Then there was a tremendous explosion, like a huge belch. It boomed, and a great gush of mud and water exploded, spreading over the hilltop. Then came another silence.

"What is it, Pete? What's happening?" Jerry demanded.

"Just watch and you'll see."

They did see. Suddenly the ground swayed again like an earthquake. There was a crashing sound, and the well exploded. A yellow geyser burst into the sky over their heads. It climbed up and kept climbing for over a hundred feet and then began cascading over. Pete ran out and the liquid fell on him, covering him until his skin glistened with the dark brown fluid. "It's oil!" he said. He tasted it and said, "First-quality crude oil!"

From down the hill, Horace Kingman and the others watched the geyser of crude oil make a plume as it issued from the earth. "Well, that's it," he said quietly. It was as if a weight had been lifted from his shoulders.

Pete had run out from under the rain of oil and grabbed Leslie again. Everybody was pounding shoulders and grinning like maniacs. They were interrupted by a tall, burly man who shoved his way through the family. He grabbed Pete by the arm and said, "Two fifty—two fifty a barrel against the first fifty thousand!"

Pete wiped the oil from his face and grinned broadly. "You got a pen?" he said.

"Right here!" the oil man said. "Sign it quick, because you're going to get lots of offers, but we'll stick with you all the way, Pete. You sure showed Kingman!"

Ted Kingman turned to see his father coming up the hill with some of his tough hands. He walked forward to meet him and said nothing, but defiantly faced him.

Horace Kingman took one look at his son and swallowed hard. "That oil needs to be capped," he said. "You might ask your friend Stuart if he needs some help."

Maury had come up beside Ted. She took his arm, and Ted turned to smile at her. He looked back and said, "This is your future daughter-in-law, Maury Stuart, Dad. I'm not asking permission."

There was something in Ted Kingman—a new toughness—that pleased Horace. He pulled his hat off and stared down at the ground for a moment. When he lifted his eyes, he said, "I'm happy to meet you, Miss Stuart." He hesitated still more and said, "I'd like to think there's another side to me than what you've seen. Maybe you would give me a chance to show it."

"I think I'd like that, Mr. Kingman," Maury said evenly. "You might start by stopping that oil. Pete's losing money."

Kingman at once yelled, "All right, you birds, get that oil well capped!"

Kingman moved closer and studied the clear face of the young woman. He put his hand out tentatively in a strange, almost helpless gesture. "I guess–I guess I've got a lot to say, but I'm not used to backing down. You might have to help me a little."

Maury saw the similarity in some of the features of the two men—and took the hand. "I think we could arrange that. Maybe you could have dinner with Ted and me tonight?"

Horace Kingman swallowed again and seemed to have trouble speaking. "I–I'd like that very much. Just tell me when and where."

"Come along, Dad. Maybe we could give those fellows a hand," Ted said. He slapped his father on the shoulder—something he had never done before—and laughed at the expression in the older man's eyes. The two of them turned quickly to where the roughnecks were tearing into the crumbled oil derrick.

Maury was still watching them when Amos came to stand by her. "Looks like you're going to have a rich family. Maybe I can put the bite on you for a few bucks now and then."

Maury turned and put her arms around him and began to cry. "Oh, Dad, I'm so happy!" she mumbled, pressing her face against his cheek.

Amos held his daughter for a while and said, "Come along. We'll go tell your mother."

Two days later, after a great deal of frantic activity, Violet was walking slowly around the pump that had been installed over the old derrick. Dent was with her, and suddenly she looked across and saw something that made her smile. "Look, there's Ray with Winona—and Maury with Ted."

Dent looked at the two couples for a long time, then turned to face her. "Looks like they're pairing off, doesn't it?" He hesitated for a moment and said, "I'd like to get out of here. Let's go back to Arkansas, Violet."

At once, she said with relief, "I'm ready, and we'll take Bailey back. He'll like it there."

"We'll go in the morning. Say your good-byes tonight." He looked around the barren land. "It'll sure be good to see some fields and hills again!"

 24 

THE END AND THE BEGINNING

President Herbert Hoover fought valiantly to retain the office of the presidency in 1932. He prophesied that a Democratic victory would mean that, "The grass will grow in the streets of a hundred cities." Most of the voters, however, remained unconvinced. Almost everyone felt that the American system needed desperate measures to be saved.

The man who offered an alternative was Franklin Delano Roosevelt. FDR—born to a patrician Hudson River family, graduate of Harvard—was different from any candidate who had thrown himself into a presidential race. Before his nomination, he appeared to many to be merely a nice man who very much wanted to be president.

He soon, however, electrified the country with a bold, aggressive campaign. Now with a wide radio network at his disposal, he set out to prove his physical vigor and exert his personal magnetism. He promised a "New Deal" to the "forgotten man." In contrast to Hoover, he promised to use the power of government to ease unemployment, to develop public power, and to sponsor a broad program for social welfare.

Roosevelt was elected overwhelmingly and was immediately faced with a fearful number of tasks. He had to restore the shattered economy and give a new sense of purpose to the federal government. Most of all, he had to restore the faith of a nation that seemed stricken by fear.

The country was in a terrible condition. Rud Rennie, the baseball writer, mentioned his journey with the New York Yankees from their training camp, describing the Southern cities as having been ravaged by an invisible enemy.

Back in the Ozarks, however, surrounded by the rolling hills and the green forest, Violet Ballard was not as aware of the political scene as were others in the country. She'd come home with Dent, accompanied by Bailey. Ray had chosen to remain at Pete's to work in the oil field, for a while at least. To Violet, coming back home was like moving out of a terrible storm into a calm, placid harbor.

Logan Stuart met his daughter early one morning, a week after her return, coming back from a walk just at dawn. As she entered the door, he admired the dark blue of her eyes as he always did. "Been out walking?" he asked.

"Yes, Pa. How's Ma this morning?"

"I think she's better. She says she's going to get up and fix dinner for us."

"I'm glad," she said. "She looks better. I think she's going to be all right."

The house shook as Bailey came walking into the room. He wore a pair of overalls, still stiff and new, and he put his fingers in the straps of the bib and grinned broadly. "I like these new overalls you got me, Violet. They just fit!"

"You look just like a farmer, Bailey," Violet smiled. "What are you going to do today?"

"Chop wood." Bailey had quickly learned how to saw down trees, and splitting wood seemed to come natural to him. He already had an enormous stack alongside the house. He moved to the door and said, "But first I'm going to milk the cow."

After the door closed behind him, Logan shook his head. "I don't know that I've ever seen such a feller for work! He's strong as a bull and he learns quick. Only thing is, he's liable to wear the mules out—as much as he likes to work!"

They laughed at the thought of it, and soon Anne came in and they sat down to the breakfast that Violet had cooked. Anne did look better. There was color in her cheeks and she had gained some weight. She appeared happier than she'd been in a long time. "Did you tell Violet about the letter Pete sent?"

"No, I haven't had a chance." Logan reached in the pocket of his overalls and pulled out a letter. "It just came yesterday. You was out at the lake fishing when it did. Never could understand anyone fishing in the wintertime. It's too cold."

"I like it. I wish it'd snow. What did Uncle Pete say?"

"He didn't say much, just a note. But lookee here." He held out a small slip of paper, and when Violet leaned over, she saw that it was a check. When she saw the amount, her eyes opened wide. Her father chuckled. "How 'bout that? It looks like it pays to have a big oil man as a brother."

"Well, that was nice of Uncle Pete. What's it for?"

"Part of it is for getting ready for the reunion. Guess we'll all be here this Christmas, kids and all. Pete told me to rent the Delight Hotel—rooms for everybody, and the dining room to have our big reunion party in."

"Oh, Pa, that'll be fun! We can have music and dancing, I bet, too."

"You bet! And I'm going to have a big tree set up right in the middle of that room to put the presents under." He looked at Anne fondly. "It'll be nice to be able to buy presents for all the young 'uns this year, won't it, Annie?"

"Yes, it will." Anne looked out the window suddenly and said, "Look, I think that's Dent."

The sound of a car stopping and then the door slamming echoed, and almost at once Dent's footsteps sounded. "Anybody home?" The door opened and Dent came breezing in. "Well, what a coincidence—just in time for breakfast."

Violet glared at him. "I don't think you've come to this house a single time except when we're eating!"

"My mama didn't raise no fool." Dent grinned. "I know where the good cooking is." He moved around the table, leaned over, and kissed Anne on the cheek. "My, you're looking right pretty this morning, Miz Anne." He winked at Logan. "You'd better watch out. One of these good-looking bachelor fellas might come along and take this young lady away from you."

"Get away from me, you crazy thing!" Anne said, but she was pleased with his teasing. She always brightened when he came into a room. "Sit down there and eat your eggs while you tell me what you've been doing."

Dent sat down and began at once to describe a hunting trip he'd made. His eyes were bright and his hair was growing down over his collar. He ate prodigiously and when Logan told him about the reunion, he nodded. "That's good. I like to see families get together around Christmas."

"Well, you'd better be there, Denton," Anne said. "It wouldn't be Christmas without you around—you and your foolishness."

"Come on out to the car, Violet. I've got something to show you." Dent got up and Violet followed him out to the car. He opened the door of the Model T and pulled out a long package. Ripping the paper off, he said, "It's kind of a pre-Christmas present. Look at that!"

Violet saw that it was a new twelve-gauge shotgun. He placed it in her hands and she looked at him in bewilderment. "What's this for?" she said.

"Why, it's for you. Me and you are going duck hunting tomorrow. Nothing like a fat, juicy duck along with some rice and biscuits."

Violet held the gun up and said, "Why, I've never had a gun before."

"It's about time you did," Dent said. "Be ready about three. I won't blow the horn. You come on out and we'll sneak off so we don't wake the folks up."

"Why, that's the middle of the night! Three o'clock in the morning?"

"That's right. I want to be in the blind when the ducks come in. We've got quite a drive to make, so wrap up warm." He reached out and pinched the lobe of her ear. "You'd better bring some vittles along, too. A body gets kind of hungry out there in the blinds." He leaned over suddenly and kissed her cheek, then he cranked up the Model T and hopped in. "See you at three!" he yelled as he tore out full speed down the rutted road.

Violet turned and went inside the house holding the shotgun.

"What in the world is that?" Anne demanded.

"A brand-new shotgun. Dent gave it to me." She smiled and said, "We're going duck hunting at three o'clock in the morning."

Anne and Logan exchanged looks as the girl left the room, carrying the shotgun with her. "What do you make of that, Annie?" Logan said. "Kind of a strange gift for a fella to give a young woman. Seems like he'd brought flowers or something if he was courting."

"I don't think Dent's courting. He's past the age for that and Violet's too young for him. He just likes her, that's all."

December twenty-fourth at the Delight Hotel was unusual. The hotel was packed. It was a small place anyhow, with only fifteen rooms, and every one of them was filled.

Amos and Rose had made the trip from Chicago with Maury and Ted. Lylah and Jesse were there with Adam, and Bonnie and Jerry had come with them from California. Owen was there with his wife, Allie, and their three children, William Lee, Woodrow, and Wendy. Logan had even moved Anne into the hotel with Clinton and Violet; Helen was there with her new husband, Gordon Sanders. Pete had brought Leslie and Stephen and Mona, and Ray had come with them from Oklahoma. Lenora was there. Gavin and Heather had come, bringing their children, Phillip and Sidney. Christie and Mario were there with their young children, Maria and Anthony. Bailey bunked with Ray and Ted, just like when they'd worked on the oil rig together.

On Christmas Eve, every light in the dining room was on. The tables were loaded with turkey, corn bread dressing, sweet potatoes, ham, and greens—not to mention the pies, cobblers, and cakes that adorned one special table. A fifteen-foot cedar tree stood at one end of the dining room, covered with the ornaments, silver rope, and lights that the children and young people had worked so hard on. The reunion had actually been going on for two days, more or less, as everyone arrived—but now after the meal, when all were as stuffed as they could be, Amos stood to his feet and pounded on the table, yelling, "Let's have a little quiet around here!"

Slowly the noise filtered down and Amos grinned. "I certainly have enjoyed listening to all of you eat," he said. "You really sounded good."

"You didn't do too bad yourself," Owen called out. "I could hear you clear across the table, Amos."

There was a great deal of banter and Amos allowed it to go on for some time. He looked across the room and his face grew thoughtful. "I don't have any long speech to make," he said. "I'm just thankful to God that we're all here. I remember," he said, "when we were just kids together. Those were mighty hard times, but God has kept us all alive and he's prospered us. I want us to take time right now to thank him for it. Owen, will you offer thanks for us?"

They all stood and held hands, and Owen began to say a fervent prayer of thanksgiving. He mentioned the names of all the children, naming a particular need of each. Ted Kingman, who had been invited specially for this occasion, stood by Maury and felt there was a warmth to the prayer and honesty that he was glad to hear. After the prayer was over, each of the sons and daughters of Will and Marian Stuart had to stand and say something. They went around laughing at themselves and remembering the good things. Finally, Amos said, "I'd like to propose a toast." They all held their glasses high. "I propose a toast to our Pa, William Stuart, and our Ma, Marian Edwards Stuart." He paused for a moment and said quietly, "They don't make them like those two very often. So, here's to them and to all of us. I would also like to invite everyone to a wedding! Jerry and Bonnie and Maury and Ted are getting married in a double ceremony next month!"

Afterward came the opening of the presents and still later, the old hotel rang with the sound of laughter and talk. Finally, the dining room emptied and the hotel grew silent. The next day, the visitors left, and the Delight Hotel was restored to its normal state. But none of the Stuarts ever forgot the reunion of 1932!

Violet was restless. She had done all of her work and now was walking through the house looking for something to sew or for something to read. Actually she wanted to do neither. She had been dissatisfied ever since the reunion. Now it was the middle of January, and she realized that she had been snappy and irritable with her father and mother, and even with Bailey. "I don't know what's the matter with me," she said aloud, stopping before the grandfather clock and looking up into the face of it. "Maybe getting older is doing this to me." As she listened to the loud *tick-tock, tick-tock* of the heavy pendulum, she remembered, when she was a child, standing in front of it, moving her head in time with it. She turned and went into the kitchen, fixed a cup of cocoa, and sat drinking it, and reflected on her eighteenth birthday celebration with the family the week before.

She was alone in the house, her parents having gone to visit friends down the road. "I ought to write a letter," she said, "there're so many to write—but I don't want to." She forced herself to pull a book off the shelf. It was a novel she hated the first time she'd read it and hated it even more as she began it again. She was glad when she heard a car come up the road. The fields were covered with snow and cars had not moved, up until two days earlier. But now the sun had melted it enough so that the snow was packed down and some travel was possible. Leaping up, she ran to the window and saw that it was Dent. Throwing the book across the room, she ran to the door to meet him. He left the engine running, and she said, "Go shut it off and I'll fix you some cocoa."

"Nope. Get your coat on."

"What for?"

"Don't ask questions, Violet. That's your problem—you always have questions." Dent, grinning broadly, turned her around and pushed her back into the house.

Violet had no idea where Dent was going this time. He'd shown up like this several times, however, since they'd returned from Oklahoma, as he had when he had taken her duck hunting. She put on her heavy mackinaw and pulled a wool cap down over her ears, and she thought about the hunting trip. She had shot at ducks and missed them all, but Dent had hit four. They had brought them home, dressed them, and all the family had eaten a fine duck supper the next night.

She left the house, walked down the steps carefully to avoid slipping on the ice, then got into the car and slammed the door. "We're not going duck hunting, I take it. I don't see your gun."

"Nope, not this time. Hang on now!"

Dent always seemed to drive, wherever he went, at full speed. He went skidding down the road, sometimes spinning the car halfway around, so that she was thrown against him. "Dent, don't drive so crazy! You're going to kill us both."

He had merely laughed at her and grabbed her around the shoulders and held her tight. "Here, I'll hang on to you. You'll be safe that way."

She enjoyed the weight of his arm around her. He held her close for a moment and she stole a glance at his chiseled features. *He looks so young,* she thought. *He'll always look that way. His daddy was the same way. He always looked young, even when he was sixty years old. The DeForge men never seem to get old. I wonder if his wife will like that!* She glanced at him again as if he might have overheard her thoughts.

Dent drove skillfully. He chatted on the way about the affairs of the small world they inhabited. He knew everyone, it seemed, not only in their little village, but all over that part of the Ozarks. They turned off the main part of the road. Violet looked out the window and saw that he was stopping in front of a fine old two-story house. "This is the Stephens's house," she said. "Why have we come here?"

"Come on, I've got something to show you," he said. He shut the engine off, leaped out of the Ford, hurried around, and opened the door. As Violet stepped out, Dent grabbed her hand and said, "Come on."

When they got to the porch, he opened the screen door and started in. Violet pulled away from him. "You can't just go in this house, Dent!" she protested.

"Aw, there's nobody here. They won't care." He pulled her inside and she saw that the furniture was all old, but of excellent quality.

"You ever been in here before?" Dent asked.

"Once or twice. It's such a nice house, so big and roomy. But where are the Stephenses? I didn't hear anything about them going on a trip."

Dent said, "Let me show it to you." He showed her the parlor, the kitchen, the dining room, and the four bedrooms upstairs—and the marvel of all—an inside bathroom with a fine enamel tub. "Look at the feet on that tub," he said proudly. "I never saw nicer claws in my life!" He banged it with his hand and said, "Now a man could come in on a cold day, fill that up with hot water, and really relax."

Violet was feeling more and more nervous. "You're crazy, Dent! Let's get out of here. If the Stephenses came home, I'd be so embarrassed! Did you bring me over to see them?"

"Let's go downstairs. I want to look at that kitchen again." He took her hand and led her downstairs, laughing at her protest. She tried to pull away and run out the front door, but he pulled her to him. She tried to get away, but his strong arms held her tight. She felt the lean, masculine strength of his body as he held her close, and she put her arms around him. Then he reached up and plucked her cap off. "I've always liked your hair," he said, reaching up and running his hand down it. "Never saw such pretty, thick, brown hair in my entire life."

Violet was mystified. "Dent! What are you doing?"

"Well, I reckon I'm holding about the prettiest girl I know real tight. How do you like it?"

"You've got to let me go, Dent. This isn't right!"

He bent his head and kissed her. His lips were firm on hers, and her arms went around his neck. She held him tightly, then finally put her hands against his chest and pushed away. He let her go and she said, "I'm ashamed of myself."

"Well, I'm not ashamed of myself," Dent said huskily. He reached out and took her hands. "I want you to marry me," he said abruptly, "and live in this house."

"Dent, what in the world!—"

"I mean that the Stephenses have been trying to sell this house for a while. I made the down payment on it." He reached into his pocket, pulled out a small box and opened it. The light caught the diamond in the gold ring. He took her hand and slipped it on her finger.

Violet stood there, her heart beating fast. She looked up at him and her lips began to tremble. She looked very young and vulnerable, and finally she whispered, "Do you really mean it, Dent?"

For once, Denton DeForge was totally serious. "Sweetheart, I never meant anything more in my whole life! I thought I was too old for you—and I guess maybe I am. You'll just be a child bride, I guess. But I love you, Violet. I guess I always have. You were like a little sister at first, but then you blossomed out and became a woman. And now, I love you like a man loves a woman. Do you love me?"

Violet pulled his head down and kissed him hard. When she drew back there were tears in her eyes. "I've loved you all my life," she whispered. "Yes, I'll marry you."

Dent hugged her tight, swung her around till she lost her breath, then he carried her over to a full-length mirror in the parlor. Standing her on her feet, he faced the mirror with her and smiled at their reflection.

"There," he said, squeezing her. "We're going to make a good-looking couple, Violet. I wouldn't be surprised," he added with a wicked wink, "if we aren't the best-looking couple in the Ozark Mountains!"

Violet's heart was so full that she could not speak. She threw her arms around him and buried her face in his chest. "If you say so, Dent, then I guess it must be! . . ."

They stood quietly, holding each other, and the only sound was the ticking of a clock on the mantel—that and the startled *meow* of a hammer-headed yellow tomcat that came out from behind the stove and stared at them. The cat yawned hugely and began lazily to stretch and scratch.